This is a work of fiction. Names, characters, organizations, places, events, and incidents are either products of the author's imagination or are used fictitiously.

Published by Sandra Owens
Print ISBN: 978-0-9997864-0-6
E-book ISBN: 978-0-9997864-1-3

Edits by: Jennie Conway and Ella Sheridan
Printed in the United States of America

Cover Design and Interior Format
© The Killion Group, Inc.

Just Jenny

Blue Ridge Valley

SANDRA OWENS

PRAISE FOR SANDRA'S BOOKS

The Blue Ridge Valley series is Sandra Owens at her finest. Filled with Southern charm and a dash of humor, she had me churning through the pages. I laughed. I cried. This series has it all.
Heather Burch, bestselling author of ONE LAVENDER RIBBON

Take everything you love about a Sandra Owens novel—the dry humor, the hot alpha heroes—and transplant them into a quirky small town, and you have the Blue Ridge Valley Series. Charming, funny, and sexy.
Jenny Holiday, *USA Today* bestselling author

Snappy dialog, endearing characters, and a delightful plot . . . I loved, loved, loved Just Jenny!
Barbara Longley, #1 Bestselling author

Welcome to Blue Ridge Valley . . . A town you'll want to visit and never leave. You'll fall in love with the quirky residents who will make you laugh, and you'll cry tears for Jenny and Dylan—two hearts in need of healing—as they find forgiveness and love.
Miranda Liasson, Bestselling author of the Mirror Lake series

JUST JENNY, set in the picturesque Blue Ridge Valley, is just an all-around good time. It's got its share of colorful characters, juicy secrets, nosy neighbors, apple pie moonshine, and a romance that will touch your heart. Small town living at its best you

don't want to miss.
Tamra Baumann, Bestselling author

"If you are a fan of this author or enjoy romantic suspense or just love your heroes to be swoon-worthy, Jack of Hearts is highly recommended."
Harlequin Junkie Top Pick

"A heated romance is at the forefront of this novel, backed by a compelling story that will lure readers into Madison and Alex's world."
Publishers Weekly

"I love this new series! It's filled with ongoing suspense and tension, then sexy hot romance, and relatable people that you want to spend time with."
Reading in Pajamas.

To sign up for Sandra's Newsletter go to:

https://bit.ly/2FVUPKS

ALSO BY SANDRA OWENS

~ ACES & EIGHTS SERIES ~

Jack of Hearts

King of Clubs

Ace of Spades

Queen of Diamonds

~ K2 TEAM SERIES ~

Crazy for Her

Someone Like Her

Falling for Her

Lost in Her

Only Her

~ REGENCY BOOKS ~

The Dukes Obsession

The Training of a Marquess

The Letter

DEDICATION

Just Jenny is dedicated to all the romance readers in the world who believe in happily ever afters...

CHAPTER ONE

~ Jenny ~

"WHAT WAS YOUR CAR DOING at Road Dogs this afternoon?"

I set the scotch neat in front of my boyfriend, although he wasn't going to be for long if he kept up this jealous, *where the hell were you* thing he'd been dishing out lately. "I'm working here, Chad. Drink this and then go away." Road Dogs was a biker bar. Not my kind of place, which he should know by now.

"Careful, Jenn." He sucked half the drink down his throat, then swiped a hand across his mouth. "Ben said he saw your car there."

"Then Ben's wrong. Ever think of that?" I walked away before I decided to punch my soon-to-be ex in the nose. I poured two glasses of merlot for the couple at the end of the bar, making small talk with them while trying to ignore Chad. The jerk was going to get me fired if he didn't leave. I'd known for a few weeks that our relationship was on its last legs, but I'd put off making a clean break.

Unless you wanted to make the forty-minute drive east to Asheville, North Carolina, Vincennes was the place to eat—and be seen—in my neck of the woods. You couldn't beat Angelo's Italian food, and if you wanted to hear the latest town gossip, you came to Vincennes. I loved working here, but Angelo hated drama. I'd told Chad that numerous times, but he didn't seem to care.

Blue Ridge Valley was a small North Carolina town close to the Tennessee state line, and good paying jobs were scarce. Many of my classmates had moved to Asheville or other big cities in North or South Carolina offering better opportunities, but I'd landed a waitressing job at Vincennes, where the tips were good. As soon as I was of age, Angelo had put me behind the bar, a job I loved and didn't want to lose. I was too close to reaching my goal to have it snatched away now.

"Another," Chad said, pushing his glass to the end of the counter.

Not happening. I leaned my face close to his, keeping my voice low. "That was not me. Go home now. Or go find some other woman to annoy. I don't really care which, but if you don't leave, I'll never speak to you again. And if you get me fired, I swear to God I'll kill you."

The two women sitting to his left—one of which I recognized as the head of our chamber of commerce—widened their eyes, and I realized I hadn't kept my voice as low as I'd intended.

"Not something you should be saying in front of witnesses, Red."

My gaze swung to the man who slid into the seat next to Chad, and I did a classic double take. He had to be a figment of my imagination. No man that drop-dead gorgeous would ever walk into a bar in my small mountain town without some kind of hot-guy alert lighting up the phones, announcing his arrival.

Stupid Chad took one look at the newcomer and apparently decided to lay his claim by grabbing my hand, bringing my fingers to his lips for a kiss. What a toad.

I almost told him off, but the lounge was busy, some people having a drink while waiting for their table, others eating their dinner at the long bar. If I said anything to make him mad, there'd be a scene, and that was the last thing I needed.

"I'll be back when you get off, babe."

"Don't bother," I said, and deciding the best thing to do was make myself scarce until he left, I headed for the kitchen.

"Jenn," Chad called after me, but I kept going.

After loading up bread and salads for the two couples eating at the bar, I peeked out the oval window of the swinging door. Chad was gone. I let out a relieved breath.

He was a good-looking guy, and he'd been nice when we'd first started dating. That was two months ago, and sometime during the last few weeks he'd started acting like he owned me. He knew my plans, ones I wouldn't change for any man. On our first date I'd made it clear that I wasn't looking for a serious relationship and why. We were only supposed to be having a little fun for a few months.

"I'm not looking for serious, either," he'd said. "My focus right now is on my career, on building my client list."

It had seemed the perfect setup. Someone fun to date until it was time to go. The fun had stopped, though, and since cavemen weren't my thing, it was time to break things off with him. I didn't doubt he'd be sitting outside my apartment when I got home, which would put him in a pissy mood. He'd been asking for a key to my place so he could wait for me in the comfort of my home, but I'd put him off each time he brought it up.

How did I get myself in these messes? It wasn't the first time I'd made a poor choice when it came to men. Once I got rid of this one, I was going to swear off the creatures. For a while anyway. I mean, what girl who loves sex—which I did—could live without them forever?

I pushed the swinging door open with my butt while holding plates of salad and breadbaskets. Once my two couples had everything they needed, I turned to the stranger who hadn't gotten any less hot in the few minutes I'd been away from the bar.

"What can I get you?"

Eyes the color of dark Tennessee whiskey met mine, rested there a few lingering seconds, then moved to the bottles lining the shelves. "I'll have a Green Man."

"Good choice." Green Man was brewed at one of Ashville's many microbreweries, and it was my favorite beer. Not that it meant anything. Liking the same beer was probably the only thing we had in common.

"No mug, Jenny," he said when I pulled one from the small freezer under the bar.

I slid the opened bottle in front of him. "My friends call me Jenn."

"He called you Jenn. I'll call you Jenny." One side of his mouth curved up. "Or Red."

That lopsided smile of his curled my toes, my resolution to swear off men forgotten. And the way *Jenny* rolled off his tongue—soft and intimate, like there was no one in the room but him and me—almost had me licking my lips. I already liked him for not wanting to call me Jenn simply because Chad had. The man was scoring points without even trying.

He held out his hand. "I'm Dylan Conrad."

And of course he would have a sexy name. I stared at that masculine hand with the blunt-tipped nails on the ends of his long fingers, thinking it would be a big mistake to touch him. With all the electricity sparking around us, we might ignite on contact, but he kept it there in the space between us. I glanced up to see him watching me, and the laugh lines at the corners of his eyes crinkled. It was as if he could read me and was amused.

You're being ridiculous, Jenn. It was only a hand he was offering, not his body, which was all hard lines and muscles. The second I put my hand in his, I almost jerked it away when some kind of weird spark actually did shoot up my arm.

I think he felt it, too, because his eyes widened for a

millisecond. If I hadn't been watching him, I'd have missed his reaction. His fingers curled over mine, his touch feeling so intimate and warm that for a moment the world around me faded away. I gave a little shake of my head, banishing any interest I might have in this man. My plans wouldn't change, even for a man with whiskey-colored eyes and a lopsided grin.

"Nice to meet you, Dylan." I pulled my hand away. Where had I heard his name? For the life of me, I couldn't remember.

He sent me that killer smile again, and I had the urge to rub my chest, right over where my heart had decided to skip a beat or two. The man was decidedly dangerous if he could make my heart misbehave like that. The big question: did I want to encourage him? I almost laughed at myself. Obviously banishing him from my mind hadn't worked if I was asking that. Brandy, one of the waitresses, brought out the dinners for my two couples, and I gratefully turned my attention to her.

"Thanks, hon," I said, getting busy filling drink orders from the waitstaff. While I mixed and shook martinis, poured carafes of wine, and uncapped bottles of locally brewed beers, I could feel Dylan's eyes on me. I couldn't resist adding a little sway to my hips when I walked to the other end of the bar to take a drink order.

He had to be a tourist, so no harm in a little flirtation. Whatever might or might not happen, though, took second place to adding to my travel account.

As soon as I had a sufficient amount saved, I was taking off to see the world. It had been our dream, Natalie's and mine, for as long as I could remember, and I had a promise to keep.

We'd grown up in the valley, but my twin and I had both had wanderlust. We'd gone to Greece, the trip a graduation present from our parents. The first week had been awesome. Then my world had changed forever. I bowed my head to clear it of memories of her. This wasn't the time or place to fall apart.

"Ready for another one?" I asked Dylan, finally turning to him once I could speak without my voice quivering. And there went that damn smile that curled my toes. It occurred to me to wonder why a man as hot as him was on vacation alone. Lots of hikers passed through Blue Ridge Valley, so maybe he planned to hike the Appalachian Trail.

"I'm good, Red." He pulled out a ten, sticking it under the empty bottle. "See you around."

I couldn't resist watching him walk away, my gaze mostly on his butt—and what a fine one it was. He was tall, lean in all the right places, and muscled everywhere a man should be. His hair was dark brown, cut close to his head. A good look on him. At the door he paused long enough to glance back and wink. Busted. He'd known I was eyeing him. My cheeks heated. I prayed he was too far away to notice my blush.

"That's one fine specimen," Brandy said, coming to stand next to me.

"Yeah, and he probably knows it." Although I hadn't got that impression, I was looking for faults. That one would do for a start. Hopefully he really was a tourist and I'd never see him again. The man would be entirely too easy to fall for.

CHAPTER TWO

~ Dylan ~

I CHUCKLED AS I WALKED TO my car. I'd felt Jenny Girl's eyes on my back and had stifled the urge to flex my ass cheeks for her viewing pleasure. If the women in this town were as pretty as the bartender, I was going to enjoy living here. Watching her was better than seeing the Energizer Bunny in action. She owned that bar and ran it like a well-oiled machine, making drinks and chatting up the customers without missing a beat. Well, chatting to everyone but me, which right there said she was too aware of me for her peace of mind.

Every time she shook a martini, her ponytail bounced against her back, and all I could think about was wrapping that long red tail around my hand and holding her still while I kissed her senseless. Yeah, parts of me long dead were coming back to life. I definitely intended to see her again.

If I had to guess, the asshole at the bar was her boyfriend, but maybe not for much longer. I hoped not. The dude needed to learn how to treat a woman. I'd stood back for a few minutes, listening to them, and it had been all I could do not to say something. With any kind of luck, I'd run into him one day when I was on the job.

To get to know my new town, I drove around a little after I left Vincennes. The main street consisted of a mile of asphalt with shops on both sides. On the north side of the two lanes, a fast-moving creek wound its way behind the souvenir and mountain crafts stores. A few restaurants were scattered about; the ones on the creek side had outside seating in the back. In the summer you could get a burger or a mountain trout dinner while watching the tubers float by.

All information I'd learned from the town's website after I'd been offered the job as Blue Ridge Valley's chief of police. The photos posted on the site had called to me, the ones of laughing people drifting down a rushing creek on fat tubes, of sunsets over the mountains, and ones showing the brilliance of fall when the leaves had turned, dressing the trees in yellows, oranges, reds, and golds. Blue Ridge Valley had seemed like a place where I might find a bit of peace.

I'd already stopped by several of the businesses, introducing myself. Except for one biker bar and one honky-tonk joint, I hadn't identified any other possible trouble spots. I'd visited both places, letting them know I had my eye on them.

The townspeople had created the perfect tourist destination. In the summer it was bikers with the low rumble of their Harleys cruising by, families renting cabins so they could explore the Blue Ridge Parkway and load up on useless souvenirs, and hikers wanting to walk parts of the Appalachian Trail or hike up to one of the many waterfalls in the area. Come fall, the leaf lookers took over, and in the winter the skiers and snowmobile enthusiasts flocked in when there was snow.

From what I'd learned researching the town, the residents and shop owners went all out decorating the place at Christmas. I'd already decided I would make myself scarce when that happened. Christmas brought back too many dark memories. Last year I'd dealt with the ghost haunting me by staying drunk from Christmas Eve until the day after Christmas.

Before I fell too deep into the memories, I pushed them

away. I'd come here to start over, and Jenny was the first woman to catch my interest since...well, just since. At the sight of a drive-through, I pulled in, ordered two grilled chicken sandwiches and a large coffee. Dinner in hand, I continued my familiarization of the area, memorizing street names as I drove over curvy roads winding their way up the mountains. Someday, if I stayed here, I'd like to buy one of those log cabins nestled on the hillsides. I wondered if I'd passed Jenny's house in my travels.

Although I didn't officially start my new job until Monday, I decided to stop by the station, see what was going on. Not much in a town like this, I figured, which after working the mean streets of Chicago for nine years suited me just fine since I was suffering from a severe case of burnout. I hoped that arresting someone for making moonshine was going to be the most exciting incident in my new career. Whether or not I'd get bored remained to be seen.

The Blue Ridge Valley police station was about a tenth the size of my old precinct. Another thing I liked. As far as I was concerned, less was best. Parked in front of it, I studied the one-story building made of limestone blocks and sporting a blue tin roof, then turned my attention to the vehicles in the lot. There were six civilian cars and two police cruisers. Shouldn't the cruisers be out on patrol? It occurred to me that not once had I passed a police car while touring the area.

I'd not stopped in yet, so they wouldn't know who I was unless they'd seen my picture in the local paper announcing my appointment as their new chief. This was going to be interesting.

Under normal circumstances I would have come here for an interview with Jim John Jenkins, the mayor, and Buddy Ferguson, the town manager. They'd come to me instead, explaining that the captain of the department expected to get the chief's job, but they felt it was time to bring in new blood. Strangely the town manager had appeared to be more on board with that idea than the mayor.

Reading between the lines, I got the impression they wanted someone from a big-city police department with no ties to their corner of the world. "We're looking for experience, forward thinking, and common sense," Buddy Ferguson had said. "Someone who can bring tried and proven ideas to our police department."

It had sounded like their police department needed fixing, which was something I was good at. The mayor had told me during my interview that they'd narrowed the applicants down to three: me, a cop from Raleigh, North Carolina, and one from Dallas, Texas.

Since they didn't want their captain to know they were looking elsewhere until they made a decision, they'd come north, all bug-eyed when I'd taken them on a tour of my Chicago police precinct. My spidey senses said there was more to the story where my new captain was concerned.

Truthfully, when I'd sent them my resume after seeing the opening posted on a site specializing in law enforcement positions, I hadn't expected to hear back from them. But I did, and here I was. Now that I had the job, I looked forward to digging in.

The photo announcing my appointment that ran in the paper here was of a younger, somewhat heavier me. I'd lost about twenty pounds in the last two years since Christine. That came from losing interest in food, but I was starting to find my taste buds again. To make this surprise visit interesting, I slipped on a ball cap and a pair of reading glasses. A glance in the rearview mirror told me that I didn't look much like the photo.

"Let's go see what I've gotten myself into," I murmured as I approached the door. It was a few minutes past ten, and I figured there'd be a shift change at eleven. Stepping inside, I stopped and scanned the empty lobby. Shouldn't there be someone stationed at the counter?

Laughter bellowed from down the hallway, and I followed the sound, noticing as I passed the counter that there were some files spread out on the desk behind it. I stopped, picked one up, and thumbed through it. It was the arrest record for one Hank Sands. The other files were the same, arrest records on various people. I glanced around again. Anyone could come in right now and walk off with these. As I'd suspected, I had my work cut out for me.

Another burst of laughter had me continuing my search for the source. I took the files with me. At the first open door I came to, I peeked in. It was the dispatchers' room, and one dispatcher sat with his back to me, the other desk empty. I listened to his conversation for a moment as he gave someone instructions to put ice on a swollen ankle, and then to call their doctor. It struck me how different that was from listening to a roomful of dispatchers in Chicago. That was definitely a welcome change.

"Damn it, Moody, I know you're fucking cheating."

The loud voice carried down the hallway, and I continued on my way. Before I reached my destination, I came to another open door and looked in. It was a good-sized room with about a dozen cubicles. All were empty except one where a blond man in his late thirties sat, flipping through a file. He looked up, studied me for a few seconds, then picked up a pair of glasses and put them on. From under a neat stack of folders he pulled out a newspaper, eyed it, then me.

"Chief," he said, standing.

I awarded him three points, which put him three points ahead of the clowns down the hall making all the ruckus. "Detective Lanier," I answered, and only got a miniscule tell from the slight widening of his eyes that he was surprised I knew his name. I'd done my homework and knew the names and faces of all my cops.

He darted a glance at the wall. "We weren't expecting you until Monday."

Obviously, considering the party going on in what I was pretty sure was my new office. I moved to his desk, perching on the end. "Working on anything interesting?"

"An old cold case," he said, sitting.

Give my only detective another point. Unless they worked for a big department and were assigned that responsibility, cops didn't have to dig into cold cases and most didn't have the time. Since time issues didn't seem to be a problem here, it appeared my detective was taking the initiative to keep himself occupied. I liked that.

"Any new leads?"

He shrugged as he removed his glasses and set them aside. Intelligent blue eyes met mine. "Not really, but something's bugging me about this one. Just have to figure out what."

If something's bothering a smart detective, someone needs to start worrying, namely the killer. "When I get settled, let's go over it. Two minds are better than one and all that." Another round of laughter and more swearing reached my ears. I glanced at the wall, wishing I could see through it and get my bearings before I descended on the ones starting off on the wrong foot with me.

Lanier, apparently pretending not to hear them, said, "That would be great. Welcome, by the way."

"Thanks. Good to be here." I turned my gaze back to him. "What am I going to find when I walk in there?"

"A whole lot you're not going to like. I think it's time for me to be somewhere else." He put his glasses into a case, opened his drawer and removed a set of keys, then stood. "You going to be around anymore before Monday?"

"Maybe. Haven't decided yet."

I followed him out, turning right when he turned left.

As I neared the end of the hall, I inhaled the strong aroma of a cigar. Before going any further, I backtracked to the outside door to confirm that I had seen a NO SMOKING sign. I had. Still carrying the files I'd picked up, I headed for my prey.

The next to last door I came to was marked as the interrogation room, and I walked past it. When I was able to see into the last room without entering, I stopped and observed four of my cops sitting around my desk playing poker. Captain Moody sat in my chair, a fat cigar hanging from his mouth as he dealt cards with the expertise of a Vegas dealer. In front of each man but one was a tumbler filled with golden liquid.

"We really shouldn't be here," said the one without a drink who I pegged as Tommy Evans, my youngest officer and newest to the department. "I heard the chief's in town. What if he decides to come by?"

I gave Tommy half a point, deciding there was hope for him.

"Fuck the chief," Moody said, balancing his cigar on the edge of my desk, then sucking up the last of his drink, which I guessed to be whiskey.

It was time to rattle their cages. Changing my mind about playing games with them, I removed my ball cap and glasses.

"Sorry, but you're not my type, Moody." I walked in, tempted to laugh when cards went flying from startled hands. Three of the men jumped to their feet, but one took his time setting his empty glass down, then picking up his cigar and clamping his teeth around it before rising. Belligerence glittered in his eyes.

I decided on the spot that Moody's employment was going to be short-term. "Gentlemen, I hope you enjoyed the fun because it's the last time. Capisce?"

Two of them nodded, and Tommy, snapping to attention, said, "Yes, sir."

Another half point to the kid. He was savable. I hadn't made up my mind about the remaining two. "Who's supposed to be out on patrol right now?"

"Me, sir, but I was called in. They needed a fourth…" Tommy trailed off as Moody shot him a death glare.

"What time's your shift over?"

"Eleven, sir."

I glanced at my watch. "You still have fifty minutes." I looked at him and raised a brow. If he was as smart as I thought, he'd recognize the reprieve I'd given him.

"Thank you, sir." He shot out of the office like a dog with his ass on fire.

Moody had stubbornly stayed on my side of the desk. The man was an idiot, and I didn't have much patience with idiots. For the moment I ignored him, turning to the other two. "Woods, Jansen, what are the two of you supposed to be doing right now?"

Woods, thirty-one and married, gave me a sheepish look. "I'm off duty. I promised my wife I'd be home by eleven."

"Looks like you're gonna be able to keep that promise. Good-bye."

Although he didn't move as fast as Tommy, he didn't waste any time leaving. I gave him half a point. "Jansen?" I said, turning to the oldest man on my force.

"I'm on the front desk until eleven, Chief."

"Could've fooled me. How long you been playing cards?" Billy Jansen was about fifty pounds overweight and had the waist of his uniform pants pushed down under his abundant stomach. I'd have to think about a training regimen for my cops.

"About an hour."

"Then you're on the desk until midnight."

He sucked in air as if breathing were a chore for him,

which I imagined with his weight it was. "But I get off at eleven."

"That would have been true if you didn't owe the department an hour." I held up the folders. "Do you always leave confidential files out where anyone can get their hands on them?"

He shared a look with Moody, which was his mistake because it got him no points. "Get outta here before I decide to keep you on the desk all night." He left with the speed of a turtle. I deducted a point, putting him in the negative.

When it was just me and the biggest problem I'd inherited with his job, I eyed Moody. "We can do this easy or we can do this hard. Which is it gonna be?"

He didn't pretend to not understand. "When all's said and done, I'll still be here and you won't."

I shifted my gaze to the cards scattered over the desk and floor. "Since you're a betting man, how much you want to wager on that?" The man didn't give a shit that his new chief had caught him breaking every rule in the book.

"You're not worth the time of day, much less my money," he said as he calmly reached under my desk, coming up with a bottle of Jack Daniel's.

I waited for him to reach the doorway. "The sign when you enter states this is a no-smoking building, Captain Moody. Lose the cigar."

I thought I heard him mutter "fuck you" under his breath. One of my first priorities would be finding out why Moody still had the honor of wearing a badge and gun.

"That went well," I said to the empty room. As I looked around, I realized I'd made my first mistake by not ordering them to clean up my office.

A few minutes before eleven, I'd cleared out the mess and was getting ready to leave. I still had boxes to unpack at the apartment I'd rented, and since I never slept much, I could get a few done tonight. As I was walking down the hallway, I heard the dispatcher on duty say the name Jenny Nance. I didn't know Red's last name, and there was likely more than one Jenny in Blue Ridge Valley, but I still went into the room.

"I'm the new chief. What's going on?"

The dispatcher glanced up at me, apparently took me at my word, and said, "Domestic dispute. Boyfriend's refusing to leave."

"Find out if Tommy's close to the station." The dispatcher got on the radio and asked for Tommy's location. He was only a few miles away. "Tell him to pick me up."

If it was my Jenny having a problem, I intended to be on the scene.

CHAPTER THREE

~ Jenny ~

"YOU'RE MAKING A SCENE, AND you need to leave before my neighbors call the police." I tried to jerk my arm away, but Chad had a tight grip on my wrist. "You're hurting me."

"Who was the man at the bar?"

"There were a lot of men at the bar tonight." I knew exactly which man he meant, but his jealousy was making me angry. As expected, he'd been parked outside my apartment when I arrived. I'd almost kept driving. My best friend's sofa was available to me anytime I wanted it. But Autumn's fiancé lived with her now, and I didn't want to intrude. Besides, no way was I going to let Chad run me away from my home.

"Don't think I didn't see the way you looked at him, Jenn."

Well, I had done a double take, but so what? My mom and dad had a you-can-look policy, and I'd always believed that it was because they trusted each other and were secure in their love. With a man like Chad, that would never happen. Would, in fact, just get worse. I was done with him.

"He was a customer, Chad. Of course I looked at him." I huffed out a frustrated breath. "You've known from the beginning that I'm leaving in December, and that there would never be anything serious between us. You agreed to that."

"I changed my mind. And this idea of yours to take off for God knows where or how long is ridiculous."

"Well I haven't changed my mind, and I could care less what you think." I tried to pull my arm away again, but he held tight.

Chad was a stockbroker in Asheville, and part of his attraction had been his claim that he was too focused on his job to get involved in a serious relationship. With his puppy-brown eyes and soft voice, my first impression of him had been that he had a gentle soul. Like I said, I'm obviously a lousy judge of men. Chad actually had the soul of a self-centered, controlling Neanderthal. And those soulful eyes that had charmed me in the beginning were starting to creep me out with the way he would sometimes stare at me, as if he owned me and needed to make me understand he was my lord and master.

"Let. Go. Of. Me." As soon as I could put some distance between us, I would tell him it was over. Again. I'd tried to get that through his thick skull as soon as I'd gotten out of my car, but he'd closed his ears to anything he didn't want to hear.

He slid his other hand up my arm. "Come on, baby, you know I love you."

When he tried to kiss me, I turned my face away. "No, you don't, but it doesn't matter. I want you gone, and don't come back. Ever."

"That's not how this works, Jenn. I say when it's over." He grabbed my hand, pulling me toward my apartment.

He was starting to scare me with the way his eyes shone with barely concealed anger. I was sure my neighbors were already peeking through their blinds, and I hoped one of them had called the police. Deciding it was time to make a lot of noise, I dug in my heels.

"Let go of me," I yelled.

A man came out from a few doors down. "There a problem here?"

"No—"

"Yes," I said, speaking over Chad's denial. "I want him to leave." This was embarrassing, but I was grateful for the man's appearance.

"This doesn't concern you." Chad narrowed his eyes at me. "Unless he's another one you've been flirting with. Are you screwing him, too?"

Seriously? I needed to have a firm talk with myself about my boyfriend choices. "Who I'm screwing or not screwing is no longer any of your business."

"The lady wants you gone," the man said.

Chad dropped my arm and stepped toward my neighbor just as bright lights almost blinded my eyes and the sharp *whoop whoop* of a siren sounded. Everyone froze.

"What's the problem here," a cop said after getting out of his car.

"No problem, Officer," Chad said.

I glanced over, and seeing Tommy Evans, I backed up until I was close to him. "The problem is I want him to leave." I pointed at Chad. "He refuses." I'd never in my life witnessed or been involved in a domestic dispute, and I took a moment to be depressed that I could no longer say that.

Chad the Idiot waved a hand at my neighbor. "That man assaulted me. I want him arrested."

Was he for real? Maybe he thought he could divert the attention from himself. "That's my neighbor, Tommy, and he was only trying to help. He didn't assault anyone."

"Name's Bob Hagan. Now that the police are here, I'll take myself off."

"Thank you, Bob," I called to him. He raised a hand in acknowledgment as he walked away.

Not knowing when to quit, Chad started arguing with the officer.

"What's his name?" Tommy asked, ignoring Chad.

"Chad Perrine. My ex-boyfriend."

"Mr. Perrine, you have two choices," said a voice from behind me that sounded familiar. "You can leave now, or you can spend the night in jail."

I swung my head around and looked into the eyes of Dylan Conrad. Why was he here?

"I knew you were fucking him," Chad the Even Bigger Idiot said.

I refused to respond to that absurd statement. "Why is he here?" I asked Tommy, eyeing Dylan.

"He's our new chief of police, and he's riding along with me tonight."

That's where I'd heard the name, from people at the bar talking about the big-city cop the town had hired. So he wasn't a tourist that I'd probably never see again. My stomach gave a flutter of excitement at that news.

To keep from adding to Chad's suspicions, I tore my gaze away from Dylan's. "I'm thinking you should choose door number one and go home, Chad. Your father won't appreciate having to drive here from Asheville to bail you out."

That got his attention. His dad owned the brokerage firm where Chad worked. I'd met the man once and had the impression he was cold and ruthless.

"It was just a silly misunderstanding," Chad said, but resentment radiated from him as he leveled his gaze on the new police chief. "I'm leaving. Talk to you tomorrow, babe."

"I'd rather you didn't." His lips thinned at that, but he headed for his car. The two cops and I watched him until he drove away. "Sorry for the trouble."

"Wait for me in the car," Dylan said to Tommy. When we were alone, concerned eyes searched mine. "You okay?"

"As long as I never hear from him again, I am." Why did this man have to be so gorgeous?

"Want to put a restraining order on him?"

"No, I don't think he'll bother me again." I wasn't so sure of that, but a restraining order seemed harsh, at least at this point. If Chad decided to cause me more trouble, I'd consider it.

He reached over and tucked a loose curl of hair behind my ear. I froze. Those whiskey-colored eyes captured mine, and I had the wild idea that he was going to kiss me.

Instead he reached into his back pocket and removed his wallet, taking out a card. "My cell number's on here. If he gives you any more trouble, call me."

When I stood there like a statue while my brain tried to start up again, he picked up my hand and closed my fingers around the card.

"See you around, Red." He chuckled as he walked away.

That low chuckle said he knew exactly what was going through my mind. When he reached the door of the cruiser, he paused and shot me one of those killer smiles, accompanied by a wink, across the roof before disappearing inside.

I expected them to drive away, but the car didn't move, and after a few seconds it dawned on me that they were waiting for me to go inside. Right, I would do just that. Spinning on my heels, I left, not giving them a good-bye wave. As soon as I walked inside, locking the door behind me, my cell started ringing. Chad's name came up on the screen, and I let it go to voice mail. Pulling up my contacts, I deleted his name and blocked his phone number, then deleted the message without listening to it.

No doubt Chad thought this was just a little bump in our relationship, but when I'm done with someone, I don't mess around. A quick peek out the window and I saw that the police car was gone.

Was I imagining Dylan was giving off signals that he was interested in me, or was he just a nice cop doing his job? Didn't really matter either way because I had a vow to my sister to keep, even if being near him made my heart do that pitter-patter thingy.

I needed some girl talk with my bestie. "Hey," I said when Autumn answered her phone. "You free for some girl time tomorrow?"

Autumn Archer, Savannah Graham, and I had been tight ever since first grade. Savannah was in New York now, fulfilling her dream of becoming a supermodel, otherwise I would have included her, too. Autumn's fiancé owned a car dealership, and since Saturdays were a busy day for him, I knew she'd be free.

"Sure," she said without hesitation. "Whatcha got in mind?"

"A day at the beach." The beach was what, back in high school, the four of us called Skinny Dip Falls, which is a half-mile hike off the Blue Ridge Parkway and easy to get to.

"Awesome! I'm in."

"I'll swing by around ten. We can pick up some snacks on the way." I'd wait until tomorrow to tell her about Chad. If I got into it now, we'd be on the phone all night. After disconnecting, I stared at the opposite wall, but it wasn't my soon-to-be ex-boyfriend filling my mind. It was a man with whiskey-colored eyes and a killer smile.

CHAPTER FOUR

~ Dylan ~

"HOPE SHE LOSES THE BOYFRIEND," Tommy said. "The dude's an ass."

I hoped she did, too. "She seems like a smart lady." Not to mention downright sexy with those deep green eyes and long hair that reminded me of red and dark gold autumn leaves. Without thinking, I'd touched her, tucking a loose strand of hair behind her ear before remembering Tommy was sitting in the cruiser watching us. Not like me to forget my surroundings.

We got back to the station a little after the shift change. Jansen was still at the front, and I'd never seen a grown man pout before. It wasn't pretty. His bottom lip was sticking out a mile. He lost more points.

"Night, Chief," Tommy said before disappearing down the hall.

"Later, Tommy." I wondered how long it would take my cops to figure out if I called you by your first name, it meant I liked you. Or maybe they'd just assume I went with Tommy because he was so young. It was a little game I'd played in Chicago, and only my partner had figured it out. That was back when I still called Jack by his first name, but those times were done. I did my best not to think of my ex-partner by any name these days.

"Who relieves you, Jansen?"

He leaned back in his chair and stuck his thumbs underneath his belt, or tried to. After some thumb fumbling, he finally gave up and crossed his hands over his beer gut.

"Payton."

"And where is Officer Payton?"

"Here, Chief."

I turned. Kim Payton stood at the end of the hallway. Word had spread that I was here if she was calling me chief without an introduction. Her uniform was perfectly pressed and creased, and I gave her a nod of approval. She was on my list of possible saves.

Yeah, I had a list with two columns. Not that I was going to make any changes immediately. I needed to get the lay of the land, but my instincts were pretty good, and I'd already divided up the department into two groups. Gone and not gone. I'd give the gone ones a chance to change my mind, but so far Jansen wasn't doing a good job of securing his future with the Blue Ridge Valley Police Department.

"You're relieved," I told Jansen, ending his punishment fifteen minutes early. See, I'm not that much of an asshole. I can be generous when the mood strikes.

"Do we lock the front door at night?" I asked Payton after Jansen waddled out.

"Never have." Eyeing the messy desk, she frowned and began tidying up.

"Then let's start with the nightly shift change. Too many crazies out there these days, and there're only two in here after eleven, the duty officer and a dispatcher, right?" She nodded. "We'll get an intercom installed so if someone comes by at three in the morning, we can check them out before opening up."

"Good idea, Chief."

Oh, I'm just full of good ideas. They had no clue. "Post a notice that I want everyone here Monday morning at seven for a brief meeting. Make sure the word gets out."

"On it." She pulled a sheet of copy paper from the desk and started writing.

I gave Officer Payton a point for her easy slide into accepting me as her new chief. I had a tendency to operate out of the box, like this points thing. It was something I'd started as the head of vice in Chicago when I'd had a problem child. The kid thought since he was the nephew of the commissioner, he could do as he pleased. I sat him down and told him he had three months to earn thirty points or I was transferring him out of vice and back onto the street. I don't remember how I came up with the idea, and no one was more surprised than me that it worked. He ended up being one of my better detectives. He was happy. I was happy. The commissioner was happy.

The difference now was that I wasn't going to tell my new department they were either getting points or losing them. Last thing I wanted was a bunch of cops kissing my ass. Each of my Blue Ridge Valley officers had six months to earn sixty points. How hard could ten points a month be, especially since I planned to be generous at giving them out?

Come time's up, I planned to sit down with each one and discuss where they stood. Then the problem ones, I'd give another six months to get their act together…except for Moody and Jansen. I was pretty sure they'd be gone before sit-down time.

"See you Monday, if not before," I told her as I walked out. I didn't look back, but I slowed my steps until I heard the click of the lock. That earned her another point.

After I got home, I sat at the kitchen counter and pulled out the notebook I'd already created, a page for each of my officers, and entered the first points I'd awarded. Already I was having fun.

Finished with that, I swiveled on the bar stool and eyed the stack of boxes pushed against one wall of the living room. Nah. Not tackling those tonight. I had all day tomorrow and Sunday, having decided I wouldn't make another appearance at the station until my official start day on Monday. I'd stirred things up enough, so I'd give my cops two days for all the gossip about me to die down.

A quick shower and I was in bed by midnight. The ceiling fan made a clicking noise as the blades turned, something I'd have to fix. I'd rented an apartment on the third floor so I could leave my windows open at night. The sounds here were foreign. No sirens, no cars passing under my window, no arguing or yelling from groups of kids out on the streets at a time when they should be tucked into their beds.

An owl somewhere nearby was asking, *Hoo? Hoo? Hoo?* That was pretty cool. A strong breeze rustled the needles of what I'd been told were eastern white pines. I grinned and closed my eyes, hoping I'd been successful in leaving my ghost behind, the one who'd paid me nightly visits back in Chicago.

An hour later I turned onto my stomach, put my pillow over my head, and cussed out that damned owl that wouldn't shut up. This nature business was going to take some getting used to. Since I was determined to adjust to my new environment, I didn't get up and close the window.

I was finally drifting off when Christine decided to pop in. *I was hoping I'd left you behind.*

She laughed, a sound I'd once loved hearing. *Nice try, Dy. I can find you anywhere.*

My therapist told me that I wasn't going crazy having these conversations with my dead wife. That was a relief, believe me. He said when I was ready to let her go, I would stop hearing her voice in my head. I'd sure as hell hoped starting over somewhere far from our familiar haunts would do the trick. Obviously not. During the day I hardly thought of her anymore or what she'd done. Nights were a bitch, though.

She'd been a beautiful woman—ash-blonde hair, sapphire-blue eyes, and a perfect body that I'd worshipped many nights—and she'd caught my attention the first time I saw her. I'd thought she was my forever. I was sure as hell wrong on that one.

Ah, Dylan, don't be so mean. You love me. I know you do.

I did once, but I got over you.

Did you really?

I refused to answer because I had a rule about lying to myself. I hoped I was. Prayed I was, but if she was still in my head… I squeezed my eyes tight, shutting out her sapphire-blue ones.

She didn't show up as often as she had after everything had happened, but I hadn't been able to put her to rest even though almost two years had passed. It was starting to piss me off. I understood it was because of how the end came, and I carried a ton of guilt that I hadn't grasped how desperate and depressed she was. I'm a cop, trained to recognize desperation in people. My rage at what she'd done had blinded me, though, and I'd turned a deaf ear to her threats.

My therapist said I'm not responsible for the actions of others, but that's damn easy for him to say when it wasn't his wife who put a gun—my gun—in her mouth and pulled the trigger.

To quiet Christine's voice, I visualized a red-haired, green-eyed, feisty bartender. That did the trick because my wife faded away, and I drifted off thinking of Red.

CHAPTER FIVE

~ Jenny ~

BECAUSE I'D BLOCKED CHAD'S NUMBER, it wouldn't surprise me if he showed up since it was a Saturday and he was off. I threw on a pair of shorts and a T-shirt, grabbed my straw hat, my camera, a cooler, and hightailed it out of here. It was still an hour before I was supposed to pick up Autumn, so I went ahead and made a stop at the grocery store. I knew what she liked, and by the time I was done, I figured I had about twice what we could eat.

After loading the sandwiches, cheese packages, and bottled waters into the cooler, I headed over to Autumn's. Although I was twenty minutes early, she was ready to go.

"It's been too long since we've done this," she said as we drove onto the entrance for the Parkway.

"Well, if a certain someone wasn't too busy planning her wedding…" I looked pointedly at her.

"Yeah, well, who knew there would be so much to do? We should have just eloped."

I glanced at my friend. "And give up wearing that amazing wedding dress? I don't think so." With her honey-blonde hair, blue eyes, and the toned body she'd dieted and exercised like a fiend to achieve, she was going to be a beautiful bride.

"Too late now, I guess, since all the invitations have gone out." She leaned over and eyed my speedometer. "You better slow down. I heard they're cracking down on speeding on the Parkway."

"No fun." But I eased off the gas. The only thing I didn't like about driving the Blue Ridge Parkway was the slow speed limit. My car was a four-year-old silver Mustang GT, and she liked to run. Okay, truth was, I liked to go fast. Probably not the best car for mountain roads with their sharp curves, not giving me much opportunity to test her limits, but I loved her. I should probably sell her before I left, but I couldn't bring myself to do it. My dad could take care of her while I was gone. Actually I think he was looking forward to getting his hands on my Mustang.

We were having unusually warm fall weather, and it looked like others had the same idea. I found a parking spot in the almost full gravel lot, locked the doors, and then we hiked down to the bottom of the falls, our totes slung over our shoulders and the cooler between us.

At the end of the easy path down, the space opened up to a large round pool of crystal-clear water. The waterfall wasn't the biggest in the area, but it was high enough so that the falls cascaded over the rocks and boulders, noisily crashing when it reached the bottom.

People had claimed their spots with coolers and towels. Some were playing in the pool—which I knew from experience was icy cold—while others were basking in the sun. We spied a flat boulder with no one nearby and headed for it.

"I can't believe how warm it is for October," Autumn said as we spread out our towels.

"Yeah, we're going to have a late leaf turning this year." The sun was warm on my face, but the cool water flowing around our rock kept me from overheating.

For a few minutes we talked about Autumn and Brian's wedding and what things she had left to do. She was getting married the second Saturday in December, and that would be here before we knew it.

I dropped down onto my back and stared up at the

fluffy white clouds floating by. "Do you ever wish you could just drift off on a cloud, go wherever it goes?"

Autumn settled onto her side, facing me, resting on her elbow. "Not even. You're the one with wanderlust. I prefer to keep my feet on the ground right here in Blue Ridge Valley." She studied me for a moment. "So you're really going?"

I turned my head toward her. "Of course I am. I promised."

She sighed. "I miss her."

"God, me, too. Every minute of every hour. I feel like half of me is gone." Which made sense, I guess, since Natalie was my twin. When she died, she'd taken a part of me with her.

Autumn's eyes misted. "I don't want you to go."

"You know I have to. I promised her I'd go to all the places we'd planned to visit together." And she'd said one other thing, which I'd never told anyone, including Autumn and Savannah, because even they wouldn't understand. Natalie had made me a promise, too. She swore she would be right there with me, that I'd feel her in my heart. I needed that, craved feeling her being a part of me again.

My plane ticket to Greece was bought and paid for. I'd be leaving right after Autumn's wedding. That was as far as I'd planned. Once in Europe, I'd hike my way around some, take buses or trains to wherever I felt drawn to go next. Where I went and when would depend on Natalie. If I felt her with me in some particular place, I'd stay longer. If not, I'd move on.

Before we both started bawling, I decided we needed a change of subject. "So, guess who was such a big jerk last night that the cops had to show up?"

She sat up. "No way."

"Way." I told her what had happened. She knew I'd been ready to break up with Chad, even warning me that he wasn't going away easily.

"What an asshat. You should take out a restraining order on him," she said when I finished.

"Dylan asked me if I wanted to."

Her eyebrows furrowed. "Who's Dylan?"

Oops. I probably shouldn't have mentioned his name. Autumn could be relentless in satisfying her curiosity, meaning about a thousand questions were coming my way. "Dylan Conrad. He's our new police chief."

"And exactly how did it come to be that you're familiar enough with him to call him by Dylan? Cool name, by the way."

"Um, he stopped by Vincennes last night for a few minutes."

"A few minutes and he's already Dylan. Give over, Jenn. There's more to this story."

It was useless to resist. "He calls me Jenny. He refuses to call me Jenn because Chad does."

"Wow. I like him already. I'd heard a big-city cop got the job. Is he cute?"

"No." She looked so crestfallen that I couldn't help grinning. "Cute doesn't do him justice. He's gorgeous."

She clapped her hands. "I knew it. With that name, he had to be. I'm hungry. While we eat, you can tell me all about him."

"Tennessee whiskey-colored eyes, huh?" she said when I finished describing him. "I need to meet this man, see if I approve of him for you."

"Autumn, I'm leaving in two months. I'm not looking for a Chad replacement."

"Who knows, maybe you'll fall madly in love and stay home. Then I won't have to miss you."

I threw an olive at her. "Not gonna fall in love."

After we finished our sandwiches, we stretched out on the rock. Autumn yawned, and within a few minutes she'd fallen asleep. I watched the clouds float by and thought about Dylan.

Everyone had a story, and I wondered what his was. Why would a man leave a big city to come to a small mountain town? It didn't make sense to me, a person who wanted out of this place. Not that I didn't love my hometown, I did, but there was a whole wide world waiting to be explored. He had to be used to a wide choice of restaurants, shops, and all kinds of entertainment.

He probably wouldn't last long here before he got bored and moved on. It occurred to me that wasn't such a bad thing where I was concerned. I could date him, neither of us with any expectations. Just have a good time together, nothing more, and then we'd each go our separate ways. Him back to Chicago or some other big city and me off to see the world.

I laughed. Already I was planning our relationship. To divert my mind from the town's new hot cop, I got out my camera and took some pictures of Autumn sleeping and then some of the landscape. Photography was my hobby. To prepare for my world tour and the photos I'd take, I'd enrolled in classes, learning about such things as light, depth, and the Rule of Thirds, which was the placement of your subject matter.

Taking pictures always worked as an escape from thinking about anything other than lining up the best shot, and it worked for me today. Dylan was forgotten as I got some terrific shots of the waterfalls and surrounding landscape.

Chad hadn't been waiting for me when I returned home, nor was his car at Vincennes when I got there. Although it surprised me he'd not made an appearance, some of the tension I'd felt from expecting another confrontation eased. Maybe he'd gotten the message. We didn't start getting busy until around five, and I spent my first hour restocking the bar.

A few minutes before five, I made a quick trip to the restroom before things started hopping. Saturday nights were always crazy, and I loved it that way. I redid my ponytail, gathering the strands that had come loose. I headed back to the lounge, happy that my ex wasn't being a PITA. Maybe Dylan would stop by tonight. Still hadn't made up my mind about him, but I was kind of excited about seeing him.

Scanning the room to see who had arrived, I rolled my eyes. Considering my poor track record with men, I should know better by now than to expect it would have been that easy. I grabbed a bottle of pale ale, opened it, then slammed it down in front of Chad.

"Hey, baby," the jerk said as if last night had never happened.

As if the police hadn't been called, totally embarrassing me. Ignoring him, I turned to Autumn and Brian as they walked up. "Hey, you two." I wasn't crazy about Brian, but Autumn loved him, so I kept my opinion to myself. Since I knew they liked eating at the bar, I set out silverware and napkins.

"Love that dress. Can I borrow it sometime?" It was the same blue as her eyes and really made them pop.

"No, you may not. Last time I loaned you my clothes, you spilled red wine down my favorite blouse."

I rolled my eyes. "That was four years ago. I've grown up since then."

She blew me an air kiss before darting a quick glance at Chad, then turning a raised brow to me. *Why's he here?* she mouthed.

"Later," I said, making the universal sign with my hand to my ear that I'd call her.

"Jenn, got a minute?" Chad said.

"Nope." I handed Autumn and Brian the specials menu. The regular one they had memorized, as had most of the locals. "Angelo's got those lamb chops tonight," I said as I poured each of them a glass of merlot. Brian perked up, which I knew he would. Angelo marinated the chops all afternoon, then crusted them to perfection over a grill. They were pretty darn good.

Brian pushed his menu back to me. "Sign me up."

"I think I'll have veal piccata," Autumn said.

"Of course you will." She rarely ordered anything else. "Savannah ever call back?"

"Nope." We'd tried calling her on my phone this afternoon, getting her voice mail. We were worried about Savannah. The first few years, we heard from her all the time. Lately, not so much, and that was worrisome. She was supposed to be home for Autumn's wedding, so hopefully we could reassure ourselves that she was okay.

"Jenn, please. I need to talk to you."

I put in the orders for Brian and Autumn before walking over to Chad. If I kept ignoring him, he'd get mad and make a scene. "I'm busy and there's nothing left to say. If you want dinner, then order something. If not, you're taking up a seat and there are people waiting."

He put his hand over mine. "I don't know what I did wrong, baby, but whatever it was, I'm sorry. Forgive me?"

The urge to bang my head on the bar was almost irresistible, but I settled for pulling my hand away. "Fine. I forgive you. Now go away." A couple I didn't recognize came in, and I moved away to take care of them. How did you break up with a guy who refused to listen?

After making drinks for the latest arrivals, I checked on the rest of my customers, refilling glasses and taking orders. I refused to glance Chad's way, but I could feel his glare on me.

While I was refilling Brian and Autumn's wineglasses,

Brandy brought out their salads. "Saw your car at the grocery store this afternoon. I walked up and down all the aisles but couldn't find you," she said.

"That's because I wasn't there."

"Well, your car was."

"No, it was with me at the water..." I glanced at Chad. Yep, he was listening. "Oh right, I did run in to pick up a few things."

Autumn gave me a funny look, knowing I was lying. That was the second time someone had said they'd seen my car somewhere I wasn't. Unless somebody had stolen my car to make a quick run to the store and then returned it, there was a person running around with one like mine. Since I didn't know of a local who had a silver Mustang, it must be a tourist.

"Jenn!"

I sighed when Chad held up his empty beer bottle. I wanted to tell him to bug off, but he was a customer and this wasn't the place to make a scene. When I slid another beer to him, he grabbed my wrist. The next time I came near him, I was going to bring a fork with me so I could stab his hand when he grabbed me.

"Come on, baby. I said I was sorry. How long you going to punish me?"

What had I ever seen in him? I glanced around the bar, and the only one paying attention was Autumn. She raised a brow, shooting a look at Brian. I gave a little shake of my head. No way I wanted Brian getting involved, which would only end with Chad mad and mouthing off.

"I'm working, so please let go of my arm."

The toad tightened his fingers just enough to hurt, then let go. "I'll be back when you get off."

My first reaction was to tell him no, but I was going to have to have a firm conversation with him, and I might as well get it over with.

"Fine. See you later."

It had turned out to be a disappointing night. Chad had shown up and Dylan hadn't.

CHAPTER SIX

~ Dylan ~

I'D BEEN SITTING IN MY car for fifteen minutes in a lot across the street from Vincennes, watching Jenny's boyfriend—hopefully ex-boyfriend—as he leaned against the hood of his Beamer. It didn't surprise me that he wasn't going to give up easily. He was the kind of man who couldn't handle a woman walking out on him. Good-looking, big ego, high-powered job, daddy's money. Yeah, I'd checked him out. My instincts had yet to lie to me, and they were buzzing over this guy.

This afternoon I'd debated going to Vincennes for dinner but had decided it was too soon to see Jenny again. Didn't want her to think I was trying to make a move on her while she was still tangled up with Pretty Boy.

I'd spent most of the day unpacking and getting my apartment in order, only leaving to go to the grocery store to pick up some sandwich supplies for dinner. My intention had been to spend the evening preparing for Monday and my first official day on the job. But having been closed up most of the day, I was going a little stir-crazy and decided to take a ride.

Since there was only one main street in Blue Ridge Valley, I couldn't help driving by the restaurant. As I passed, I saw Chad Perrine turn into the parking lot shortly before their closing time. I pulled into the lot across the street, turned off my lights, and eased into a space that allowed me a good view. I wasn't going to try to fight Jenny's battles for her, but if things got nasty, I'd be nearby.

Perrine straightened when Jenny appeared. Had she made up with him? *Don't break my heart, Jenny Girl.* I watched her body language, pleased that she stopped a few feet from him, putting her hands on her hips. I wished I could hear the conversation, but I was at least able to keep an eye on her, make sure the discussion stayed civil.

They talked back and forth for a few minutes, then Perrine reached for her. She shook her head as she backed up. When he stepped toward her, I put my hand on the door handle. Jenny reached into her purse and pulled out her cell phone, backing up some more as she said something. My guess, she was threatening to call the cops. Smart girl. He got in his car and slammed the door, spinning his tires as he took off.

"Real cool, dude."

I decided I'd follow Jenny home, make sure the man didn't decide to show up there. She disappeared around the back of the building where I assumed she parked. A few minutes later a car came into view.

"I'll be damned," I murmured. We had matching Mustangs. Amused, I stayed far enough behind her so she wouldn't notice me. After she arrived home and disappeared into her apartment, I stuck around for ten minutes or so, just to make sure Perrine didn't show up. Once I decided he wasn't going to make an appearance, I headed back to my place.

Monday morning I made sure to get to work before the seven o'clock shift change. I figured it was safe not to have any cars out on patrol this early for the forty-five-minute meeting I had planned, so when the cops coming off shift and those going on were all gathered, I gave them my spiel. The ones on the three to eleven were also here, and as I introduced myself, my gaze slid over the group both seated and standing around the lobby. Everyone except for Jansen looked crisp and sharp.

"I'm sure all of you know my name by now, but if you missed that bit of news somehow, I'm Dylan Conrad, your new chief. I'm a fair man, but..." I scanned the room, meeting each of their eyes. "But my word is law. Are you paying attention? I hope so, but I'll repeat it one more time so there's no misunderstanding." I turned my gaze on Moody and Jansen, who were sitting together, both with bored expressions on their faces. They were going to find themselves very bored when they were out of a job.

"My word is law. No ands, ifs, or buts." Moody narrowed his eyes, and I deducted five points. The man was digging a deep hole but was too stupid to know it.

"I won't be making any changes right away... Actually, that's not true. From this moment on, there will be no more poker games in this building. There will be no cursing, not even a 'damn' when on duty. My favorite word is 'fuck,' but you'll never hear me say it again when I'm on the clock."

"This is fucking bullshit," Jansen muttered.

Why was I not surprised he'd be the one to test me? "You're suspended for the day without pay, Jansen. Go home." I deducted a thousand points, making sure he'd never dig his way out. Jansen leaned back on the chair he was squeezed into, crossed his arms over his belly, and glared at me.

"You have a very short memory, Officer Jansen. My word is law. You're now suspended for three days. If you're smart, which I have my doubts about, you'll leave this second. If you don't, my next offer is a week's suspension."

He heaved his massive body up and stomped out. I heard a snicker and turned my attention to Reddick. "Something funny, Officer Reddick?"

His eyes widened. "No sir."

"Didn't think so." He was surprised I knew his name, but I knew the names of every man and the two women sitting or standing in this room, even the ones I hadn't met. They didn't know how much I loved assigning myself homework. Except for the few who'd had contact with me last Friday night, they didn't know what to expect. As I continued on with my little speech, I began to see respect in most of their eyes. My work here was done, at least for this morning. Other than Moody and Jansen, I gave each one of them five points as a bonus because I was feeling generous.

"Bottom line, ladies and gentlemen"—I gave a nod to my only two women officers—"this police department is going to be the pride of Blue Ridge Valley. You do your job and do it right, I'll have your back. That is my promise to you. If you have any questions, now's the time to ask them."

One of the women raised her hand. "Yes, Officer Griffin?" Again, the wide eyes of surprise that I knew her name.

"Ah…maybe it's too soon to complain, but we hate our uniforms. Is there any chance of getting new ones?"

"We as in all of you?" Everyone nodded. I hated their uniforms, too. The shirts were a puke green, the pants a muddy brown. I sure as hell wouldn't want to wear that uniform. "That's on my list. I can't promise you how soon it will happen, or if it even will, but I'm working on it."

"Thank you, Chief."

"Anything else?" Tommy raised his hand. "Tommy?"

Officer Kim Payton scrunched her eyebrows together, giving Tommy a quick glance when I called him by his first name. I gave her a point for being observant.

"I'd like to propose a rotation schedule for cleaning the break room. Right now it's up to Sarah and Kim…I mean Officers Griffin and Payton to do it. I don't think that's fair."

"They do it 'cause they're the only women we got," Moody said.

Sexist pig. I took fifty points away from him—no, make that a hundred. Ignoring Moody, I said, "First, you're free to use each others' first names. Second, work out a rotation schedule, Tommy, then post it."

The two women exchanged grins. I figured with that one act alone, I'd won their loyalty. "If that's all, you're dismissed. For those going on duty, be careful out there." I loved that line from the old cop show, *Hill Street Blues.*

For the rest of the day I spent my time in the office, getting it organized. Moody had been the interim chief for six months, and the place was a mess. What a surprise. By six I had everything organized the way I wanted it and, when my stomach growled, decided to call it quits for the day. Someone from the Ladies Auxiliary had dropped off a large pan of lasagna to welcome me aboard, so I hadn't even left for lunch. I'd carved out a chunk for myself and then gave the rest to my cops.

Vincennes was closed on Mondays or I would have had dinner there, but instead I grabbed a burger at a drive-through and, after wolfing it down, made a few more stops around town to introduce myself. I wanted the people in Blue Ridge Valley to know their new police chief was interested in them and their well-being.

Tomorrow I'd have a police radio installed in my car, but for now I was using a handheld. When it crackled to life, reporting a fight at Hideouts, the honky-tonk bar, I headed there.

The first thing I saw when I pulled into the parking lot was Jansen beating on a guy half his size. I assumed the guy trying to pull them apart was the bouncer. A siren sounded, and moments later a police cruiser raced up.

"Tommy," I said when he exited the patrol car, "come help me pull Jansen off that dude before someone gets hurt."

"You got it, Chief."

Between the two of us and the bouncer, we separated Jansen and the other man, but Jansen was an idiot—which I already knew—and he tried to break away and go after the man again. Jansen was beyond reasoning with.

"Give me your handcuffs," I said, talking to Tommy behind Jansen's back. He slipped them to me, and I clamped one on Jansen's arm, then realized there was no way I'd get his fat arms behind his back and be able to cuff him without another pair, maybe two more.

"Help me push him to the cruiser." Between the two of us, Tommy and I managed to get him next to the back door. Jansen was still spitting mad, and the fool hadn't even realized I'd cuffed him to the door handle of the cruiser until he tried to go after the other man again and was jerked back.

"The fuck?" Jansen said, trying to tug his arm free.

I didn't bother deducting points because as of now, the man was no longer one of my cops. "What's this all about?" I asked the man I took to be the bouncer.

"John Mackey," he said, holding out his hand, which I shook. "You're the new police chief, right?"

I nodded. "Dylan Conrad."

"Thought so. So, your cop comes in on occasion. Don't know what started it, but he followed Jordy out and tried to beat the shit out of him." He glanced at Jordy. "Sorry, don't know your last name."

"Neiman, Jordy Neiman. I bumped into the dude, apologized, but he didn't want my apology."

"Asshole stepped on my foot."

I walked back to Jansen. "Not another word." He spit on my shoe, and I grabbed his earlobe and twisted it until he squealed. "You do that again, I'm going to throw you in a cell and lose the key."

Returning to Neiman, I said, "Do you want to press charges?"

"No, man. I just want to leave. That was what I was trying to do when he tackled me."

That wasn't the answer I wanted, but I let it go. I did get John Mackey to agree to give a statement to Tommy tomorrow, which would still suit my purpose. "I want you to write out what you saw from the time you arrived, Tommy. I'll do the same."

"You gonna fire Jansen?"

I eyed Tommy. "Would you?"

"Definitely. He's trouble."

"That he is. Speaking of trouble, guess we're about to find out how much when we try to get him into the back of your patrol car. Give me your stun gun."

Turned out with the stun gun pointed at him and my threat to use it, Jansen was as manageable as a puppy.

CHAPTER SEVEN

~ Jenny ~

"WE SHOULD HAVE GONE TO Asheville," Autumn said, shaking her head at the sundress I held up.

"You're being too picky. I'm going to start calling you Bridezilla." We'd made the two-hour drive to Knoxville because Autumn had gotten it in her head that she'd find exactly what she needed in Tennessee. The shop we were in had some adorable women's clothing, but apparently Autumn didn't think so. Shopping wasn't my favorite thing in the world to do, but she was my bestie, so sacrifices were called for.

She stuck her tongue out at me. "You haven't seen anything yet. I'm just getting started on my bride bitch."

"Heaven help me then." I held up another dress. She wrinkled her nose. "Jeez, Autumn. You'll be on your honeymoon. You probably won't have any clothes on half the time." I grinned when she giggled. "Besides, you're going to Hawaii. All you really need are bathing suits."

"I just want everything to be perfect, and that includes my clothes."

"And it will be. You wouldn't allow it to be any other way." Her interior designer eye extended to her wardrobe. I often wished I could put outfits together the way she did. Give her a plain, shapeless dress, a scarf or two, a funky belt, a few accessories, and she'd turn them into something that looked right out of a fashion magazine.

"Am I really turning into a Bridezilla? I'm trying not

to."

A little. "No, you're being entirely sane about your wedding and honeymoon."

She elbowed my arm. "Liar."

"Let's wrap this up for the day. We'll get back to the valley just in time for dinner." Truthfully, what I wanted to do was warn her again about Brian's roving eye, but I kept my mouth shut. I'd tried to tell her a few times, but she didn't want to hear it.

"Jenn?"

"Mmm?"

"I'm so glad we're friends."

"Me, too." I hugged her. "Now, let's go feed me. I've worked up an appetite helping you spend money."

Natalie and Savannah should be here. Like most teenaged girls, the four of us had spent hours planning our weddings, describing our wedding gowns, and dreaming of the exotic locales we'd go on our honeymoons. At one point we'd pinkie swore that no matter where we might be in the world, we'd come back when one of us was getting married.

When Autumn got engaged, Savannah had said she'd arrange her schedule to be here three weeks before the wedding, so she could spend that time with Autumn and me, doing things like helping Autumn shop. Now she was flying in the day of the rehearsal and leaving the morning after the wedding. As for Natalie, she would never come home again.

"Why are you so quiet?" Autumn asked as we drove back to Blue Ridge Valley.

"You wore me out, I'm hungry, and my feet hurt." I didn't tell her that Natalie and Savannah were on my mind. The time leading up to her wedding was supposed to be happy and fun, and I didn't want her to be sad, too.

We ended the day by having dinner at Fusions, the second-best restaurant in the valley, Vincennes being the best. But the last thing I wanted to do was hang out where I worked. We'd finished eating and had relocated to the restaurant's lounge a few minutes before Brian joined us for a drink, after which he'd take Autumn home.

"Hey, babe," he said, giving Autumn a kiss. "Jenn, how're they hanging?"

"Same as always." Brian claimed I had balls. He'd come to that conclusion not long after I met him when I'd threatened his if he ever made my friend cry. So far, he still had his balls, but if he kept staring at my butt whenever he thought no one was paying attention, he wasn't going to have them for long.

We'd just ordered our drinks when Dylan Conrad walked into the lounge. He paused in the entryway, his gaze scanning the room. The man was so freaking hot. At seeing me, he smiled, making my heart thump in my chest.

"Mind if I join you?" he said, coming to a stop behind the empty chair at our table for four. "Unless you're expecting someone."

That was said to me. "Nope. Have a seat, Chief." I had a sudden fantasy of playing cop and criminal with him, me being the bad guy and him having to frisk me. I hoped my cheeks weren't as red as they felt. He sat next to me, and I caught a whiff of man and something spicy. I also hoped I didn't start drooling.

His eyes danced with amusement. "Introduce me to your friends, Red."

Oh. Right. I was sitting here staring at him like an idiot, and now I knew for sure my face was beet red. "Ahem, this is my best friend, Autumn Archer, and her soon-to-be husband, Brian Stratton. Guys, this is Dylan Conrad, Blue Ridge Valley's new police chief."

"Welcome to Blue Ridge Valley," Autumn said. "I've heard great things about you."

Dylan sat back in his chair. "Oh?"

I kicked her under the table. That devilish gleam in her eyes meant she was up to no good.

"Yep. You have really pretty eyes, by the way. Jenn said they were the color of Tennessee whiskey, and she's right."

I kicked her again. Harder.

Dylan turned those beautiful eyes on me. "You been talking about me, Red?"

He was fighting a smile, so I knew he wasn't mad. Still. "Nope. I hadn't noticed what color your eyes were until now. One thing you need to learn about Autumn is that she likes to stir the pot."

"That's true," Brian said.

Autumn punched his arm. "Hey, whose side are you on, anyway?"

"Yours, babe. Always yours."

I hated when he called her that. Mostly because I'd heard him call other women *babe*.

Dylan glanced at me and winked, and what was it about a sexy man winking at you that made your heart flutter? Thirty minutes later we were all laughing like old friends, and I could tell Brian and Autumn liked him. I didn't blame them. I sure did. The question was, what was I going to do about it?

"Isn't this cozy?"

Well, hell, if it wasn't Chad the Stalker. What a surprise. I glared at him. "Are you following me now?"

"Of course not. I just want to talk to you." He scowled at Dylan.

Dylan put his arm around the back of my chair, pulling me next to him. "Jenny's with me now, Mr. Perrine. I don't take kindly to you harassing my girlfriend."

Huh? What was he up to? Autumn glanced at me, the same question in her eyes. I shrugged, telling her I had no idea.

"Is that true, Jenn?" Chad said.

"Ah, yeah. It is." Why not agree if it would make him go away?

"Is there anything else you wish to say, Mr. Perrine?"

Man, Dylan's voice had gone stone-cold. So had his eyes. A little thrill shot up my spine. I'd never had a man step in as protector before. It was kind of cool in a medieval-knight-in-shining-armor way. I wondered if he had a white horse stashed away somewhere.

"No? Then I suggest you leave before I decide to arrest you for being a public nuisance."

Chad's fists clenched at his sides, and for a second I thought he was going to do something stupid like punch Dylan. But with one last glare at me, he walked away.

"Wow," I said, watching Chad's retreating back.

"That was crazy cool," Autumn said. "You ever talk to me with that menacing voice, I promise I'll skedaddle away as fast as my legs can carry me."

Dylan grinned. "He didn't quite skedaddle. Maybe I need to practice making it scarier."

"That turn you on, babe?" Brian said. "I can talk plenty scary if that gets you off."

Along with the way I'd sometimes catch Brian checking out my butt, that was another thing about him that rubbed me wrong. He was always making inappropriate comments.

Autumn punched his arm. "Behave."

How did she not see that deep down he didn't respect women? I wanted to shake her. Back when he'd asked her to marry him, I'd tried to tell her my concerns, but she'd insisted I was imagining things, had even accused me of being jealous that she was engaged. Believe me, I wasn't, considering her fiancé was Brian. Maybe I was wrong and they'd have a good marriage. I sure hoped so.

Brian put his arm around Autumn's shoulder. "It's getting late, babe. You ready to go?"

I glanced at my watch, surprised to see two hours had passed. They said their good-byes, and suddenly I was alone with a man I wouldn't mind having as a boyfriend. A temporary one.

"You don't like him much, do you?"

The man was observant, for sure. I shrugged. "I think she's making a mistake, but it's her life."

"True."

The waiter appeared, and Dylan and I both declined another drink.

"But I will have a cup of coffee and a slice of pecan pie," he said. He glanced at me. "Join me?"

"Sure. Coffee for me, too, and a piece of that chocolate volcano thing you guys do."

"That sounds good," Dylan said after the waiter left. "I went for the pie because I've never had pecan pie before. Thought I should try it."

"I like a man who's adventurous where food's concerned. Chad wouldn't…" I about bit my tongue off. Why was I even thinking of Chad when I was with a man like Dylan Conrad? "Sorry, I shouldn't have—"

"No problem." Dylan put his hand over mine. "If you need to talk about him, I'm a good listener."

Was this man for real? Guys hated it when you mentioned previous boyfriends around them. That had been my experience, anyway. I glanced down at the hand covering mine, liking how big and strong it was. And warm. And how would that hand feel roaming over my body?

"Jenny?"

"Mm?" And the way he said my name made all my nerve endings tingly, not to mention other parts of me.

"Tell me what you're thinking right now."

I lifted my eyes to his and saw the heat in them that matched what I was feeling. "You tell me," I whispered, knowing he could.

Before he could answer, the waiter returned with our coffees and desserts, and the moment was lost. One side of his mouth curved in that half smile that made my stomach twitchy. I exhaled a silent breath, trying to get my heart to calm down when he turned his attention to his pie. If he had leaned his face down to kiss me, I would have let him.

When we finished our dessert and coffee, he walked me out, and I came to a halt at seeing two silver Mustang GTs sitting side by side. So someone did have a car like mine. That explained why people kept thinking they saw me in places I wasn't.

"Whose car is that?" I wasn't even sure which one was mine, and I peeked in the window of the closest one. The locks popped up, startling me, and I jumped back. At hearing Dylan chuckle, I glanced over to see him pointing a remote at the car. "Yours?"

He grinned. "It is. Like it?"

"What's not to like?" I couldn't decide if I liked that we had the same cars. Seeing the silver Mustangs sitting side by side, it was like they were a couple. I wasn't ready to be the other half of a couple with any man now that I'd gotten Chad out of my life, and this...well, it seemed like some kind of sign. Maybe I should sell mine after all and get an early start on my world tour.

"Hey, where'd you go?"

"What?"

"Just now." He tilted his head and peered at me. "What were you thinking?"

That I can't decide whether to run from you or climb you like a tree. "Have you ever traveled? You know, like to other countries?"

CHAPTER EIGHT

~ Dylan ~

"YEAH. WHY?" I HONEYMOONED IN Paris with Christine, but I wasn't going to talk about that. Her question had come out of nowhere, and I waited to see where she was going with it.

She shrugged. "Just wondered. My dream is to go on a world tour. I'm leaving right after Autumn's wedding. My flight is booked and paid for. I'm saving as much as I can between now and then so I can travel as long as possible."

I leaned against the door of my car and crossed my arms over my chest. "When's the wedding?"

"Second Saturday in December."

So she'd only be around two more months. Probably for the best. I found her too intriguing. "Where do you want to travel?"

Her eyes lit up. "Everywhere! The Netherlands, Peru, China, Ireland, Scotland." She laughed. "You name the place and I want to go there."

Damn. I wanted to take all that energy and excitement to bed with me. "You'll get to all those places, Red, if you're determined to make it happen." I could see that it wasn't just idle talk, that she would live out her dream.

"I know. It's just seems like it's taken forever to save the money I need, but I'm almost there." She eyed her car. "I've thought about selling my Mustang, but there's no way I can bring myself to sell Lady."

"You named your car?" This girl kept making me smile, and even though I was rusty at it, it felt good.

"You didn't?"

"Didn't know I was supposed to. How about Gaga? Then together we'd have Lady Gaga." I loved how she laughed—deep, throaty, and sexy.

"Please don't name your car Gaga."

"Pity. I was rather liking it." She took a few steps toward her car, and I wanted to ask her to come home with me, help keep my ghost away.

"Well, it's getting late. I guess I should head home."

Did guess mean she really didn't want to leave? I was out of practice and didn't like being unsure of myself. Put me in a roomful of misbehaving cops and I was confident I could whip them into shape, but I was at a loss as to how to go about seducing one slip of a woman.

"Good night, Dylan."

There was no one else walking by, and damn if I was going to let her go without at least a kiss. I followed her to her car, opening the door for her.

"I think I should kiss my new girlfriend good night."

A wide grin split her face. "You mean pretend girlfriend. Thank you, by the way."

"You're welcome." I did some fast thinking. She fascinated me, and I wanted to get to know her. "You know, it might not be a bad idea for us to continue the ruse for a while. Make sure he doesn't doubt that you're no longer available."

"After tonight he's probably given up."

"Maybe, but we can't be sure." Was I pushing too hard?

"True, and he is stubborn. I guess it wouldn't hurt to be seen together now and then."

I hoped for more than now and then, but it was a start. "Can I kiss my *pretend* girlfriend good night?"

"Will it be a pretend kiss?"

"Red, when I kiss you, there will be no pretending about it." I'd asked her twice now, and she'd evaded answering, which I took as her answer. I hid my disappointment, smiled at her, and said, "Good night, Jenny."

"Wait," she said when I stepped away.

"Hmm?" I paused, waiting for her to speak.

She grinned, then tapped her lips with her finger. "Aren't you forgetting something?"

"Am I? What's that?" After her evasion, I wanted her to say it, to ask for a kiss.

"My kiss."

"Ah, that." I walked back to her, put my hands on the roof of her car, caging her between my arms, and lowered my face until our mouths were only inches apart. "To set the record straight, this kiss is going to be real."

"Yes, please."

That made me smile. She was simply adorable. I brushed my lips over hers. Her mouth was soft and warm, and although I'd only intended a brief good-night kiss, just one taste of her and my intentions flew out the window.

I moved to one corner of her mouth, teasing her with little flicks of my tongue. Her breath hitched, and when she tried to meld our mouths together, I dodged her attempt, moving to the other side of her lips, then gently nipped on her bottom lip.

She let out a soft whimper, and I was lost. I swept my tongue into her mouth, finally and fully tasting her. And forgetting we were standing in a restaurant's parking lot, I plastered my body against hers as our tongues tangled in an age-old dance. It had been so long since I'd had a woman's soft body pressed against mine, and I desperately wanted her. Right here. Right now.

Before I truly lost my mind and ravished her in a parking lot, I lifted my head, smiling down at her. It was only because of my training that I was able to project an image of control. Inside I was a trembling mass of desire. At least I wasn't the only one affected by that kiss. Her chest heaved as she sucked in air.

"Good night, Red." I wondered what she'd say if she knew she was the first woman I'd kissed since burying my wife.

"That was nice," she said, then ducked into her Lady car.

I grinned as I watched her drive away. Nice, huh? "Next time we kiss, Jenny Girl, I'll do better than nice." I gave her a ten-minute head start, and then I drove by her apartment to assure myself that she was tucked safely inside, no ex-boyfriend giving her trouble.

With nothing else to do in my new small town, I turned the car for home. Not having restaurants and clubs on every corner was going to take some getting used to, but I didn't regret leaving Chicago. My ex-partner was still on the force, and seeing him every day, imagining his mouth on my wife, thinking of the two of them in bed together—I just couldn't do it anymore.

When I'd discovered their affair, I'd gone ballistic. What man wouldn't when walking into his bedroom and finding his wife and best friend tangled up in the sheets? I was supposed to be out of town, and I had been. Unfortunately for them, I'd cut out of the criminal behavior workshop a day early. Surprise!

When I started thinking of ways I could get away with killing my former friend, I knew it was time to leave. The only thing I didn't blame him for was my wife's suicide. That was all on me, and why she still haunted me. She begged me to forgive her, but I had my pride. I couldn't even look at her without seeing her and Jack together.

Before that day, she had been my everything. I moved into the guest room because I couldn't bring myself to get back in that bed, and when she pleaded with me to go to counseling with her, I refused.

From the moment I first saw Christine, I was entranced,

and even though she'd taken a rusty knife and cut out my heart, I had still loved her. But I couldn't stand the thought of touching her, and my confusion had eaten me alive. I still wanted her, yet I didn't. It hadn't made sense.

What had I done to drive her into another man's arms? She tried to tell me once how and why it happened, but I couldn't listen and had walked out of the house. There was no reason she could give me to make me forgive her. I don't know why she put my gun in her mouth and pulled the trigger. Was it because she couldn't stand the thought of a divorce, which I'd asked for? Or was it guilt that drove her to it? Since she hadn't left a note, I'd never know.

Christine had never been an easy woman to love, but I'd loved her all the same. She had been high maintenance, but I'd believed I was up to the task. When she needed reassurance that she was pretty and desirable, I gave it to her. When she had crying spells for no reason that she could explain, I'd held her, doing my best to soothe her. She'd had bouts of depression throughout our marriage, but anytime I suggested she see a therapist, she'd adamantly refused. I should have pushed the issue, insisted that she go. But then she'd seem okay, and I'd let it drop. Shame on me for that.

There were times when she went on shopping sprees that could have bankrupted us if not for her father's money. I didn't care. That money was there for her to spend. Her father, a former senator, doted on his only child, and had accused me of wanting to marry her for her money. That burned because he refused to see that I understood her—or thought I had until she cheated on me and then took her life. I wanted nothing to do with his money and had never touched a penny of it.

When he'd died, everything went to her since her mother had passed when Christine was in high school. My wife was a millionaire several times over, and now I am. I still refuse to touch a penny and never will. After I buried her, the first thing I did once her will was read was set up a foundation in her name for college scholarships for underprivileged kids in Chicago.

Back in my apartment, I went straight to the shower. As I toweled dry, I wished I hadn't thought about Christine. She always appeared whenever she was on my mind, and I wasn't looking forward to going to bed knowing she'd show up. To delay the inevitable, I opened the windows and listened for my owl. When I heard his *hoos*, I turned on the fan and got in bed. I had sleeping pills my therapist had prescribed, and those kept her away, but I hated taking them. They made me groggy for a few hours after waking.

My therapist had urged me to contact one of the specialists in grief counseling on the list he'd given me. All of them were in Asheville, and I wasn't willing to take time off from my new job right now for appointments that would take up half my day. I had also been hoping that Christine would stay in Chicago and not follow me to Blue Ridge Valley. If she persisted in hanging around, I was going to have to give in and make a damn appointment.

"You're starting to piss me off, Christine," I muttered as I drifted off.

You kissed her.

Hello, Christine. I've been expecting you. We really have to stop meeting like this. Isn't there a white light or something you're supposed to disappear into?

Are you going to kiss her again?

I hope so.

I don't want you to.

And I didn't want you to kiss Jack, but you did, so you lost the right to tell me who I can't kiss.

Apparently she didn't like that because she disappeared. Half-awake now, I sighed, pumped up my pillow, and listened to my owl.

CHAPTER NINE

~ Jenny ~

CRAP. FIVE MINUTES TO CLOSING, and Chad the Persistent showed up. Apparently he didn't care that I had a new boyfriend. I was meeting Dylan at Fusions for a drink as soon as I was done here. The last thing I needed was a confrontation with my ex-boyfriend, emphasis on the ex. All the tables were empty, and there was only one couple left at the bar finishing up their last drink.

Dylan had surprised me by stopping in for dinner and asking if I'd like to meet him after I got off. I'd given Dylan a lot of thought after he'd kissed me two nights ago. A whole lot of thought. Even though we'd pretended to be a couple the other night, he would be a fun guy to hang out with. The man made me laugh, and that was pretty awesome.

I'd told him my dream of going on a world tour, and unlike Chad the Jerk Who Refused To Go Away, he'd seemed to understand why I'd want to do such a thing. The last thing I wanted was to ruin my good mood by getting caught up in an argument with Chad.

Before he could start in on me, I went to the table in the back corner where Brandy was filling salt and pepper shakers. I slid onto the chair across from her. "I need a favor."

"Sure."

That was typical Brandy, agreeing without even knowing what I was going to ask. She was such a sweetheart. "I don't want to deal with Chad tonight. Would you ring out the couple at the bar so I can slip out the back?"

Big brown eyes peered back at me. "I thought he was your boyfriend."

"He was and now he's not, but he's refusing to believe I broke up with him."

She glanced over at the bar. "He's watching you. Go on and get out of here. I'll take care of everything. Susan's still here, and Angelo's cleaning the bathrooms, so if he tries to cause trouble, we'll deal with him."

"Thanks. You know I love you."

She grinned. "Love you back."

Without glancing behind me, I walked into the kitchen. In the back room I got my purse out of my locker, then jogged to my car. When I arrived at Fusions, I saw Dylan's car and parked next to it. I lowered my visor. Ugh. My hair was a mess of curls. I fished my brush out of my purse, tamed my wild hair as best I could, and then applied some lip gloss. The black T-shirt with *Vincennes* above my left breast couldn't be helped as it would take me too long to go home and change. Maybe I should start keeping a spare outfit in my car if Dylan was going to make a habit of inviting me out for a drink when I got off work. A girl could hope.

At first I didn't see Dylan when I walked into the lounge, but then he stood and smiled, waving me over to a booth. Mercy, that man's smile slayed me every time.

"Hey," he said when I reached him.

"Hey back." I slid onto the leather seat across from him. A full bottle of Green Man beer sat on the table, so I guessed he hadn't been waiting long.

"What would you like?"

"Same as you." I wasn't a big drinker, sometimes a glass of wine or a beer. Much more than that, I'd be dancing on the table. Instead of waiting for a waitress, he went to the bar and got my beer. "Thanks," I said when he slid it over to me. He lifted his bottle, holding it toward me. I picked mine up and clinked it against his. "To my new friend."

He grinned. "To the possibility of more than a friend?"

Now he had me confused. Weren't we just supposed to be having a pretend relationship? Be seen together a few times so that Chad got the message? Not that I wasn't interested in more, but I had no clue where Dylan was coming from. Maybe he was only flirting and didn't mean anything by the question.

"Well, you did ask me to be your pretend girlfriend." If I wasn't mistaken, he seemed disappointed in my answer.

"That I did."

There was something about this man that made me feel all marshmallowy inside. What I really wanted was someone to have fun with until it was time to go see the world, and I suddenly wanted that someone to be Dylan. Only one way to find out if he was interested.

"Okay, let's back up a minute. I'm just a small-town mountain girl, easily confused. Exactly what did you mean when you said, 'To the possibility of more than a friend?' I think I understand…well kind of, but maybe you should clarify things for me."

He studied me a moment and then smiled, and God help me, I smiled right back at him. Because that oh so charming boyish expression on his face was impossible to resist. Honestly I was finding everything about him irresistible.

"I don't think you're confused at all, Red," he softly said. "Tell me you don't feel the attraction between us."

I refused to say a word, which seemed to amuse him.

"Your silence answers my question. Do you have a leave date for your world tour?"

I nodded, wondering where he was going with this. "Mid-December."

"So about two months." He reached across the table

and covered my hand with his. "Proposition. Spend that time with me. Teach me about your town and the people, and we'll see how it goes from there."

He meant sex eventually. I think. Maybe I was putting the cart before the horse, but I wanted to make sure there was no misunderstanding. "I guess this is where I should say that I don't jump into bed with the first guy that comes along." That just wasn't me.

"Meaning me?"

I nodded. As much as Dylan intrigued me—and I was pretty sure it would happen, hoped it would—I wanted to feel comfortable with it, with him.

"Okay, I can respect that. How do you want to go about this?"

This conversation was definitely odd. "Um, I don't know. I've never negotiated a temporary fling before." But it was kind of fun.

He grinned. "That makes two of us. Tell me how you'd like to go forward from here."

I liked that he was asking, letting me do this at my comfort level. "Basically I want to get to know you better, for you to know me."

"Anything else?"

"Only that you don't push me before I'm ready."

"To the first, that's a fair request, and to the second…" He stared at his beer bottle as he traced the lip with his finger, then he raised his eyes to mine. "I don't make love to a woman unless she wants it, too."

I believed him. And the way he looked at me when he said that last part, heat flaming in his eyes, sent a shiver through me that started somewhere near my chest and went all the way down to my toes.

"So how was work?" He leaned back and stretched his arms along the back of the booth, then about charmed my panties off with that killer smile. "This is me getting to know you better."

I blinked at the sudden change in our conversation. The man was constantly surprising me. I liked that. A lot. "Work was the same as always. Well, until Chad showed up." Dylan went from relaxed to alert and tense in a nanosecond. I waved a hand at him. "Stand down, tiger. I didn't even talk to him. He came in a few minutes before we closed, and I snuck out the back."

"I think you should reconsider getting a restraining order."

The last thing I wanted to talk about was Chad. "I'll think about it if he keeps coming around. So, how do you like Blue Ridge Valley? It has to be a cultural shock, coming from a big city."

"Tell me about it. The hardest thing is the nights. It's so damn quiet." He chuckled. "Except for my owl."

"Your owl?" Who had an owl for a pet?

"Yeah. He's very vocal at night. I guess he's hunting?"

"Oh, I thought you meant you had a pet owl." I shrugged. "I think they hunt at night. I guess it would be a lot different here than in a big city like Chicago. You'll get used to it."

"It's already better than my first night here." He paused and took a sip of beer. "So tell me where this travel bug you have came from."

"Growing up, we always went somewhere for two weeks every year for vacation." I twirled my beer bottle. "Sometimes the beach. Sometimes a state park. We would get so excited. When we were old enough, my parents let us help plan where we'd go."

"Us?"

"Me and Natalie, my twin." I still couldn't talk about her without tearing up, but she was a big part of why I planned to take off on a world tour. It was impossible to explain everything to Dylan without including her. Everyone in the valley knew about her, and eventually he'd hear the story. I'd rather he hear it from me.

I blinked away my tears. "When we were fourteen, we did my mom's dream trip, Ireland and Scotland. It was awesome. Natalie and I decided that one day we'd travel around the world. We wanted to see everything. The Mayan ruins, the Great Wall of China, the changing of the guard at Buckingham Palace. We wanted to swim in the Mediterranean Sea and eat olives while sitting at a sidewalk cafe in Greece."

"I wish you could see how your face lights up when you talk about"—he made air quotes—"seeing the world. I'm glad you have someone to go with you who loves to travel as much as you."

"That's just it. I don't." Willing myself not to cry, I trailed my finger through the moisture ring from my beer bottle. "Natalie died." I lifted my gaze to Dylan's. "She made me promise to still go, to travel for both of us."

"Saying I'm sorry is inadequate. Believe me, I know. But I am sorry you lost someone you loved."

He glanced away, and I wondered who he'd lost. "Yeah, it was really hard, but she's not gone." I tapped my heart. "She'll always be a part of me."

"Another round?" our waitress asked, coming up to the table.

We both passed, and to change the subject before I embarrassed myself by crying, I said, "What about you? What kind of things do you like to do?"

"In Chicago I went to restaurants, the theater, museums when I had the time. My hours were sometimes long, but I liked to explore when I could. Here? Haven't figured that out yet, aside from work. What's there to do in Blue Ridge Valley?"

"Lots of things. I could be your guide if you want."

He locked his eyes on mine. "I want."

The way he said that, his voice low and husky, made my stomach flutter. "Well, there's a car and motorcycle show at the fairgrounds this weekend if you're interested."

"A girl after my own heart."

"Because I like cars?"

"Among other things. And yes, I'm interested."

"Awesome. Saturday or Sunday? Which would work best for you? I'm free both days until four, then I have work."

"Sunday."

"Sunday it is." I had my hand resting on the table, and he reached over, putting his over mine. I lifted my eyes, and my breath hitched at the way he was looking at me. As if he'd like to devour me whole.

"The other night when I kissed you?"

I nodded.

"You said it was nice. I want to kiss you again, Red. Show you I can do better than nice."

Well, wow. "Maybe I'll let you kiss me again." I grinned. "You know, just to prove you can do better."

He laughed. "That's as good a reason as any."

"Right now, though, it's late and I'm tired. I should be getting home."

"Stand by and I'll walk you out." He went to the bar and paid the tab. I hoped I knew what I was doing because I sensed he was a man who could rock my world. I was busy admiring the back of him, specifically the way his butt looked in those jeans, when Chad the Absolutely Impossible To Get Rid Of slid into the booth across from me.

"I knew you were screwing around on me," he said.

I opened my mouth to tell him off, then closed it. What good would it do? Obviously he closed his ears whenever I said something he didn't want to hear. Dylan was headed back to the table, his narrowed eyes focused on Chad. Before he could reach us and the new police chief found himself in a fight with my ex-boyfriend, I snatched up my purse, slid out of the booth, and grabbed Dylan's hand.

"He's not worth it," I said, tugging him along with me. That he came willingly increased my opinion of him. He could easily take Chad on, by either beating the crap out of him or putting him in jail. But he let me lead him away, not at all worried about losing his man card. I liked that.

"It's time to take out a restraining order, Jenny."

He was right, but I didn't like it. I only wanted Chad to leave me alone.

"I just want to talk to you, Jenn."

Dylan's fingers tightened around mine when I stopped, and I was sure he'd finally lose his cool. Instead he looked at me and raised a brow. I understood his question. He was asking if I wanted him to deal with Chad. I shook my head before letting go of his hand and turning.

"So talk," I said to Chad the Stupid. Because he really was, considering he was bothering me when I was with the head of a police department.

Chad shifted his gaze from me to Dylan. "Alone."

"Not going to happen. If you have something to say, tonight's your last chance because I'm going to take out a restraining order on you first thing tomorrow morning."

Dylan put his hand on my lower back, caressing me with his thumb, and I understood the message he was sending. He was letting me know he was there for me if I needed him. He could easily step in and try to take control, making this some kind of male-versus-male fight over the girl. A lot of men would probably do just that. Seeing how he handled himself in an awkward situation, I liked him even more. And I was already liking him a lot before this little scenario happened.

Chad's face turned red. "A fucking restraining order, Jenn?"

CHAPTER TEN

~ Dylan ~

I FISTED MY HAND, HOLDING ON to my temper by a thread. What I wanted to do was knock the asshole into next week, but unless she asked me to step in, this was Jenny's battle.

"You're such a jerk, Chad." She stomped off to her car. "Coming, Dylan?"

I glanced over at her. "You bet." But first I had something to say to Mr. Perrine. "You come around her one more time, you're going to find yourself a guest in my jail. It comes to that, you're going to be real impressed by all the things I'll be able to think of to charge you with. Capisce?"

His eyes glittered with hatred, and I wondered if he was going to turn into one of those stalkers that can't stand not having the woman he's fixated on. He walked away without answering, and I hoped he believed I wouldn't hesitate to make his life miserable if he didn't leave Jenny alone. The idiot spun his tires, throwing up gravel, as he left the parking lot, and I shook my head. "How old are you anyway, dumbass?"

I walked over to Jenny. "You okay?"

"No, I'm furious." She glanced up at the sky. "If I go home now, all I'll do is stomp around my apartment half the night, calling Chad every bad name I can think of." She paused again, looking out on the road thoughtfully. "There's someplace I go when I need to think. Would you come with me?"

"I'm all yours." It was definitely an honor to be invited to her special place. I followed her to her car, sliding onto the passenger seat. She rolled down her window, so I did the same. The night wind felt good. Although I was curious where she was taking me, I didn't ask. She had the radio on an oldies station—something on satellite since apparently it was impossible to pick up the Asheville stations where we were. As we drove away from town, the radio blaring and the mountain air blowing in, it almost felt like I was back in high school and on a date. Except the girl was driving. Surprisingly, I liked it.

"Where's a good place to get doughnuts around here?" I asked.

She glanced over at me, then burst into laughter.

"What?" I gave her innocent, wide eyes, but I was pretty sure I could guess the reason for her amusement.

"Cops and doughnuts."

Yep, I'd called it. I couldn't stop a grin. "Hey, it's a thing." It had been a long time since I'd been this relaxed and happy. It felt good.

"Mary's Bread Company has doughnuts every morning except Sundays until eleven. They're amazing."

"I've seen the place." It was a nondescript building about the size of my living room, easy to miss if you weren't looking.

"Mary makes great coffee, too. What's your favorite doughnut flavor?"

"There's only one kind of doughnut worth eating. Glazed." Sprinkles and icing were just wrong.

"Then be there any time between seven and eight if you like them hot."

"Seriously? She has hot glazed?" At Jenny's nod, I moaned. "I might have to marry Mary." That set off another round of laughter. "Now what?"

She shook her head. "You'll see."

I was intrigued, and the first chance I got, I'd be showing up for my hot doughnuts and a look at Mary. We turned onto a dirt road that curved its way up. Not used to mountain roads, I gripped the window ledge. I also considered praying we didn't go over the side, but I was going to trust that Jenny knew what she was doing.

"Thank you for not going all macho and knocking out a few of Chad's teeth, by the way."

"I figured you'd ask if you wanted me to butt in." But I'd sure as hell wanted to.

"Definitely. After tonight I don't think he'll bother me again, but I'll get a restraining order just to be safe."

Finally. "That would be wise."

"Here we are." Jenny slowed the car and cut the engine. The headlights were still on, illuminating the flat surface where we were parked. Off to the left were waist-high boulders, and to the right, the land disappeared.

Jenny opened her door. "Come on. You're going to love this."

I wasn't so sure about that, but I followed her to the back of her car. She opened her trunk, grabbing a blanket and flashlight. Being a city boy, communing with nature wasn't high on my bucket list.

"Are we going hiking in the middle of the night? Like through the woods? Aren't there bears?" I had my gun on me, but maybe I should have studied up on bears. "How many bullets will I need to take down a pissed-off bear?"

She laughed. "You're hilarious."

"Wasn't trying to be funny, Red." I trailed behind her to a boulder near the edge. "What are you doing now?" I asked when she turned on the flashlight, illuminating the rock.

"Making sure there aren't any snakes."

Oh, hell no. I backed up a few steps. Give me a shootout with a bad guy any day, but snakes? Nope. Not happening. "Tell me again why we're here."

"You'll see."

She spread the blanket over a rock that might or might not have snakes hiding in it just waiting for a couple of dumbasses they could bite. She patted the space next to her. I took a moment to debate the merits of being a wuss versus manning up and climbing onto a possibly snake-infested boulder. It was probably a lot easier to shoot a bear than a snake, and I made a mental note to find a shooting range that had small, slithering targets I could practice on. But I was a lawman, and it was my duty to protect citizens and pretty girls, so I pushed myself onto the rock.

"Shouldn't we leave that on?" I said when Jenny turned off the flashlight.

"No, we can't see the stars when it's on."

But we could see the damn snakes. "Is that what we're doing, stargazing?" I didn't think I'd ever done that before, not that I could remember. The lights were never off in Chicago, so we never bothered looking up at night.

She lowered onto her back. "Come look."

On my back beside her, I lifted my eyes to the night sky. "Wow," I whispered.

"Amazing, isn't it?"

"Yeah." We fell silent, both of us entranced by the glittering diamonds on black velvet. It helped that the moon was a mere sliver in the sky, allowing the stars center stage. I slipped my hand over Jenny's, and she laced her fingers around mine.

"Someday I'll stand under the stars in Greece or Ireland or China."

I lifted onto my elbow and peered down at her. "You're serious about this world travel thing?"

"Definitely."

It was too dark to see her well, but I could see the gleam of her teeth as she smiled, and the outline of her hair spread out over the blanket, and I could smell her scent. Something earthy, like a combination of cinnamon and vanilla beans and rain. Made my mouth water. She lifted her hand and pressed her palm against my cheek. I took that as permission and lowered my mouth to hers.

Her lips were soft and warm, and when she parted them, I slid my tongue over hers. My body hummed with longing for this woman. I put my hand on her hip, pulling her closer. Her breath hitched, and she grabbed the front of my shirt, fisting her fingers in the material.

Oh yeah. I sucked her bottom lip into my mouth, then let go, chuckling when she made a little growling noise. She paid me back by clamping her teeth lightly down on my lip, giving a little tug.

I gathered a lock of her hair, wrapping it around my hand and tugging her head back. "Still think my kiss is just nice?"

She grinned. "Jury's still out."

We'd see about that. "You better take a deep breath, Red, because you're not coming up for air until I get my fill of you."

"Is that so?"

"I don't say things I don't mean." And I proved it to her. We made out like teenagers for a good thirty minutes, and by the time I pulled away, breathless, I was so hard I could hammer a nail with my dick. The last thing I wanted to do was stop, but if I didn't, I wouldn't be able to.

Although she'd been just as into our kissing as me, her hands had never strayed below my chest, which told me she wasn't ready. She'd asked me not to push her, and never mind that I'd never be able to walk straight again, I would honor her request.

Even though I wasn't going to get what I wanted tonight, I still considered it a victory. There had been times when I'd doubted that I'd ever want another woman. That was how bad my wife had fucked up my head. It was a relief to know my manly parts were still alive and operative.

"Does the jury have a verdict yet?"

Jenny sat up, then leaned down and brushed her lips over mine. "The defendant wins the case. He's a damn great kisser."

I kept my hands at my sides when she circled my mouth with the tip of her tongue, otherwise I'd start stripping off her clothes. My control was hanging on by a thread—a very fragile one. She slid off the rock and walked to the edge, and I followed her. And yes, it was impossible to walk normally.

"That's our little town down there," she said.

Below us was a scattering of lights on the valley floor. "If that was Chicago, the entire valley would be lit up like it was daylight."

"Do you miss Chicago?"

I put my arm around her shoulders and tucked her into my side. "Some things, but I'm glad I'm here." Especially since meeting a red-haired bartender who longed to travel the world. I was going to miss her when she left.

CHAPTER ELEVEN

~ Jenny ~

SUNDAY MORNING I CHANGED CLOTHES three times before deciding on a white, spaghetti-strap sundress with cherries on it. My Vincennes' everyday uniform was a black T-shirt and black pants, so having enough black in my life, whenever I dressed for anything other than work, I went with colors. A pair of comfortable red, flat-heeled sandals, and my hair up in a ponytail to keep it off my neck, and I was almost ready for Blue Ridge Valley's annual car and motorcycle show.

The forecast was for unusually warm temperatures for this time of the year, getting up into the midseventies and sunny. That called for some suntan lotion on my bare shoulders and arms, and I was trying to reach the middle of my exposed shoulders when the doorbell rang.

"It's open. Come on in," I said after looking in the peephole to make sure it was Dylan. When he entered, I held up my lotion-slicked hands. "Sorry. I couldn't turn the knob. Give me a minute to get the rest of this lotion on, then we can go."

"Let me."

He took the tube from my hand when I tried to reach my back. Goose bumps rose when he rubbed the cool lotion over my skin. It had been three days since I'd seen him—since we'd made out like teenagers—and I hadn't been able to stop thinking about kissing him again.

"You look very pretty today, Red."

He put his mouth on my neck, just behind my ear, and

my "Thank you," came out all breathy.

"You smell good, too," he said, taking a deep breath. He stepped around me, fingering a strand of hair I'd left down.

"So do you." And God did he ever. I didn't think he wore cologne. It was more like bay rum–scented soap and maybe a spicy aftershave. Whatever it was, it was mouth-watering sexy. The whole package was sexy, actually. He wore jeans, topsiders, and a sky-blue polo shirt that he filled out very nicely. And that lopsided smile could melt a girl's heart.

"I'm ready."

He brushed his thumb across my bottom lip. "First I have to do this."

Our eyes locked as he lowered his mouth, and when our lips touched, I put my hands on his upper arms. His muscles flexed under my fingers, and I longed to run my hands all over his body, exploring all the places he had muscles. Butterflies fluttered their wings in my stomach, making me feel twitchy all over.

He lifted his head, then tapped my nose. "Now we can go."

"If my knees can still hold me up." Because they'd gone weak with that kiss. If he could do that to me with only a kiss, I was pretty sure we were going to be dynamite together in bed when things progressed that far. But I wasn't ready for that yet. I wanted to get to know him better, and I was enjoying the anticipation of it happening. The building sexual tension between us was exciting, and I wanted to draw it out a little longer.

He smiled as if I'd pleased him. "Not sure my knees are working much better than yours, but I'll hold you up if you'll return the favor."

I grabbed the red straw hat I'd put on the coffee table. We held hands, leaning against each other in pure silliness, laughing that we made it to his car without falling on our faces. It only took ten minutes to get from my apartment to the fairgrounds, and Dylan spent the time quizzing me on Blue Ridge Valley.

"So let me get this straight," he said as he pulled into a parking space. "Betty Kirkland owns the Mountain Crafts store and she hates Virginia Stanley, the owner of All Good Things because Virginia was voted homecoming queen forty-six years ago, but Betty thinks Virginia bought the votes with laced brownies? And the feud is still going on?"

"That about sums it up."

He leaned his head back against the seat, closed his eyes, and gave a full-bellied laugh. When he opened his eyes, he looked at me and grinned. "I'm going to love this town."

"Wait until I tell you about Hamburger Harry, famous for his moonshine. No one has ever seen him eat anything but hamburgers, and that's saying a lot because he's eighty-three. He'll probably be here today."

"Please don't tell me I'm going to have to arrest an old man named Hamburger Harry."

"Don't feel bad. It won't be the first time he's been arrested. Judge Padgett said to him once, 'Hamburger, if you'll promise me you won't ever make moonshine again, I won't send you to jail,' and Hamburger said, 'Well, George, I cain't rightly tell you that 'cause I'm a honest man and that would be fibbin' and my mama teached me better'n that.' True story."

I loved listening to Dylan laugh. It was contagious, and we both sat in his car with tears streaming down our faces. When I'd told Chad about Hamburger Harry, he'd said it was the stupidest thing he'd ever heard, that they should just put him in a cell and throw away the key. First off, Hamburger wouldn't hurt a fly, and second of all, his apple pie moonshine was to die for. I loved that Dylan thought the story was hilarious.

Two hours later I liked him even more. He'd let me

take the lead, saying, "This is your town, Red, so I'm yours for the day. Introduce me to people, and then whisper their story in my ear." I could do that.

The first people we came to were Adam and Connor Hunter. The twins were sprawled in lawn chairs behind their classic Harleys. "Adam, Connor, this is our new police chief, Dylan Conrad. Dylan, if you ever want a to-die-for log cabin built, the Hunter twins are your men."

Adam and Connor were the hottest bachelors for a hundred miles. Every woman in striking distance had tried to catch one of them, including Natalie and me when we were fifteen. We'd thought it would be really cool for twins to marry twins, had even planned our double wedding to them. Savannah had managed to catch Adam, then had broken his heart when she'd left him to go find fame and fortune in New York.

Dylan launched into a manly discussion with the twins, one that involved the cost of lumber and land prices and the best kind of roof to put on a cabin. I pretty much zoned out of the conversation, happy to do nothing more than observe Dylan. He was amazing the way he fit in. I fished my camera out of my purse and shot some pictures of him and the twins.

After leaving Adam and Connor, we checked out the cars. We oohed and awed, both of us agreeing that the 1966, perfectly restored, white-with-red-upholstery Mustang convertible should win the Classic Car Class. I wasn't at all surprised to learn that the Hunter brothers owned that one. Last year their entry had been a '69 Dodge Charger that I would have almost given up my world tour to own. I said almost. I loved cars, but I wasn't that far gone.

"Let's have pulled pork barbeque sandwiches." At Dylan's raised brow, I said, "When in North Carolina…" Someone needed to teach the man about good southern food. Who better than me?

We got our paper bowls filled with the sandwiches and fat, soft fries, taking them to one of the picnic tables. I rolled my eyes when he scraped the cabbage off his bun. "At least try it that way," I said.

He eyed the cabbage, shifted his gaze to me, opened his mouth, and then shut it. The cabbage went back on his bun.

Have I said how much I liked this man? "It's not going to kill you."

"Not so sure about that, Red. Anything else I should do before I eat it?"

"Just this." I picked up the red sauce and slathered it over his pork, then added a dash of hot. "Now have at it." I tossed a handful of paper napkins his way. "Oh, and you'll need these."

I scored it a victory when he deemed the pulled pork with cabbage on the top good. We'd just gotten a funnel cake—my festival weakness—to top off our lunch when there was a commotion near the stage where a band was setting up. Of course Dylan's attention zeroed in on the crowd gathering around what appeared to be a fight. I couldn't see over the heads, but I could hear the yelling. Dylan headed that way, and holding on to my funnel cake, I followed him. Two cops, Sarah Griffin and Tommy Evans, were already pushing through the crowd when we got there.

"Stay here," Dylan said, then elbowed his way past the people egging on the combatants.

I didn't try to follow him because that would mean I'd probably get my funnel cake dumped on the ground. That wouldn't have made me happy. Dylan let his officers do their job while he forced the crowd back by putting his arms out and backing up. When one man tried to push back, Dylan said something and the guy shut his mouth as he stepped away.

Sarah and Tommy got the two men wrestling each other on the ground apart. Dylan still did nothing more than maintain crowd control with brute strength and words I couldn't hear. I'd expected him to jump in and, if nothing else, help Sarah because she was a female, but he didn't. It reminded me of how he'd stayed out of my confrontation the other night, yet had stood behind me, letting me know with the touch of his hand on my back that he was there if I needed him.

Was the man for real? As I munched on my powdered sugar–coated cake, I ran a critical eye over him. Tall—at least six feet—whiskey-brown eyes that I'd noticed had gold flecks in them, and muscled—but not overly so—in appearance, he was a man who would catch the eye of any red-blooded woman.

Of course, I thought he was hot, but it was his personality that intrigued me. No one was perfect, and I knew me. I'd be obsessed now with finding his flaws. I also thought there had to be a story behind him leaving a big city like Chicago for a small mountain town like Blue Ridge Valley. Maybe he'd been married and there had been a nasty divorce. Or had there been some kind of on-the-job scandal?

The crowd had dispersed, leaving him standing with the two men who'd been fighting and his two cops. It figured that it was the Emery brothers. Those two practically had a cell at the jail with their names on it. Now that the yelling had stopped, I could hear their conversation. Apparently Dick had knocked over Ted's beer. *Good grief, just go get another one, guys.*

Dylan glanced over at me and winked, sending my stomach into a somersault. *Don't you dare go and fall for the man, Jenn.* No, I wouldn't do that because I had a world to see and a promise to keep. So what if he made my heart flutter when he looked at me with that crooked smile? It was lust I was feeling, nothing more.

CHAPTER TWELVE

~ Dylan ~

I LEFT THE EMERY BROTHERS FOR Sarah and Tommy to deal with now that we'd managed to separate them. According to my officers, this was typical behavior for Dick and Ted, and I could expect to see them in my jail on occasion. Tommy told me they were always fighting each other for the slightest offense, but if you messed with one, you'd have them both trying to take you down.

I walked back to Jenny. "You save me some of that, Red?"

She peered down at the paper plate, empty except for one small bite left. "Oops." She held out the plate.

"Yum," I said, munching on the sugary concoction.

"We can get another one."

I laughed at the hopeful look on her face. "You eat any more of that and you'll be so high on sugar your feet won't touch the ground." It was funny how she kept making me laugh. She'd already taught me two things. I still had a libido, and I could still laugh. Hadn't been sure either of those things would happen again.

"Oh, I see someone I want you to meet."

She took my hand, pulling me toward the stage. As we passed a trash can, I dropped the paper plate into it. The man she led me to sat on a metal folding chair next to the stairs that led up to the stage. He wore coveralls, had a scraggly gray beard that reached halfway down his chest, and hair as white as snow. Even sitting down, I could see that he was rail thin. At his feet were a violin case and a filthy white canvas tote.

"There's my honeypot," he said, breaking into a wide, toothless smile at seeing Jenny.

Honeypot? Oh boy, I couldn't wait to call Jenny *honeypot.*

"Hamburger, I'd like you to meet Dylan Conrad. He's the new police chief. Dylan, this is Hamburger Harry."

I'll be dammed, the infamous moonshiner in person. Rheumy pale blue eyes gave me the once-over. I wasn't sure what to call him. Hamburger? Just couldn't bring myself to do it.

"I heared we got us a new sheriff in town."

Well, I wasn't a sheriff, but I let it go.

"You like bluegrass, boy?"

Truthfully I preferred my grass the usual green. "Haven't given it much thought." That seemed a safe enough answer. From the amusement in Jenny's eyes, I figured I was missing something in this conversation.

"Hamburger plays a mean fiddle. We'll stick around, let you hear some honest-to-God bluegrass music." She grinned back at Hamburger Harry when he gave her another one of those gummy smiles. "You up first as usual?"

"Sure am. Got sumpin' for ya." He reached into the ratty tote, then narrowed his eyes at me. "Turn around, lawman."

Oh hell. He had a bagful of moonshine. "Ah…" I scratched my head. "I think I'll get a beer." I was going to have to have a talk with the old coot about bringing moonshine into public places, but today wasn't the time. I'd probably have a riot on my hands if I tried to arrest him, especially since there was a crowd gathering in front of the stage, obviously waiting to hear him since he was first up.

"Get me one, too," Jenny said.

I waved a hand in acknowledgment as I headed for the

beer stand. It wasn't that I had anything against alcohol of any kind, but moonshine was deemed illegal, and I was duty bound to uphold the law. As I headed back with our beers, I couldn't help but laugh, remembering my wish that the worst thing I had to do in my new job was arrest moonshiners. That qualified as a "be careful what you ask for."

By the time I made it back to Jenny, Hamburger Harry, his violin case, and his tote were gone, thank God. I handed Jenny one of the bottles. "Please tell me you don't have a jar of moonshine in your purse."

She smirked. "I think this would be a good time to adopt the don't ask, don't tell policy."

I groaned. "You do know I could arrest your pretty ass on the spot, right?"

"Will you handcuff me?"

A picture flashed in my mind of Jenny handcuffed to my bed, and my first groan was nothing compared to this one. I leaned my mouth close to her ear. "Wicked girl."

"You have no idea." She stepped in front of me, leaning her head against my chest. "Now pay attention."

"Yes, honeypot." She kicked me, making me laugh. I wrapped my arm around her chest, holding her to me.

Hamburger Harry came out onstage, and the crowd went wild. Obviously they'd heard him play before. The moonshiner lifted his fiddle, tucking the end under his chin, and began to play. For an old man he had a lot of energy. The music was fast and twangy, like folk music on steroids.

My attention was drawn to his feet. He wore a pair of scuffed, high-top boots that tied, and he was doing some kind of shuffling fast step. I'd never seen anything like it. Although it wasn't music I'd want to listen to on a constant basis—the fast pace would wear me out—it was definitely interesting.

Hamburger Harry played for an hour, the crowd growing larger with each passing minute. Pretty impressive for an eighty-three-year-old man.

"Oh, there's Granny, Hamburger's mother." Jenny pointed to an old woman now sitting in the chair Hamburger Harry had occupied earlier.

I blinked at seeing a woman with the craggiest face ever, a corncob pipe stuck between her lips. She had on a print dress that came down to the top of her black, high-top boots. "If Hamburger's eighty-three, how old is she?"

"Ninety-eight. She was fifteen when he was born. She had six husbands and fourteen more children, but outlived them all except for Hamburger so far. According to her, she's lived this long from drinking her son's moonshine."

Christ, if I arrested Hamburger and put a stop to his moonshining, Granny would die. "I think I've had enough of the small-town experience for one day. What say we go to the Cheery Cherry and have an ice cream cone?"

"Yes!" She handed me her unfinished beer. "A Cheerwine float for me… No, a hot fudge sundae. Or maybe a banana split without the bananas."

From the light in her eyes at the mention of ice cream, I was beginning to realize Jenny Girl had a sweet tooth. I dumped our beer bottles in the recycling can, then took Jenny's hand.

"A banana split without bananas, Red? That's just not right." She peered up at me with those green eyes that sparkled with so much life—as if she wasn't going to waste a minute not enjoying the world around her—and in the middle of a crowded festival grounds on a warm fall day, I had an epiphany. I wanted to see that kind of light back in my own eyes when I looked in a mirror. There had been a time when I'd thought the world was fun, and I wanted that me back.

"I hate bananas. Can't stand the smell of them. Can't

stand to watch someone eat them." She shuddered.

"I happen to like them, but I promise I'll never make you watch me eat one."

"You're my hero," she said.

Her comment was meant to be flirty and fun, but my dead wife's last words to me flashed through my mind, mocking me. *"You stopped wanting to be my hero, Dylan."*

That had enraged me. My team had been working a case for several months, putting in long hours to bust up a gambling ring that had preyed on elderly men and women who hadn't had the money to lose in the first place. She knew that because I always talked about my cases with her, unlike some of my cop friends who shut their wives out of what was happening on the job.

"I'm your husband, not some caped hero who never does a damn thing wrong," I'd snarled. "I'm tired, frustrated with this case, and... You know what? I'm not talking about this anymore." She wasn't the one who came home early and found me in bed with another woman, yet there she sat like a wounded little bird, curled up on the sofa with her legs tucked under her, tears streaming down her cheeks because I couldn't forgive her for fucking my best friend.

"Where are you going?" she'd asked when I put on my winter coat.

"Out." It was Christmas Eve, and I spent it drinking myself into a stupor in my favorite neighborhood bar. When I got kicked out at closing, I dragged myself home, only to find a three-ring circus happening in our apartment. My neighbors were crowded around the entry, and when they saw me, silence fell as they parted like the Red Sea, making a path that led to the door. Standing just inside watching me was my precinct captain, pity shining in his eyes. Through the opening, I could see other cops, EMTs, and a gurney, a white sheet draped over it. No one had to tell me what had happened.

Guilt ripped my legs right out from under me, and I fell to my knees. I'd walked out on her when she'd needed me the most. She had tried to talk to me, and I had refused to listen. Because she'd had bouts of depression throughout our marriage, I should have recognized that she was capable of such a dramatic act. I also knew her intention had been to punish me. Well, it sure as hell worked.

"You okay?"

Jenny's voice penetrated the movie reel playing in my head, and I blinked Christine's face away. "Sure, why?"

"You kind of spaced out there for a minute."

"A little too much sun today. Let's go get that banana-less banana split." I could tell she wasn't sure she believed me, but she smiled and squeezed my hand. It was the best hand squeeze I'd ever had because I knew she was telling me that she wouldn't pry, but she was there for me.

As we approached my car, I spied Captain Moody several rows back in what appeared to be a terse conversation with Mayor Jim John Jenkins. I was trained to recognize body language, and there was no doubt in my mind that my police captain intimidated the mayor.

"What do you know about those two?" I asked Jenny.

She wrinkled her nose. "Moody's an ass, and our mayor couldn't find his balls if they were dangling in front of his face."

I burst into laughter. Couldn't help it. Miss Jenny Nance was a treasure. Someday, when she finished seeing the world and decided to settle down, some man was going to be damn lucky. I wrapped an arm around her shoulder. "I like you, Red."

"I like you, too, Chief."

My laughter had caught the attention of the mayor and my officer, and both glanced over at us. Moody smirked, as if he didn't give a shit that I'd caught him towering over the town's mayor. Mayor Jenkins slinked down until the cars hid him from view. Maybe he was looking for his lost balls.

Moody tried to engage me in a stare down, but I rolled my eyes, letting him know that I thought he was an idiot. He might very well be one, but that little episode between him and the mayor confirmed what I'd thought from the beginning. Moody had something on Blue Ridge Valley's mayor, and I was going to find out what.

CHAPTER THIRTEEN

~ Jenny ~

THE DAY HAD BEEN PERFECT. I didn't want it to end, and when Dylan pulled up in front of my apartment, I invited him in. "You can't stay long. I have to get ready for work."

He gave me that lopsided smile that I was coming to adore. "Kick me out when you need to."

I had the unsettling thought that I wouldn't ever want to kick him out. I blinked away any notion of Dylan permanently in my life and headed to the kitchen.

"Taste this," I said, returning with a shot glass filled with golden liquid. Dylan eyed the glass with suspicion, which I found amusing. I hadn't missed his dilemma when Hamburger had reached his hand into his legendary canvas bag, the one every person born in the valley knew held moonshine.

The thing about Hamburger, he rarely sold the mason jars filled to the brim with some of the best 'shine this side of the Mississippi. He used to, but after his last arrest and a stern warning by Judge Padgett, Hamburger had started giving the stuff away. It was beside the point that every one of us lucky enough to get a jar of Hamburger's liquid gold never charged him for whatever he bought or consumed when in one of our establishments. Mountain bartering at its best.

"I'm not stupid, you know," Dylan said, taking the shot glass from me. "I'm aware of what this is." He drank it anyway, tossing the contents down his throat.

I waited for his reaction and wasn't disappointed at seeing his eyes widen.

He licked his lips. "That tasted like apple pie."

"Good, huh?"

"Very, but honeypot?"

I sputtered a laugh. "Mmm?"

"Next time you give me some of that, lie. Tell me I'm drinking a flavored fruit drink or something."

Although he winked when he said it, I knew he was half serious. Hamburger Harry's moonshine was obviously a quandary for Dylan, but he'd get used to small-town ways soon enough.

"Will do, Officer. Now give me a kiss so you can take off."

"I can do that."

He prowled toward me, a wicked gleam in his eyes. Before he even touched me, my body hummed with anticipation. Because I already knew that he had the ability to make my knees weak, I backed up against the wall so I'd have something to lean on. He chuckled as he put his hands along the sides of my head, his gaze capturing mine.

"I want my mouth on yours, Red. I want my mouth on your neck and shoulders, on your breasts and the sweet curve of your ass. I think a lot about tasting you. All over. It will happen, but not tonight."

"When?" I rasped. No man had ever sent damp heat to my core with only words the way Dylan just had.

"When you're ready."

He covered my mouth then, stopping me from yelling, *Now! I'm ready now.* His tongue swept inside, and he tasted like apple pie, sweet and tangy. I wrapped my arms around his neck, and he pressed his hips against mine, letting me feel how much he wanted me.

I moaned. The little bit of my brain that still worked suggested that I call in sick and let Dylan spend the night showing me what he could do with his talented mouth. It was tempting, but I'd never missed a day in the three years I'd worked at Vincennes, and Dylan was right. I wasn't ready for him yet. I needed to get my head straight on what I wanted where this man was concerned. He was different. Special. That scared me because I could fall for him real hard. I couldn't allow that to happen.

He lifted his head and stared at me, and I loved how his eyes had gone darker and dreamy-like. "I've never been kissed by a cop before you. I rather like it." There went that grin that made my heart flutter.

"I've never been kissed by a mountain girl before you. I very much like it." He kissed my nose. "What nights are you off?"

"Mondays and Tuesdays."

"Let me pick you up Tuesday and take you to my apartment. We can cook a couple of steaks on the grill. You do eat meat, right?"

"I sure do, and I'd like that." Plus, I was dying to see his place. You could get to know a lot about a person by their stuff. Yet… "Is all this still pretend? You know, you and me just being together to make whatshisname go away?"

He rocked his groin against me. "Does that feel pretend, Red?"

Since my mouth was incapable of forming words, I just shook my head.

"Good. I'll come get you at five if that's okay."

"Five works." He laid one more delicious kiss on me, then walked out the door. I slid down the wall on legs that had given up their job of supporting me.

On Monday mornings I always made a stop at Mary's Bread Company to get a box of assorted doughnuts and three ready-made honey ham and cheddar cheese sandwiches on sourdough. Knowing I'd walk in the door around eight, Mary had my order ready to go.

Although there were six pastries in the bag, I was never charged for the two pecan bear claws. Those were my dad's. Twelve years ago he had been serving his last term as the mayor of Blue Ridge Valley. One of the town's wealthy and influential commissioners had wanted the land Mary's bakery shop was on and had tried to force something called eminent domain—which we'd never heard of here in our small part of the world. Once everyone understood what it meant, there was a firestorm.

I don't even remember why the commissioner wanted Mary's land, but oh man, the yelling that went on at the town hall meetings for over a month. The commissioner had a lot of people who owed him favors, so it was him and his group against my dad, Mary, and everyone else.

From the time Natalie and I entered high school, Daddy made us go to open town meetings, saying that it was important for us to understand the workings of our community. Sometimes we found them interesting, and sometimes they were so boring that we could barely keep our eyes open.

During the time of the Eminent Domain War, or Mary's Last Stand as it became known, we would sit, wide-eyed, watching people's faces turn red and the spit flying out of their mouths as they nearly came to blows. Daddy refused to back down, though, even when the commissioner threatened to take over the town and run my father out with his tail tucked between his legs. My dad's only defense for standing his ground was that what they were trying to do to Mary wasn't right. After months of fighting, the commissioner finally gave up and, in a snit, sold his house and moved away. "Good riddance," everyone said.

In Mary's eyes, Daddy's a hero. In mine, too. From then on, pecan bear claws—his weakness—have been free, no matter how hard he at first argued with Mary that he was just doing his job, and she should take his money. And every Monday morning I pick them up, along with the pastries for me and Mom, and the sandwiches, and take them to my parents, spending most of the day with them. After we have our coffee and Mary's treats, I work in the yard with my dad for a few hours until lunchtime.

"Tell your daddy I put extra pee-cans on his claws, Miss Jenny."

"I sure will." She put extra pecans on his claws every week, but she liked reminding him. I pulled a twenty and a ten from my wallet and handed it over. Even though I only had sixty-seven cents due back, I knew better than to tell her to keep it.

The bell over the door tinkled. I glanced over my shoulder, expecting to see Mrs. Hershel. She usually came in around the same time I did, and I would always brace for a smothering hug. It wasn't Mrs. Hershel, but I'd definitely be good with a hug.

"Morning, Dylan," I said.

He smiled, his eyes lighting up at seeing me. "Jenny."

That was all he said, but it was the way he drawled out my name, making it whispery, that had me inhaling air back into my lungs. He wore a dark blue suit, light blue shirt, and a gorgeous blue and red tie. Sunglasses were pushed up on his head, and the whole effect was of a CEO billionaire like those on the covers of some romance books. I wished I had my camera with me.

Mary cleared her throat, reminding me that she was there. "Ah, Mary, I'd like to introduce you to our new police chief, Dylan Conrad. Dylan, Mrs. Mary Ballard." I kept my gaze on Dylan, wanting to see his reaction to Mary.

CHAPTER FOURTEEN

~ Dylan ~

IT WAS CLOSE, BUT I managed not to show any surprise at Blue Ridge Valley's famous baker. "Mrs. Ballard, it's a pleasure to meet you. I'm going to be one of your best doughnut customers," I said to the top of her purple head. I doubted she reached the five-foot-tall mark, and not much more than her nose, eyes, and hair were visible over the top of the counter. Her eyes were heavily shadowed in purple, and each ear had a row of pierced rings along the shell. I estimated her to be in her sixties.

I glanced at Jenny to see amusement dancing in her eyes, and I remembered saying that I'd marry Miss Mary for her doughnuts. My lips gave an uncontrollable twitch imagining Mary Ballard in my bed. I think Jenny was holding her breath in an effort not to laugh.

God, I loved this town.

"Mr. Ballard kicked the bucket back in '92, and nobody calls me Mrs. Ballard anymore. I'm just plain Mary. What flavor doughnut you like, Chief?"

There was absolutely nothing plain about Miss Mary. "Hot glazed for doughnuts, and…" I eyed the gigantic muffins. "What are those?"

She glanced at the ones I pointed to. "Apple cinnamon with walnuts. Eat this one now," she said, handing me a glazed doughnut that was warm in my palm. "Take this one for later." She put another one in a bag. "No money today, Chief. They're a welcome present."

"Thank you, Mary." I bit off half of the warm doughnut, moaning at how it melted in my mouth. "I've died and gone to heaven."

Mary beamed, her purple-shadowed eyes shining with pleasure. "My Larry always did love those the best. Glad to meet another man who appreciates them."

She'd found a fan in me. "I also want three dozen assorted to take to the boys and girls at the station, and I will pay for those. Make sure you put an apple cinnamon muffin in the box."

Doughnuts paid for, I walked Jenny out. "You're evil, Red." We hadn't made it two steps out of Mary's sight when Jenny doubled over in laughter.

"If you could have seen your face," she gasped.

"You could have warned me, you know."

"No way. It was too much fun watching you try to keep a straight face."

I took out the apple muffin, biting into it. "Oh my God, this is good. I might marry her anyway, purple hair and all."

"Just so you know, next week her hair and eye shadow will be green or red or maybe blue. It changes every Monday."

"Even better. She'll keep me on my toes."

Jenny gave me a toothy grin. "Now I know how to bribe you, Chief. Give you a box of warm glazed doughnuts and apple muffins and you'll be putty in my hands."

I was pretty sure I was already putty in her hands. "I'm an officer of the law, madam. I can't be bribed."

She made a snorting noise. "We'll see. You look really nice today, by the way. Very CEOish."

"Thank you." It wasn't my usual attire. Normally I'd have on a pair of tan cargo pants and a dark brown or olive-green polo shirt with the Blue Ridge Valley police logo on the chest, bought with my own money because I refused to wear those crappy uniforms the city supplied. I was working on getting my officers something similar.

Today I had a meeting with the mayor and town manager, thus the monkey suit.

A powder-blue Mercedes convertible turned into the lot, parking next to my car.

"Oh crap," Jenny said.

I raised a brow. "Something I should know?"

"Man-eater alert."

The woman who exited the Mercedes was stunning. I guessed her to be in her mid-twenties, about Jenny's age. Sleek blonde hair in a blunt cut just below her ears, eyes as blue as the sky above me, tall with a body curved in all the right places. Her sight zeroed in on me as she sashayed—that was the only word for it—straight for me.

"She hates me, so I'm outta here," Jenny said.

I grabbed her arm. "Oh no you don't." The type of woman aiming for me made me want to run for the hills.

"This isn't going to be pretty," she grumbled.

Probably not.

"Introduce me to your friend, Jenn."

What? No *hello, Jenn. How are you?* No pretense of having good manners?

"Stephanie, this is Dylan Conrad. Dylan, Stephanie Jenkins."

"Jenkins as in Mayor Jenkins?" I said.

"My daddy."

Oh joy. "Pleased to meet you, Stephanie. Sorry to run, but I've got a meeting." Which was true, but it wasn't until later in the morning.

She put her hand on my arm, stopping me. "We're having a barbeque Saturday afternoon. I'll have Daddy give you directions to our house."

Did I miss something? Like an actual invitation that I could decline? Apparently Miss Jenkins was used to taking a lot of things for granted. I had a bad feeling that she was going to be trouble.

It was definitely time to run for the hills. "Ladies, have a nice day." Hopefully Jenny wouldn't be too mad at me for abandoning her to the man-eater. It occurred to me that I didn't have Jenny's phone number. I should have gotten that when we were together yesterday so I could text her a silly smiley face or something.

"Those doughnuts from Mary's?" Tommy asked, eyeing the box in my hands when I walked into the building.

"That they are." I handed him the box. "Put them in the break room." I'd gotten plenty to go around, but even so, I rolled my eyes when he took four out. "Hungry this morning?"

"Always hungry," he said around a mouthful of chocolate-covered doughnut.

"You're on the desk today, right?" He nodded. "When Captain Moody comes in, tell him I want to see him."

"Will do, Chief."

I walked down the hall, stopping at the doorway to the bull pen. "Morning, everyone."

"Morning, Chief," four voices rang out.

"Anything going on I should know about?" I was on week two, and we'd settled into a routine. The day shift was already out on patrol, but the night shift had started hanging around, waiting for me to come in. We'd shoot the breeze for a few minutes, catch up on any problems that might have come up overnight, and then they'd be on their way.

"It was quiet last night," Officer Griffin said.

"Good to hear, Sarah." I'd already started using hers and Kim Payton's first names, along with Tommy's and Gene Lanier's, my only detective. Those four were the cream of my police force, all of them sharp as tacks. Each were well on their way to earning the sixty points I'd set as a requirement to keep their jobs. Hopefully the others would get there before the deadline.

"Was that a box of doughnuts from Mary's that Tommy just walked by with?" Gene said.

"You have good eyes, Gene." Four cops flew past me, following Tommy like bloodhounds on the scent. "All right then. Guess we're done here," I said to the empty room.

My meeting agenda with the mayor and town manager was a review of my first week and a discussion of my plans for the department. I picked up the briefcase I'd stored under my desk and put three folders into it, things I'd worked on the last few days to prepare for my meeting. After a quick review of the list I'd made, I stuck it on top of the folders. It was going to be an interesting meeting, and I was going to find out just how much authority I actually had.

"Damn it, Tommy, you eat all the chocolate ones?"

I glanced up at hearing Moody's voice. The shit was about to hit the fan.

"You wanted to see me?"

Moody stood in my doorway, a cup of coffee in one hand and a cream-filled doughnut in the other. There was nothing wrong with that, but I couldn't help thinking if my new boss wanted to see me, I would have lost the coffee and doughnut. Also, I would've made sure there wasn't a blob of white cream on my chin.

"Come in and close the door." When he was seated, I said, "Captain Moody, it appears that you've forgotten that we don't use curse words when in uniform, even among ourselves." I could have let that go, considering what I had coming his way, but the man irritated me to no end.

"Whad I say?"

Whad? The man was dumber than a fence post, but that was the least of his problems. "You said 'damn it.'"

His thick brows furrowed. "I thought it was 'fuck' we couldn't say."

And I was going to bang my head on my fucking desk.

"We do not use any curse words when on duty, Captain, even something as innocuous as 'hell' or 'damn.'" When his brows scrunched together again, I figured he was trying to puzzle out what *innocuous* meant. Whatever.

"We have a problem, several in fact." I had to look away when he crammed the rest of his doughnut into his mouth.

"Like what?"

"Like this contract with Ed's Garage." I slid a copy of the contract across the desk, but he didn't pick it up. I didn't blame him because it was a snake that was about to bite him.

He eyed it warily. "What about it?"

"The department is paying Ed's Garage at least twice what we should be for the maintenance on our vehicles." And since Ed was Moody's cousin, I could guarantee Moody was getting a cut. Unfortunately I couldn't prove it. Yet. I was working on it, though.

"It's the going rate. You calling him a cheat?"

That was exactly what I was calling him. I wished I could say that my captain was smart enough to be nervous, but the dumbass was getting mad. The next sheet I slid his way was the breakdown of costs I'd gotten last week from the head of Chicago PD's motor pool.

"Captain Moody, those are the going charges for maintenance and repair items in the city of Chicago, where they pay union rates." I pushed the page closer to him, but he refused to even glance at it.

He glared at me. "Just because—"

"You can sit there and talk yourself blue in the face, but there's nothing you can say to convince me that we should be paying Ed's Garage double what a big city does. Here's how this is going to play out. Can I assume that there is an Ed at Ed's Garage?"

Moody gave a curt nod.

"Then Ed has a choice. We have nine months left on

our contract with him. We will honor that on the condition he charges us the same rates as Chicago PD pays, minus ten percent. When he asks why the discount, it's because he doesn't have the overhead that a big city does. If that is unacceptable to him, then the contract is null and void."

"You can't do that, *sir.*"

"Oh, but I can." He'd practically spit the *sir* at me, and without doubt more colorful names for me were circling around in his head. "According to the fine print, we have the right to audit his books and invoices at any time during the length of the contract. Do you think he wants that?"

Silence greeted me. "Didn't think so. When we finish here, you and I are taking a ride over to Ed's Garage to explain things to Ed." I wasn't about to let Moody get there before me. If Ed cooperated, I'd let him finish out the contract, but it wouldn't be renewed. There were two other garages I'd scouted out that I'd ask to bid on the contract.

"The next item we need to discuss is the building's cleaning service."

Because I was watching for a reaction to that one, I was rewarded with pure hatred in his eyes before he blanked them. "You can tell your sister that her cleaning services will no longer be needed unless she's willing to accept the job at twenty dollars an hour." The fifty we were paying her now was ridiculous. "You might remind her that even that is more than she'd get for the same job anywhere else."

"You can shove the job..." He clamped his mouth shut.

I wasn't even deducting points from the man anymore. Why bother? He was gone as soon as I could make it happen.

"Is that all?" he said, standing.

"No, there's one more thing." I waited for him to sit again, stifling a smirk when he eyed the door as if he'd like to run straight through it, leaving the outline of his body in the wood. "There will be no more lunches or dinners charged to the department's entertainment account. In fact, we no longer have charge privileges at any restaurant in town."

After I'd discovered he was entertaining his family and friends, charging it to the department—and why did a small-town police department even have an entertainment budget?—I'd spent all afternoon on Saturday visiting restaurants. They weren't any happier now than Moody was. Not surprising considering how much money that was not his that he'd spread around.

The only response he gave was to press his lips together so hard that they turned white. Those three things were all I'd found so far, but I wouldn't be surprised as I dug deeper to find more ways he'd figured out how to fleece the department.

"Now we're done. Let's go have a little talk with Ed."

"We can't afford new uniforms," Mayor Jenkins said.

"Yes, we can." My little trip to Ed's Garage with Moody had gone as expected. There'd been a lot of sputtering and denials, but Ed had come around to my way of thinking when the subject of an audit was brought up. Now I had a mayor I hadn't quite figured out yet how to deal with. I was pretty sure I could count on Buddy Ferguson, our town manager, as an ally, and I hoped to have that confirmed by the end of this meeting.

"The budget that was submitted three months ago wasn't worth the paper it was printed on." I handed both men copies of my new budget, then sat back and gave them a few minutes to review it.

Ferguson was the first to look up at me, and I acknowledged the approval in his eyes with a slight nod. "As you can see," I said when the mayor set the page down, "several line items have been cut from the original numbers."

"You don't want to piss Ed off," Mayor Jenkins said. "He keeps our police cars on the road."

I didn't care if Ed of Ed's Garage was pissed or not. The bastard was a crook, along with his cousin, my police captain. "We worked things out this morning. Ed rethought his pricing. With the new contract and the other items adjusted to reflect actual costs, there's room in the budget for new uniforms and a pay raise for those officers deserving one."

It had been over a year since anyone had an increase in their paychecks, and that was never going to happen as long as Moody continued diverting money into his pockets. That was stopping as of today. I wanted my officers to take pride in themselves and their police department. Happy cops made for good cops.

"This budget will have to be approved," Mayor Jenkins said, and I heard the dismissal in his voice.

I knew that, but he could give it the stamp of approval, fast-tracking a vote from the town manager and city commissioners, or it could get lost somewhere under a pile of papers on his desk.

"We can put it on the agenda for next Thursday night." Ferguson tapped his pen on the table as he leveled his gaze on me. "It's our monthly review session. The mayor, me, and the commissioners."

The town manager had just let me know he was onboard. Mayor Jenkins was glaring at Ferguson. It was time to play my trump card. "Buddy, could you give the mayor and me a few minutes?"

"I think we're done here." Ferguson gathered up his papers and folders. He stood, putting his hand on the mayor's shoulders. "Jim John, we said we'd give Dylan a chance to prove himself or fall flat on his face. Put him and his amended budget on the review meeting agenda."

They had said that when I'd interviewed. One of my conditions before I'd signed a one-year contract with the town of Blue Ridge Valley was that within reason, I had a free hand to set up the police department as I saw fit.

"You're making changes too fast," the mayor said when we were alone.

He and I both knew that wasn't his problem with my new budget. I was tempted to come right out and ask what Moody had on him, but he'd deny it to hell and high water.

"Another year under Moody's control, and he would have run your police department out of business. You brought me here to do a job, and I need to know now if you're going to let me do it."

Jenkins sighed. "Of course, I am. I just think you should ease into things. We'll talk about this some more, maybe schedule it for next month's meeting."

I thought the mayor was caught between a rock and a hard place. Not my problem though. "Easing into things isn't my way, Mayor." I'd hoped not to have to resort to playing dirty, but I was willing to if it meant getting my police department in shape. "This morning I was cleaning out some files, and I came across this." I laid the arrest report on his daughter in front of him.

A muscle in his jaw twitched. "What do you plan to do with it?"

My guess was that he'd thought it had been destroyed. I'm also sure Moody was keeping it for leverage. "It's a copy. Do whatever you want with it."

"And the original?"

I really hated dirty games, but the only way to fight a fire was with fire. "Locked away for now. You help me get my budget put through Thursday night, I'll give it to you." The last thing I wanted to see was respect in his eyes for doing this, but there it was. I was playing the game the way he understood it. Christ, I hated politicians and their backroom deals.

"Done."

"A word of warning. If I or one of my officers ever catches your daughter driving while under the influence or finds drugs on her person, I will see that she is prosecuted."

His eyes narrowed. "Don't threaten me, Mr. Conrad. And you don't have to worry. She's cleaned up her act."

I hoped so. Stephanie's arrest had been buried, and she hadn't even gotten a slap on the hand for getting caught driving while high on coke. Even worse, a gram of cocaine had been found in the pocket of her jeans. But I was willing to give her a clean slate.

"I guess I'll see you Thursday night, unless you want to meet one more time to go over everything before the review meeting."

"No. Present it as is."

"Thank you." I stood. "As far as my officers are concerned, their raises were your idea." I could afford to be gracious now that I'd gotten what I wanted, and it also helped get the bitter taste out of my mouth for having to resort to dirty play.

I had made it to the door when he told me he expected to see me at his Saturday barbeque. Damn, I guess Stephanie got to her father.

CHAPTER FIFTEEN

~ Jenny ~

AFTER GETTING THE YARD WORK done, I came in with my dad for lunch. On my plate was a present wrapped in Christmas paper. "What's this?"

My dad pulled out my chair. "It's your Christmas present." He nodded at my mom. "You tell her."

I slid onto my seat and waited for my parents to sit. Christmas was a hard time for us. My parents had loved Christmas as much as Natalie and me and had always made it a special time for us with lots of family traditions. The first Christmas after Natalie had died, we couldn't bear to stay home and had gone to a beach in Florida where it was warm and hadn't felt at all like Christmas.

We'd continued doing that, but this year I wouldn't be with them. Because we no longer celebrated Christmas, I had been able to book my flight to leave the day after Autumn's wedding without feeling guilty for not being here for the holidays. My parents were leaving for Florida the week before Christmas.

My mother leaned her elbows on the table and folded her hands in front of her. "Open it first, and then I'll explain."

I eased a finger under the tape. I was one of those people who opened gifts carefully so I could save the bows and wrapping paper. Natalie would always tear into her packages with impatience, eager to see what was inside. Halfway through getting my present open, I paused, smiled, and then tore into it the way Natalie would have.

"That was so Natalie just then," my dad softly said.

When I glanced up at my parents, both had smiles on their faces and tears in their eyes. I blinked against the stinging in mine. I opened the box, and inside was a white envelope. Inside that was a check. I pulled it out, looked at the amount, and gasped.

"I can't take this." I waved the check for ten thousand dollars in the air. "This is too much."

"Yes, you can, honey." My mother cleared her throat. "We'd planned to give each of you five thousand dollars toward your world tour, and we still want to do that. Half of that is for you and half for Natalie. You'll just be spending it for her now."

I burst into tears. My parents pushed their chairs away and came around the table, pulling me into their embrace. From the day Natalie had been diagnosed with a grade IV brain tumor—one her specialist had likened to a runaway freight train with no hope of stopping it—bone-deep sadness had permeated our home. She'd been given eight months to live, but she'd managed to last for eleven. Those extra three months had been a wonderful gift.

Because I was her identical twin, my parents had insisted I get tested nine ways to Sunday to make sure I was okay. I was, but the realization that life was fragile and could be stolen away at any moment had only made me more determined to follow my dream, mine and Natalie's. I was doing it as much for her as for myself.

"I'm blessed to have you both as my parents," I said through my tears.

My dad rested his chin on my head. "We were the ones blessed to have you and Natalie as our daughters, sweetheart."

I gave a broken laugh. "Can't argue with that." We hugged once more and then returned to our seats. "Remember when Natalie was mad because I got chosen to spend the day with you, Daddy, on take-your-daughter-to-work day?"

He grinned. "Yeah, I flipped a coin and you won. I told her that the next year, it would be her turn."

"Oh, I was so angry with her for what she did," my mom said.

"You were?" I snorted. "I'm the one she pretended to be for my English test and purposely failed it." I'd been so tempted to tell my seventh-grade teacher that I'd been with my daddy, and that it had been Natalie taking the test, but then she would have been in even more trouble.

My mom, my dad, and I laughed, and it felt really good. We reminisced some more as we ate lunch, and then we ended the day sitting on the sofa together, paging through the family album, something we hadn't done since Natalie died. It would have hurt too much, but today, the remembering was healing.

And soon I would stand on a distant shore and feel her with me again like she'd promised.

"Nice place," I said Tuesday night after walking into Dylan's apartment. "Autumn's fiancé lived here before he moved in with her."

"It will do until I build my log house. If I'm still here next year."

"If you're still here?" I followed him into his kitchen. The living room area and kitchen was a great room with tall windows that looked out over a gorgeous mountain view. There was a fireplace against one wall, and I could imagine curling up on his leather sofa, a fire burning, sipping a glass of wine while watching the snow fall.

"My contract's for one year. If they're happy with me, they'll extend it. If not, they won't. Red wine or a beer?"

"I think wine tonight." I scooted onto a stool at the

granite-topped island. It would be awesome to live in a place like this, but I was saving my pennies. My apartment was a tiny one-bedroom, the cheapest I could find that I was willing to live in. No view, no fireplace, no cathedral ceilings.

"So you have to prove yourself? I didn't know that's how it worked."

He kicked off his shoes, pushing them against the wall with his foot, then pulled the white button-down shirt out of his jeans. Why I found that totally sexy, I don't know. Taking my cue from him, I slipped off my sandals.

"For the first year. If they offer to renew my contract, it will be for five years at a time." He grabbed the bottle of wine in one hand and two wineglasses in the other. "Let's sit on the balcony."

"I envy you your balcony," I said. "And your view."

"It is nice, isn't it?" He poured wine into each of our glasses, then handed me one. "My view in Chicago was of the Sears Tower, and I didn't have a balcony. I'm enjoying this one."

He seemed subdued tonight, and I wondered if he was missing the city or maybe his friends. What if he had a girlfriend? But would he take off and leave if he did? And I didn't see him as the kind of man who would mess around on a girlfriend.

"What made you decide to leave Chicago?" The silence stretched as I waited for him to answer, making me wonder if he was going to tell me. It was a simple question, or at least I'd thought so.

"My wife died. I decided it was time for a change of scenery," he finally said.

His voice was flat, his gaze on the mountains rising up on the other side of the valley. I waited for him to say more, but when he didn't, I let it go even though I was really curious. How long ago had she died? Had he loved her, mourned her, cried tears for her? How had she died? Suddenly in a traffic accident or slowly because of some god-awful disease like cancer? I'd lived through Natalie's suffering and understood that kind of heartbreak. But I didn't ask any of those questions. It was obvious the subject was closed.

"I'm glad you chose Blue Ridge Valley."

The hint of a smile appeared on his face. "I'm even happier with my decision after meeting you, Red."

Well. Okay then, Dylan. Just go and wake up the butterflies nesting in my stomach. We fell into silence again, but it was a comfortable one this time. I sipped my wine, watching Dylan out of the corner of my eye. He seemed to be sloughing off whatever had caused him to be moody.

"Hear that? That was my owl." He put his feet on the railing, tipping his chair back.

"I love listening to them. There's one that lives somewhere near my parents' backyard. I actually saw it once, sitting on a tree stump. He just sat there, staring at me with big, unblinking eyes."

"Haven't seen mine yet. Are there certain species of owls that live in the Blue Ridge Mountains?"

"Beats me. We'll have to google it sometime."

Dylan set down his empty wineglass, reached over, and rested his hand on my thigh. Mercy, I loved it when he touched me. He made me tingly whenever he did.

"I'm sorry for my shitty mood. I have a lot of things on my mind, but I'm better now that you're here."

I put my hand on top of his, giving him a smile. "I aim to please."

"Trust me, Red, you please. Getting hungry?"

For you? God yes. "I could eat."

"How good are you at making a salad?"

"I'm a master salad maker."

"We'll leave the rest of the wine and glasses here for

later." He stood, pulling me up with him, then tugged me against his body. "First, I need a kiss."

I lifted onto my toes and put my mouth on his. He groaned as he wrapped his arms around me, pulling me tighter against him. Our noses bumped, and he chuckled, angling his head as he took possession of my mouth. His kisses were lethal, setting my body on fire, making me ache for him. He devoured my mouth, possessing me like no man ever had. It was entirely possible I'd never kiss another man again because after Dylan, why bother? I put my hand on his chest, felt his heart pounding against my palm, and my own heart thumped hard, answering his.

"Dinner," he gasped, pulling away. "I promised to feed you."

"Okay." His kiss had stupefied my brain to mush, and that one word was about all I was capable of. The man did love to kiss. He took my hand, leading me to the kitchen, which gave me time to recover from the hottest kiss on record. I was also worried. I liked him too much. That was a problem because I didn't want to take off on my world tour, my heart missing a man, any man.

CHAPTER SIXTEEN

~ *Dylan* ~

I'D ALMOST LOST CONTROL. THAT wasn't me. I was always in control, but Jenny Nance was getting under my skin. Kissing her had set my blood on fire, and I'd come close to taking her down to the floor of the balcony with me. I'd almost called her and canceled tonight. The sour taste still in my mouth with how I'd strong-armed the mayor to get my budget on Thursday night's agenda, topped by catching Moody stealing the department blind, had put me in a bad mood.

As if that wasn't enough, I hadn't slept well. I'd gone so far as to take out my phone to call Jenny before remembering I didn't have her number. So here she was, and I was glad. Already my mood had improved, and not just because I'd kissed her. Being with her soothed me.

"Want some music?" I asked, letting go of her hand when we walked into the kitchen.

"That would be nice."

She opened the refrigerator, pulling out the makings for a salad. I liked that she didn't wait to be told what to do, and there was another thing I realized I liked about her. Jenny Nance was comfortable in her own skin, knew who she was and what she wanted. Like her travel-the-world dream. Nothing was going to get in her way of that. Good for her.

It also meant that she wasn't looking for a man to put a ring on her finger, which made being with her for however long we enjoyed each other's company easy. I wouldn't hurt her, and she wouldn't hurt me.

When she'd told me about her twin sister, I'd wanted to wrap her in my arms and take the hurt away. But I knew firsthand that there were no words or actions that could ease the pain of losing someone you loved. I understood why she was so determined to see the world. She had an unbreakable promise to keep.

"Jazz, blues, or R&B? Sorry, I don't have any bluegrass CDs."

"I can only listen to bluegrass at a festival. You pick." She rummaged in one of the kitchen drawers. "Where're your knives?"

"Second one down." I went into the living room and put on some blues. "What's your favorite music?" I asked, coming back into the kitchen. *And please don't say country.*

"Some country, and I also like southern rock—you know, Lynyrd Skynyrd, The Marshall Tucker Band, ones like those. Oh, and soft rock and love songs." She glanced up from dicing a tomato. "Really, there's not much music I don't like... except rap. Not crazy about that."

"That makes two of us." Conversation was easy with her, and by the time we finished dinner, I knew her favorite color, purple, her favorite food, lobster drenched in warm butter, and the food she hated the most, green peppers. She had me laughing with her stories of some of the residents of Blue Ridge Valley.

"Here's another one," she said, amusement lighting up her green eyes. "Every Sunday, Preacher Seamus calls on someone to open his service with a prayer. One time he asked Old Man Pickens. Everyone bowed their heads and waited. And waited. And waited some more. Then people started peeking their eyes open just in time to see the ass end of him crawling out the window.

"He's never been seen at the Baptist church again. He converted to Methodist with a promise from Reverend

Joe that he'll never be called on to speak a prayer. Now Preacher Seamus claims Reverend Joe owes him one parishioner. Reverend Joe asked for a volunteer to switch to Baptist, but none of his people want to change because the Baptists don't dance or drink." Her lips twitched. "At least not in public."

"That's hilarious, Red. I don't think I'll ever get tired of your hometown stories." I was definitely glad I hadn't canceled our dinner. She insisted on helping me clean up the kitchen, and we had that done in short order.

"You cook a good steak," she said as I poured her a glass of wine after we'd returned to the balcony.

"That's about the extent of my cooking abilities. Wait, I can make a mean omelet, too." I glanced over at her. "You ever decide to stay over, which is my greatest wish, I'll prove it."

"No green peppers?"

"For you, I'll leave them out."

She laughed. "You're sweet, you know that?"

"I've been called a lot of things, but sweet has never been one of them." I noticed that she was snuggling up into herself. The temperature had dropped considerably since we'd been out earlier. "Cold?"

"A little."

I patted my leg. "Come over here." Without hesitation she set down her wine and then straddled my lap. "Hello," I said, my gaze on her mouth.

"Hello to you. Want to kiss me?"

"Silly girl." I slipped my hand under her hair, cradling her neck, and tugged her to me. She nestled against my chest as I claimed her mouth. I let go of her neck and wrapped my arms around her back. She was soft and warm, and tasted like the wine she was drinking. It wasn't long before I was burning for her, but I didn't know how far to take this. If she wasn't ready yet, then I needed to stop now.

"Jenny…" When she started to unbutton my shirt, I caught her hand. "Are you ready for this? For us?"

Her gaze locked on mine. "I think so."

I had no idea what her hesitation was all about, but *I think so* wasn't good enough. "No, Red, we're not doing this until you know it's what you want." I pulled her head to my shoulder. "The second you're sure, you call me. I don't care if it's four in the morning, okay?"

"I'm sorry, Dylan." She picked at the top button of my shirt. "I honestly don't know why I'm hesitating. I want you. I really do. It's just that… well, it's different with you."

"How so?" I wrapped a lock of her hair around my finger while wondering if I'd ever walk normal again.

"You're different from any man I've been with before. Not that there's been many, but you're special."

No, I wasn't. "Jenny, I'm just a man doing his best to get along in this world. Don't make me something I'm not."

She lifted her head from my shoulder, her eyes studying me as if she could see my deepest thoughts. I hoped the hell she couldn't. If so, she would see a man who'd failed to listen to his wife's cry for help. I had to live with that every fucking damn day. To hear anyone say I was special made me want to smash my fist through the wall.

"I think you misunderstand." She put her hand on my cheek, and I forced myself not to lean into her palm. "I'm not saying you're special, you know, like some kind of superhero. I mean that I like you a lot, and I don't want our sleeping together to be nothing more than a matter of getting our jollies off."

I tried not to laugh. I really did. "Get our jollies off?"

She punched my arm. "That wasn't meant to be funny, Dylan."

"Yet it was." I gave in to temptation and pressed my face against her palm. What was it about this woman that soothed my soul?

"Okay, it kind of was. I don't want you to fall in love with me because nothing's going to stop me from going on my world tour, but for me, sex with a man has to mean something."

And here I was, planning to give her the don't-fall-in-love-with-me lecture. "You're a constant surprise, Jenny Girl. Let's make a promise now. No falling in love for either of us." I held out my hand, and we shook on the deal.

"But we can definitely like each other, right?" She bit down on her bottom lip as if worried about my answer.

"We sure can." She had no worries about that on my side, and when she smiled, I smiled back.

"Does this mean we've gone past the pretend stage?" She tilted her head, studying me. "I mean, that's part of my hesitation. You know, it's not real if it's make-believe."

"We left pretend behind at the restaurant when we decided we wanted to get to know each other better, don't you think?" I regretted I'd even used that word with her, since she seemed to be hung up on it. "Are you okay with that?" *Please be okay with it, Jenny Girl.*

"As long as we both agree to the rules. We can't go past the like-each-other stage. No messy love business."

I tapped her nose. "By the rules. Got it." Why did that make me a little sad? It was what I wanted, too. "Since you're working the rest of the week, would you like to do something on Saturday?"

"Have you seen one of our waterfalls yet?"

"Nope. You want to be my waterfall tour guide?" I'd thought when I first met her and realized she was interested in me that we would have a few tumbles between the sheets, then both move on. Instead I was dating her, romancing her, and I was enjoying it. Yeah, there'd be a long shower for me tonight that included a little hand relief, but when Jenny and I did have sex, I was pretty sure she would be worth waiting for.

"Want to watch a movie? I'll make us some popcorn."

"Yay!" She hopped off my lap.

"I take it that's a yes?" She was grinning like a kid. A few times when she'd do or say something that reminded me how full of life she was, I'd start to compare her to Christine, especially at the end. But every time I shut that thought down. She wasn't Christine, and I wasn't going to start comparing them.

I let her pick the movie, expecting something romantic. She surprised me again when she found *Arsenic and Old Lace* on a cable channel.

She squealed. "This one is so funny. Have you seen it?"

I hadn't, and that was all it took for her to insist that I had to watch it. She was right. It was hilarious. We made out a little more during the commercials, and too soon the movie ended and it was time to take her home. I didn't want to and almost asked if she wanted to spend the night, just sleep, nothing more. But my reason was selfish, and it wouldn't be right to use Jenny to try to keep Christine's ghost at bay, so I didn't.

I was pulling out of my parking lot when my phone rang, which reminded me that I needed to get Jenny's number.

"Talk to me," I said when Tommy's name came up on the screen. He wouldn't be calling this late at night if there weren't a problem.

"Chief, I think you better come over to Jansen's house."

"He causing trouble?"

"Not anymore. He's dead. His wife shot him. Now she's threatening to shoot herself."

An image of Christine on that gurney flashed in my mind, making my stomach take a sickening roll. "Location?" I memorized the address, then told him I was on my way. "You know where Crooked Creek Road is?" I asked Jenny.

"Yeah, why?"

"We've got a situation. You mind riding along? When we get there, you can take my car and go on home. I'll hitch a ride back with Tommy."

CHAPTER SEVENTEEN

~ Jenny ~

"NO PROBLEM," I SAID, WONDERING what the situation was, but Dylan didn't offer any more information. He'd gone real quiet, in fact. "Go through town, take the first left after the post office."

He flipped a switch, and a flashing blue light on the dash came on. We sped through town, and speed demon that I am, I thought it was cool. It only took ten minutes to get to the address, but my excitement at racing through town died at seeing two other police cars and an ambulance parked out front.

"What's going on here?"

Dylan parked on the grass in front of the house. "Don't know yet."

I was pretty sure he knew more than he was saying, but I let it go. Obviously something was seriously wrong, and I didn't want to distract him.

"Wait here," he said before jumping out of the car, then jogging up to Tommy Evans.

While they talked, Dylan kept glancing at the open door to the house. I craned my neck, trying to see inside, but the only view I had was of the foyer and what I assumed was a coat closet door. Neighbors were gathered on the street, and I turned on the ignition long enough to roll down my window.

"I heard two shots," one of them said.

"I thought it was three," another stated.

Someone was shot? I tried to think if I knew anyone

who lived on Crooked Creek Road, but no one came to mind. It appeared that Dylan forgot I was in his car because he headed for the open door of the house without looking back. Was I supposed to go ahead and drive home? He'd told me to wait, so I didn't know what to do. Finally I settled on waiting a little longer to see if he came back to the car.

The people on the street quieted as Dylan stood at the open door, talking to someone. I strained to hear him, but couldn't. Why didn't he go on in? Tommy, along with a female cop I recognized as Kim Payton, and two EMTs watched from the sidewalk leading up to the house.

Something was going on, and I tried to think of a reason Dylan wouldn't go inside. Was there a hostage situation? That would explain what I was seeing. I already knew someone had a gun from what the neighbors had said. The idea of that made me nervous. What if Dylan got hurt?

Fifteen minutes passed and still Dylan talked. Then he disappeared inside the house. I wanted to yell at him to come back out. Tommy and the other cop approached the door, their hands on the guns still in their holsters. I put my hand over my chest, pressing it against my rapidly beating heart. My shoulders hunched, preparing to cringe at hearing gunshots.

There wasn't a sound, not from the neighbors huddling nearby, not from the EMTs whose gazes were focused on the open door, the same as mine, and not from the two cops with their shoulders pressed against the doorframe. I'm not even sure any of us were breathing. Maybe another twenty minutes passed, and then the cops disappeared inside.

Not long after, Kim poked her head out, gesturing to the EMTs. They rolled their gurney into the house. I still wasn't sure if Dylan had meant for me to go, but I couldn't. Not without seeing him walk out, safe and whole. An SUV with a logo on the side identifying it as the county coroner pulled onto the driveway, parking behind the police car. A woman exited, a black bag in her hand.

Oh God, someone was dead. The only reason I was able to stay in the car and not run searching for Dylan was that there had been no gunfire since he'd walked into the house. Shortly after the coroner entered, the EMTs came out, rolling the gurney to the ambulance. Shocked, I stared at Gertie Jansen as they pushed her past me. I hadn't known the Jansens lived here, but I did know her. She was in my mother's book club and had been to my parents' house on several occasions.

Her head was wrapped in gauze and one eye was swollen shut. She had obviously been beaten. Had her husband done that to her? I'd heard he had a hot temper, but to do that to his wife? Now I understood why Dylan had been quiet on the way here. Was Mr. Jansen dead?

The ambulance sped off, siren blaring. I should probably leave, but I couldn't make myself do it. Dylan wouldn't take this well if his officer was dead, and I wanted to be here for him. So I waited.

"I thought you'd left."

I jerked awake at hearing Dylan's voice. He sat in the driver's seat, staring out the windshield. I hadn't heard him get in the car. "You said, 'wait here,' so I did."

He pinched the bridge of his nose. "Sorry. I should have told you to go home."

I'm glad he didn't. I think he needed me, even if he didn't realize it. "Do you want to talk about it?"

"What I want to do is forget the last two hours." He shifted in his seat, facing me. "Will you come home with me? Stay the night? No sex, just be with me."

"I don't—"

"Forget I asked." He turned the key in the ignition.

I put my hand on his leg. "I'll come home with you if

you'll tell me why you want me to." His Mustang rumbled, vibrating under me, wanting to go do its job of carrying us away. "Why, Dylan?"

He gripped the steering wheel so hard that his knuckles turned white. "Because I can't be alone with myself tonight."

But why? I decided it didn't matter why because I couldn't leave him to face whatever demons were plaguing him. And he had demons. That I could plainly see. "I'll come with you if you'll promise to talk to me," I said. Whatever was going on with him, he needed to get it off his chest. I knew all about holding things in. If not for Autumn and Savannah forcing me to talk about losing Natalie, I think I might have exploded from grief.

His eyes flared as he looked at me. "You drive a hard bargain, Red. Come home with me and maybe I'll tell you why I need you tonight."

It was like spinning the roulette wheel at Harrah's in nearby Cherokee. You win. You lose. But what the hell. I was willing to gamble for the first time in my life. "Take me home with you, Dylan."

He exhaled a long breath, and I had the thought that he'd believed I would refuse. I probably should have, but he needed me. Without another word he made a U-turn, heading back toward town.

"Would you like to make a detour to your place, get some things?" he said once we'd passed the shops and restaurants.

"Sure. That would be great." He went silent again. It was killing me not asking any questions. What had happened in that house that had upset him? Without knowing, I had no idea what to say.

He didn't get out of the car when we arrived at my apartment. It only took me a few minutes to throw a toothbrush and some makeup into a small case. I grabbed something to sleep in, a pair of jeans, a T-shirt, and undies, stuffing them into a tote along with the makeup bag. When I came back to the car, Dylan was on the phone. I tossed my overnight bag into the back seat. It was impossible not to listen to his conversation.

"Get her a good lawyer," he said.

Gertie? I'd come to the conclusion that Gertie had shot her husband.

"No, we're not going to question her without an attorney present. You saw what he did to her."

I found that interesting and insightful. Obviously he meant Gertie, and from watching police shows on TV, I would have thought he'd want to interrogate her as soon as she was able to talk, hoping that she didn't ask for a lawyer. Instead he was protecting her.

Dylan intrigued me more every day. I was learning that he was a complicated man, which only made me want to peel away his layers, learn what made him tick. He rolled down the windows as we traveled to his place, leaning his face toward the opening as if he needed the fresh air in order to breathe.

Something was eating at him, something more than what had happened tonight. Why I felt that, I wasn't sure, but I hoped he would open up when we got to his apartment.

The first thing he did when we walked inside was to go straight to the kitchen, where he filled a tumbler with scotch. I dropped my overnight case onto the counter and waited for him to tell me why he was pouring scotch neat straight down his throat.

CHAPTER EIGHTEEN

~ Dylan ~

WHY HAD I BROUGHT JENNY home with me? This was a night to down this bottle of scotch until I was too drunk to see Jansen's wife holding a gun under her chin, her hands trembling so hard I was afraid she'd accidently shoot herself.

Was that how Christine had held my gun, her hands shaking, before pulling the trigger? I'd never know, but now that image was in my head where I feared it would live forever. At least I didn't have to witness Mrs. Jansen blowing her brains out. I'm not sure I'd ever be right if that had happened.

"Dylan?"

I set down the empty glass, resisting the urge to refill it. What I should do was put Jenny in the car and take her back home. I wasn't good company tonight, and she didn't deserve my black mood.

"I need air," I said, walking past her to the balcony. She followed me out, and as I stood at the railing, my hands gripping the metal, she wrapped her arms around me, resting her head on my back. I sucked in air like a suffocating man, but I didn't dare close my eyes. When I did, it was Christine's face I saw transposed over Jansen's wife's. As Jenny held me, the warmth from her body slowly seeped into my skin and I could breathe again. Was I a bad man for needing Jenny here with me when I was battling my demons?

For months after Christine had taken her life, I'd had

episodes like this, where I couldn't get air into my lungs. A word that reminded me of her, a picture, a woman with her hair color would steal my breath, and not in a good way. After many sessions with my therapist, the attacks had faded, and I'd hoped they were gone forever. Guess not.

I turned in Jenny's arms. She was rainbows and sunshine, and I wanted to crawl into her skin and live there. "I should take you home."

"You invited me to stay with you tonight. You can't take it back now." She took my hand, pulling me to the patio chair. "Sit."

I did. She disappeared into the apartment, coming back with two glasses and the scotch bottle. If she planned to get me drunk, I was onboard. She poured three fingers into both glasses, handing one to me.

"Drink."

"Yes ma'am." I liked how she was bossing me around, taking away my making any decisions.

"Don't pour it down your throat like you did the last one. Sip it."

I held the glass up in a salute. Obeying her, I only sipped. It surprised me that I was good with her taking over. That wasn't normally me. I was used to being in control, being the one to lead others. Somehow, though, she knew just what I needed tonight. For that, I owed her some kind of explanation.

"Mrs. Jansen shot and killed her husband tonight after he almost beat her to death."

"I kind of figured that out." She reached over, putting her hand on my leg. "Although that's awful, that's not what has you so upset."

She was intuitive, my Jenny Girl. I swallowed the rest of my scotch. Talking about Christine wasn't easy. The only people I'd told everything, other than my therapist, were my brother and my former captain. But sitting here with

Jenny, my owl hooing in the distance and the scotch loosening my tongue, I wanted to tell her.

"Mrs. Jansen still had the gun in her hand that she had shot her husband with. She held the barrel against her throat, threatening to pull the trigger." And I thought she'd fully meant to, even though I'd begged her to give me the gun, promising her that I would get her help. Finally, desperate to find a reason to stop her, I'd told her about Christine, then I'd told Gertie Jansen that if she made me watch her pull that trigger, I'd see her face every night in my dreams along with my wife's. When she'd finally held out the gun for me to take, I'd wanted to fall to my knees and weep.

"What aren't you telling me?"

I turned my hand over, lacing our fingers, and told myself to just spit it out. "My wife did the same thing, only she followed through." The scotch in my stomach threatened to come back up, and I swallowed hard.

"Oh, Dylan. How awful for you."

Surprised, I looked at her. "Why do you say awful for me? Shouldn't you be saying how awful for Christine?"

"Because she's not here to say it to. Yes, how awful for her, but you're the one left to live with what she did. My mother's brother committed suicide. It devastated the ones he left behind who loved him. My grandparents and my mother lived…still live with the guilt that there was something they should have done to prevent it. I know you feel the same way."

She'd named my problem, and all I could do was nod.

"Did you see her do it? Was that why Gertie holding a gun to her throat upset you tonight?"

"No, I came home to find my captain and some cops in our apartment, waiting for me. She was still in there. They wouldn't let me see her because she didn't have a face left." I was going to be sick and sucked in air in an attempt to settle my stomach.

Jenny stood, put her hand on my neck, and pushed. "Put your head between your knees and take deep breaths."

I felt like a wuss, but did as she said. After a few moments of deep breathing, the nausea went away. Embarrassed, I stood, going to the railing. "I should have seen the signs," I said with my back to her.

"Hindsight is always perfect, Dylan. But here's the thing. She made the choice to do what she did, not you."

I gave a bitter laugh. "You're starting to sound like my therapist."

"If so, maybe you should consider listening to us. Do you know why she did it?"

Yes, because I'd stopped loving her. "I don't want to talk about this anymore."

"Okay."

Again, she surprised me by not insisting it would be good for me to get it off my chest or some such nonsense. I faced her. "If you want me to take you home, I'll understand."

"Oh no you don't. I already told you that you can't take back your invitation. Go take a shower while I tidy up. I'll meet you in your bedroom." She gave me a push. "Go."

I gratefully went.

As hot water rained down on my head, I closed my eyes, grimacing that I'd let my guard down with Jenny. She didn't need my shit dumped on her. I wanted to blame it on the scotch, but I hadn't drunk enough to get all chatty. It was her, Jenny Girl. It was the way she listened without offering advice or platitudes, the way she'd said what Christine had done must be awful for me. For me! It was the way she'd held my hand and taken care of me. I shouldn't like that so much.

It wasn't that I was still in love with my wife. I wasn't. I would always love her, though, but for the way we'd once been, not how we'd ended. By then, I hadn't liked her very much. Standing in Jansen's living room, talking myself blue in the face, trying to convince Mrs. Jansen to put the gun down, it struck me that I hadn't tried that hard to get through to Christine.

To give myself some credit, if Christine had put my gun in her mouth in front of me, I sure as hell would have found a way to stop her. But she'd waited until I'd stormed out to perform the final act of her life, leaving me to wallow in a truckload of guilt.

The water turned cold, and I ended my shower. With cuddling up to Jenny's soft, warm body in mind, I decided to shave so I wouldn't irritate the skin on her neck and shoulder where I wanted to plant my face. The eyes that reflected back at me in the mirror didn't seem to be as haunted as they must have been when I'd walked out of Jansen's house.

"Hunka, hunka," Jenny said, her gaze roaming over my body when I walked out, wearing a white T-shirt and black boxers.

She fanned her face, making me grin, something I definitely hadn't thought I'd be doing tonight. I'd debated what to wear to bed. I'm a sleep-in-the-nude guy, but that seemed presumptuous for our first night together, especially when sex wasn't on the agenda.

She'd changed into a pair of yellow girl boxers and a yellow spaghetti-strap top. Her red hair curled around her shoulders and down her back, and she could have been a goddess come to life. Seeing her sitting on my bed in her sexy little nightclothes, her legs crossed under her, was all my dick needed to stir awake. After my meltdown I would have thought nothing could turn me on tonight, but I was wrong.

I'd promised her we would just sleep, though, so I slipped under the covers to keep my erection from being on display. Pushing up against the headboard, I wondered what to say. Should I apologize for my behavior earlier? Pretend it had never happened? While those questions ran through my mind, Jenny reached over to the nightstand on her side of the bed, then settled next to me with a plate of chocolate chip cookies and a glass of milk in her hands.

"I nosed around in your pantry and found cookies. They'll help us sleep." She handed me a cookie and took one for herself. "That's my story, and I'm sticking to it," she said, giggling. "We'll share the milk."

So we sat in my bed munching on store-bought cookies and passing the glass back and forth, telling each other stupid jokes. Yeah, dumb jokes. Her idea. She wanted to see which of us could come up with the most moronic, groan-inducing one.

She took the empty plate and glass, putting them back on the nightstand. "Okay, I got one. Two cannibals are eating a clown. One says to the other, 'Does this taste funny to you?'"

Her green eyes sparkled with delight at hearing me give her my best groan for that one. "You win," I said. This had been the best time I'd had since… No, I wasn't going there. Not after Jenny had managed to bring me back from the edge of a deep black hole.

I turned off the lamp, eased my head down onto my pillow, and patted the space in front of me. "Come here, Red. Put your back to me." When she was stretched out in front of me, I wrapped an arm around her, resting my hand on her stomach. She felt good here, snuggled up next to me, and she smelled so damn good.

I closed my eyes, breathing her in. "Thank you, Jenny Girl," I whispered.

CHAPTER NINETEEN

~ *Jenny* ~

I KNEW WHAT DYLAN WAS THANKING me for. When my uncle had swallowed a bottle of pills, Natalie and I had felt helpless as to how to help our mother and grandparents deal with their grief. In our need to do something, to learn the right things to say, we'd devoured books on the stages of grief and how to cope. We'd learned that all you could do for someone was to be there for them, to listen without offering all the clichés such as time heals, blah, blah, blah.

In one book, something about laughter had caught our attention. A woman the author had interviewed said that she started to come out of her depression from losing her husband when her best friend had managed to get her to laugh again. I'd remembered reading that and wondered if it would work with Dylan.

While he was showering, I'd come up with the idea of milk and cookies and stupid jokes. Fortunately he'd had the bag of chocolate chip cookies, so I went with it, and now he was thanking me. He'd scared me there for a while, and he'd also left me with more questions than he'd answered.

As I listened to his breathing relax into that of sleep, I placed my hand over the one he had against my stomach. It was a big hand. A strong one. I was getting to know him, and I had no doubt that his mind was strong enough to get him through what had happened.

He cared—too much, maybe—about those under his

protection. I couldn't guess what had brought his wife to believe she couldn't face another day, and hoped someday he'd tell me. But I did know one thing. Dylan was a good man, not one who would drive a woman to take her life. I just knew that in my heart. Maybe she had a chemical imbalance or maybe suffered from chronic depression.

Or I could be totally fooling myself, seeing only what I wanted to see where Dylan Conrad was concerned. Men were good at hiding their dark side. Take Chad. Who knew those puppy-dog brown eyes hid a total jerkface? With Dylan, his eyes said *this is me, take me with all my faults or don't.* I decided I'd take him.

His big body was curled around mine, and as he held me in his arms, I whispered, "I'm ready, Dylan." He was asleep and didn't hear me, but I'd said the words for me. Everything about this man called to me, and I suddenly wondered what I was waiting for. He wanted me, and I wanted him, and I couldn't think of a single reason to wait any longer.

My being with him wouldn't change my plans. He wasn't that important to me. I wouldn't let him be. But as long as he wanted to be with me, I was his. Until I left. I drifted off, wishing he'd stayed awake long enough to make love to me.

The aroma of coffee and bacon drifted into my nose, and I rolled over, yawning widely. When I opened my eyes, my gaze settled on the window and a view of the mountains that I didn't have from my bedroom. It took a few seconds before I remembered I was in Dylan's bed. I stretched, wishing he were still next to me so I could tell him I was ready. We'd have morning sex, which I loved because joining my body with a man's when sleep still held us both in its thrall was dreamy good, like a scene seen through a hazy camera lens. Soft and magical.

The sheet where he'd lain was cool when I put my

hand on it, so he'd left some time ago. The bed was so snuggly, though, that instead of getting up like I should have, I curled my body into a ball and drifted back to sleep.

"Wake up, Red."

"Mm?" I stretched like a lazy cat. Not a morning person, the one thing that could get me out of bed was the smell of bacon. I opened my eyes to see a piece held under my nose.

"Oh no you don't," Dylan said when I snapped at it, trying to get it in my mouth. He pulled it away. "Up with you. Breakfast is ready."

"Meanie," I grumbled when he pulled off the covers. But bacon. Yeah, I'd get up for that. I brushed my teeth, combed my hair, slipped on the jeans and T-shirt I'd brought, and then headed for the kitchen.

"Morning, Jenny."

Dylan put an omelet, bacon, and toast in front of me. I might marry this man, after all. Never had any guy I'd dated made me breakfast, even after we'd had sex. What kind of creature was this man?

"Got one for you," he said.

"One what?"

"A dumb joke that will beat yours. What happens when a frog's car breaks down?"

"It gets toad away."

"No fair." He grinned, and I saw a wholly different man from the one who'd broken down last night.

"All's fair in a bad joke war." I wanted to tell him I loved the light in his eyes I was seeing, but that would only remind him of last night.

"So no rules? I like it."

"Uh-oh, I think I've created a bad joke monster."

"Entirely possible. Listen, about our waterfall plans for Saturday. I've been issued an invitation with the implication that I couldn't refuse to attend that barbeque the mayor's daughter mentioned Monday morning."

Did I say that I didn't like Stephanie? She was making a play for Dylan, just like she'd gone after my high school boyfriend, he of the cheating heart. "The mayor speaks, people listen." I hated how snarky that came out, especially when Dylan raised a brow.

"Of course you have to go." I smiled to show him I meant it.

"It's at four. Are you ever able to get a weekend night off? I'd like you to come with me."

"I wasn't invited." That would really get Stephanie's goat if I showed up on Dylan's arm.

"I'm inviting you."

It was tempting just to see the look on Stephanie's face. "Let me see what I can do."

He reached over and put his hand on mine. "Try hard. I need you to protect me from man-eaters."

Who could resist that lopsided smile? Not me, obviously. "I'll let you know tomorrow." I never asked for time off, so Angelo should give me the day, although he wouldn't be happy about it. No one sold as much behind the bar as me.

"Good. Now give me your phone number so I can call you."

The talk at the bar Wednesday night was nothing but Billy Jansen and his wife. Some claimed knowledge that he hit Gertie regularly. Others said that wasn't true, that it was losing his job that set him off. One jerkface blamed Dylan.

"If that new big-city cop hadn't a fired him, he wouldn't a done what he did. No man likes not being able to support his family. That's what drove him to beat on Gertie."

I wanted to throw a mug of beer in his face. Normally I kept my mouth shut when customers talked, no matter what they said, but I couldn't let that go.

"Freddie Barnes, you and the whole town knows Billy Jansen was a hothead. If the new chief fired him, then he had a good reason." I slid his beer to him instead of dumping it on him like I wanted to. Freddie was one of the councilmen, and in his position he should keep his mouth shut.

A few people nodded in agreement, sharing stories of times Billy's temper had gotten out of hand. Some I'd heard, but many I hadn't, and none of them were good. Maybe Gertie did the world a favor. I felt sorry for her and hoped she didn't end up going to prison. She was a nice woman.

I had my back to the bar, ringing up a meal ticket, when it got real quiet. A glance in the mirror behind the shelves holding liquor bottles had me holding my breath. Dylan had just walked in, and the only empty seat was next to Freddie. He slid onto the bar stool, gave me a wink when I glanced at him—which made my heart merrily beat—then glanced around at the people who were silently staring at him.

Dylan held out his hand to Freddie. "Dylan Conrad. I'm Blue Ridge Valley's new police chief."

"I know who you are." Freddie glared at Dylan's hand.

I think everyone at the bar held their breath along with me, waiting to see how Dylan would react to the snub. Any other man would have dropped his hand by now, but Dylan, holding his smile, kept his stretched out toward Freddie.

"Freddie Barnes." A collective exhale of breaths—including mine—sounded when Freddie finally shook Dylan's hand.

"I hear those boiled peanuts of yours are addicting," Dylan said. "Never had 'em boiled."

"You come by my peanut stand tomorrow, city boy, I'll show ya what you been missing."

I put a bottle of Green Man beer in front of Dylan while he listened for the next ten minutes to Freddie give a detailed account of how much salt went in the peanuts, how long they needed to boil, and how much wood it took to keep the boiling pot going at just the right temperature.

God bless Dylan. He didn't yawn once. When Freddie's meat-loaded pizza arrived, interrupting his discourse on how to make perfectly boiled peanuts, Dylan caught my attention. "Could I get an antipasto plate, Red?"

"You bet." I wanted to crawl across the bar and kiss him silly, but settled for giving him a smile, which he returned.

Even though I was busy filling drink orders and delivering meals, I listened as Dylan charmed every person at the bar, including Freddie. He took his time eating his antipasto, waving good-bye as people left. Was he hanging around, waiting for me to get off?

Turned out he was. "Are you really going to eat boiled peanuts?" I asked as I wiped down the bar.

"Well, I was until you made a face asking that question. They're not good?"

"My mother loves them. You boil them in salted water until they get soft and mushy. They're one of those things you either hate or love."

"I'm committed to giving them a try, it seems. I'll let you know what I think. Were you able to get Saturday off?"

"I'm all yours."

A wicked grin curved his lips. "Promise?"

I put my elbows on the bar and leaned toward him. "How about I'm yours for the whole weekend? We'll go to the"—I glanced around to make sure no one was nearby—"mayor's stupid barbeque, then Sunday morning you can make me breakfast, and then we'll go on our waterfall adventure."

"Now there's an offer I can't refuse." He trailed a finger along my arm, raising goose bumps. "How long do these barbeques last? I'm asking because the whole time we're there, all I'm going to be thinking about is how soon we can leave so I can be alone with you."

"How fast can you eat a plate of ribs?"

"Pretty damn fast if you're the reward."

"I like how you think, Mr. Policeman."

"Angelo wants to know if you've closed out the register yet," Brandy said, coming up next to me. Her gaze darted between Dylan and me.

"Brandy, this is Dylan Conrad, our new police chief. Dylan, Brandy Morrison, waitress extraordinaire." Brandy was a tiny thing, maybe five foot, long brown hair she always wore in a single braid down her back, and soulful brown eyes. She was as shy as a mouse except when waiting tables, then look out. She was born to be a waitress, and if you asked her, she'd tell you that was all she ever wanted to do.

"A pleasure, Brandy," Dylan said, holding out his hand.

Her cheeks turned pink as she shook his hand. "Me, too," she mumbled.

Dylan and I exchanged an amused glance. Brandy was a sweetheart, and I loved her. Taking pity on her, I said, "Go tell Angelo I'll be closed out in five."

She took off like her little butt was on fire.

Dylan watched her go. "What just happened?"

"Put a hot guy in front of her and she gets tongue-tied unless she's taking your food order."

His eyes shifted to mine. "You think I'm hot?"

I snorted. "Hotter than a firecracker lit at both ends." I walked away to his laughter.

"Red?"

"Yeah?" I kept going but glanced at him over my shoulder.

"Bet I can make you go boom." He winked, then walked out.

There wasn't any doubt in my mind, and Saturday night I was going to test that claim firsthand.

CHAPTER TWENTY

~ Dylan ~

HOO. HOO. HOO.

Unable to sleep, I listened to my owl. I'd gone to Vincennes to see if I could get Jenny to come home with me tonight. There'd been no visits from my ghost while Jenny slept in my arms, and I selfishly wanted her with me every night.

Instead I'd left without asking her. Christine was my problem to deal with. When Jenny was in this bed with me, it would be because it was what we both wanted, not for her to stand sentry while I slept.

Hoo. Hoo. Hoo.

Was he out hunting? I hoped he had success finding a mouse. As I drifted off, I imagined I was flying through the night with him. When I was a kid, I used to have flying dreams but hadn't had one as an adult. They were fun, and I wished I still had them. After having one, I'd wake up exhilarated, as if I were on top of the world. I hadn't felt like that in a long time. A few times with Jenny I'd come close to believing I could be happy again.

The owl swiveled his head, studying me with big round eyes. "*Hoo,*" he said.

I looked down at the ground, far below. Even asleep, I knew I was dreaming, but I held on to the illusion. "I just want to fly with you for a few minutes."

The owl blinked, and I took that as acceptance. We flew over the tops of trees, down into the valley, and then traveled up the side of the mountain looking for mice.

"There," I said, pointing to the ground in a clearing where a mouse scurried across the grass. The owl swooped down as I hovered above, excited about his catch.

"You can't fly, Dylan. Silly man."

"Yet I am. Go away, Christine."

She yanked on my arm, bringing me back to the bed. *"I can't go away. We have unfinished business."*

Maybe we did. *"I'm sorry for not being there for you when you needed me. I live with that regret every day."*

She smiled the way she used to when everything was right between us. *"That means everything to me, but can you ever forgive me for what I did?"*

I hadn't thought I ever could, but a woman with red hair and laughter dancing in her green eyes crystalized in my mind. The truth settled in my heart. If I couldn't forgive Christine, I'd never let her go, and I didn't want her standing between Jenny and me. For the first time, I was ready to let go of my wife.

"I loved you with everything I was, Christine. You know that. I never gave us a chance to find our way back to what we'd had together. For that, I'm sorry. I don't hate you anymore. You'll always own a piece of my heart, but we need to let each other go."

"But can you forgive me?"

If she'd asked me that one day ago, my answer would have been no. I'm not sure what changed. Maybe that I was tired of holding on to my misery. Maybe because I'd flown with an owl, reminding me that I liked being happy. Or maybe it was because I wanted that green-eyed girl in my bed without a ghost between us.

"I forgive you, Christine. I do."

She disappeared. I knew she'd never come back.

The clock said it was 3:00 a.m. when I eyed it. As I sat there in the middle of my bed, I made a mental rundown of my vitals. My breathing was calm, my heart softly beat, and my mind was blessedly free of the guilt that had lived with me for the past two years.

My therapist had told me that her visits were a creation of my mind and that this would happen when I could both forgive her and myself. He turned out to be a smarter man than I'd given him credit for.

"Be at peace, Christine," I whispered, sitting there alone in the dark.

Hoo. Hoo, the owl said, sounding as if he were right outside my window.

I smiled, wondering if he knew I'd flown with him tonight. Christine would always be a part of me, would always own a piece of my heart. That I hadn't lied about. But she was finally resting in peace. I punched my pillow back into the shape I wanted, then went back to sleep, dream-free.

"So you're just going to let her go free after she murdered Billy?"

I came close to telling Moody that he needed a good mouthwash and get the hell out of my face. Since I was in my new Zen state, I just shrugged. "I'm not her judge or jury, Moody. She made bail and she has an attorney."

He fisted his hands as if he planned to plant one on my face. I could look mean when the situation called for it, which this did. Narrowing my eyes, letting them go cold, I poked him in the chest. "Back off. That's an order."

"You son of—"

"I don't think you want to finish that sentence, *Captain*"—emphasis on the Captain because his ability to use that title was limited to how soon I could fire him—"because if you do…"

Okay, I'd lost my cool, which wasn't at all cool. I took a deep breath. We were in the bull pen with my other cops looking on, and I'd almost told my captain that I was going to knock him on his damn ass. Every single one of them looked ready to start placing bets on the outcome of a fight between Moody and me.

"In my office," I said to Moody. "The rest of you, find something constructive to do." Apparently they knew I meant business because they scurried off like rats. I stalked Moody down the hall, closing the door behind me after we'd both stepped into my office.

The only thing this man understood was brute force. I invaded his space, backing his fat ass against the wall. "You want to take me on, be at Valley Gym tonight at six. Otherwise, Captain, you need to keep your mouth shut. Don't ever disrespect me like that again."

He clamped down on his bottom lip so hard that a trickle of blood dripped down his chin, but he kept his mouth shut. Lucky for him I'd woken up in a good mood, willing to give him leeway that I wouldn't have yesterday.

I stepped back. "Do we understand each other?" I didn't doubt that there were a thousand words he wanted to spit at me, but he only nodded. "Good. See yourself out."

Since I'd made the challenge, I was at Valley Gym at six, but Moody never showed. At least he wasn't totally stupid. I worked out for an hour before going home. Christine didn't visit that night, and I knew she wouldn't be back again. Nor did I fly with my owl, which was disappointing.

Dressed in a dark gray pin-striped power suit, white shirt, and red tie, I walked into the town hall building Thursday night, taking a seat near the front. Two councilmen were already at the table, deep in conversation, one of whom I knew was Adam Hunter, since I'd studied up on the councilmen.

The meeting wouldn't start for another five minutes, so I took out my phone, tapped the screen for a few seconds, then decided what the hell.

Thinking about you and fireworks

She would be busy at the bar and wouldn't see my text until later. Would she answer? I switched the phone to vibrate, then dropped it into my coat pocket. Although I'd been tempted to stop by Vincennes for a quick bite before this meeting, just to see Jenny, I'd resisted. Absence made the heart grow fonder and all that. I was hoping she'd miss me between now and Saturday.

The mayor came in, gave me a curt nod as he passed to take his seat at the table. So Jim John was still annoyed with me for how I'd pushed my way into this meeting. He'd get over it soon enough. Buddy Ferguson and Freddie Barnes walked in together. I nodded to them both.

Peanut Man was a sly fox. I'd stopped by his stand—Friendly Freddie's—this morning as promised, and he hadn't said a word about tonight's meeting even though he was aware I was on the agenda. I'd had Buddy make sure each councilman had a copy of my new budget to study. Although I knew Freddie was one of the three—having done my homework—I hadn't mentioned it either.

As for boiled peanuts, they were just weird. Not bad tasting, but peanuts should be dry and crunchy, not wet and mushy. I'd sat on a barrel for an hour, eating the damn things while listening to Freddie tell me the story of his life.

According to him, forty years ago he'd been a highly successful stockbroker in New York, then one day for no reason that he could point to, he quit, loaded up his belongings, moved to Blue Ridge Valley, and opened his stand, selling boiled peanuts, molasses, honey, and cheap souvenirs. It was anyone's guess how much of what he said was true.

An older woman was the last to come in, and she took a place at the end of the table, opened a stenographer's notebook, and wrote something. They still had their meetings recorded in shorthand? Who did that anymore? I smiled to myself, charmed by my new town.

Jim John opened the meeting by pounding a gavel on a block of wood as if the room were full of people, getting another private smile from me.

"Record that the monthly town council review meeting began promptly at six in the evening and all members are present," he said.

I glanced at the stenographer to see her nodding her head as her hand flew over the page.

"We have a guest tonight, our new chief of police, Dylan Conrad. He will review and answer questions on a revised budget. Mr. Conrad, you have the floor."

"Gentlemen, thank you for adding me to your agenda tonight. I trust you've taken a look at the revised budget I've submitted." I quickly reviewed the changes I wanted, then asked for questions.

"I told y'all when we renewed our contract with Ed's Garage that the old cuss was a crook," Adam said. "I vote we approve the new budget."

"About time our officers got rid of those baby-puke green uniforms," Steve Sutton, owner of three motels, said. "I approve it."

Freddie Barns sat back in his chair, eyeing me. I braced for whatever trouble he was going to throw my way. After spending time with him this morning, I'd come to the conclusion that he liked stirring things up.

"The chief liked my peanuts. I vote aye."

I choked on a laugh, covering it up with a cough. Looked like I needed to learn to love boiled peanuts if that was all it took to get Freddie's vote on something I wanted.

Jim John banged his gavel three times. "I approve. Your revised budget is accepted, Chief. Anything else?"

"No." I stood. "Thank you for making time for me." As

I left, the first thing I wanted to do was call Jenny and tell her of my success, but she still hadn't answered my text, so I went home and celebrated with a glass of wine on my balcony with my owl hooing in the distance.

CHAPTER TWENTY-ONE

~ Jenny ~

I WAS HAPPY TO FINALLY BE home. We'd been unusually busy tonight, and we got out later than usual. I was bone-tired. All I wanted was to get off my feet, a good soak in a hot bath, and sleep. While the tub was filling, I added a few capfuls of scented bath oil, then went to the kitchen and poured a glass of wine. I retrieved my phone from my purse, taking it and the wine back to the bathroom.

After slipping into the tub, I turned on my phone. It pinged, and I grinned when I saw I had a text from Dylan. I laughed when I read it. So he was thinking of me and fireworks? After considering a response, I texted back.

Boom!

A minute later my phone pinged again.

Where are u

Home

Can I call u

Yes

My phone rang, and I swiped my thumb over it. "Hey."

"Hi, Red. Hope I'm not interrupting your sleep."

"Nope. I'm treating myself to a bubble bath."

Silence, then, "You're in the tub?"

Wow, his voice just dropped about two octaves. "Ah… yeah."

"Naked?"

"No, Dylan. I'm wearing all my clothes."

He laughed. "Sorry. I went dumb there thinking of you naked."

I let out a dramatic sigh. "You're such a man."

"Last I checked, but maybe you should have a look, just to make sure."

"Well, if you're in doubt…"

Another laugh, one that sounded a little strangled. "Considering what thinking of you wet and naked does to me, definitely not in doubt."

He sounded happy tonight, and I thought about asking him if he wanted to come over, but decided against it. It was late and I was tired. Plus, I liked him thinking of me wet and naked for the next couple of days before we saw each other again.

"You have a good day?" I asked. I knew he was making some kind of presentation at the monthly council meeting. In a small town, nothing's secret.

"Very. Met with the councilmen tonight and got my new budget approved, but back to you naked in the tub."

"Ha ha. Nice try, Mr. Policeman. I'm going to hang up now. See you Saturday."

"Sweet dreams, Jenny Girl."

The dream I had of Dylan that night wasn't at all sweet. I woke up hot, sweaty, and aching. If Dylan was anything like my Dream Lover Dylan, I was definitely going to explode.

For the barbeque, I decided to go cowgirl. It was a risk because I knew that since we were still having a warm spell, Stephanie and her friends would be decked out in sundresses or adorable little shorts and cute, flowery blouses. My outfit—white jeans, red cowboy boots, red midriff tie top, and black cowboy hat—was going to stand out, but I'd always been one to go against the crowd. Especially Stephanie's crowd.

From the day she laid eyes on Natalie and me in first

grade, she'd hated us. I'd never been sure exactly why, but if I had to guess, it was because of the twins, Adam and Connor. At that time they lived next door, and Natalie and I were total tomboys. Natalie and I, along with Autumn and Savannah, were the only girls they let into their tree house.

Stephanie wanted them for her friends, mainly because they were cute boys and she was boy crazy, even then. She saw Natalie and me in her way, and because she was mean to us, Adam and Connor didn't like her. But that was just my guess as to why she'd always had it out for us. For all I knew, maybe she hated red hair.

As far as I was concerned, that was old history, but Stephanie still held a grudge. Since I wasn't stupid, I always watched my back around her. The doorbell rang, and I took a last look in the mirror, adjusted my cowboy hat, then went and opened the door.

Dylan pulled his sunglasses down his nose, his gaze roaming over me. "Smokin'."

I grinned. "I could say the same about you." He wore jeans, a blue button-down with the sleeves rolled up, a black belt with a silver buckle, a silver watch on one wrist, and a black leather band on the other. Just looking at the man sent tingles racing through me, especially after the dream I'd had.

"Before we go, there's something I have to do," he said.

"What's that?"

"Just this." He stepped inside, closed the door, and then backed me against it. "I got to kiss a mountain girl recently, but I've never kissed a cowgirl before. I need to correct that."

He ducked his head under my hat, put his hands on my hips, and covered my mouth with his. As he deepened the kiss, he dug his fingers into my hips, holding me still when I tried to rub against him.

"Be still, or we'll never make it to the barbeque," he

said, his voice gravelly.

"I don't think I can. Be still. Not when you're touching me." It was true. With his hands on me, I just wanted to climb up him and wrap my legs around his waist.

He tapped my nose with his finger. "Then we better go before we decide there's something else we'd rather do."

I brushed my thumb across his bottom lip, damp from our kiss. "Actually there is something I'd rather do."

"You're killing me, Red," he said, then sucked my thumb into his mouth.

And now he was killing me. "The sooner we go, the sooner we can leave." I grabbed the overnight bag sitting by the door. "I plan to save a horse by riding a cowboy tonight."

He grinned. "Then I'll need to borrow your hat later. Make me officially a cowboy." He took the tote, slinging an arm around my shoulder as we walked to his car.

The man was a toucher, and as far as I was concerned, he could put his hands on me whenever and wherever he wanted. And I really would have been good with staying home and as far away from Stephanie as I could get. Although I was pretty sure I could have seduced him into forgetting about going to the barbeque, he needed to be there. I'd deal with Stephanie like I always had—by ignoring her.

Ignoring Stephanie and her friends turned out not to be so easy when they swooped down on Dylan within minutes of our arrival, effectively pushing me out of the circle they'd made around him. We'd been handed mint juleps on arrival by a server holding a trayful of them, and I wanted to splash mine in Stephanie's face. And who served mint juleps at a barbeque anyway? Where the hell was the beer?

As soon as I spied Adam and Connor, I headed for them, even though Dylan sent me a help-me look. I gave him a what-am-I-supposed-to-do shrug. I could have gone one-on-one with Stephanie, but her and her four minions? Not even going to try.

"Hey, you two," I said, giving Adam a hug, then Connor.

"Here's my favorite cowgirl," Adam said, wrapping an arm around my shoulder. "You gonna let her steal your man?" he whispered in my ear.

I laughed. "I'm not claiming him as my man, but I do know he's going home with me, so she can just go and eat her heart out."

"What secrets are you two whispering about?" Connor said, hauling me away from his brother and tucking me next to him.

"I just told him that I was going to marry him instead of you."

"The hell you say. I'll knock his teeth out first."

"I guess I'll just have to marry you both." For a brief second I had an erotic fantasy of the black-haired, blue-eyed twins making a sandwich out of me, which would have been totally hot if it hadn't sent me into a fit of laughter.

"Want to share?" Adam said.

"Not really." I put the still-full mint julep on a table. "Where'd you get the beer?" I asked, eyeing Connor's.

"I'll get you one." He winked as he headed away. "Love the hat, by the way."

A few minutes and he was back with an icy bottle. I took a few swallows. "Much better."

Adam pointed at Dylan with his beer bottle. "Maybe we should go save him."

Poor Dylan. Stephanie had her arm wrapped around his, talking a mile a minute. He glanced over at me, narrowing his eyes, and I took pity on him.

The mayor's house—a sprawling brick ranch—sat on

about an acre of land, with a rushing stream behind the large deck we stood on. The Blue Ridge Valley Country Club set were all here, most of whom I knew well enough to say hello to. Not my crowd, but they'd expect Dylan to join their ranks. Honestly, he really wouldn't have a choice even if he weren't interested.

"How's Savannah?" Adam asked as the three of us headed off to save Dylan.

"Autumn and I are a little worried about her. She's not keeping in touch like she's supposed to, and when we do talk to her, she seems evasive. She'll be home for Autumn's wedding, so we'll get to see firsthand what's going on with her."

Adam got silent after that. He and Savannah had been an item in high school, but she'd moved to New York to become a famous model, leaving him behind. If not for her mother interfering and pushing Savannah to go, I think she might have stayed. I know she loved him. I was the only one who knew Mrs. Graham had paid Adam a visit, convincing him that he was standing in the way of Savannah's dream, and if he didn't let her go, Savannah would end up resenting him. I knew that because I'd stopped by his house the night he'd broken up with her, and it had all come pouring out.

"Great to see you again, Dylan," Adam said when we reached the group.

"Same here." Dylan held out his hand, forcing Stephanie to let go of him. As he and Adam shook, he subtly sidestepped, putting some space between her and him. He took another step away to turn to Connor.

Dylan laughed. "I don't know which one of you is which, so I'll just say it's good to see you both."

"I'm Adam," Connor said.

"Stop messing with him, goofball." I squeezed into the space Dylan had created between him and Stephanie. "For today, just remember that Adam's wearing the white shirt and Connor the green one. And anytime Connor tells you he's Adam, it'll be just the opposite, but you can always trust Adam."

Amusement sparkled in Dylan's eyes. "You do realize that doesn't help. If he says he's Adam, but Adam always says he's Adam… You follow my reasoning there, Red?"

That made me laugh. "True." I could always tell the twins apart, but a lot of people couldn't except for those who knew what to look for. "Okay. I'll let you in on a secret. Adam always wears a sapphire stone earring and Connor an emerald one."

He eyed each of the twins' earrings. "Ah, good to know."

"You on the way to a rodeo, *Red*?" Stephanie said, her nose wrinkling as she gave me the once-over.

I hated how she turned Dylan's pet name for me into a joke, but I'd learned long ago not to take her bait. "No, but I do plan to save a horse tonight." Dylan covered up a laugh with a cough. On the other side of him, the twins gave dual snorts.

She furrowed her brows. "Whatever."

Well, that went right over her head, but she'd never been the fastest bunny in the forest. The mayor and his wife came out the back door, and seeing an excuse to get away from Stephanie's toxic presence, I grabbed Dylan's hand.

"We should go say hi to Mayor Jenkins." He came readily along, and after a few minutes of chatting, we headed for the food table.

The rest of the afternoon went easily enough. Adam and Connor mostly hung with us. I loved how my two friends got along so well with Dylan. We mingled, introducing Dylan to various people, and I was impressed with how at ease he was with the country-club crowd. Actually he seemed to win the approval of everyone he met, from

Hamburger Harry to the mayor and his friends. He sure had mine.

After we finished eating, Dylan leaned over, putting his mouth close to my ear. "Let's get out of here. Go save that horse."

"What's your hurry? Is there a cowboy needing riding?" I whispered back.

Under the table he put his hand on the inside of my thigh and squeezed. "Needing it like the air he breathes."

Okay then. "We'll catch you guys later," I said to the twins as I pushed my chair back. We'd done a good job of avoiding Stephanie until the band that had set up while we were eating began to play.

"Dance with me, Dylan," Stephanie said, coming up on the other side of him. She grabbed his arm and tugged.

He flashed me an apologetic smile as he was dragged to the dance floor set up on one end of the deck, and yes, the mayor's deck was that big. "Bitch," I muttered.

"I heard that," Adam said.

"Yeah, well, he doesn't have to look like he's having fun." One thing I had to give Stephanie was that she was a good dancer, and as it turned out, Dylan was, too. There were several couples dancing, but everyone sitting around was watching Dylan and Stephanie. They were so good together that it looked like they'd been dance partners for years. I didn't want to be jealous, but there it was.

"You don't have to worry about her, Jenn."

I shot Adam a grateful smile. He disliked Stephanie probably more than me. After his junior year in college, he'd dated her when he'd come home for the summer. Why, I don't know, because by then he knew what she was like, and I don't think he was particularly crazy about her. More like he was bored and she was just someone to pass the time with until he returned to school. Or maybe he was trying to get Savannah out of his system. Who knows?

Stephanie had other ideas, though. She'd decided he was husband material, and when her hints that they should get engaged fell on deaf ears, she claimed she was pregnant.

"I'm going to have to marry her," Adam had said to Connor and me as he paced across his living room floor. "No baby of mine is going to be raised without a father."

"Did you use protection?" Connor asked. "And if you say no, I'm going to disown you."

Adam had glared at his twin. "Always. You shouldn't even have to ask me that."

"I haven't trusted Stephanie since first grade when she put salt in my milk," I said. "Here's what you need to do before you agree to anything. Make an appointment with Dr. Saltzman for a pregnancy test. Then wait and tell her where you're going when you're on the way there, but not before."

Adam did exactly that, and as he pulled into the doctor's parking lot, Stephanie confessed she wasn't pregnant. To this day, he credits me with saving him from a life of misery.

The band started right in on a second song, and when it appeared that Dylan was headed back to me, Stephanie danced in front of him, blocking his way. He laughed and kept on dancing. She turned, bumping her butt against his groin while her gaze landed on me, a smirk on her face. I was going to kill her.

"Easy," Connor said, putting his hand on my arm when I stood.

He was right. If I killed Stephanie in front of all these witnesses, Dylan—being the police chief and all—would have to arrest me. There would go any chance of saving a horse tonight.

"Let's go dance, peanut." Connor pushed me toward the dance floor, but I planted my feet, refusing to move.

"You know I can't dance," I muttered. Yeah, I danced

when I was with friends and had had a little to drink. But no way was I going to put myself next to Dylan and Stephanie, who could go on a dance show and win without even trying.

Connor took my hand and tugged. "Trust me."

Of course I trusted him, so I let him drag me to the dance floor. He leaned over and said something to one of the band members, then led me to a spot near Dylan and Stephanie. Dylan smiled and winked when he saw me, but I was miffed with him. Turning my back, I gave Connor a what-now look.

The fast song faded out, changing to a slow one. I grinned at my friend. Slow dancing I could do without embarrassing myself. That was great except that meant Dylan would now be slow dancing with Stephanie. I scowled at Connor.

"Trust me," he said again, reading my mind.

He pulled me into his arms. We'd danced for maybe a minute when he twirled me right up to Dylan. "Change partners with you," he said.

Stephanie shook her head. "I don't—"

"You bet," Dylan said, pulling away from Stephanie's clutches. He wrapped an arm around my waist, pulling me close. "Thanks for rescuing me."

Well, it was technically Connor, but who was I to argue? "I wasn't sure you wanted to be rescued. The two of you were great together." Although I about choked on the words, it was true.

"She's an excellent dancer, and I love to dance."

My heart sank to my stomach. "I can't dance," I blurted.

He leaned his head back and peered down at me. "If that's true, what do you call what you're doing right now?"

"I can't fast dance. I mean I can, but I look spastic." *Shut up, Jenn.* My cheeks heated. Why did I care what he thought of my two left feet? It wasn't like I was going to marry him. "And stop laughing."

"I can't help it. You're so adorable." He slid the hand he had at my back up to my neck, pulling my face closer to his. "About that horse needing saving."

"Let's blow this joint, cowboy." He danced me right off the deck, and as soon as we turned the corner of the house, we ran hand in hand for his car.

CHAPTER TWENTY-TWO

~ Dylan ~

I SUDDENLY BECAME NERVOUS WHILE WE were driving back, so I poured Jenny and myself a glass of wine when we got to my place. The last woman I'd bedded had been my wife. Jenny was the first woman to wake the little man up. What if that was an illusion and when it came time to perform, he outright refused?

That hadn't crossed my mind until Stephanie had twerked her ass all over me, and I hadn't felt any response at all. Maybe it was simply because she wasn't Jenny. I hoped that was the reason, and I'd find out soon enough. First, I needed to relax and get rid of the anxiety of disappointing Jenny.

"I still haven't gotten used to seeing the sunset in the mountains," I said when we went out to the balcony.

"Don't you have sunsets in Chicago?"

She took a sip of her wine, peering at me over the rim. That look she was giving me was sexier than any of Stephanie's bumping and grinding. I thought Jenny had been a little jealous, but she had nothing to worry about where the mayor's daughter was concerned.

"Of course we have sunsets in Chicago, silly girl. The buildings block them, or we just forget to look up. Everyone's always in a rush to get somewhere. To work, back home, to dinner, wherever. Who thinks of stopping for a few moments to enjoy a sunset?"

"That's sad."

Actually it was. I was still getting used to the slow pace

of these mountain people. It drove me crazy at work when some of my cops took their time carrying out an order. Outside of the police station, I was learning to enjoy the slower pace.

"Is there something at the edge of the woods there?" I pointed where I'd seen movement.

Jenny stood and went to the railing. "It's a deer. A buck. Come look," she whispered.

I joined her, and sure enough there was a buck with a set of antlers like I'd never seen before. I wished I had binoculars and made a mental note to keep a pair out here.

"Eleven points. Impressive."

"What does that mean?" I wasn't a hunter, couldn't stand the thought of killing something, which was interesting considering my job. I'd had to shoot a man once who pointed a gun at me, and I hoped to hell I never had to do it again.

"His antlers. He has eleven points on them. Eight points is more common."

"Ah, I see."

"I'll be right back. Don't let him go anywhere."

She skipped off, and I eyed the deer, wondering how I was supposed to keep him from going anywhere. The buck was staring toward the building, only his face and neck visible. Except for the vague outline of the front half of his body, the rest of him was hidden by the dark of the forest and the night.

In less than a minute Jenny was back, her camera in her hand. After fiddling with a few knobs, she put it to her eye and started snapping picture after picture. The big guy's ears perked up, and I wondered if he'd heard the click of her camera. But no, from below my balcony, another deer, one without antlers, trotted into view, heading for the buck.

"His lady," Jenny whispered, the camera still to her eye.

"He's watching out for her."

The two deer pressed their noses together for a few seconds, then the buck turned, disappearing into the forest, his lady following. "Wow. That was pretty cool."

"Yeah, it was. I got some good shots. Take a look tomorrow, see if whoever lives below you puts food out for them. Some people do. Or they just like the grass under your balcony."

Now I wanted to put food out so they'd come back. "Do they hang around where people live? I would have thought they'd stay in the forest."

"If there's food or good grass."

"So now I have an owl and some deer?"

"And probably some bears with how close to the forest these apartments are. If you ever see a cub, stay far away because the mother will be nearby. She won't take kindly to anyone getting close to her baby." She stepped back, started taking shots of me. As soon as I realized what she was doing, I stuck out my tongue and crossed my eyes.

She laughed. "That's the one I'm going to enter in *The Valley News* monthly photo contest."

"Oh no you're not." I reached for the camera. "You always have this on you?"

"Yep. Never know when I might want to take a picture of a hot guy."

She backed up, her green eyes flashing with mischief as she held the camera behind her. There was nothing a man loved more than a chase, and I prowled toward my prey. Although I could easily take her camera away, I decided I'd steal a kiss instead.

I grabbed her cowboy hat, tossing it onto the chair. She backed up another step. A few more and she'd be against the wall where I wanted her. I kept coming at her, my eyes locked on hers until she was trapped.

"Now where you gonna go, Red?" When she giggled

as she tried to slide sideways, I put my hands on the wall. "Gotcha," I said, lowering my mouth to hers.

Kissing Jenny Girl was like falling into a vat of my favorite ice cream and drowning in the pleasure of all that decadent taste. She let out the sweetest sigh as she wrapped her arms around my neck, one hand still holding tightly to her camera. I took advantage of that sigh and slipped my tongue into her mouth.

When I grew hard, I realized I'd worried over nothing. Whether I'd respond to another woman the way I did her, I didn't know and didn't care. I'd always been a one-woman man, and apparently, she was meant to be my one woman for as long as it lasted between us.

I trailed kisses over her cheek, finding my way to her neck. Her skin was soft and as smooth as silk. And warm. I wanted to spend all night licking her. When she rubbed against me, I almost lost it right then and there.

"Easy, Red, or I'm going to embarrass myself."

"I don't think I can be easy. I want you." She put her hand on my jaw, pulled my face up, and stared hard into my eyes. "Now."

That did it. I scooped her up, taking long strides to my bedroom, where I dropped her onto the bed. "Don't move." For my entry back into the living, I wanted everything to be perfect. I put on a long-playing soft jazz CD, retrieved our wine and some candles, and returned to my bedroom. The glasses I put on the nightstand, then I lit the candles, placing them around the room. All the while, Jenny's eyes tracked me.

"Take off your shirt, Dylan," she said after the last candle was lit.

I paused at the foot of the bed, smiling at the bossy woman. If she wanted my shirt off, off it would go. Holding her gaze, I made a show of slowly unbuttoning my shirt. "Happy?" I asked as I dropped it to the floor. The little hellcat smirked.

"Halfway happy. You still have your pants on."

"And you still have everything on. I'm thinking tit for tat is only fair." I loved how her eyes always seemed to shine when I amused her.

"Can I move?"

"What?"

She grinned. "You said don't move. If you want my shirt off, I'm going to have to move."

"Move," I growled. I'd never before in my entire life growled at anyone, but this one? I'd howl at the moon if that was what it took for her to take off her damn shirt. Her lips curved into a sultry smile that would steal any man's heart. Then her shirt and bra were gone and my mouth went dry.

"You're beautiful," I said—actually whispered—as my gaze worshipped all that she'd revealed to me. Rosy, pert nipples that I was going to have my mouth on very, very soon filled my vision.

"Your pants," she said.

I couldn't get them and my shoes off fast enough.

"And your briefs, although you look pretty darn sexy in them."

I shook my head. "Nope. Your boots and jeans first." We were daring each other with each piece of clothing, almost like we were playing strip poker. I'd have to play that sometime with her.

Her breasts bounced as she tugged off her boots, making my heart thump in my chest in anticipation. Jenny Girl was fucking killing me, and she didn't even know it. It hit me that I could probably fall in love with her given time, but she had plans that didn't include me. I just had to make sure she didn't take off with my heart in her backpack on her traipse around the world. I could do that. I would do that.

Stripped of everything else, she sat on my bed wearing nothing but a red thong. Be still my heart. I walked around to the side of the bed, sitting on the edge. "You take my breath away," I said, sliding my hand along her thigh.

She put her hand on my neck, leaned toward me, and put her lips at the corner of my mouth. I let her play until she licked across the seam of my mouth. I couldn't stand it anymore.

"Come here." I tugged her down with me to the bed. Finding her mouth again, I took my time savoring her taste, breathing in her scent. She nestled against me, and I slid my hand down the curve of her spine until I reached her ass, splaying my fingers over one firm cheek.

The candles I'd set on the nightstand flickered light and shadows over the creamy white skin of her breasts. "Need those in my mouth," I murmured. She gasped when I swirled my tongue around the little bud, then moaned when I sucked hard on it. Ah, so damn good.

"Dylan."

That was all. Just my name, but the needy sound of it was enough to drive me wild. I rose onto my elbows and stared down at her. Her eyes were filled with desire, and her mouth was parted as she breathed heavily in and out.

"It's been a long time for me, Red. I'm going to apologize in advance for how fast this first time is going to go." I brushed my mouth over hers. "But I'll make it up to you. I promise."

She smiled. "We have all night."

"That we do." I pushed my briefs down my legs and kicked them off, then reached into the nightstand, pulling out a handful of condoms, dropping all but one.

"Pretty optimistic, aren't you?"

I glanced at the pile of condoms and laughed. "Probably not that optimistic." I hooked a finger under the elastic of her sexy thong, wanting it off. To make sure she was ready for me, I slid a finger inside her. Oh yeah. She definitely was.

She held out her arms. "Inside me. Now."

"Yes, ma'am." I moved between her thighs, and after I rolled the condom on, I lowered my body over hers. She spread her knees, and as I sank into her, she wrapped her legs around my ass. Heat spiraled up my spine, and I clenched my entire body to keep from coming right then.

Heaven. It was fucking heaven being inside my Jenny Girl. She lifted her hips to meet mine, matching my rhythm. With each stroke I drove deeper, and the pressure built inside me until I couldn't hold out any longer. I found Jenny's mouth, our tongues dancing around each other as I lapped up her moans.

"Ahh," I said into her mouth as I erupted, waves of pleasure, one after the other, washing over me. My heart pounded in my chest. "I'm sorry." And I was. She hadn't climaxed.

"Hey, remember we have all night?"

I smiled against her neck. "I remember."

"Just do better next time, cowboy. We're trying to save a horse here."

The woman definitely knew how to make me laugh. "That horse has nothing to worry about."

When I could move again, we raided the kitchen, bringing a container of ice cream and two spoons back to the bed. Once our bellies were satisfied, I took my time exploring Jenny's body, learning what made her shiver with pleasure. Her taste, her scent, the way her silky skin felt under my palms was intoxicating. I wasn't sure I'd ever get enough of her.

We dozed off sometime after midnight. I was spooned behind her, my nose buried in her hair so I could breathe her in, and as sleep took me, I wondered how I was going to let her go when it was time.

My phone interrupted my sleep, and I rolled over, looking at the clock to see it was two in the morning. Calls that came in the middle of the night were never good. I sat up, grabbed my cell, and went into the living room to keep from waking Jenny.

"Talk to me," I said when I saw Kim Payton's name come up on my screen. She and Tommy were still on night shift.

"Chief, I'm really sorry to be calling at this hour."

"No problem. What's going on?"

"Ah, Tommy and I are at the scene of an accident involving the mayor's daughter. Captain Moody's here, too. Apparently Stephanie called him. We're pretty sure she's drunk, but Moody's refusing to let Tommy give her a Breathalyzer."

And here was my first test on how I was going to treat the mayor's daughter. The answer? Just like I would anyone else. "Tell Captain Moody I said—"

"That's not all. Sean Lamar was in the car with her and wasn't wearing a seat belt. He was thrown out. He's in pretty bad shape. They've called for MAMA to take him to Mission in Asheville."

Shit. MAMA was the hospital's medical helicopter. Blue Ridge Valley had a small hospital, but they didn't have a trauma center. "Tell Captain Moody I'm on the way and that I said to let you and Tommy do your job." I'd find out who Sean Lamar was when I got there. After getting the address, I returned to my bedroom to put on some clothes.

"Are you leaving?"

I'd tried to be quiet, but it was better that I could tell her where I was going. "Yeah. There's been a bad accident. Go back to sleep. I don't know when I'll get back." I gave her a kiss before heading out. Until I found out more information, I chose not to tell her about Stephanie.

When I reached the scene, Stephanie was in the back

of Kim's cruiser with Kim standing guard at the back door, and Captain Moody was in Tommy's face.

"I don't care what the chief said. I'm taking her home," Moody said.

So intent on intimidating Tommy, he didn't hear me walk up behind him. "Captain Moody, your presence isn't needed here." He spun, opened his mouth, then closed it. I could see he was making a visible effort to control his temper.

"You need to let that girl go home," he said after a few deep breaths. "She's upset enough."

"I'm sure she is, but she's not going anywhere until we get a blood test done on her. You, on the other hand, can go home. As for your not caring what I say, we'll discuss this in my office Monday morning at nine."

"The mayor's not going to be happy about this," he yelled as I walked away.

Too true. I ignored him and went to Kim. "You handcuff her?" Kim nodded, eyeing me as if she wasn't sure she should have. "Good. Take her to the hospital. Get a blood test done and have them check her out to make sure she doesn't have any internal injuries. After that, take her home. We'll decide what to charge her with depending on the results."

"Yes sir."

Stephanie banged her head on the window, trying to get my attention. I ignored her, too. Moody had moved to his car, but he was sending me death glares. Like I cared. Tommy was now at Stephanie's Mercedes, and I joined him. "Looks like she took the curve too fast."

Tommy nodded. "She denies it, but my guess, she was doing over sixty. The posted speed limit here is thirty-five."

Stupid woman. The car was wrapped around a tree on the passenger side. If her passenger had been wearing his seat belt, he would have been killed instantly. One of the rare times not wearing one might have saved a life.

"I'd say it's totaled. Who's Sean Lamar and where is he?"

"The ambulance took him to the ball field where the helicopter will land. His parents own the Apple Orchard Motel and Gift Shop."

"How old is Sean?"

"Twenty-four. He's army, stationed at Fort Bragg. He was home for the weekend. Stephanie said they'd been at Hideouts and were heading back to her place."

The honky-tonk bar. I glanced at my watch. The bar would be closed by now. "Tomorrow night when you go on duty, go there first. Find out how long they were there and how much they were drinking." I hadn't met the Lamars yet, but I could see a lawsuit against Stephanie in the making. "When you get to the station tonight, write up a report while everything's still fresh in your mind. This could get nasty before it's all over. I want every word she said, everything you saw here documented. That includes everything Moody said or did."

Tommy eyed me with approval. "Yes, sir."

"And Tommy, no talking to anyone about this. Not even to other cops, capisce? Tell Kim she's under the same orders. Tomorrow morning I'll get an accident investigator out here."

He nodded. I trusted Tommy and Kim to keep their mouths shut, but Moody? Doubtful. The rumors would fly, and we didn't need to be contributing to them. I went back to my car and got the camera I kept in the glove box. After getting pictures of the Mercedes from all angles, I lowered the camera, taking one last look at the mangled car. It was hard to believe that Stephanie had walked away without an apparent scratch. The next thing I had to do was what I hated the most, but it couldn't be put off any longer.

"Tommy, follow me to the station so I can drop off my

car. We'll go together to notify Sean's parents."

What a shitty ending to what had been one of the best nights I'd had in what felt like forever.

CHAPTER TWENTY-THREE

~ Jenny ~

I OFFERED TO CANCEL OUR SUNDAY waterfall trip thinking Dylan would prefer to get some sleep, but he refused. He didn't return until this morning, and I could tell he was tired.

"Thanks," he said when I slid a plate of scrambled eggs, bacon, and toast in front of him. "This and a quick shower, I'll be good as new."

"It must have been a bad one if it had you out this long." He still hadn't told me anything, and as small as my town was, I worried that it involved someone I knew.

His eyes searched mine. "As I understand the bartender rules, you're bound by oath to keep anything said to you while serving beers confidential, right?"

Kind of a weird question, but I'd play along. "Absolutely, and I've never once broken a confidence."

"Then put yourself in bartender role and grab me a beer."

"Sure." Now I was really worried. I'd already noticed that Dylan wasn't a big drinker unless he was upset about something. One or two beers or the occasional glass of wine at most, so if he wanted a beer at nine in the morning, that didn't bode well.

"Breakfast of champs," I said, sliding the bottle across the counter.

He downed half of it in one swallow, then pushed it aside. "I've ordered the cops at the scene not to talk about it, so I shouldn't either, but you're going to hear about it soon enough. Whatever rumors surface, here's what I know as of now. Stephanie Jenkins and Sean Lamar were returning to her place after spending time at Hideouts. Unfortunately she wrapped her car around a tree. She's okay, but Sean is in critical condition at Mission Hospital in Asheville."

"Holy shit," I whispered.

"That about sums it up." He slid his empty plate to the side and pulled his cup of coffee in front of him.

"Sean's a really sweet guy. God, I hope he's going to be okay." I noticed Dylan's cup was empty, and I refilled it. "It's been maybe two years since I've seen him. I'd heard he was back from Afghanistan. Honestly I can't figure out why he was with Stephanie. He was never a big party person like her."

"His parents said he's changed since returning from his last tour. That he seemed angry and withdrawn."

"You saw them?"

"Yeah." He scrubbed a hand over his face. "The part of my job I hate the most. Take me to your waterfall, Red. Show me something beautiful today."

"I can do that. While you're taking a shower, I'm going to call my parents and let them know. They're friends with Frank and Judy and will probably want to go to the hospital to be with them. Don't worry," I said when he seemed about to speak. "I'll just say he was in an accident. Frank and Judy can tell them however much they want them to know."

He gave me a dog-tired smile. "I trust you to know what to say."

Dylan's shower done and my call made, we walked out to his car. I held out my hand. "Keys. I'm driving." Without a word he handed them to me. The man was so different from others I'd dated. Chad would have argued, no matter he was dead tired and had drunk half a beer. He'd see it as an insult to his manhood or some crap like that.

"Top down?" he asked.

"Definitely." It was another warm day, perfect for a convertible. This warm spell wasn't going to last much longer, but I was going to enjoy while it did. I dug out a band from my purse, pulling my hair into a ponytail.

On the way out of Blue Ridge Valley, we stopped at the grocery store and bought a small Styrofoam container, a couple of bottled waters, some presliced cheeses, crackers, strawberries, a package of blackberries, a half-dozen chocolate chip cookies, and a small bag of ice. On the way to the checkout line, I spied a rack with cheap straw hats and grabbed one. Dylan chose a ball cap with a North Carolina Panthers' logo on it.

As I pulled out of the store's parking lot, I debated which waterfall to take Dylan to. I decided on one of my favorites, Soco Falls, which was actually a duel falls located between Maggie Valley and Cherokee, right off the Blue Ridge Parkway.

Dylan fell asleep within minutes of our driving out of town. I couldn't stop glancing over at him, thinking how much younger he looked when all his worries and responsibilities weren't etched in weary lines on his face.

My heart ached at the thought of leaving him. But traveling the world had been my dream for so long that I didn't know how to give it up. And then there was my promise to Natalie that I had to keep. So I would go, and I seriously doubted Dylan would be waiting for me when I got back. He was simply every woman's dream man, and he would find someone to love him the way he deserved. And I would be happy for him. I swore it.

I turned off the ignition after parking as close as I could get to Soco Falls. I was going to let him sleep a little longer, knowing he needed it, but when the Mustang's engine noise cut off, he jerked upright.

"Did I drool?" were the first words out of his mouth.

"Yes, and you snored, and then drooled some more."

He lowered his chin, eyeing his shirt. "Did not." He massaged his eyes with his fingers, then scrubbed at his face.

I knew he'd showered, but I hadn't noticed until now that he hadn't shaved, too intent on watching how peaceful he looked in sleep. That day-old bristle on his cheeks made me want to jump his bones, but when he'd slept, I could see the boy in him. I wish I'd known him when he mischievously drove his mother mad. I wanted him to tell me about those days, yet I didn't because then I'd fall in love with him.

"We're here," I said instead of putting my mouth on his like I wanted to. We gathered our cooler and hats, and I wished we'd taken my car because I always kept a blanket in it. I had plans for him, so we'd make do.

It only took about five minutes to reach the observation deck, and I stepped back to let Dylan take his first look at the double waterfalls.

He didn't say anything at first, then he glanced at me with awe in his eyes. "I've never seen anything so beautiful."

"I know." I loved that he saw the beauty that I did. "Come on. We have a ways to go." The trail down was slippery, and the only way to get to the bottom safely was to hold on to the rope the park service had put up. Dylan held our cooler in one hand, white-knuckle gripping the line with his other. We laughed like silly kids as we slipped-slid our way down.

At the bottom he dropped the cooler to the ground, snaked his arm around my waist, pulled me against him, and kissed me with the same exhilaration that strummed through my body. He'd come back to life after a horrible night, and I was glad he hadn't taken my suggestion to stay home and get some sleep.

"Wow," I said when we came up for air. "If this is what going to a waterfall does for you, we'll have to do it often. I have a whole list of them we can visit."

"It's not just the waterfall, Red."

He didn't have to explain. I could see the desire for me in his eyes. I took his hand, leading him to a spot I'd seen on the way down. The rock was flat and dry, perfect for a little picnic and a little loving.

"Thank you," Dylan said once we were seated on the rock.

"For?"

"For bringing me here, for being you."

Just go and melt my heart, Mr. Policeman. I leaned my cheek on his shoulder, and he rested his chin on my head. We sat like that for a while, listening to the crash of the water onto the rocks. I could feel the tension seeping out of his body as the sun warmed our faces. He sank down onto his back, bringing me with him and cradling my head with his arm.

"I think I could live here if we could get pizza delivery," he said.

"And chocolate chip cookies. And a hamburger once in a while."

He laughed. "You're complicating things, Red."

There was something in his tone of voice that made me think he wasn't talking about pizza delivery. His fingers played with my hair, and I closed my eyes, sighing from the tingles he was sending around my head.

"Mm, that feels good."

"This world tour of yours. How long are you planning to be gone?"

"I don't know. I'm leaving that open. A year. Two. Until I get tired of traveling, I guess." But I was going to miss him. I almost wished we hadn't met until after I came back. There was no way a man like him would sit around for a year or two, waiting for me to get the travel bug out of my system. I'd never expect him to or ask it of him.

There was no one else at the bottom of the falls, and we were hidden from view of anyone on the observation deck. I swung a leg over Dylan's waist, straddling him. His eyes, hooded and half-asleep, tracked my movements. I put my hands on either side of his head, bracing them on the rock, lowered my face, and brushed my lips over his. He put his hands on my hips as I played with his mouth. I loved kissing Dylan Conrad. His lips were full, soft, and delicious.

"I wish we had a tent we could crawl into so we could strip off our clothes and make love here next to the waterfalls." I dropped kisses to both sides of his eyes. The mountain water cooled the air around us, but my body felt like someone had turned on the furnace. Simply being near this man sent heat to every bone and nerve ending living inside my skin.

"I'm a transplanted city boy. I've never been camping, but I think I'd like wrestling around in a tent with you." He smiled. "We'll have to give it a try sometime."

There were all kinds of things I wanted to do with him, places I wanted to take him, things I wanted to show him. When the voice in my head said that there wasn't enough time left to check off everything on my list, I pushed it away.

We were in the here and now, and when I left, it would be with beautiful memories of this man, whether we ever got naked together in a tent or not. He slipped a hand under my T-shirt, cupped my breast with his palm, and flicked his thumb over my nipple.

"Copping a feel there, Chief?"

"Uh-huh."

I laughed. "I love an honest cop." His erection pressed

against the vee of my shorts, and I rubbed against him, teasing him.

"You're treading on dangerous territory, Red. You keep that up, and I won't care that we're out in the open and someone could come down here any minute." Even as he spoke the words, he arched his hips, pushing back at me.

As if he'd conjured company by mentioning the possibility, I heard voices. Dylan put his hands on my waist and lifted me to the side of him. By the time the family of four reached the bottom of the trail, Dylan and I were innocently enjoying our picnic. But, mercy, those hot looks he was giving me were setting me on fire.

"I think we should go back to your place and take a nap," I said as I popped the last bit of cheese in my mouth.

He smirked. "If you say so."

Yeah, we might be in his bed, but we weren't going to be napping.

CHAPTER TWENTY-FOUR

~ *Dylan* ~

MONDAY MORNING, I WAITED FOR Moody to appear. He was late, and as usual where he was concerned, I was irritated. Already on my third cup of coffee, I replayed my weekend in my head. Jenny and I had gone back to my place, made love, and then had actually napped for a few hours. When she said she should go home, I'd convinced her to stay. I could get used to having her in my bed every night.

When I'd kissed her good-bye this morning, I'd almost asked her to come over tonight when she got off work. I liked having her with me, but I resisted asking. We'd spent the weekend together, and it was better that I give her space. Didn't want her getting tired of my ugly face.

Moody's voice floated down the hall, and I swiveled my chair to face my computer. By the time he walked in, I was creating a form for my officers to fill out with their uniform sizes.

"I'm here," he said, standing in the doorway.

"Sit." I kept on working for another five minutes, letting him stew. Playing games with people wasn't normally my thing, but Moody brought out the worst in me. At what I estimated to be his tenth loud sigh, I shut down the monitor.

"Captain, before we're done here, one of two things is going to happen. You are either going to give me your word that you accept me as the police chief, or you're going to put your gun and badge on my desk."

He sputtered and his face turned red. I held up my hand. "I'm not done yet. This department's a joke. Since you've acted as the interim chief for the past six months, some of that is on you."

"You son of—"

"Careful. Here's the thing, Moody. Together, you and I could make the Blue Ridge Valley Police Department something that our officers and our town could be proud of. You're either with me or against me. Which will it be?" He'd been with the department longer than any other officer here, and for that reason alone, I was giving him one last chance.

"You let a murderer walk free. You arrested a poor girl who was traumatized. How the fuck do you expect me to be with you on anything?"

Stupid ass. I deducted a million—no, a trillion—points. "If by a murderer you mean Gertie Jenkins, her guilt or non-guilt is up to the courts. And by the poor girl, if you mean Stephanie, the court will also decide her guilt or innocence based on the evidence, not me. That's how the law works."

I wanted to knock some sense into him with my fist. Never had a man working for me frustrated me the way Moody did. "Time's up. Do I have your support?"

Moody shot up so fast you'd think his chair was on fire.

"I don't have to take this shit from you." He paused at the door, giving me a hard stare that he probably thought would have me shaking in my boots. "You can expect a call from the mayor."

I rolled my eyes at the empty doorway. According to the addition I'd made to my contract before I scrawled my John Hancock on it, if Jim John wanted me gone before my year was up, he would have to give me a letter terminating my employment signed not only by him but the town manager and all three commissioners. It wasn't going to be so easy to get rid of me. I was pretty sure I had all but Jim John on my side. And that was only until I found out what Moody had on the mayor.

By the evening shift change, I hadn't heard a word from Jim John. Nor had I seen Moody since our morning meeting. Truthfully his absence made for a much improved atmosphere in the building.

As the evening officers arrived and the day shift returned to the station, I gathered them in the lobby. "I have some good news," I said, getting their attention. "As soon as you fill out the form Tommy's about to pass out and get it back to me, we'll be able to order your new uniforms, courtesy of your mayor."

Whistles and enthusiastic clapping filled my ears. "You'll get one dress uniform, one logoed black leather jacket, five dark blue polo shirts with our logo, and three pairs of black cargo pants." I held up a picture the uniform company had sent me.

"Those are awesome," Sarah Griffin said, and everyone vigorously nodded.

They were. I'd like that uniform for myself, but settled for what I'd already picked. Wearing something different from my officers set me apart, which was an important thing to do, and giving them the super cool uniform scored me points.

"The second bit of news you're going to like, your next paycheck will have a five percent increase." I waited for the huzzahs and cheers to die down. There was enough money in my new budget to give them even more, but they didn't need to know that.

"This is the only time there will be across-the-board increases. From here on out, your raises will be based on your job performance. Your first review will be six months from today. Whether you get a raise at that time will depend on you."

Fortunately my new police department wasn't unionized. In Chicago I'd never be able to get away with that. As they filed out, either to go home or on shift, each man and woman came up and thanked me. I felt pretty damn good.

Gene, my sole detective, the last to leave and the last to comment, said, "The mayor thought of this? Not likely."

"Could be likely. Guess you'll never know." He rolled his eyes, making me chuckle. I followed Gene to his desk. "You in a hurry to get out of here?"

"I got some time."

"Good. Grab that cold case file you're working on and bring it to my office." I stopped in the break room, got an RC Cola, which I'd seen Gene drinking previously, a bottle of water for myself, and a half bag of pretzels I saw on the counter.

"Tell me about the case," I said, digging into the pretzels.

"Six years ago, Old Man Scroggins's prize bull went missing—"

"Say again."

Gene's lips twitched. "Yeah, it's a prize-bull cold case."

"That's what I thought you said. Go on." God forbid the guys back in Chicago got ahold of this. I'd never hear the end of it.

"The Angus stud bull was valued at five thousand. Scroggins got a hundred-dollar stud fee per cow, plus room and board for forty-five days. He had a waiting list, people lined up, wanting their cows covered by that particular bull."

I grinned. "Covered meaning getting it on?"

"You're having too much fun with this, Chief."

"Impossible not to." A missing prize bull beat a murder cold case any day. "Any suspects?"

"Scroggins accused his neighbor, Roland Hancock, of stealing Beauregard and eating him."

I tried to keep a straight face. I really did.

"Thought that would tickle you," Gene said when I laughed.

"Sorry, this is too good. I assume Hancock's place was searched?" I paused before adding, "Of course, if he ate the evidence, I guess there was no proof?" Gene sat back in his chair, and I could tell he was trying hard not to laugh. I couldn't resist throwing out the line from an old commercial. "So, where's the beef?"

That finally did it. He slapped his palm on his leg as he burst into laughter. "Stop it, Chief," he gasped.

I shrugged. "I'll try. If the bull's been missing for six years, do you really think you'll find it now?"

"That's not the problem as much as there's been an ongoing Hatfield and McCoy situation between the two families ever since. Patrol's out there two or three times a month because one of them's taken a potshot at the other, or some such nonsense. The day's going to come when one of them gets hurt if we don't put a stop to it. Roland didn't steal that bull, much less eat it, but Old Man Scroggins can't seem to get that through his hard head."

"And you know that how?"

"I grew up with Roland. We played ball together. He was the pitcher. I was his catcher. He won us the state championship our senior year. I know him. He didn't do it, Chief, but he's getting real tired of the old man messing with him, so I told him I'd look into it."

I took the file from Gene. "Whose case was it?"

"Captain Moody's. He was the detective back then."

"Of course he was." Opening the folder, I flipped through the meager report. "Not much here, but I'll go through it with a fresh pair of eyes. Not sure we'll get anywhere, but who knows, right?"

Gene stood. "Thanks, Chief."

"No, thank you. Seriously. I never thought I'd be investigating a kidnapped bull case." Damn, I loved this town. "Now go home to your wife and kids, Gene." By the hint of a smile, I knew he'd figured out when and why I used one of my officer's first names.

After he left, I put my feet on my desk, leaning back in my leather chair. After reading the report twice, I recalled something I'd seen in another of Moody's old notes on another case. After double-checking that I'd remembered right, I closed both folders, locking them in my desk. Beauregard hadn't been turned into hamburger patties, and I knew who had him. Damn Moody and his incompetence.

CHAPTER TWENTY-FIVE

~ Jenny ~

"YOU SO DID NOT!"

I shot Autumn a wide grin. "Did too."

She reached across the table, poking me in the arm with a finger. "You actually spent the entire weekend with our new police chief?"

"Uh-huh."

"Oh my God. He's so hot. Is he really that hot? I mean in bed? He's definitely hot to look at. Are you going to see him again? What did—"

"Autumn, shut up." I had to laugh. Her eyes were about to bug out. "Yeah, he's that hot. In bed and out."

It was Tuesday, my day off, and we'd gone to Asheville to do a little shopping in Biltmore Village and have lunch. She was collecting more items for her trousseau—I didn't even know brides did that anymore—and as long as we were spending her money, I was good.

I took a bite of the fried green tomatoes and moaned. "So freaking good." We were at the Red Stag Grill in the Village. One thing I loved about eating with Autumn was that we always shared our food. Today we were splitting the fried green tomatoes and a bohemian hunter's platter.

"Back to your police chief." Autumn forked the last olive on the hunter's platter.

"Hey, I wanted that."

"Too bad." She popped it into her mouth, then pointed her fork at me. "Talk."

"He invited me to go with him to the mayor's barbeque Saturday afternoon, and I didn't go back home until Monday morning. That's pretty much it."

She smirked. "I highly doubt that." Her expression turned serious. "That's awful about Sean. Is he still in critical condition?"

"Yeah. I talked to my parents this morning. They said there's been no change. The good news according to the doctors is that he lived through the night."

"Damn Stephanie. I bet she was drinking."

I wasn't going to repeat anything Dylan had said to me in confidence, even to my best friend. "I guess we'll find out soon enough what happened. Nothing stays a secret in the valley." When the waitress brought our check, I grabbed it. "My treat today."

"Okay. I'll get the tip." She put a ten on the table.

We were on our way out when Chad and his father walked in the door. Crap. Their office was downtown. What were they doing in the Village? Before I could take off for the bathroom or a back door if there was one, Chad saw me.

"Jenn!"

He rushed over, taking both my hands. I wanted to jerk them away, but his father was watching, and I didn't want to embarrass Chad. Stupid softhearted me.

"Hello, Mr. Perrine," I said when he approached. "Nice to see you again." Not really. I'd never liked him much.

He gave me a curt nod. "Jennifer."

I eased my hands out of Chad's. "Ah, Autumn and I were just on our way to…" I gave her a helpless glance.

"On our way to an appointment for my wedding dress fitting." She glanced at her watch. "We're going to be late, Jenn, so we really need to go."

I'd never been good at lying, and Autumn knew it. She, however, could come up with a story on the spur of the moment to cover any situation. That particular talent had kept us out of trouble with our parents many times growing up.

"Yeah, we have to go." When Chad seemed about to protest, I grabbed Autumn's arm and we took off. Mr. Perrine had never liked me, probably thought a bartender wasn't good enough for his son. I'm sure he was happy to see me out of the picture. Chad called after me, but I kept going.

"Of all the gin joints in all the towns in all the world, he walks into ours," Autumn drawled, deepening her voice.

I laughed at her impersonation of Rick Blaine from *Casablanca.* Autumn loved old movies, and I'd watched probably every classic in the world with her through the years. If you didn't know Autumn, with that gorgeous blonde hair of hers, those sky-blue eyes, and a smile that could melt the hardest heart, you'd think she was an angel. So not true. Growing up, Autumn had always been the instigator in any trouble she, Natalie, Savannah, and I got into. She was also the one who, when we got caught, could talk our parents into going easier on us than they should have.

"Speaking of old movies, I got Dylan to watch *Arsenic and Old Lace* with me the other night," I said as we headed to the first store.

"Did he like it? If he didn't, you're not allowed to see him anymore."

Ha! Like that would stop me from seeing him. "He thought it was hilarious."

"'Look. I probably should have told you this before but you see… well… insanity runs in my family… It practically gallops,'" Autumn said, quoting a line from the movie in her best Mortimer Brewster voice. She sighed. "God, Cary Grant was so sexy."

"I bet if he were still alive, you'd leave Brian for him."

She vigorously nodded. "Without looking back."

Too bad he wasn't still alive then. We didn't see each other as much since she'd met Brian, and I missed that, especially with Savannah in New York now. I suppose that was what happened when you grew up and life took you on different roads, but that didn't mean I had to like it.

"I hate buying bathing suits," she said when we walked into the first store.

She had a list of things she'd need for her honeymoon, and since Brian was taking her to Hawaii, she had three suits on the list. A one-piece, a conservative two-piece, and a bikini. "Covering all possible scenarios?" I asked, leaning over her shoulder and reading the items on the screen of her phone.

"Exactly. Brian has friends who live in Hawaii, and we've been invited to a pool party, so a one-piece for that. The bikini's for Brian." She shot me a wicked grin.

"He's going to look funny wearing it."

"Smart-ass." She held up a yellow suit.

"Not your color. Here, this one." I handed her a blue bikini that was a perfect match to her eyes.

"Ooh, nice."

"I still don't understand why you think it would be bad luck to move into your new house," I said as she loaded her arms with bathing suits to try on. The house was gorgeous, but Autumn had this weird idea that she should only live in it as Brian's wife, so they were residing in her apartment until the wedding.

"I just do, okay? We'll spend our wedding night in it, then leave for Hawaii the next morning." She grabbed my hand. "I'm so happy, Jenn, that it scares me. Like everything's too good to be true."

"Hush! You're not going to wake up and find out it's all a dream." I pinched her. I didn't like the ominous shiver that tickled my spine at her words.

"Ouch." Laughing, she rubbed her arm.

"Just wanted to prove you're awake and this is real." The second she smirked and waggled her eyebrows, I knew something outrageous was about to come out of her mouth.

"Well, I am pretty sure I was awake last night when Brian brought whipped cream and cherries to bed with us."

I put my hands over my ears. "TMI!"

Her eyes sparkled with happiness and the mischief that was always in those blue orbs. "You should try it sometime…well, not with Brian. I'd have to kill you. With your sexy police chief. Bet him how many cherries—"

"Autumn! Stop it." We looked at each other and burst out laughing.

I'd stand as maid of honor when my bestie got married. Savannah would be home for Autumn's Christmas wedding, and I couldn't wait for the three of us to be together again. Autumn and I shopped till we dropped, and then I drove us back to Blue Ridge Valley, where we were meeting Brian at Fusions.

"Why don't you call Dylan, see if he wants to meet us for dinner?"

"He's probably busy." We weren't in a relationship, exactly. Not of the boyfriend/girlfriend kind. We were just having some fun until it was time to go, so I didn't feel comfortable asking him out on a double date with my friends.

"Doesn't hurt to ask." She grabbed my phone out of the console cupholder.

"Don't you dare." Although I kind of hoped she would. If he didn't appear to appreciate being called, I could always blame it on her. She punched in my pass code. Autumn was always forgetting her phone, so since she often used mine, she knew my code.

"Voice mail," she whispered. "Hi, Dylan. This is Autumn, Jenn's friend. We're on our way to meet Brian at

Fusions for dinner. Thought you might want to join us."

"I can't believe you did that."

She snickered. "Yes, you can."

"Truth." Would he show up? I hadn't heard from him since he'd kissed me good-bye yesterday morning. Maybe he'd only been looking for a quick tumble in bed with no plans to see each other again, but I hadn't gotten that impression. This was me we were talking about, though, and we'd already established that I was a lousy judge of men.

"I don't think he'll come," I said as I parked next to Brian's shiny new Lexus.

"Guess we'll know soon enough. Don't tell Brian about that scrap of black silk masquerading as lingerie I bought, okay? That's a wedding night surprise."

"My lips are sealed."

CHAPTER TWENTY-SIX

~ *Dylan* ~

I WAS IN THE SHOWER WHEN Jenny's friend left her message. My plan for the night had been to finally get the last of my stuff unpacked, but that lost its appeal as soon as I listened to Autumn's invitation to dinner, giving me a chance to see Jenny.

Several times during the past two days, I'd picked up my phone to text or call her but had stopped myself. I had no idea how she felt about me. Sure, it was obvious she enjoyed my company, and I wasn't even questioning that she thought the sex between us was good. Damn good.

There was actually another consideration that played into my resolve not to get too involved with Jenny. She was leaving soon, and she didn't know when she'd be back. Who knew what men she'd meet on her world travels? What if she fell in love with a dark-eyed Italian who whispered sweet accented love words into her ear or some damn Scotsman in a kilt that she couldn't resist finding out what he wore under it?

I wasn't going to be the man left behind who'd eventually get a letter saying, *Sorry, but...* So I hadn't called her. She was going to stay a woman I enjoyed hanging out with and, yes, having sex with. When she left, though, she wasn't going to take my heart with her. But I couldn't resist the lure of seeing her, so I dressed, then headed to Fusions.

I parked close to Jenny's car, and feeling a little more excited than I wanted about seeing her, I walked inside.

"Chief, you haven't been back for more doughnuts. Why not?"

Someone tugged on my shirttail, and I looked down to see Mary. "Because they're so good I won't be able to fit in my uniform if I come by every day. I'll stop in tomorrow. Promise."

The tiny, turquoise-eye-shadowed-today woman grinned up at me. "How many you want me to have ready for you?"

I had to laugh. "You're quite the saleswoman, Mary. Three dozen. Assorted." My cops were going to love me if for no other reason than I brought them the best doughnuts in the world.

"See you in the morning." Her turquoise-colored hair bounced around her neck as she walked away with amazing grace on lime-green stilettos that should have toppled her onto her face. I watched her climb onto a bar stool in the lounge next to an elderly gentleman who seemed delighted to see her. I shook my head as I grinned. Crazy town.

"I'm meeting some people," I said to the hostess, glancing past her. "There they are, in the booth by the window."

She motioned for me to go in, then turned her attention to the couple waiting behind me. As I headed to where they were seated, I scanned my surroundings—the way any big-city cop would automatically do—noting who was sitting where and if anyone looked like trouble in the making. It was a habit I'd probably never be able to break.

My gaze landed on Jenny, sitting with her friends. Was she expecting me, or had Autumn called on the sly, hoping to play matchmaker? Jenny saw me coming toward her and smiled. Damn if my heart didn't do a little dance at seeing her.

"Hello, Red," I said, sliding into the booth next to her.

"Autumn, Brian, good to see you again."

Autumn grinned. "I was hoping you'd get my message."

"It was a surprise, but a good one."

"Well, Jenn wanted to call and invite you, but she has this weird idea that girls shouldn't call boys."

Jenny sputtered a laugh. "Autumn! I did not say that."

"I've ceased being surprised by anything Autumn says or gets up to," Brian said.

I glanced at Jenny and winked. "You have permission to call this boy anytime you want."

She put her hand on my thigh. "Good to know."

I liked the way her cheeks pinked in a cute little blush. I also liked the feeling of her hand on my leg, and when she removed it, I reached for her hand and put it back. She ducked her head, but I caught the pleased smile on her face.

"So, Dylan, when you going to come by and trade in that boy-toy car of yours for one of the best rides on the road? I can have you in a Lexus GS or LS in less than an hour."

"When Jenny trades hers in, I will."

Jenny shook her head. "So not happening."

I gave Brian a shrug. "Guess that answers your question."

"Speaking of cars, Stephanie's Mercedes is at my dealership until the insurance adjuster comes to look at it. After that, it'll go to the junkyard," Brian said. "After seeing it, it's hard to believe anyone survived."

"Why your place? I would have thought it would go to the Mercedes dealership."

"I'm the closest, and the car's not salvageable, so it didn't matter where it went."

"Do me a favor and take some pictures of it from all sides. I took some at the scene, but I'd like some in full daylight."

"Done." Brian took out his phone. "Give me your e-mail, and I'll send them over to you tomorrow."

"You must think our little town is nuts considering what's happened this past week," Autumn said after I gave him my addy. "Usually the most exciting thing going on around here is when someone stumbles on another one of Hamburger Harry's stills."

"You're forgetting that I came from Chicago, where there are over five million calls to 911 a year. Believe me, my first weeks on the job have seemed tame compared to what I was used to. I'm actually looking forward to seeing one of Harry's infamous stills."

The more time I spent with them, the more I liked them. Autumn was a riot, and Brian was a man I could hang with on a Sunday afternoon, drinking a beer and watching a ball game. And then there was Jenny.

All through our meal, amid the laughter and good-natured teasing, I'd been aware of her, from her cinnamon-and-vanilla scent to the heat of her body. I'd pressed my leg against hers, keeping it there. Touching her both calmed and excited me, if that made sense.

What struck me, sitting in this booth with people whose company I truly enjoyed, was that I hadn't come here expecting to make friends right away. I especially hadn't expected or planned to meet a woman who would catch my interest the way Jenny had.

All I'd really wanted was to get the hell out of Chicago, where I hadn't been able to find peace of mind since Christine's death. I was beginning to believe I'd found my little slice of heaven here in the valley.

As we were walking out, my phone pinged with a text. "Sean Lamar has been downgraded from critical to serious," I said after reading it. I'd asked Tommy to keep me posted on Sean's condition. Turned out Tommy and Sean had been high school buddies, and Tommy had spent today at the hospital, keeping vigil with Sean's parents.

"That's great news," Jenny said.

Brian and Autumn headed to his car. I walked Jenny to hers. "Want to come over to my place?" Now that she was here in front of me, I didn't want to let her go.

She slid her hands up past my shoulders, wrapping them around my neck. "Have you ever spent an entire day with Autumn?"

"Can't say I have." I put my hands on her hips, pulling her against me.

"She's a force of nature. A whirlwind. An energy suck."

"I take it you're telling me you're tired?" I tried not to let my disappointment show.

"Dead on my feet. I'm sorry."

"Don't apologize." I kissed her, loving how she melted into me. We finally came up for air, and I put my hands on her shoulders, turning toward her car. "Go home and get some sleep, Red. I'll see you on Sunday, if not before." What I really wanted to do was take her home with me, and even if all I could do was watch her sleep, I'd be happy.

When she was inside her car, I tapped on the window. "Remember, you have permission to call this boy anytime you want."

Her eyes turned soft. "I just might do that."

I watched her taillights until they disappeared. As I approached my car, a black dog crawled out from under it. I'd never had a dog, so I was wary of them, especially one as big as this creature. He or she was pitifully thin, and I hoped it wouldn't come at me. The thing was blocking my car door, and I took a slow step back. The dog whined, then rolled over onto its back. Although I didn't know much about dogs, I recognized the submissive gesture and saw that it was female.

"Ah, hell." At the sound of my voice, the dog's tail swept back and forth across the pavement. I crouched and held out my hand. She flipped back over and stretched her neck, sniffed my fingers, then licked them.

"Ah, hell," I said again. No way I was going to be able to leave her here to starve or get run over. "Hey, girl." She scooted closer. I wasn't sure what breed she was, but she wasn't someone's lap dog. And she stank to high heaven.

I stood and opened my car door. She jumped in, parked herself on the passenger seat, and looked at me as if to say, *Let's go.*

"You're really not the girl I wanted to take home with me tonight," I told her. "The one I had in mind smells a lot better than you, let me tell you."

I would swear the dog's mouth lifted in a smirk.

Turned out she was a purebred Labrador retriever, and according to the animal doctor I'd taken her to the next morning, she was a dog that was as loyal to her owner as they came. "She's maybe a year old and has been on her own for at least a few months now, if not longer," the vet had said. "She's not wearing a chip, and I doubt you'll find her owner, if she ever had one."

When the veterinarian had offered to find her a home, I'd put a protective hand on her head. "Then I'll keep her." At hearing myself uttering those words, I decided that the mountain air had screwed with my brain. Back in Chicago, if I'd found a starving dog, I would have taken it straight to an animal shelter.

There in that sterile white room, the dog had grinned up at me as if I'd made her the happiest creature on the face of the earth with that statement. Apparently I was a sucker for mountain girls.

I'd left her at the vet's for the day to get a flea bath and whatever shots she needed. When I'd stopped by that afternoon to pick her up, you would have thought she had won the lottery the way she barked with joy at seeing me. I was kind of happy to see her, too, especially since she no longer stunk like last week's garbage.

I named the damn—always grinning—dog Daisy because daisies were cheerful flowers, so the name suited her. At home she'd stared morosely down at her empty bowl after chowing down, then lifted her black head and grinned hopefully at me. She could eat like there might not be a meal tomorrow, but I couldn't blame her. I didn't know how long she'd gone hungry, and I couldn't resist pouring a second helping of the food the vet had told me to give her.

"New police dog," I said the next day to each raised eyebrow I passed as Daisy trotted loyally next to me through the police department. The only person who had anything to say against her was Moody.

"The fuck a dog's doing here?" he said.

"My office. Now," I snapped.

When I sat at the chair behind my desk, Daisy parked herself with her back against the wall where she could see both Moody and me. Her chocolate-brown eyes were trained on him, and it was the first time since finding her that there wasn't a grin on her face. Smart dog.

I pulled an envelope out of my drawer and wrote his name on it, then turned it to face him. "Captain, this is your last warning. The next time you utter a curse word while on duty, you'll either put a hundred dollars in this envelope or face one day's unpaid suspension. Your choice."

He sneered. "What, you lining your pockets now at my expense?"

Ignoring him, I said, "The money will go to a local women's shelter." I leaned back in my chair, giving him a hard stare. "My patience only goes so far. You need to keep that in mind before you go spouting off your mouth again."

Later that night Daisy and I did an Internet search for local dog trainers. If she was going to hang around the department during the day, I wanted to make sure she behaved. There was only one that I could find in this area, and I called him, only to learn that he was booked up for two months. He said Daisy and I both would get one-on-one training, and I liked that. I gave him my name and contact information, and asked him to put us on his schedule.

The next day my detective and I were going to rescue Beauregard, the prized bull. "You know where we can borrow a truck and horse trailer?" I asked Gene.

"Yeah, why?"

"So we can take Beauregard home." I couldn't stop my smirk when his eyes widened.

"You know where he is?"

"Pretty sure I do."

It took him a few hours to return with the truck and trailer. "Where to, Chief?" he said after Daisy and I were loaded up, her in the back and me in the passenger seat.

"You know where Granny lives?" I thought Gene's eyes were going to pop out of his head.

"Hamburger's ma?"

"One and the same. Head for her place." I hoped I was right or I was going to look like a fool. Granny lived twelve miles from the Scroggins' farm, not too far a distance for a loose bull to roam. I didn't think so, anyway.

"Okay, here's the scoop," I said. "On the same day Beauregard went missing, two people on the path to Granny's called in a report of a bull in their yard, but by the time an officer arrived, there was no sign of any bull. Then the following day, Granny's closest neighbor, Clyde Anderson, complained about a bull trying to get to one of his cows. Anderson ran it off with his shotgun, firing over the bull's head."

"How did no one know this?"

"Hard to believe, but Moody apparently never connected Scroggins's Beauregard to the errant bull." *Errant* was definitely a good word for Beauregard. "Moody got the call, but the bull was gone by the time he arrived. A week later Anderson reported that he'd seen the same bull following Granny around like a puppy."

"And you know all this how?"

"Because I stumbled on Moody's report from Anderson, which he was either too lazy or too stupid to connect to Beauregard." I shouldn't be slamming one of my cops to another, but whatever. It wasn't like Gene didn't already know and agree with me. "Moody did go talk to Granny. According to what she told him, she'd raised the bull, and he took her at her word."

Gene snorted. "More like she promised him a lifetime supply of moonshine if he'd go away and forget what he saw."

"That occurred to me." Gene turned onto a rutted dirt road. Every tree in sight had a NO TRESPASSING sign on it. Underneath many of those signs were ones that said, TRESPASSERS WILL BE SHOT.

"Getting a little nervous here," I said, wondering if I was about to get in a shoot-out with a crazy old bull-stealing lady.

Gene laughed. "She'll have a shotgun pointed at us when we pull up, but she's not stupid enough to shoot the police chief and his detective." He eyed the dog poking her face between us. "New uniforms, raises, a police dog. Can't wait to see what you give us next."

My detective was trying to calm me down, so I decided to take him at his word that I didn't need to draw my gun. "Going to be hard to top all that," I said. "My bag of tricks might be empty."

He snorted. "Somehow I doubt that."

Since I was still working out the details, I decided not to mention the SWAT team I was considering creating. Even though we were a small town, there should be a team trained for hostage situations.

The lane we drove on was overgrown with weeds, some a good three feet tall. We went around a curve, passing bushes that probably hadn't been trimmed in years, if ever, and the house—cabin was more like it—came into view. The place was run-down and looked as if it could fall in around the inhabitants at any minute. An old refrigerator lay on its side in the yard, and a nasty-looking fabric couch was on the sagging porch.

"People actually live here?"

Gene nodded. "There are places like this all in these mountains. People who don't want to be bothered."

I had no intention of bothering any of them as long as they didn't break the law. Not a minute after we pulled up, Granny came around the side of the cabin, pointing an ancient shotgun at us, a big, black bull following her like a loyal puppy.

"That's Beauregard," Gene whispered reverently.

I prayed that Granny didn't shoot me.

CHAPTER TWENTY-SEVEN

~ *Jenny* ~

I HEARD THE NEWS FROM COUNCILMAN Freddie Barns, the first to arrive at Vincennes. Soon after the bar and restaurant were jam-packed, everyone wanting to get in on the latest big story. The gossip was flying, and who knew what was true and what wasn't? Until I heard it straight from Dylan, I'd take most of it with a grain of salt.

What was apparently true was that Dylan and Gene Lanier were hailed as heroes for finding Beauregard, now and forever after to be known as The Drifter. For six years, two families had hated each other for no good reason.

All the waitstaff were run haggard trying to keep up with orders, while Angelo worked in the kitchen, helping to get the food out. Apparently crazy bull stories made people hungry for pizzas, pasta, and beer. The bar was three-deep, and Angelo had called in Brandy from her day off to help me. At the end of the night my boss was grinning like a madman as he counted the day's receipts. I thought he wished bizarre things would happen every day.

We were an hour later than normal getting out for the night, but I'd racked up a week's worth of tips in six hours, so I wasn't complaining even though my back and feet were. My plan was to go straight home and luxuriate in a hot bubble bath, a glass of wine by my side. That changed when I walked out to my car to see Dylan leaning against it. Sitting at his feet was a skinny black dog.

"A friend of yours?" I asked, walking up to Dylan. He looked worn-out, and I had the crazy desire to sit on a sofa with his head in my lap while I soothed the tired lines from around his eyes.

He glanced down at the dog. "This is Daisy. Daisy, meet my friend, Jenny."

At the sound of her name, she looked adoringly up at him. I knelt. "Hello, Daisy. What a beautiful dog you are." She wagged her tail as she arched her neck, sniffing the fingers I held toward her. "Labrador?" I asked, peering up at Dylan.

"That's what the vet said."

"They're good dogs. I had one growing up." I scratched Daisy around her ears, and her eyes rolled back in ecstasy.

"Never had a dog before. She adopted me."

I stood. "Can't say I blame her. Hear you had an interesting day."

He chuckled. "That's putting it mildly." His gaze locked on mine. "Daisy and I came to invite you home with us. She thinks I need some TLC considering I spent the afternoon chasing an ornery bull."

I leaned forward and sniffed him. "You stink."

"You would too if you'd been wallowing around in manure. After delivering Beauregard the Bull back to his rightful owner, I spent the evening negotiating peace between the Hatfields and McCoys. Guess I should have taken the time to go home and shower first, but I didn't want to miss you."

I lifted onto my toes and kissed him, then wrinkled my nose. "Go home, take a nice hot shower, and I'll be at your place in about an hour. I need to run by my apartment, get the smell of pizza and garlic off, and grab some clothes."

"Thank you, Red." He took a step away, then paused. "If you…" He shook his head.

"If what?"

He hesitated before saying, "If you want, you can leave some things at my place. You know, some toiletries and spare clothes."

I blinked. That one had caught me by surprise. Did I want to do that? It felt like a step toward commitment. A part of me wanted to do a little dance because that would mean he wouldn't bring another woman to his apartment. The other part dinged warning bells in my head. Ones that said, *This is a man you could fall head over heels for. Can you take off for parts unknown if you do?*

"Forget I said that," he said when I hesitated.

"No can do now that it's out. I need to think about it, okay?"

He did pull me roughly into his arms and kissed the daylights out of me. "Think hard, Red."

With that, Blue Ridge Valley's stinky police chief and his new dog walked away, leaving me sucking air into my lungs. I still hadn't come to a decision by the time I pulled into my parking space. I wanted to take some things to his place and I didn't. No man had ever wormed his way into my head the way Dylan had, not even the jerkface who was leaning against my front door.

I sat in my car, staring at Chad. Why couldn't he just go away? Since the last thing I wanted was to get into another fight with him, I locked my doors, then called Dylan.

"Please don't say you're not coming over," he said on answering.

"Could you head to my place? I have unwanted company waiting for me."

"Your ex?"

"The one and only. I've locked myself in my car." The sound of a siren came through the phone.

"Be there in five. Don't get out of your car."

"Not going to," I said to dead air. There was something pretty cool about dating a cop who could come to your rescue with lights flashing and sirens blaring. *Oh, Chad, you stupid fool.*

I sat right where I was, and when he realized I wasn't getting out, he headed toward me. Grabbing my purse, I fished around in it until my fingers closed around my mace. As long as he didn't get crazy on me and break my window, I'd wait for Dylan to get here. If not, Chad was going to need an eye doctor. I'd never gotten around to filing a restraining order on him, but I'd correct that as soon as I saw Dylan.

Chad tapped on my window. "Jenn, can we just talk? I love you." He pulled on my door handle. "Please, unlock your door and talk to me."

I held up the mace. "I swear I'll spray you," I yelled.

He put his hands at the bottom of my window, his puppy-dog eyes pleading with me. "I messed up, baby. I know that. Just give me a chance to make it up to you."

I turned my radio up so loud that my car vibrated. That was probably why I didn't hear Dylan's car screech to a halt next to me. All of a sudden Dylan was there, forcing Chad away with nothing but his body. All I could think was wow, Dylan hadn't even laid a hand on Chad yet was herding him out of my sight.

"Tell him as of right now, there's a restraining order filed against him," I called to Dylan after I rolled down my window.

"You heard the lady," Dylan said as he pushed Chad to the back of my car.

I looked in my rearview window, seeing that they were having a heated conversation. I really didn't care what was being said between them. While their attention was on each other, I slipped out of my car and ran into my apartment. I had a moment of thinking I should just lock my door to men in general. But no, Dylan needed some TLC tonight. And not only that, I tossed some toiletries and some extra clothes into a tote to leave at his place.

I'd thought about it on the drive over, deciding that

leaving some stuff at his place was simply a matter of convenience. It didn't mean that when it was time to leave, I would hesitate to do so. With that clear in my mind, I stepped out of my apartment after a quick shower and change of clothes, a canvas bag in my hand.

"Oh, I thought you two would have headed home by now," I said at seeing Dylan and Daisy waiting outside my door as if they were standing guard.

Dylan threw an arm around my shoulder. "He won't bother you again."

I believed him, unless Chad was stupider than I thought. Dylan and Daisy walked me to Dylan's Mustang, one on either side of me as if both were protecting me. When I tried to head for my car, Dylan herded me toward his.

"I'll bring you home in the morning, okay?"

I shrugged. "Sure."

He took my tote from me. "Does this have girlie things in it?"

"You mean like things I might leave at your place?"

"Yes, Red. That's what I mean."

"Maybe." Why not? I could take them back as easily as I brought them.

Suddenly his mouth was on mine. I guess that answer made him happy. He sucked my bottom lip into his mouth, and at my soft moan, he pulled away.

"Let's go home."

I liked the way that sounded a little too much.

He opened the door. "In the back, Daisy," he said when the dog jumped onto the passenger seat.

The dog gave me a baleful look before scrambling between the seats. "Poor Daisy. Did I steal your place?"

"She'll get over it." Dylan reached back and gave the dog's head a pat. "Looked like you were busy tonight. When I pulled in, the parking lot was packed."

I was glad he'd brought it up since I was dying of curiosity. "Everyone wanted to either hear the gossip about Beauregard, or they wanted to be the one to tell what they'd heard. Seems you and your detective are heroes for finding him. That's what they're all saying, anyway."

Dylan laughed. "Beauregard doesn't think so. He's head over heels in love with Granny. Wasn't real happy about being taken away from her."

"Did she know the bull was the missing Beauregard? It was common knowledge when he disappeared that Mr. Scroggins accused Roland of taking him. I can't see how she didn't hear anything about it."

"To quote Granny when I asked that exact question, 'I ain't knowed nothing about it. The bull showed up one day 'n' stayed.' Then she crossed her arms over her chest and glared at me, saying around the corncob pipe in her mouth, 'I'm a law-uring up now, sonny boy, so dontcha be asking me no more questions.' So I didn't. If she wasn't admitting to anything, what was I going to do? Throw her in jail? The entire town probably would've turned on me."

Dylan grinned at me when I laughed. "They likely would have because that would have upset Hamburger, and we can't have our moonshiner unhappy."

"God forbid. Then all y'all would have been asking, who shot the sheriff?"

"You said 'y'all.' We'll make a southern boy out of you yet."

He winked. "After the time I spent with Granny and Old Man Scroggins today, I can y'all with the best of them."

"So all's good and peace has been restored in the valley?" At his nod, I put my hand on his thigh. "It was a nice surprise to see you waiting for me."

"I just wanted to be with you tonight, Red. Even if all we do is hold each other."

How was I supposed to guard my heart when he said things like that?

As soon as we got inside his apartment, I sent him to take a shower. I doubted he'd had a chance to eat dinner, so I rummaged in his fridge, looking for something I could make for him.

"Ah-ha," I said to Daisy at finding cheese and bacon. In the pantry I found a loaf of sourdough bread. "Perfect."

When Dylan walked into the kitchen, I glanced over to tell him to sit down at the counter. The words died on my lips.

He had on a pair of black lounge pants that rode low on his hips and nothing else, leaving his beautiful chest on full display. My fingers tingled, wanting to touch him, to explore every inch of his incredible body.

"Ah...I've made you a little something to eat. Figured with everything going on today that you probably didn't have time to grab something."

A slow smile curved his lips. "Is this the beginning of my TLC?"

"Could be. Sit." Daisy eyed him as if she wanted to go to him—not that I blamed her—but I had bacon that I'd been feeding her little bites of. The bacon won out.

He slid onto the bar stool. "You didn't have to cook for me."

"Wanted to." I cut the grilled cheese and bacon sandwich in half, piled some chips on the plate and put it in front of him. "Beer?"

He wrapped his hand around my wrist, pulling me to him. "That would be my second choice."

"What would be your first?" I asked even though I saw the answer in his eyes. He slowly slid his hand up my arm, and after spreading his fingers around the back of my neck, he pulled me to him.

"You," he whispered. His mouth covered mine, teasing me with little flicks of his tongue over my lips.

I couldn't resist any longer. I had to touch him, and

I trailed the tips of my fingers across his chest and ribs, marveling at the smoothness of his skin over all those muscles. He slipped one hand under the back of my shirt, and as he kissed me, he stroked along the curve of my spine. His other hand fisted my hair, keeping me right where he wanted me.

A wet nose pushed against my knee, making me laugh. "Someone's jealous." I stepped away. It was either that or climb right on top of him. The only reason I didn't—and I didn't think he'd mind at all—was because he'd had a long, exhausting day, and he really did need something in his stomach.

I grabbed a bottle of beer from his fridge and opened it. "Here you go." After giving it to him, I opened another one and sat across from him.

He picked up one of the sandwich halves. "You're not eating?"

"Had a couple of slices of pizza while I was working." Since I was coming straight to Dylan's, I had changed into a pair of lightweight sweatpants, and a long-sleeve cotton top with five buttons that I'd left undone. I hadn't bothered putting on a bra since I was sure it'd come right back off soon.

As Dylan ate, his gaze kept landing on the exposed flesh where my shirt parted at the top. The man wasn't only hungry to fill his belly. I could see that in the way his eyes devoured me. He tore off a small piece of crust, tossing it in the air. Daisy deftly snapped it up.

I tsked. "You're going to spoil her." Never mind that I'd been sneaking her bacon.

"Maybe she deserves a little spoiling." He studied the dog looking back at him with pure adoration. "I don't think she's led a charmed life."

That was obvious by the ribs showing through her skin. It wouldn't be long before she fattened up under Dylan's care. In the short time I'd known him, I had already learned that he was a giver, taking care of those he felt responsible for. He'd told me how he'd convinced the town council and mayor to approve new uniforms and raises for his officers. Whenever Chad had shown up, causing me trouble, Dylan had been there for me, making sure I stayed safe. Who had taken care of him?

He finished the last bite of his grilled cheese, and I took the plate to the sink. After tossing the two beer bottles in the trash, I crooked my finger. "Follow me." As I walked down the hall toward his bedroom, I heard the soft pad of his bare feet and the clicks of Daisy's toenails on the wood floor.

"What are you up to, Red?"

He was only inches behind me, and his warm breath tickled the hair on my neck. "Just a little TLC, Chief." I glanced over my shoulder. "Tonight I'm going to take care of you." Because someone should, and I wanted that someone to be me.

CHAPTER TWENTY-EIGHT

~ *Dylan* ~

I don't know why Jenny's words touched something deep inside of me. Without asking what I wanted or needed, she'd known. She'd sent me straight to the shower so I could get the stink of a bull off. I had turned the shower on as hot as I could stand it, letting the heat and water cleanse me. Feeling somewhat better, I'd walked into the kitchen to find that she had the perfect meal waiting for me. Now I was following her to my bedroom, so she could take care of me. Whatever that meant. Sex, hopefully.

When I'd left the station, it had been with the intention to go straight home, take a shower, and then fall into bed. Wrestling bulls was hard work, and I was dead tired. Without even thinking about it, though, I'd made a detour to Vincennes, hoping I could talk her into coming home with me. I'd wanted to tell her about my day with Beauregard the Bull, then spoon my body around hers while I slept.

My gaze roamed over her back and ass, and I chuckled at the part of me that was making itself known, protesting the idea of doing nothing but holding her. Stepping next to her, I tucked her hair behind her ear for no other reason than I wanted to touch her. "Thank you," I said softly.

"For?"

"For being here with me tonight, and for the best grilled cheese sandwich I've ever had."

Her eyes turned soft as she smiled. "You're welcome."

Daisy whined, begging for attention. I'd forgotten I had

a dog. "Get in your bed, Daisy." I walked over to the large dog bed I'd bought yesterday. Had it only been yesterday? It seemed like a hundred years ago. She'd wanted to get in bed with me after I'd brought her home, but that was one thing I was going to put my foot down about. She gave me a baleful look but stepped onto the bed, making a few circles before settling down to work on her dog bone chew.

"Good girl." I turned to go back to Jenny and stilled. She'd taken off her top and stood at the edge of my bed, crooking her finger at me the way she'd done in the kitchen when she'd told me to follow her. Her lips curved into a smirk, telling me she was fully aware of what she was doing to me.

I walked toward her, my eyes locked on hers. I reached for her, needing to touch those breasts that were calling to me.

She shook her head. "Not yet. Get in bed. On your stomach."

"Have I told you that I like this bossy side of you?"

"I'm real good at bossy. In the bed, Dylan."

"Yes, ma'am." I wasn't sure what she was up to, but I was definitely curious to find out. "Can I take my pants off?"

"Not yet." She pointed. "Bed."

I did as ordered. She picked up a bottle of lotion from the bedside table that she must have put there while I was in the shower. "Am I about to get a massage?"

"You are." She straddled my back. "Did you know I'm a licensed massage therapist?"

"Can't say I did." I glanced back at her and came close to flipping over and putting my mouth on one of those beautiful breasts. "Were you a topless masseuse? Because if you were and I'd known…ah, that feels good."

"No, silly man. You're my first topless massage. What's this?" She pressed her fingers to my side. "You have a big bruise here."

"Courtesy of one pissed-off bull. I'm pretty sure he aimed to kill me, but Granny grabbed his nose with her fist and walked the damn thing right into the trailer."

"Didn't Gene go out with you? Where was he?"

"Up a tree where Granny's hound dogs had chased him."

Her hands stilled. "You're kidding, right?"

"Red, I couldn't make this shit up if I tried." She laughed so hard that she fell over onto the bed.

I turned onto my side, grinning at her. All afternoon I'd held in my amusement at the entire situation. Granny glaring at me with her pipe sticking out of her mouth because I'd come to take her pet bull, Gene hanging from a tree limb, pants torn, as three flea-bitten hounds tried to climb up after him, and then to top it all off, Hamburger showing up, trying to bribe me with moonshine. A lifetime's supply in exchange for not taking away Granny's bull.

I couldn't hold it in any longer, and Jenny and I laughed until tears poured from our eyes. "I got Mr. Scroggins to agree to let Granny visit Beauregard twice a week," I said when I could speak again.

"Visiting hours for a bull. That's hilarious." She giggled. "On the plus side, if he goes missing again, you'll know right where to find him."

"True."

"You're a good man, Dylan Conrad. Now roll over again so I can make you feel better."

The massage was sigh-inducing pleasurable, and my eyes drifted closed. When she was done, I planned to thoroughly show my masseuse my appreciation for all that she'd done for me tonight.

Sunlight lasered bright beams right through my eyelids.

I blinked my eyes open and stared at the ceiling fan blades circling slowly overhead for a moment. The last thing I remembered was Jenny straddling my back, her clever fingers soothing my aching muscles.

I was embarrassed that I'd conked out on her last night. Turning on my side, I faced her. She was on her stomach, her beautiful red hair hiding her face. The cover was pushed down to her waist, and I lifted it to see if she'd left her pant bottoms on. No, she hadn't, but I saw the thin waistband of her thong. The sight of her perfect bottom was all it took to wake up the little man.

Jenny wasn't a morning person. She slept hard, so I didn't worry about waking her as I kicked off my pajama bottoms, then dug out a condom from my nightstand and put it on. There was nothing better than lazy morning sex, and no better way to wake up Jenny Girl.

I pressed my body against hers, nuzzling her neck and smiling into her hair at hearing her sigh. She grumbled something when my hand traced the shape of her back and ass. "Grouchy girl," I murmured.

She snuggled her face into her pillow. "Mawh wah."

"Is that so?" I slipped my fingers between her legs and then inside her panties. It only took a few minutes of playing with her before she was wet and ready. She turned her face toward me, peeking at me with one eye half open.

"You got something in mind this morning, Dylan?"

"I sure do. Panties off." She lifted her sexy ass so I could pull them down. "Sorry I fell asleep on you last night."

She gave me a sleepy smile. "That's okay. I think you're about to make it up to me."

"I'm going to do my best. Turn over on your side with your back to me." She pushed her body against me, and I put my hand on her hip as I slid into her. "I wish you could be me for a few minutes so you'd know how good it feels to be inside you."

"I don't think it could possibly be better than how I'm feeling."

Maybe, but I didn't think so. She took my hand and moved it to her breast. I buried my face against her neck and breathed in her scent as I made love to her. There was no rush to reach the end, no need for hard and fast. That was what I loved about morning sex, the softness of it.

"Dylan," she whispered.

That was it, just my name spoken softly as she came. It was sexy as hell, and I let go, climaxing with her. I kissed her neck, holding her close. She fell back to sleep, and lying there next to her, I wondered if I liked her in my bed a little too much. She had plans that didn't include me, and I didn't want to be left behind, missing her. One woman I'd loved had already left me, and I had no desire to lose another.

The trick was to not fall in love with Jenny, and I'd thought I could guard my heart against that happening. Now I wasn't so sure I could do that if I kept seeing her.

Disturbed by my thoughts, I slipped out of bed. After dressing, I took Daisy for a long walk. I honestly didn't know what I wanted to do about Jenny. I liked being with her. She was funny and caring, and then there was the sex. We were good together, whether we were going at it like frenzied got-to-have-it-right-now bunnies or like the sensual half-asleep coupling this morning.

"What should I do, Daisy?" She paused in sniffing a bush to look up at me, gave me what appeared to be a doggie shrug, then went back to sniffing things that were more interesting than my girl problems.

We were on a nature path that circled my complex. It took a good twenty minutes to walk it, and we were five minutes from making it back to where we'd started when Daisy growled. Her fur rose in a razor-sharp line down her back, and she stepped in front of me, forcing me to stop.

"What's wrong, girl?" The dog's behavior was scaring me, and I regretted that I hadn't brought my gun with me. I wouldn't make that mistake again. Daisy let out another growl as she pushed against me, forcing me to step back.

Then I heard it. A sinister *shhhhhhhhhh* sound, something like dried beans being furiously shaken in a paper cup. The leaves in the path two feet from where we'd been moved, and the pointed head of a snake lifted, his tongue flickering in the air. Behind him his tail rose, the rattlers making their get-away-from-me-or-you'll-die warning. The middle part of the body was still hidden by the leaves, but the head was large and it looked to me like it was a big, full-grown bastard.

"Fuck me," I whispered. Daisy pushed me back again, and I gladly let her. Two more steps and I would have gotten way more up close and personal with a snake than I ever wanted to be. Having grown up in a big city, the only snakes I'd ever seen had been in a zoo behind glass. I hadn't even liked them then, and I sure as hell didn't like having a close encounter with one.

Daisy and I kept backing away. The snake slithered out from under the leaves, and I estimated it to be a good four to five feet long. It disappeared into the brush, leaving me with a pounding heart. As soon as it was gone, Daisy started back down the path. I debated going back the way we'd come, but we were almost to the end. Daisy didn't seem concerned, so I'd trust her instincts, especially since she'd kept me from ending up in the hospital.

"Good girl, Daisy." I scratched around her ears, where she loved it the most, making her feathery tail wag. We finished our walk with no further deadly encounters. As we emerged from the woods, I looked up to see Jenny standing on my balcony, watching us. She smiled and waved, and all I could think about was getting her back into bed.

"A timber rattler," Gene Lanier said. "They're common in this area."

We were sitting in my office that afternoon, going over the Gertie Jansen case. I'd told him about my early morning encounter, and didn't at all like hearing timber rattlers were common. Daisy and I liked that path, but I didn't care for meeting up with another snake.

"All I know is that's the last time I'll walk in the woods without my gun." I glanced at Daisy, curled up in her dog bed in the corner of my office. She was my hero of the day, and I'd given her extra treats when we'd gotten inside my place, and then I'd sweet-talked Jenny back into bed.

"People don't usually smile when talking about rattlesnakes, Chief."

Thinking of loving on Jenny tended to make me smile, but I wasn't about to share that. "So you don't think the prosecutor's going to press charges against Gertie?" I hoped not.

"That's the vibe I'm getting." Gene stood and closed the door. "Moody's raising all kinds of stink about Gertie not already being in jail."

"Screw Moody. He's in my doghouse for too many things to count."

"I stopped by Gertie's on my way home last night," Gene said. "The guilt of what she did is eating her up."

"The man about killed her. She was justified in doing what she had to do to protect herself." From what we'd learned, Jansen had beat on his wife on a regular basis. I'd seen too many battered women in my line of work who'd lost their lives because they'd let a man treat them like a punching bag. As far as I was concerned, good for Gertie Jansen.

"I've made an appointment for her with a therapist who specializes in helping battered women. My wife's taking her this afternoon."

"You're a good man, Gene." Truthfully, other than Jansen and Moody, I had a pretty damn good police force. Jansen's fate I wouldn't have wished for, but I planned to do whatever I could to see that his wife stayed out of prison and got the help she needed.

Gene shrugged as if he'd not done anything out of the ordinary. "She was my babysitter, so I've known her a long time. She should have left Jansen years ago."

"Unfortunately that's too often the case where battered women are concerned."

"Sadly true. At least we settled a long-running dispute yesterday, so not every situation turns out to be tragic."

I eyed him with a smirk. "I was pretty impressed with your tree-climbing skills."

His cheeks turned pink. "How much to keep that to yourself, Chief?"

"There's not enough money in the world." I chuckled when he narrowed his eyes. "Besides, Hamburger Harry and Granny witnessed your ass hanging out of your torn pants, so it's not just me you have to worry about." I had no intention of repeating the story—other than to Jenny, and I trusted her not to spread it around.

"Won't matter if you do." He let out a sigh. "Hamburger's a storyteller. He's probably already put his own spin on it and telling anyone who'll listen."

"Well, if it makes you feel any better, no one will hear it from me. If those dogs had come after me, I would've been up that tree with you."

My phone buzzed, Kim Payton's name coming up on the screen. The information my officer gave me wasn't surprising. "Stephanie Jenkins tested twice the legal limit," I told Gene after disconnecting.

"I figured she would. How do you want to handle it?"

This was the touchiest of the situations we had going

on. "We're going to have to charge her with a DUI, of course. Let me talk to the mayor first, tell him what's going to happen." Jim John definitely wasn't going to be happy.

What I'd rather do was find Jenny, take her back to my place, and lock the door against the world for at least a week. Even that wouldn't be enough time with her, though. Gene left, and I swiveled my chair to face the window, my gaze on the mountains rising up behind the town. I loved it here, wanted to make a home here, a wife, kids, all that jazz.

If Jenny weren't leaving soon, I'd want to explore that possibility with her. But she was, and already there was going to be a small hole in my heart that she was going to leave behind. I think if I asked her to stay, she would consider it, but I wouldn't. If she did, a year from now, ten years, or twenty, she'd regret not following her dream. Nor would I tell her I'd wait for her. She needed to go, free of any baggage. If she met someone on her travels and fell in love, I wouldn't have her feeling guilty over me.

I had two choices. Stop seeing her or make sure I guarded my heart. Since I didn't want to stop seeing her, guard my heart it was.

CHAPTER TWENTY-NINE

~ Jenny ~

I LICKED MY CANDIED APPLE, GLANCING up when Dylan groaned. "What?"

"It's the way you close your eyes when your tongue slips out and licks that thing." He leaned his mouth to my ear. "Puts dirty pictures in my mind."

"Men." I rolled my eyes.

He chuckled, bumping my shoulder. "We can't help ourselves."

We were at our town's annual Christmas Festival. Every year on the last weekend in November, we blocked off the main street of town. Artisans and food vendors set up tents, and the merchants decorated their storefronts for the Christmas season. We kicked it off on Saturday morning with a parade, which delivered Santa to his throne, and ended the festivities Sunday night by lighting the large tree in front of town hall.

Usually it was cold and everyone would be bundled up, drinking hot cider. But not this year. We'd only reached sweater weather temps. A cold front was headed our way, though, and I looked forward to it finally feeling like Christmas.

We drew thousands to the event, some from as far away as Georgia, Tennessee, and South Carolina. Dylan had been the officer in charge yesterday, but today he was playing tourist. Even so, his eyes were constantly scanning the crowd, watching for trouble. We'd been doing the festival for twenty-three years now and had never had a problem.

I guess his Chicago cop's mind was used to always being on alert.

We crossed paths with one of his officers, and Dylan stopped to talk to him. I'd eaten my candied apple down to the core and looked around for a garbage can. My gaze fell on a man standing at the corner of a nearby tent, staring at Dylan. Something about the expression on his face caught my attention. My first thought was, if looks could kill… Disturbed by the hatred I saw in the man's eyes, I tugged on Dylan's sleeve.

I glanced up at him. "Do you know that guy over there?"

"Where?"

When I turned back, the man was gone. I shrugged, figuring I'd imagined he was glaring at Dylan in particular. "He's gone. Let's go see how much money Autumn talked Brian into spending on that carved herd of horses." They'd come with us but had stopped to talk to an artist about doing a special-order wood piece for their new home. Still disturbed by what I might or might not have seen, I kept my eye out for the man but didn't see him again. It had to have been my imagination.

Spending the day at Dylan's side, seeing him at work even when he wasn't supposed to be working, gave me new insights into the man. It seemed he'd already learned the names of most of Blue Ridge Valley's residents, and he stopped to talk to each one when we came across them, asking about their kids or grandchildren or even their dog.

Everyone had apparently heard about Daisy, the new police dog, and wanted to know where she was. Unsure how she'd react to crowds, Dylan had left her home. That seemed to be a disappointment to all those wanting to meet her.

It was obvious that the town loved their new police chief. As for me being with him, I was getting mixed reactions. No one said anything, but I was good at reading people's faces. By the stink eye the single women gave me, they didn't like that he'd been claimed. I didn't blame them. What they didn't know was that they'd have their chance with him once I was gone. That made me want to gouge their eyes out.

"How do you already know everyone's names and stuff about them?" I asked after a while.

He slung an arm around my shoulder, tugging me closer. "Homework, Red. I've done my homework."

"Well, I for one am impressed."

"Come over tonight after you get off, and I'll really impress you." He peered down at me and waggled his eyebrows, making me laugh.

Too soon it was time for me to go home and get ready to go to work. Dylan walked me to my car, as I'd driven so he could stick around and keep an eye on things. He backed me up to the door, then gave me a searing kiss.

"Will I see you tonight?" he asked when we came up for air.

I put my hand on his jaw. "Looking forward to it."

He pressed his face against my palm. "Not as much as me."

I walked out of Dylan's shower, wearing nothing but a towel. He wasn't in the bedroom, so I went looking for my sexy man. I found him in the living room, sitting in a leather chair, wearing nothing but the black lounge pants I loved on him.

"Come here, Red."

"Give me one good reason."

He cocked a brow, spread his legs, and pointed between them.

I cocked a brow right back at him. "Are you saying

there's something between your legs I might be interested in?"

He smirked. "I think you already know the answer to that."

Truth. I walked halfway to him, then stopped and dropped the towel, swallowing my own smirk when his breath hitched. Power over a man was a heady thing, and right now, based on how hard he was gripping the arms of his chair and by the heat shimmering in his eyes, I had the power.

"Jenny Girl," he murmured when I stepped between his legs.

He put his hands on my thighs, pressing his fingers into my skin. His touch, the heat seeping into my pores where Dylan's palms pressed against me, the way he looked at me... All of it almost brought me to my knees. I didn't love him. I didn't.

How many times had I told myself there wasn't a man in the world who could keep me from making Natalie's and my dream come true? Not even this man. I did not love him. But I could someday. If he was still around when I came back.

Words tumbled from my mind to the back of my teeth, words that would beg him to wait for me. I somehow managed to stop them. It wouldn't be fair to ask such a thing from this beautiful man who deserved more than a promise that I'd return to him someday.

Dylan couldn't know that all he'd probably have to do to get me to stay was ask. I blinked away the tears that were burning my eyes, forcing a smile. "Is that a gun in your pocket, or are you just happy to see me?" I said, doing my best to imitate Mae West's voice in whatever that movie was I'd watched with Autumn.

"It's definitely not a gun." Dylan pulled me onto his lap. "Did you have fun today?"

"Yes." He settled one hand under my hair on the back of my neck while his fingers caressed my breasts, moving from one to the other. It was impossible to think when he touched me like that. I settled against him, resting my head on his shoulder.

His eyes deepened to a dark, shimmering brown. "You're so damn gorgeous, Jenny Girl."

"You're not so bad yourself, Chief."

He leaned toward me, melding our mouths.

His kiss was hot and possessive, and after a few minutes he pulled away, staring at me. It seemed as if he wanted to say something, but then he gave a little shake of his head before standing with me still in his arms. He carried me into his bedroom and made the sweetest love to me, as if I were a precious treasure.

When he fell asleep, I lay there, listening to him breathe. Although I rarely allowed myself to think of the night Natalie died, I let the memory come back. I needed to do it to strengthen my resolve to keep my promise to her.

I knew the end was close, and I spent every second with my twin. I'd crawl in bed with her at night and hold her in my arms. Sometimes we'd cry, other times we'd talk of our dream to travel as soon as she was well. Although I knew better, I desperately wanted her to believe she would. To have hope for a future.

"When we get to Scotland, I want to sneak into a haunted castle," I said one night, snuggling in bed with her.

"Who's haunting it?" she asked.

"A sexy, kilt-wearing Highlander lost in time, trying to find his lover. He stands on the castle wall every evening playing his sad song on his bagpipes, hoping she will hear and come to him." I held a cup of hot chocolate to her lips, letting her sip. "The minute he sees you, though, he'll forget all about her."

She laughed, then began to choke. I scooted behind her

and massaged her back and shoulders. I'd gotten certified soon after we'd learned she was sick so I would know how to ease the pain in her failing body with soothing massages. "Take a deep breath," I whispered, moving my hands to her head and neck.

"Maybe we can be ghosts together, him and I."

I squeezed my eyes shut against the burn of tears. "No, he's going to take you back in time with him, where you'll become a hearty Highland lass."

"Jenn?"

"Yeah?" I didn't like the sadness I heard in her voice.

"Promise me you'll travel the world for me, see all the things we've talked about. Promise you'll make our dream come true."

I wrapped my arms around her, pulling her back against my chest. "I swear it, Nat. I'll make our dream come true if you'll promise you'll be with me."

"I swear it," she said. "We're a part of each other. No matter what happens, I'll always be with you. You'll feel my spirit with you in all those places you're going to go. I just know it."

My identical twin died that night in my arms. I'd made her a deathbed promise, one I had to keep because she'd promised in return that I'd feel her with me in all those places we were supposed to go together.

Vincennes was busy. Many of the tourists who'd come for the festival had stayed on for a few days. Naomi Reeves and Gloria Davenport were seated at the bar, having a glass of wine while waiting for a table. Naomi owned *The Valley News*, our town's little weekly newspaper. Mostly it was a gossip rag—who had dinner at the country club, who was getting married or divorced, who died. Gloria was Naomi's only reporter at-large. No bigger gossips existed east of the Mississippi River than those two.

"I hear you and the new police chief are an item," Gloria said when I refilled her wineglass.

Twenty years from now, Dylan would still be the *new* police chief. "We've gone out a few times." That was common knowledge, so no use denying it. I wasn't about to admit we were an item, or she'd have our wedding announcement in next week's paper. Gloria nor Naomi worried too much about whether the gossip they reported was true.

Gloria nudged Naomi's arm. "I got a good picture of them on Sunday. He had his arm around her, and she's looking up at him like a woman in love. It can be the lead-in to the festival recap."

Oh God. Just shoot me now. If I tried to talk them out of doing that, it would only make it worse. Leaving them to their plotting, I turned to greet the man sitting next to them.

"What… what can I get for you?" I hoped the man I'd seen staring at Dylan at the festival hadn't noticed my stutter. He leaned back on the stool and studied me. It made me feel like I was a bug under a microscope. There was something very off about him.

"Whatever you have on draft," he finally said.

"Sure, coming right up." The man was handsome—blond hair, blue eyes, built similar to Dylan—but I didn't like him. His eyes were cold, soulless, and they stayed on me as I filled his mug. He was seriously creeping me out. I put the beer in front of him, hoping he wasn't staying for dinner.

"What's your name?"

"Jenn." The last thing I wanted to do was tell him my name, but he hadn't actually done anything wrong.

"So, Jenn, you and Dylan Conrad? Are you his girlfriend?" He took a swallow of his beer, his eyes on me over the rim of the mug.

"What's it to you?" I took a step back, not liking this man at all.

Gloria leaned toward him. "They're an item. I have the pictures to prove it."

I shot her a death glare, but she was oblivious, lapping up the chance to dish out the latest gossip. I darted a glance around the bar and wanted to groan. Gloria didn't have a quiet voice, and our conversation had caught everyone's interest.

Naomi leaned her head around Gloria. "Do you know our new police chief?"

The man nodded, but his gaze stayed trained on me. I knew down to my bones that he was about to say something I didn't want to hear. And whatever it was, I especially didn't want Gloria and Naomi to hear it.

"He killed his wife, Jenn," he said before I could slap my hand over his mouth. "I'd advise you to be very, very careful where Dylan Conrad's concerned. I'd hate to see your pretty picture in the obits." With that, he put a ten on the counter, nodded to Gloria and Naomi, and then walked out.

Naomi and Gloria let out simultaneous gasps. "Biggest news story ever," Naomi gushed, almost falling off her stool as she twisted around to watch him leave. Then her gaze landed on me. "Who was that man?"

"A crazy person, that's who."

"Did he say our new police chief killed his wife?" someone farther down the bar said.

Naomi grabbed Gloria's arm. "This calls for a special edition."

"It's not true," I yelled as they raced away. Everyone at the bar was staring at me. "It's not true," I said again, as much for myself as for them.

I pushed away the whispering voice in my head that

asked me how well I knew Dylan. There was no way the man I'd seen fall apart when he'd told me about his wife had killed her.

Dylan needed to know what had happened here tonight. Like right now, before any more damage was done to his reputation. I went looking for Brandy.

"Tell Angelo I have the flu," I said when I found her, tossing the key to the liquor closet at her. I left without knowing or caring who'd cover the bar for me. I'd never walked out like this before, but I had to get to Dylan. If I got fired for leaving, so be it.

CHAPTER THIRTY

~ Dylan ~

"IS IT ME OR THE water you like?" I asked Daisy when she followed me into the shower. It was probably a little of both. The silly dog seemed to have fun catching the water, snapping at the drops as they fell on her face, but she also didn't like letting me out of her sight.

I'd hoped to see the mayor by now, but he'd gone out of town with his wife and Stephanie. They'd left Monday morning before I could talk to him to let him know we were going to arrest his daughter. Since he'd taken her with him, we were going to have to wait for them to come back to pick her up. He'd finally answered my text late this afternoon, letting me know they were returning sometime tonight and scheduling the meeting I'd requested for tomorrow morning. I wasn't looking forward to it.

My doorbell rang as I was drying off Daisy. "You expecting company, girl?" She gave an excited bark, running to the door, anticipating Jenny since she was the only one who ever came here. I slipped on a pair of jeans and a T-shirt, wondering who was showing up this time of night.

Jenny would still be at work, so I wasn't expecting her yet. But there she was, on the other side of my door when I opened it.

"Oh God, Dylan. Something awful happened."

My smile at seeing her died as she rushed by me. "Daisy, down." The dog loved Jenny almost as much as she did me.

"It's okay." She knelt. "Hey, girl. I'm happy to see you, too, but I have to talk to your daddy." After giving Daisy a good scratch behind her ears, she stood.

I tracked her movements as she paced my living room. "What's going on?" She stopped, facing me. When she started chewing on her bottom lip, I frowned. "Jenny?"

"You remember when I asked if you knew some man when we were at the festival?"

"Not really."

"Okay. See, there was this guy, and he was watching you. I thought it was weird because I got the impression he didn't like you. But then he disappeared and I decided I was imagining things."

"But you weren't?" I had no idea where she was going with this, but whatever it was, it had her upset.

"No, but I sure wish I had been." She twisted her fingers around each other.

"Come sit and tell me what this is all about." I took her hand, leading her to the sofa.

She sat, leaned forward, and put her hands over her face. "I don't know how to tell you this."

The hairs on the back of my neck tingled as my gut said this was something to do with me. Even so, I was at a loss as to what could have her so upset. "Jenny, just say it."

When she lifted her head, tears shimmered in her eyes. "The man I saw, he came into Vincennes tonight."

"What did he look like?" I feared I already knew the answer.

"Blond. Good-looking, but his blue eyes were like glaciers. Oh, and he had a small scar at the side of his right eye."

"Jack." Fucking Jack. The scar was from a gang member who'd taken exception at being arrested.

"He said… he said that you'd killed your wife. I know that's not true, but unfortunately Naomi and Gloria from *The Valley News* heard him, along with the people at the bar tonight. They're going to publish a special edition about you. I'm so sorry, Dylan."

Ice-cold arms wrapped around me. My heart stopped beating. I couldn't breathe.

"Dylan?"

The pity in Jenny's eyes was unbearable. I somehow managed to get my legs to work, walking out without a backward glance. Daisy managed to slip out before I could close the door on her. Whatever. I didn't have my car keys on me, so I just kept walking, Daisy trotting loyally by my side.

Why hadn't I anticipated Jack would show up to cause trouble? Daisy ran over to sniff around a tree at the edge of the complex's parking lot, and I stopped, absently watching her. Although Jack damn well knew I hadn't killed Christine, he blamed me for driving her to take her own life. The tension between us had grown to the point where I knew we could no longer work together. Needing a fresh start—not to mention getting away from my former best friend before I crossed an unforgivable line—I'd put feelers out and learned about the opening for a police chief in Blue Ridge Valley. I hadn't expected to like it as much here as I did, and now he was going to take that away from me, too.

"Dylan?"

I closed my eyes at hearing Jenny's voice. She was just another thing I was going to lose. Maybe I wasn't meant to be happy. "You should probably go home, Red. I'm not good company right now."

"You have to fight this. You can't stand by and do nothing while he spreads lies about you," she said, ignoring me. "Why would he say such a horrible thing?"

Stubborn girl. I'd finally put Christine's ghost to rest, and the last thing I wanted to do was talk about her to the woman I was falling for. That Jenny put such trust in me, refusing to believe Jack without even knowing the truth, put a lump in my throat the size of a baseball. She deserved an explanation whether I wanted to talk about it or not.

Daisy rushed to the next tree, and I followed her with Jenny close to my side. One thing Jenny apparently had was patience. She didn't say another word, simply waited me out. I slid my hands into my front pockets and looked up at the sky. It was a clear night, much like the one when Jenny had taken me to the top of that mountain to stargaze.

I let out a weary sigh, tired of all the shit in my life. There was enough money in my bank account to last a few years without touching Christine's money. Maybe I should become a beach bum. Find a run-down bar on a lonely beach somewhere to buy where I could listen to people with sadder stories than mine. And now I was feeling sorry for my pathetic self, and I hated that I'd let things come to this. I should have settled this thing with Jack long before now.

I glanced at Jenny, still waiting for me to talk. She had her arms wrapped around herself. "You're cold." We'd both walked out without our jackets. "Let's go in, and I'll tell you my sad story."

Back inside, Jenny wanted to shower and change before we talked. "I smell like pizza," she said. She lifted onto her toes, brushing her lips over mine. "Why don't you pour us a glass of wine, or something stronger if you prefer."

If I started on something stronger, I might not stop, so wine it was. While I waited for her, I called my—and Jack's—old boss. "It's Dylan," I said when Garrett answered.

"You shithead. Took you long enough to check in. How's Nowhere, USA?"

Garrett Caulder rode his cops hard, demanding they give their best to the job. There wasn't a man on the force who didn't both despise and love him at the same time. He could make you feel like dirt on the bottom of his shoes if you screwed up, but you never doubted he had your back. I'd become a damn good cop under his tutelage.

"You just gonna breathe in my ear all night, Conrad? It's kind of hot, but since you don't dance to my tune, I'm thinking you're not trying to turn me on."

I sputtered a laugh. "It's great here, or it was until Jack showed up."

"Fuck me."

"No thanks, but yeah, the situation isn't good." I told him what had happened.

"Jack put in for vacation, said he was going to Montana to visit his family."

"This isn't Montana, yet here he is." I pulled the stopper out of an already opened bottle of wine.

"He's been obsessed with you since...well, since everything went down. He'll talk smack about you to anyone who'll listen, but we all know the truth."

"I wasn't sure I'd ever be at peace again, but I was finding it in my little corner of the world—"

"Dylan, you gotta take the bull by the horns on this one, you understand?"

"Not really, unless you mean I should put him out of his misery." Rumors had a way of taking on a life of their own, and considering everyone sitting at the bar had heard Jack's accusation, talk of me killing my wife would spread through these mountains like wildfire.

Garrett gave that booming laugh of his. "Tempting I'm sure, but no. Okay, my brilliant mind has been at work while you were talking, and here's what we're gonna do. First thing tomorrow, sit down with that mayor you introduced me to when he was here and tell him what happened. Get him to agree to hold a town hall, where you're going to tell your story to the good people of Blue Ridge Valley."

"You know I don't like talking about Christine."

"Then you'd better start looking for another job."

"Fine. I don't see that I have a choice."

"That's right. Besides I'm flying down to stand by your side and back up everything you say."

I swallowed past the lump in my throat. Even when I didn't work for him any longer, he had my back. "You don't have to do that."

"When have you known me to do anything I didn't want to do?"

Never. "Thanks. I'll owe you big."

"Shut up, Dylan, before you make me cry."

I laughed, something I hadn't expected to do tonight. "That'll be the day. One other thing. Is Jack still driving the same car?" I doubted he would have flown down, not wanting to go through all the red tape to carry his gun aboard a plane. And I knew he wouldn't come here unarmed.

"Yeah. I'll e-mail you the license number and my flight info when I have it."

"Thanks. For everything."

"I got your back, Dylan. Always have."

"Never doubted it." I hung up as Jenny walked into the kitchen, her wet hair curling around her face and flowing down her back. Christ, she was beautiful. Instead of cutting myself open for her, spilling my guts, I should be in bed, holding her in my arms, lost in her sweet body.

She scooted onto the stool at the kitchen counter, pulling the glass of wine I'd poured toward her. I'd drunk one glass while I was on the phone with Garrett and was on my second. Maybe I should have gone for the hard stuff.

"What happened with your wife, Dylan?"

I drained the rest of my wine, then set the glass on the counter. "Long story short, I came home from a business trip a day early and found Christine in bed with my partner, Jack." I'd expected to see shock on her face, but all I got was a nod.

"I thought it might be something like that. I can't imagine how you must have felt to be betrayed by both your wife and your partner."

I'd felt like my heart had been carved out of my chest with a dull razor blade, that was how.

"Were you and Jack close before that happened?"

"Like brothers." I'd lost my wife and my best friend that day.

"I assume he was in love with her, otherwise he wouldn't be here trying to make your life miserable."

"He says he was. I told her I wanted a divorce, but she begged me to stay with her, said she loved me and couldn't live without me. I just didn't realize she meant that literally."

"Did he know she didn't want a divorce?"

Telling Jenny all this wasn't turning out to be as difficult as I'd thought it would be. It was because of her, though, the way she understood and saw things, along with how she didn't dramatize what she was hearing. I moved to the counter, pulling a stool around so that I was facing her.

"I don't know what Christine told him, but I'm guessing not. I tried to tell him after… you know, after she did what she did, but he called me a liar. After that I didn't bother trying to repair the damage to our relationship. It eventually became clear that one of us was going to have to leave, and I decided a change would be good for me. So here I am."

I didn't tell her about the childish games Jack had played afterward. The flat tires, not telling me about meetings, having my utilities cut off, or telling our cop brothers that I'd killed Christine and then made it look like she'd taken her own life. After all, he'd told anyone who would listen, it was my gun they found next to her. Garett had put a stop to the crap Jack was pulling at work, but I never told my boss about the other stuff because even after everything had gone down, I still felt sorry for Jack. He'd loved Christine, too. We'd both lost her.

Jenny smiled as she reached across the counter and put her hand over mine. "I'm glad you picked here."

"It was good while it lasted, but the people of Blue Ridge Valley aren't going to want a murderer for their police chief." Her hand was warm where it rested on mine, and I just wanted to take her to bed, curl up with her, and pull the covers over our heads.

"You're not a murderer. I don't ever want to hear you say that again. You have to fight this, Dylan. It's not right that he can keep taking everything you love away from you. We need a plan." She squeezed my hand. "I'll be right there with you, and together we'll make sure everyone knows the truth."

Damn burning eyes. She smiled, and there was something about the way that smile seemed special, as if it was meant just for me, that made my heart beat faster. Sitting in my kitchen talking about both the woman and the best friend I'd once loved, it hit me like a ton of bricks dropped on my head. I was well on the way to being in love with Jenny Girl. That wasn't supposed to happen.

"There's a plan in the works, but I can't talk about all this anymore tonight." I stood and walked behind her, putting my arms around her. "Help me forget for a few hours. Give me some of that TLC you excel at, and tomorrow morning I'll tell you what I'm going to do."

She tilted her head up, a smile on her face and desire in her eyes. "You got it, Chief."

"Thank you." I stepped away and held out my hand. "You're pretty special, Red." That was as close as I would ever come to telling her that I was falling for her. She came to me without hesitation, and as we walked to my bed room hand in hand, I tried not to think about how much I was going to miss her when she left.

CHAPTER THIRTY-ONE

~ Jenny ~

DYLAN WOKE ME UP EARLY. "Up and at 'em, Red. We have places to go, people to see."

I pulled my pillow over my head. "Go away, evil man."

It was his laughter that caught my attention. He'd fallen asleep before me last night, but he'd been restless, tossing and turning so much that I'd almost relocated myself to the couch. I hadn't because I was afraid he'd wake up and need me.

My pillow was yanked away. "Up, Red. Coffee's on, breakfast in twenty."

I opened one eye, peeking at his hot ass as he walked out of the room. As if Dylan's early morning chirpiness wasn't bad enough, I got dog-breath licks across my face from Daisy. "You Conrads are the devil's minions," I told her, pushing her nose away. She gave me a pitiful whine, making me feel bad about hurting her feelings.

Nineteen minutes later I walked into the kitchen, inhaling the aroma of coffee. "Gimme, gimme, gimme." I held my arms out, heading for Dylan like a zombie.

He smiled at my silliness, but I noticed it didn't reach his eyes. His early morning cheerfulness was an act, maybe as much for himself as for me. "What's the plan for today?"

"First, breakfast." He put a bowl of cereal and some toast in front of me.

"Do you know where *The Valley News* office is?" he asked, sitting across from me.

"Yeah, why?"

"I want you to go there this morning. Tell those two women if they'll hold off on publishing their so-called special edition, that I'll give them an exclusive interview. I don't want to go myself so that they don't try to get me to do an interview right then."

"No problem. I can do that. Why would you want to talk to them, though?"

"A man I respect above all others told me I need to take the bull by the horns. He's right. If I'm going to be front-page news, then my side of the story needs to be told, but not until I get a chance to sit down with the mayor."

"Makes sense, but we need to do more than that." I popped the last piece of toast into my mouth while Dylan hadn't done much more than stir his spoon around in his cereal. No surprise that he didn't have an appetite this morning. "We need to make a list of who we know we can recruit to support you. Autumn and Brian, for sure. Definitely Adam and Connor... What?" He was staring at me with a kind of wonder in his eyes.

He put his hand on his chest, patting himself right over his heart. "Jenny Girl, you slay me."

"Why?" I whispered. Something like snapping live wires latched around my heart, stealing the air out of my lungs. He didn't mean he loved me, right? That wasn't supposed to happen.

"Because you believe in me."

"Of course I believe in you," I said, not liking my disappointment that he hadn't declared his undying love for me. If he had, I'd probably have gone running out of his condo.

He stood, took my hand, and pulled me into his arms. "Thank you."

When his mouth fused with mine, setting me on fire, I closed my eyes, sinking against him as his tongue invaded my mouth. Everything about this man called to me in the most elemental way. I wanted to climb up him, wrap my legs around his waist, and never let him go. Minutes later he pulled away, leaning his head back and peering down at me. Both of us were breathing hard.

"Have I told you how much I love kissing you?"

I shook my head. "No, you've never told me that."

"How remiss of me." He trailed his knuckles down my cheek. "I do, you know."

"I'm pretty fond of kissing you, too."

"Then we'll have to do more of it. In the meantime, however, I have that meeting with the mayor in an hour, so I'm going to jump in the shower." He gave me a wicked grin. "I'd ask you to join me, but then I'd never get to that meeting."

"Well, darn. How about we make a shower date for tonight?"

"You're on, but meet me for lunch. You can tell me how it went at the newspaper, and I'll bring you up to speed on what's happening."

I watched him walk away. "You have a mighty fine butt, Chief," I said before he disappeared from sight. And did he ever.

He glanced over his shoulder, giving me a wink, making my stomach flutter. Dylan Conrad was a good man, and I'd be damned before I'd let my town destroy him. Since I was already dressed, I grabbed my purse and headed out to complete my mission.

The Stop the Press Operation was a success. Naomi and Gloria had agreed to hold off their *exclusive* in return for an interview with Dylan. My next stop was to my parents. My dad had been the mayor twelve years ago, and he still had influence. If I told him Dylan was worthy of his attention, he'd believe me.

"Exactly how well do you know our new police chief?"

my mom asked as soon as I told my parents Dylan's story.

"Ah... well, I've been dating him." I hadn't mentioned that little fact previously, not wanting my mother to get excited that there might be grandbabies in her near future. She would be thrilled if a man came along and swept me off my feet to the point that I forget about taking off to see the world.

Although my dad worried about me being off on my own like that, he understood and supported me. Natalie and I had gotten our wanderlust from him. He'd joined the navy because he'd wanted to see the world, and he had. We'd poured through his photos of his travels many times, listened to his stories about the things he'd seen and the people he'd met, and our dream to do the same had been born. From there our love of travel had grown with each vacation our parents took us on.

"We already knew that, Jennifer," Mom said. "You should know by now that nothing's a secret in this town. We've been wondering when you would bring your young man by to meet us."

My mom only called me Jennifer when she was miffed. I should have realized she would have heard I was seeing Dylan since we'd openly dated. And I hadn't brought him to meet my parents for several reasons. They hadn't taken to Chad the one time I had brought him over. Dylan, though, they would love him, but I didn't want him to think that I thought we were serious enough to do the meet-the-parents thing.

"What can we do to help?" my dad asked.

That was why I loved him so much. Not once did he question my belief that Dylan was a good man deserving our support. "I'm not sure yet. Dylan's talking to Jim John this morning. Other than the interview with the newspaper, I don't know what else he has up his sleeve, but I'm sure he has a plan. I'm meeting him for lunch at the Blue

Ridge Café. Guess I'll find out then."

"No," Mom said. "Tell him to come here. We need to meet him, and we can talk without nosy ears listening in."

"That's a great idea." I leaned over and kissed her cheek. "You're an awesome mom, you know that?"

She grinned. "I know."

"Who else are you going to talk to?" my dad asked.

"I was thinking Autumn, Brian, Adam, and Connor to start."

Daddy nodded. "Good people for Dylan to have at his back. How about we do this. Call in an order for several large pizzas and see if they all can come to lunch."

"I like how you think." Hopefully Dylan would be okay with us springing a lunch meeting on him like this. He wouldn't like talking about his personal life, but since the rumors were no doubt spreading already, this would give him the opportunity to set the record straight with the people he could count on for support.

After ordering an assortment of pizzas to be picked up at noon, I got on the phone to my friends, all of whom were free for lunch and very curious about being called to a secret meeting. Once I confirmed everyone could make it, I texted Dylan, asking him to meet me at my parents and giving him their address.

My dad had just returned with the pizzas when Dylan arrived. If the people sitting around my parents' dining room table surprised him, he hid it well. It was probably a cop thing, something he'd learned how to do over the years.

He slipped off his Windbreaker, and I took it from him. Every time I saw him in his uniform—the cargo pants, the police department logoed shirt that stretched across his chest and broad shoulders, the leather belt holding a gun, handcuffs, and other police paraphernalia—I had a strong desire to play cop and bad girl with him.

Autumn punched my arm, bringing me out of my fantasy trance. My cheeks heated, and I think everyone but my parents guessed my thoughts if the amusement in my friends' eyes were any indication. I sure hoped my parents hadn't caught the direction my dirty mind had taken.

"Mom, Dad, this is Dylan Conrad. Dylan, my parents, Porter and Anne Nance."

"A pleasure to meet you both," he said, shaking hands with my dad and then giving my mom one of his killer smiles. "Ah, I see where Jenny gets her beautiful looks."

She actually giggled. No doubt she already had us walking down the aisle. I put my hand on Dylan's arm. "You already know everyone else."

"I do, and it's great to see everyone again."

"Well, let's eat while the pizzas are hot." As we took our seats, he glanced at me. I could see the question in his eyes, wondering what was going on. "This is your support group. Everyone in this room believes in you, and after we eat, we're going to have a strategy session. I'm calling it Operation Save Dylan's Ass."

"Jennifer!"

I glanced at my mom. "Well, it is a very nice ass, definitely worth saving."

Dylan sputtered a laugh. "Thanks, I think."

We dug into the pizzas, and I stayed mostly quiet, preferring to observe Dylan. I already knew he was at ease with my friends and that they liked him. It was the way he was with my parents that fascinated me. If I hadn't known he was a big-city boy, I would have thought he'd grown up in these mountains. He was respectful toward them, yet got into a heated discussion with my dad about the Chicago Bears versus the North Carolina Panthers.

At one point my mother mouthed, *He's a keeper.*

Yep, she was hearing wedding bells. The pizzas had been demolished, and I stood, collecting plates. When my mom and Autumn tried to help, I shooed them away.

"Get settled in the living room, y'all. I'll be along in a minute." Surprising me, Dylan stayed behind, helping me clean up. After the pizza boxes were dumped in the trash and the plates loaded in the dishwasher, Dylan pulled me to him.

"Thank you," he said, wrapping his arms around me.

"For?" He slid his hands down my back, resting them on the curve of my butt. I loved when he touched me. His hands felt so big and strong, his body always like a furnace, warming me.

"For this." He leaned back and peered down at me. "For rallying the troops. For believing in me."

I lifted onto my toes, putting my mouth close to his. "Of course I believe in you." I kissed him then, and if we weren't in my parents' house, our friends waiting for us, I would have wrapped my legs around his waist and begged him to make love to me right there, pressed up against my mom's kitchen sink.

Before we got carried away, forgetting where we were, I let go of him. "Guess we should join the others."

"Ah, I need a minute, Red."

We both looked down at the tent in his pants, and I giggled. I patted the bulge pressing against his zipper. "Someone wants to come out and play."

"Little hellcat." He pushed my hand away. "Go. I'll be right behind you."

I glanced over my shoulder. "Promises. Promises." I put a little sway in my hips as I walked out, smiling at hearing his groan.

"Where's Dylan?" my mom asked when I walked into the living room.

"He's…ah, getting something to drink?" Dang, I hadn't meant to make that a question. At Autumn's smirk, I crossed my eyes, making her laugh.

Mom's gaze darted from me to Autumn. "What's so funny?"

"Beats me," I said. Dylan came in, taking a seat on the chair next to me. My parents had a large L-shaped sofa. Autumn, Brian, and the twins had taken over the long side and my parents on the short half.

Now that we were all gathered, I was nervous about how they'd react to hearing Dylan's story. I was also worried about Dylan and how hard it would be for him to talk about his wife and what she'd done. I guess I shouldn't have been. As I was trying to think of how to start, Dylan put his hand on my arm.

"Have you told everyone why you asked them here?"

I shook my head. "I wanted to wait for you."

"Then let me explain."

CHAPTER THIRTY-TWO

~ Dylan ~

I UNDERSTOOD JENNY'S PURPOSE IN BRINGING her friends together, I truly did. And it humbled me that these people were ready to stand with me before they even knew what I had to say. But that was because they believed in Jenny, not me.

Christine's story and mine was deeply personal, one I'd never expected to share. Jack had forced my hand, though, so here I was in a room with people I barely knew—except for Jenny—about to bare my soul. I didn't like it.

Instead of running out like I wanted to do, I told these people about my wife. When I finished, Jenny's mother had tears running down her face, and I didn't like that either. "So that's it," I said, spreading out my hands.

"And your old partner's here now, stirring all this up?" Jenny's father asked.

"Yes, sir. Or he was last night when Jenny saw him. I have my officers watching for him, although I didn't tell them why. If he's staying in a motel around here, I'd guess he's using an assumed name."

"We need to draw him out," Adam said, his emerald earring twinkling.

"I agree, and I'm working on that. This morning I met with the mayor."

That had been one of the most difficult conversations of my life. Jack coming to what I considered my new hometown, a place I'd fallen in love with, had forced me to put the situations with Stephanie's arrest and Moody on the back burner. That didn't sit well. I had a job to do, but first I had to deal with my past.

"And?"

I glanced at the hand Jenny had put on my arm. She had no idea what her touch did to me, even one simply meant to let me know she was here for me. "And I told him everything. He's not real happy with me right now, mostly because I'm airing my dirty laundry in public."

"He said that?" Jenny asked.

"Yeah. He thinks it's going to make him look bad for hiring me."

Jenny's father made a snorting noise, drawing my attention. "Jim John has his own share of dirty laundry, so don't let him give you any shit." He glanced at his wife. "Sorry, I couldn't think of a better word."

Did Porter know what hold Moody had over the mayor? I needed to find a moment alone with him, see if he'd tell me anything. "Since he wants to make sure that his new police chief hire doesn't come back to bite him, he agreed to my request for an open town meeting. I'll answer anyone's concerns."

"I don't think I like that," Jenny said.

Autumn nodded in agreement. "What you told us isn't anyone's business. Some of these yokels around here will see it as some kind of gladiator-versus-the-lion event and just for the fun of it, they'll be rooting for the lion."

"Now you're scaring me," I teased. I couldn't help but smile at her analogy. Truthfully she'd pretty much hit the nail on the head. That was how I saw exposing my past to the people of Blue Ridge Valley, the very ones I'd taken a vow to keep safe. Unfortunately it had to be done.

"But clever not to act like you have something to hide," Connor said.

I nodded, glad I'd gotten the twins' earring colors down. "Not so sure it's as clever as it's unavoidable. Jenny said everyone at the bar heard Jack, so you know the talk has started. The smartest thing to do is meet it head-on and hope the dust settles. My boss at Chicago PD is flying in to back up my story."

"What can we do?" Adam asked.

"Spread the word about the town meeting. It's tomorrow night at eight. If anyone has time, you can help me put up a few posters announcing the meeting. Also, keep an eye out for my former partner." I scrolled through my phone, pulling up the picture of my former friend that I'd downloaded this morning. As it was passed around, I described the car he was driving. "If you see him, please call me. It would be best if you didn't try to engage him in any way. If he should say anything to you about me, tell him about tomorrow night's meeting."

Jenny scrunched her eyebrows together, puzzlement clear on her face. "You want him there?"

"Oh yeah." I was counting on it.

Three hours before the town meeting, I picked up my old boss at the Asheville airport. Other than the people I'd had lunch with, no one else, not even the mayor, knew Garrett was coming. Compared to either of Chicago's two airports, finding a parking spot outside of baggage claim was a breeze. I leaned against my car, Daisy at my side, watching for the man who'd helped to mold the cop I was today.

Garrett walked out the door with three big dudes wearing Harley-Davidson jackets, all of them laughing. Knowing my old boss, he was telling them a dirty joke. Garrett spied me, waved to his new friends, then headed my way.

"Good to see you, Cupcake," he said, dropping his tote bag and wrapping me in a bear hug.

The man always made me laugh, except when I'd displeased him. "I was hoping you'd forgotten my nickname by now."

"Not a chance." He let go of me and eyed my dog. "And who do we have here?"

"This is Daisy."

"Hello, Miss Daisy." He held out his hand, and she put her paw in it.

I figured by the time we got back to Blue Ridge Valley, the two would be fast friends. We loaded up and headed home. What would he think of my little town? He'd tried to talk me out of quitting and moving here, saying that I'd be bored out of my mind within a week. Truthfully I'd feared he'd be right, but I didn't miss the senseless gang wars, watching kids without a future shooting each other without an ounce of regret, or seeing Jack's face every day.

"You run down Jack yet?"

"Yep. He's staying at a motel outside of town." He had been spotted by one of my officers yesterday afternoon. I'd followed my former partner back to the motel. As tempting as it had been to confront him then and there, I'd reined myself in.

"Think he'll hear about the meeting?"

"After he disappeared into his room, I stuck fliers announcing the meeting on all the cars, including his."

"You clue in your department to what's going on?"

"Not yet. I wanted to wait until you were here to talk to them. We're headed to the station now." And wasn't I looking forward to that? "Daisy, you're being rude." She had her face stuck between the seats, wanting attention from her new friend.

"Tell Cupcake to leave you alone, Miss Daisy." Garrett scratched her chin, sending her eyes to rolling back in her head.

"Christ, man, please don't call me Cupcake in front of my cops."

Garrett gave one of his deep belly laughs. "I'll try to resist."

"How's Derrick?"

"Lovely as ever. He'd be perfect if he'd stop trying to keep bad guys out of jail."

The man had actually sighed at hearing his husband of six years' name. They

were as different as night and day. The two of them—Garrett, the hard-ass cop and Derrick with his public defender's liberal heart—should be like oil and water, but somehow they made it work. Derrick reminded me of the actor Henry Cavill, but with the most piercing green eyes I'd ever seen.

Garrett, on the other hand, looked more like a pit bull and had the tenacity of one. He worked out every day, had the body to prove it, and had the face of what I thought of as an MMA fighter's—strong jaw and chin, almost black eyes that could snare you in their glare, and leathery skin that could take a hit without splitting open.

"Now that we've gotten my love life out of the way, let's talk about yours. You still doing the celibate thing? Not good for you, man."

"There's someone."

Not surprisingly, he went into pit-bull mode on hearing that, plying me with questions. I told him about Jenny and her dream to see the world.

Garrett glanced behind him. "You seeing what I'm seeing, Miss Daisy?" Daisy gave him one of her doggy grins.

"What?" I said when he winked at my dog as if the two of them shared a secret.

"Your eyes light up when you talk about your Jenny. You're in love with her."

I glanced at him. "I guess I am, or at least getting there. Nothing will come of it since she's leaving soon." And I had to figure out how to put a stop to wanting more than she was willing to give.

"You need to romance the hell out of her. You know, sweep her off her feet until she forgets about taking off on you. Either that or quit your job and go with her. You got plenty of money to see you through a life of leisure."

I didn't admit that I'd briefly considered doing just that before dismissing the idea. First, Jenny had never indicated she wanted me tagging along on her travels, and second, I had a contract to honor... if I still had a job after all was said and done.

"It's really pretty here," Garrett said, glancing around as we exited the interstate. "If I ever get Derrick to take time off, we should come here for vacation."

I snorted. "Good luck with that."

"Yeah, the man's gonna end up dying at his desk, which is really going to piss me off."

"Maybe you should try kidnapping him."

Garrett's eyes lit up with unholy glee. "Damn, Cupcake, that's a great idea."

And it wouldn't at all surprise me if Garrett did just that in the near future. I pulled into the department's parking lot. "Well, here we are. You have no idea how much I don't want to do this." All my officers' cars were in the lot as I'd told them there would be a short meeting before the shift change.

"Chin up, my friend. Out of the three people involved, you were the only one innocent of any wrongdoing."

That wasn't true. I was guilty of turning my back on Christine when she'd needed me the most. But Garrett would argue with me if I voiced my regret, so I only nodded.

"Anyone going to have a problem with what you're going to tell them?" Garrett asked as we walked toward the door.

"One for sure. Moody, my captain. I'm working on

kicking his ass out the door. Other than him, I'm hoping not." We stopped outside the entry while I filled him in on my issues with Moody.

"He definitely needs to go. You can't have him going behind your back, attempting to undo all you're trying to accomplish"

"I know. It was on my list to deal with today. Then Jack showed his lovely face." The last thing I wanted to do was to walk into that building and talk about Christine to my cops. Daisy inserted herself between us, her doggy gaze locked on me. She whined, apparently picking up on the tension radiating from me. I put my hand on her head, letting her know that whatever happened, she was mine.

We walked into the lobby, and all my cops gathered there fell silent. My stomach decided this was a good time to act up, and I wished I had some antacids. The speech I'd prepared deserted me at seeing the people I'd come to care for waiting to hear why they'd been called to a special meeting. I'd come here wanting to be the one to make them proud of being a Blue Ridge Valley police officer, but I was about to be their biggest disappointment.

Garrett bumped his arm against mine, and I could almost hear him saying, *Chin up, Cupcake*. Daisy—the dog that loved every single cop here except Moody—all of a sudden was shaking like a leaf as she pressed herself against my leg. Damn it. She was picking up on my negative vibes. I straightened my spine, making a point of meeting the eyes of each of my cops.

I saved Moody for last. When our gazes collided, I saw from the victorious gleam in his eyes that he'd somehow managed to run into Jack. He knew and was already gloating. This would be my first test on how people would react to what I had to say. I cleared my throat.

"We'll keep this brief so the next shift can head out. I… ah… If you haven't already, you're going to hear some rumors concerning me the next few days."

Moody's grin was pure evil. "You gonna tell us how you killed your wife?"

Every man and woman in the room swiveled their heads, staring at him as if he'd lost his mind. A few gasped. "No, I'm going to tell you about the day she took her own life. Christine, my wife, was very depressed, so much so that she decided she couldn't face another day." I refused to besmirch her memory by telling them she'd had an affair. That was none of their damn business.

"That's not the way I heard it, *Chief*."

Moody's sarcastic emphasis on Chief wasn't lost on me. "Then you heard wrong. The man who told you that has a problem with me and is simply trying to cause trouble."

"Why should we believe you?"

I wanted to put my fist through Moody's face. Knocking him out cold would shut him up.

"Because he's telling the truth," Garrett said.

Moody frowned. "Who the hell are you?"

Tommy took a step forward. "I believe you, Chief." Several of my officers nodded in agreement.

I shot Tommy a grateful nod. "I'm sorry. I should have introduced my friend here. This is my former boss, Captain Garrett Caulder of the Chicago PD. He was also the lead investigator on my wife's suicide. He's here to answer any of your questions."

"How do we know he's really who you say he is? Maybe you're paying him to back up your story."

Now you've done it, Moody. I swallowed a snort, knowing what was coming.

Garrett eyed my captain as if he were studying a slug under his shoe that he was about to smash. "Exactly who are you?"

Moody puffed out his chest. "Captain Ralph Moody. This is my town, and we don't much like strangers."

"You thinking of using that thing to run me off with my tail tucked between my legs?" Garrett asked, eyeing the hand Moody had put on his gun handle. He glanced at me, his eyes dancing with mischief. "Damn, Chief, this is fun, like being in a Clint Eastwood movie. Is this where I get to say, 'Go ahead. Make my day?' I wish you'd told me how much fun I would have here. I woulda come sooner." He turned back to Moody. "Do I get till sundown, hoss?"

Moody scrunched thick eyebrows together. "I don't like you."

"Seems we have something in common after all. I don't much like you either." Garrett turned away from my captain, as if bored with the man. "Do any of you have any questions about what you just heard? If so, now's the time to ask."

When no one spoke up, he said, "You can trust your new chief. He's a good man and a damn good cop. If anyone still has any doubts"—he glanced pointedly at Moody—"he wasn't home when it happened. A neighbor heard the shot and called it in, then stood outside the door until the cops arrived. No one entered or exited. End of story."

With that said, he walked out, leaving me to wrap things up. Maybe I should reconsider asking Jenny if I could tag along on her world tour. Take off with her and forget about everything threatening to steal my new life.

Moody stepped in front of me. "How do we know he's telling the truth? I talked to Conrad's former partner. He says different."

"You're such an ass, Moody," Tommy said.

"Hear, hear," someone muttered.

I swallowed a grin that the youngest and shyest member of my force had the balls to risk Moody's wrath. Or maybe it was that Tommy trusted me to have his back, because I did.

"If we're done here, those off shift go home, and those heading out, be safe out there."

Every single one of the cops in the room—except for Moody—lined up to say something to me as they headed out. Things like, "I'm standing with you," from Gene Lanier. "You got us cool uniforms," Kim Payton said. "And you got Kim and me off break-room cleanup duty." Sarah Griffin added as my two female cops high-fived me at the same time, making me lift both my hands for them to slap.

It went on like that for a few minutes, until Moody, Daisy, and I were the only ones left in the room. Daisy growled when he glared at me.

"If you think this is the end of it, you're a fool," the man said, a sneer on his face.

He was trying to rattle me, but I refused to bite. "Some free advice, Moody. A wise man never counts his chickens before they hatch."

For the first time since I'd heard Jack was in town, doing his best to smear my name, I was happy. Except for Moody, every one of my cops had backed me, Garrett had flown seven hundred miles after one phone call to guard my back, and Jenny had believed in me without hesitation. Not only that, she had recruited her friends to stand up for me. Even if things didn't go the way I hoped tonight, I was blessed. Not a state of mind I'd ever expected to achieve after what I'd gone through.

"I'm bringing your former partner to the meeting tonight. We'll see how long you last here after he tells everyone what you did."

"I should have let you have at him, Daisy," I murmured after he walked out. "If it doesn't go well tonight, you'll still love me, right?" She slobbered doggy love all over my hand in response. I glanced at my watch. "Well, girl, time to face the music. You're going to have to stay in the car, okay?" In truth I felt like I was facing my execution, but I'd do it with my head held high.

CHAPTER THIRTY-THREE

~Jenny~

I'D THOUGHT WE SHOULD ALL sit together right up front—me, my parents, Autumn, Brian, and the twins—like a brick wall surrounding Dylan, protecting him. My dad said no, that we needed to spread out, be in positions to counter anyone deciding to start trouble. That made sense, but I'd claimed a seat in the front row, needing to be as close to Dylan as possible.

That there had even been a special town meeting called, forcing Dylan to speak of things that were no one's business, infuriated me. I couldn't begin to imagine how difficult this was going to be for him. Glancing behind me, I saw that the meeting hall was packed. Apparently the entire town had heard about the meeting, because all the seats were taken and people were lining the walls.

"Idiots," I muttered.

"Did you say something, dear?"

I glanced at Gloria. "No, not a thing." She and Naomi had come early to get front-row seats, and she had a notepad on her lap, ready to write down everything Dylan said. On the other side of her, Naomi was fiddling with a recorder. Dylan had promised to give them their interview as soon as the witch hunt was over, and that made me angry too. They were like vultures circling the carcass. From the glee in their eyes, I'm sure that was how they saw tonight's event.

"Has he confided in you?" Naomi asked, leaning around Gloria.

"Why would he tell me his personal business?" *Hint, hint, nosy woman.*

Gloria rolled her eyes, implying I was being silly. "Because the two of you are an item? Don't bother denying it, Jenn. The whole town knows you spend nights at his place. Perhaps that's not wise of you." She patted my hand. "Not if he killed his wife."

"He didn't kill his wife!" The noise of conversations buzzing around us fell silent at my shouted words, and I could feel the eyes on me of those who'd heard me. I had to go outside and get some air before I suffocated. "I'll be right back." To further claim my seat, I left my jacket on the metal chair.

It was cold when I stepped out, but I didn't really feel it. The burning rage inside me kept me warm. When I saw the mayor's car turn into the parking lot, I stepped to the side of the building, not wanting to have to acknowledge him. He should have put a stop to this circus, should have stood up for his police chief, but the man would never do anything that might harm his reelection chances. No way was I going to vote for him again, though.

After the mayor and his wife disappeared inside, I came out of hiding. Stephanie wasn't with them, which pleased me. I didn't want her here, witnessing Dylan's trial. Because that's what it was. The town was putting him on trial, and I hated that the people I'd known all my life were eagerly awaiting his arrival so they could hear all the juicy details.

Another car pulled in, the twin to my Mustang. I hadn't met the man who'd come all the way from Chicago to stand by Dylan's side. The lot was full, what with everyone and their brother here, but I waited for him to find a place to park. I wanted to meet Dylan's former boss, assure myself he was up to the task of helping to get Dylan out of this mess.

"Hey, you," I said, walking up to Dylan when he exited

the car.

"My favorite redhead." He brushed his lips over mine, then glanced around the parking lot. "Looks like the whole damn town is here."

"Yep. They're all waiting for the star of the show to arrive." He must have heard the bitterness in my voice because he gave me a gentle smile.

"It's okay, Jenny. It was all probably going to come out eventually. Better now. Get it over with, so I can move on." His gaze lifted toward the west, where the sun was setting behind the mountain. "Either here or somewhere else."

That shouldn't bring tears to my eyes since I'd be leaving soon, and whether Dylan was here or not wouldn't matter. But he loved this town, and as much as he tried to hide it, he was hurting. I could see it in the way his smile didn't reach his eyes.

"Is this the lovely Jenny?" a man asked, walking around the front of the car.

Dylan nodded as he put a hand on my shoulder. "Jenny, Garrett Caulder. Garrett, I have the honor of introducing you to a very special lady."

His words warmed me, as did the way he tucked me next to his side. I ran a critical eye over Garrett Caulder. The first thought that came to mind at seeing him was that he belonged in a boxing ring. He had the appearance of a bruiser with his rugged features and a nose that had obviously been broken at some point. And his body… he looked like he could take on Rocky without breaking a sweat.

When Dylan had told me about him, it was obvious this man had Dylan's utmost respect. "Mr. Caulder, a pleasure to meet you." I held out my hand.

He wrapped two big hands around mine, a grin on his face. "None of that Mr. Caulder shit, beautiful Jenny."

His eyes were warm, and even though I'd just met him,

I found that I liked the man. Dylan had warned me that his former boss had a foul mouth, though. I hoped he'd tone it down when we got inside, if he talked. This was the Bible Belt, and at least half those inside would take offense. "Garrett then. You have a packed house waiting for you, Dylan."

"Guess we better get to it then," Dylan said.

As we turned to leave, Daisy whined from inside the car. I glanced over at her. "You should bring her in with you." People around here were dog lovers whether it was their house dog, yard dog, or hunting dog. Daisy would steal their hearts.

"You sure?"

When I nodded, he gave me a happy smile. "Can you really help him?" I asked Garrett while Dylan was busy putting the leash on Daisy.

"I guess we'll know soon. I'd take him back to the Chicago PD without hesitation, but he seems to love it here." He eyed me with a smirk on his face. "Now I know why."

Heat traveled up my neck to my cheeks, but before I could think of a response, Dylan joined us. Obviously Dylan had told Garrett that we were seeing each other, and I wondered what had been said about me.

Dylan eyed the door to town hall, letting out a long breath. "Let's do this."

I wanted to pull him back to his car and take him away so that he didn't have to walk inside that building. Instead I slipped my hand into his, squeezing his fingers. No matter what happened next, I wanted him to know that I thought… What did I think? I wasn't sure anymore.

How could I get on a plane and leave this beautiful man behind? Even the idea of doing that made me question my sanity. I missed the first step leading up to the door.

"You okay?" he asked when I stumbled.

No, I wasn't okay. I would be leaving him in a little over

a week, and I wanted to plop my butt on the floor and have a good cry. "I'm fine," I lied. Tonight wasn't about me, though, so I put aside my misery.

Conversations stopped midsentence as soon as we walked in. Dylan held his head high, his posture perfect, and he looked so good in a dark charcoal pinstripe suit, a white button-down, and a red tie. Like the CEO of a billion-dollar conglomerate. Although I wasn't sure how many CEOs had a dog as their faithful companion. As if Daisy sensed the importance of this night, she held her elegant head high as she pranced along beside him. But her ears were laid back, signaling her displeasure at the tension filling the air.

Dylan squeezed my hand before letting go. Once again I had the urge to pull him out of the room so that he didn't have to go through this. Instead I walked with him toward the front, proud to be at his side. When we reached the first row, I slipped back into my seat. Dylan walked to the front where the mayor stood. Garrett moved behind them, leaning against the wall with his hands in his pockets.

"Who's that?" Gloria asked.

"He's a captain with the Chicago Police Department, Dylan's former boss."

She leaned close. "I'll need to interview him, too."

Like I had any control over Dylan or Garrett. I didn't answer her, mostly because Dylan glanced at me, and all other thoughts flew right out of my head. Without thinking about what I was doing, I tapped my chest, right over my heart. The way one side of his mouth quirked up in a lopsided smile brought tears to my eyes. How was I supposed to walk away from this man? But I would. I had a promise to keep.

Jim John banged on a block of wood with his mayoral gavel, the same one my father had used when he held the office. I'd always thought that was Jim John's favorite part of being mayor, being able to make enough noise to get everyone's attention onto him.

"There have been some concerns expressed about our new police chief, Dylan Conrad. He's agreed to answer any questions you might have." He stepped off to the side.

That was all he was going to say? What a toad. He knew the truth, and he should have shown more support for his police chief. But he was putting a protective wall between them. A just-in-case one should Dylan fail to win over the town. Maybe I'd talk my dad into running again in the next election. Hell, I'd run to make sure Jim John didn't get reelected.

Dylan kept his face carefully blank, but Garrett narrowed his eyes at our mayor. Maybe he'd go over and punch Jim John in the face. One could hope. I glanced back at Dylan as he stepped forward. He appeared to be relaxed, but I knew him. The tension lines at the corners of his mouth and eyes gave him away.

"For those I've not met yet, I'm Dylan Conrad. To give you a little of my background before I open the floor to questions, I began my career in law enforcement with the Chicago Police Department after obtaining a degree in Criminal Justice from the University of Illinois in Chicago. I spent a little over two years on street patrol before moving to vice as a detective, heading up that department for the past year."

I wasn't sure, but it seemed like he'd moved up the ranks pretty fast. That didn't surprise me, though. Dylan was a highly intelligent and focused man. If the people of this town didn't realize how lucky we were to have him, then they didn't deserve him.

"Now I'll take your questions."

The man was definitely smart. I'd expected him to say something about his wife and what had happened, but he was going to force others to bring that up. He darted a glance at me, and I saw the question in his eyes. I gave him a little nod of approval. Yes, he was perfectly handling what was an unfair situation.

"I have a question, Chief," Connor said, standing.

What was he doing? I frowned at my friend. We were here to support Dylan, not give him a hard time.

Dylan nodded. "You have the floor, Mr. Hunter."

"We are…unfortunately, I have to say, called out too often to rescue a tourist who has fallen from the top of a waterfall or gotten lost while hiking. We're experienced at handling those operations, but I'd like to see an advanced training program put in place for these kinds of rescues. For the police department and fire department personnel, along with volunteers like Adam and me. Do you have any plans for something like that?"

If I were sitting next to Connor, I would have kissed him. I should have known to trust him.

The first real smile I'd seen from Dylan tonight formed on his face. "Actually I do. A few days ago I talked to a friend who runs a training program like that in Denver. He's agreed to help us develop one for our town as soon as we get approval from the town council."

I shifted in my seat to see the reaction to that, pleased to see quite a few people nodding their heads in approval. Gloria raised her hand, and I wanted to grab it and pull it down. The wariness returned to Dylan's eyes, but before he could call on her, my dad stood.

"Chief, it's my understanding that our police officers haven't received a raise in over a year. These men and women are dedicated to protecting and serving our community. I know you are bound by budget restrictions, but have you looked into a way to scrounge up a little money to give our officers a much deserved raise?"

"Yes, Mr. Nance, that issue has already been addressed."

"We got a raise last week," someone in the back yelled.

Applause broke out, and I leaned around Gloria to see a line of cops standing against the wall, all of them clapping. My father had already known the answer to his question when he asked it. It had come up at our strategy meeting at his house.

Gloria raised her hand again, but Autumn beat her to the punch when she stood. "Our police department's uniforms have to be the ugliest ones in the world. They look like baby poop." Laughter broke out in the room. She grinned. "I know, right?" She glanced around, getting nods. "Anyway, can you do something about that?"

Another question that had been answered at our meeting. I had never been so proud of my family and friends.

"We found a little money to spend on new uniforms, Miss Archer," Dylan said. "In about three weeks, you'll see them for yourself." That got another round of applause from the cops lining the wall.

"Well, I hope they're cool ones." Autumn looked over at the officers, raising a brow.

"They're awesome," one of the female cops said.

It struck me, listening to Dylan answer the questions that he never said *I did this* or *I did that.* His answers had a way of including his whole department, as if they were a team who'd accomplished these things together. He was such an amazing man.

Having learned her lesson, instead of raising her hand, Gloria stood. My heart thumped hard in my chest. If that was my reaction, I couldn't imagine what Dylan was feeling.

CHAPTER THIRTY-FOUR

~ Dylan ~

ALTHOUGH I APPRECIATED WHAT MY self-appointed support team was doing, the question hanging in the air wasn't going to be avoidable for long. As soon as the woman from *The Valley News* stood, I knew the time had arrived to talk about Christine. I hated that I had to. Jack should be glad he wasn't standing in front of me right now. I'd expected him to be here but hadn't spotted him in the crowd. The place was packed, though, so he might be nearby.

Jenny had shown me photos of the two women from the paper so I could memorize their names. The one standing was Gloria Davenport, and I nodded at her. "Ms. Davenport, you have the floor."

"Mr. Conrad, while your background is impressive, if the rumors—"

"This is bullshit!"

Gasps sounded from the crowd as everyone craned their heads to watch Moody storm down the aisle. I glanced at Jenny, needing her to ground me before I lost my cool. Our eyes locked, and as she'd done earlier, she put her fingers to her chest, right over her heart. Calmness settled over me, and I held her gaze a few more seconds before turning my attention to my enraged captain.

Still standing, Gloria Davenport snatched the phone her boss handed her and started snapping pictures. I was actually glad she was doing that. It reminded me that my actions, along with Moody's, would be plastered on the front page tomorrow. Moody wasn't going to look real pretty in his with that red face and fire blazing from his eyes, but mine would show nothing but professional behavior, even though there was a storm raging inside me.

Garrett slipped up beside me in a show of support. It would have been nice if the mayor joined me at the front, but that obviously wasn't going to happen. It was disappointing that the man who'd hired me couldn't be depended on when it counted.

No matter what happened, I had accomplished some good things in my short time here, along with making friends I could count on. And although I'd never tell her, I'd also fallen in love with a redheaded mountain girl, learning that there was life after Christine after all. It was a good thing to know.

"Captain Moody, did you have a question?" My composure seemed to enrage him even more.

"You're goddamn right I have a question."

It was tempting, but I decided not to remind him that there was no cursing when we're in public. That would only infuriate him more. "And your question is?"

"Why don't you tell everyone how you killed your wife?"

You could have heard a pin drop as everyone in the room waited for my answer. "Captain Moody, that is a question I can't answer because I *did not* kill my wife. Do you have anything else you want to ask me? If not, I believe Ms. Davenport from *The Valley News* was about to ask a question."

His face turned so red that I thought he might have a heart attack. "You're a fucking liar, Conrad."

"That cost him 50,000 points," I murmured to Garrett, one of the few who knew about my point system. When the room quieted again, I decided it was time to introduce Garrett, letting him explain about Christine.

"I have a witness," Moody said before I had a chance to let Garrett take over. Moody looked to the right, and from the middle of the seats, Jack stood.

And...showtime. I stuck my hands into my pants' pockets to hide my fists. No matter what came next, I was determined to keep my cool. Garrett bumped my shoulder, reminding me that he stood beside me. I hadn't asked him to interrupt his schedule to come support me, but as soon as he knew what I was facing, he'd jumped on a plane.

"Hello, Jack," I said to the man I'd once loved like a brother. "Heard you were in town." Suddenly I felt like I was in some kind of western movie, about to have a shootout at the O.K. Corral. An absurd laugh bubbled up inside me, which I managed to morph into a cough.

"I got this," Garrett said. "Introduce me."

I could do that as soon as I found my voice. I cleared my throat, then cleared it again. "You've probably been wondering who this is." I put my hand on Garrett's shoulder, while at the same time staring hard at Jack, not wanting to miss his reaction. His eyes darted between us, anger on his face at seeing Garrett standing by my side. Jack leveled his gaze on me with a hatred that was beyond anything I'd ever thought to see from him.

"So you're going to lie for him?" he said, his eyes focusing back on Garrett.

I held up a hand. "Before I was interrupted, I was going to introduce my former boss, Garrett Caulder, my captain at the Chicago Police Department. Since he headed up the investigation, Captain Caulder will answer any questions you have about the death of my wife." I stepped back before I said something I shouldn't.

Jack came forward, his furious gaze never leaving my face. The Jack I'd known, the one who'd been my best friend, had never had a hair out of place or a wrinkle in his shirts. This Jack was disheveled, his hair in dire need of a cut, and I wondered when he'd last washed it. His eyes were wild, as if he were losing it. Suddenly all I felt was sadness. For me, for him, and for Christine.

"I can make this real simple and short," Garrett said. "Christine Conrad was severely depressed and took her own life. End of story."

"Because he refused to give her a divorce." Jack lifted an accusing finger toward me. "He drove her to it."

Moody frowned. "You said he killed her."

"Well, he might as well have. She loved me, Dylan, and you wouldn't let her go."

Not true, but I didn't think it would serve any purpose if I tried to tell him again that I'd wanted a divorce and she'd begged me to reconsider. As I scanned the faces in the room to see their reaction, I was surprised by the way everyone was staring at Jack with displeasure. I'd forgotten we were in the Bible Belt, and it seemed they didn't approve of a man having an affair with a married woman. That was my guess, anyway.

"Bah," Moody grunted before stomping out.

He also got frowns as he stormed toward the exit. Garrett went to Jack, slipped an arm around him, whispered something to him, and then led him out. Well, that felt rather anticlimactic. To be honest, I'd half expected Jack to shoot me.

I wasn't sure what to do. Grabbing Jenny and hauling her out with me probably wasn't a good idea, no matter how much I wanted to do exactly that. Excited conversations buzzed as everyone talked about what had just happened. I glanced at Jenny and got a big smile. I smiled back.

Yeah, it had turned out okay. Unless Jim John figured I'd caused too much drama and decided to fire me. Since I didn't want to stand here all night, I took a step toward the mayor, intending to ask if we were done.

"Well, that was entertaining," Mary said from her seat

near the front. "Come by in the morning, Chief. I'll have a bag of hot doughnuts waiting for you." Tonight her hair was bright orange with black streaks, and her eye shadow was sparkly orange. If I got to stay here, I might marry her after all if she promised unlimited access to hot glazed doughnuts and apple cinnamon muffins.

Adam stood. "Chief, I just want to say that from everything I've heard the last few weeks, you're just the man we need. Welcome to Blue Ridge Valley."

"Hear. Hear," someone said, and I glanced toward the voice to see that it was Freddie Barnes.

I guess all those boiled peanuts I'd forced myself to eat paid off. Jenny's parents, Connor, Brian, and Autumn all stood, clapping their hands. Jenny popped up to join in the applause, a brilliant smile on her face. Others began to stand, and once it seemed the residents of Blue Ridge Valley had decided I was worth keeping, Jim John walked over and slung an arm over my shoulder, grinning like a damn politician who'd just won the election. It was a close call, but I managed not to roll my eyes.

Someone—I think Jenny's father—had gotten us the private room at Fusions to celebrate the success of our plan to save me. The people sitting around the table owned tonight's victory more than I did.

I raised my glass. "To good friends you can count on to have your back." They were all here—Jenny, her parents, Brian and Autumn, and Adam and Connor. The only one missing was Daisy since I'd dropped her off at home before coming here. She'd won over her own admirers as I'd tried to make my way out of the meeting, everyone wanting me to stop so they could pet the town's new police dog.

"That's us!" Autumn exclaimed.

"Sure is." Grinning at her enthusiasm, I clinked glasses

with my friends. The lump that had been sitting in my stomach like a lead ball for the past two days was gone, and I was definitely up for some celebrating.

Jenny leaned into me, and I smiled down at her. "Thank you, Red. I think tonight would have gone south without you marshaling the troops."

She put her hand on my thigh and squeezed. "Nah. You would've pulled it off. We just made it easier."

I wasn't so sure I would have, but it was over and done with. My plans for the night were to enjoy drinks and dinner with my new friends, then figure out a way to get Jenny alone. Garrett was spending the night at my place, was actually supposed to join us for dinner, but I hadn't heard from him since he'd left the meeting with Jack.

Our waiter came and took our orders, and after he left, Jenny's father said, "Not to throw a damper on the party by bringing this up, but you need to get Moody out of your hair. As long as he's around, he's going to do his best to make your life miserable."

"Don't I know it? It's number one on tomorrow's to-do list." My phone buzzed with an incoming text. It was from Garrett, asking me to meet him outside. "I'll be back in a minute."

Garrett stood by Jack's car when I came out. "Gonna have to pass on dinner." He flicked a thumb toward the window, and I glanced inside to see Jack sitting in the passenger seat, his chin on his chest and his hands cuffed in front of him. "I'm driving him home tonight."

"Does he really need to be handcuffed?" It wasn't a picture I'd ever expected to see—my former friend and partner wearing a pair of cuffs.

"I decided it was a good idea when he went for my gun, saying he wanted to be with Christine."

"Jesus," I whispered. "He needs help."

Garrett nodded. "And I intend to get him help, but he's

done as a cop. I can't have someone I don't trust on the force."

"Of course not. It's just… I mean, how the hell did it come to this?" Had I failed both my wife and my best friend? What should I have done differently so that she wasn't dead by her own hand and he wasn't sitting handcuffed in a car with his head hanging down in defeat?

"Stop it."

I jerked my gaze to Garrett's. "What?"

"Stop blaming yourself. Life is nothing more than a series of choices. You do this and your day is better for it. You do that and it all falls down on your head." He put a hand on my shoulder. "They both did that when they should have done this. You played no part in their choices, Dylan. You get what I'm saying?"

"I'm trying to." I knew he was speaking the truth, but believing I hadn't somehow played a part in this tragedy would take some work. "Can I talk to him?" Even after everything that had gone down, I still missed the friend I'd once had.

"No. He won't hear you. Right now the only thing he hears is the voice in his head that says you kept him from the woman he loves. Maybe someday he'll be in a place where he can listen, but that day isn't now."

The half glass of vodka and cranberry juice I'd drunk curled into a sour ball in my stomach. "No, I guess not. Listen, call me when you get back to Chicago, let me know you're okay."

Garrett blew me a kiss, making me laugh. "Worried about me, Cupcake?"

"Not really. You're one mean sonofabitch. Call me anyway."

He opened the car door. "I'll do that." I didn't miss his worried glance at Jack. "I'm going to drive straight through."

I was glad to hear that. "Come back on a vacation with Derrick. We'll hang out and drink ourselves stupid, and I'll tell you the story of Beauregard the Bull."

"I'll definitely come back for a bull story."

He grabbed me, pulling me into a tight hug, slapping his hand on my back. There was no other man I respected more than this one, and seeing him again made me wonder if I'd made the right decision to leave the Chicago Police Department. But I was happy in Blue Ridge Valley, more than I'd thought I'd be.

I loved my cops and their wide eyes when I'd done something special for them. I loved Mary with her ever-changing outlandish hair and eye shadow colors, loved that I had to worry about an outrageous moonshiner deciding to sell his goods again instead of giving them away. That apple pie flavor Jenny had given me to taste had been crazy good.

"Love ya, man," I said, my voice gruff with emotion.

Garrett laughed as he let go of me. "I know."

I snorted. "Asshole."

He slipped onto the driver's seat, grinning up at me as he lowered the window. "Go back to your lady. If you let her slip out of your hands, then you're not the man I thought you were."

"Drive safe." He gave me a salute, and I watched the car until the taillights disappeared. As for the girl, I would let her slip out of my hands. But not tonight. Tonight she was mine.

CHAPTER THIRTY-FIVE

~ Jenny ~

"COME HERE, JENNY."

I eyed Dylan from across the room. He'd been quiet ever since we'd finished dinner and left the restaurant. Quiet but vibrating with energy… or maybe tension? I wasn't sure.

At every opportunity tonight, he'd touched me. A hand on my leg at dinner, his fingers brushing my back as we'd walked out of the restaurant, playing with my hair on the way back to his place. I'd also caught him watching me, his eyes dark and hungry. My girl parts were humming so loud it was amazing he couldn't hear their mating song.

For some reason, though, I felt like playing hard to get. So I turned my back on him, got a glass from the cabinet, and filled it with ice and water.

"Jenny."

"Mmm?" I didn't turn around.

"Come. Here."

Okay, I turned around. How could I not when his hot command sent the humming to a full-blown singing choir now living in the region below my stomach? He was shirtless, perched on the arm of his sofa. My sight landed on his chest, and I choked on the water I'd just drunk. A million years from now, I doubted I'd ever tire of looking at those broad shoulders and that dusting of dark brown hair above both his nipples.

A knowing smile crossed his face. "Come to me, Jenny."

Like a woman tranced by a supernatural, I went to him.

He spread his legs, and I walked right between them. I'd never given up all of me to another man before, but for tonight, Dylan had from me what no other man ever had.

"Good girl," he said, his voice not much more than a whisper.

"I want to be bad."

He chuckled. "And you're going to be a very bad, bad girl. Take off your shirt."

This man. Oh God, this man. I was lost in his hungry eyes, in the feel of his hands sliding up my thighs, in his heat and masculine scent. I was lost, and I wasn't sure I ever wanted to find my way again. When I had my T-shirt lifted halfway up, he brushed my hands away and took over. He tossed the shirt over his shoulder.

"Beautiful," he said right before he latched his mouth onto my breast.

Hallelujah, my hundred-member choir sang, their joyful voices filling my ears. My knees buckled when he bit my nipple, sending lava-hot fire through my bloodstream. He wrapped an arm around my thighs, and with only the strength in that arm, held me up. His mouth moved to my other breast, and okay, he'd not even reached the mother lode and I was ready to die a happy woman.

"Dylan," I said. It was a whisper of my need for him, a plea for more. Without warning, he stood, scooping me up as he rose. I buried my face against his neck, inhaling his essence into my lungs as he carried me to his bed. Someday when I stood on a beach in Greece or Italy or Monaco, wishing he were with me, I wanted to remember everything about him.

He lowered me, then stood at the edge of the mattress, staring down at me with those eyes that seemed to want to eat me up. "All I thought about during dinner, Red, was you and me in my bed."

"I kind of got that."

He sat next to me. "Did you?"

"Yeah. The way you kept looking at me, like I was your favorite dessert."

"Go on." He put his hand on my knee, wrapping his strong fingers around it.

"That gave you away. A choir of needy singers took up residence..." I pointed *down there*. "They're feeling kind of achy."

He stared at me in confusion for a second, and then he smiled. His smile morphed into laughter. He fell onto the bed, his body parallel to mine. "Christ, Jenny Girl, no wonder I lo—" His mouth snapped shut.

I froze. *Don't say it. Don't say it. Please don't say it, Dylan.* I had plans. I would leave him. Love couldn't happen between us.

"That I love how your mind works."

Air escaped my lungs, relieved that he wasn't in love with me. So why did I want to cry? I told my mouth to smile and it did. "My mind is a thing of mystery."

"Mysterious is hot," he said. "You're hot. That goes for your mind and those needy singers. What exactly do they need? This?" He skimmed his fingers up to the hem of the boxer shorts I'd put on after my shower.

"You're getting warm."

"Ah, that's good intel." He tugged on my shorts. "I think these need to come off."

My gaze focused on his chest while I lifted my bottom so he could slide the boxers off. Unable to resist, I reached my hand out to touch his stomach. My fingers slid over skin that was both firm and soft. He let out a breath when I reached a nipple and flicked my fingernail across it.

He leaned over me, stopping when his face was only inches from mine. Our gazes locked on each other, and then he lowered his mouth to mine. His tongue pressed against the seam of my lips, and I parted my mouth, inviting him in. My hips involuntarily bucked when he slid a finger inside me. I softly moaned against his lips. He toyed with me, bringing me to a trembling mass. Just when I thought I would step off the cliff, he removed his finger. I squeezed my legs together, trying to hold on to his hand.

"Not yet, Jenny Girl." He stood, slipping his pants over his hips, letting them pool at his feet.

He was magnificent. Jaw-dropping, mouthwatering, just plain crazy hot. The sex lines on his hips caught my eyes, and I lifted my hand to trace one. He stilled, watching me with that intense focus of his. Maybe it was a cop thing, the way he could zero in on his target, seeing nothing else. The only thing on his mind right now was me, and I loved that about him.

His skin quivered under my touch, one side of his mouth curved up in a wicked half smile, and raw hunger shimmered in his eyes, so dark now they were almost black. He'd always been attentive, his attention on me and only me, when we were in bed together, but tonight felt different. As if something had changed between us, gotten more serious. A part of me that I couldn't suppress wanted that kind of relationship with him, but I couldn't break my promise to Natalie.

"Where's your mind right now, Red?"

I blinked, pushing away the doubts I'd been having lately. Nothing had changed. Thinking it had was only my imagination working overtime. "My mind is wondering why you're not in this bed with me."

He grinned as he slid next to me. "Let me show you where my mind is, beautiful girl."

"Yes, please." He put his thumb on my bottom lip, and keeping my eyes on his, I sucked it into my mouth. I wished I could take a picture of him right now to keep with me. In some country, on some night when I was missing him—because I knew that was going to happen—I'd take it out and remember how he watched me, his eyes all soft and hungry for me.

"You're killing me, looking at me like that," he whispered into my ear.

"I don't think I've ever killed a man before just by looking at him, but I'm sure going to try to render you comatose tonight." I slid my hand down his chest, past his stomach, to his hard shaft, and wrapped it around him. He groaned right before his mouth crashed down on mine.

Hours later I lay on my side, watching Dylan sleep. I wanted to memorize everything about him. How the tension lines next to his eyes had disappeared, making him look younger. How his mouth was slightly parted, his full lips one of my favorite features. They were lips that begged a girl to kiss them. I smiled, thinking that I pretty much *had* rendered him comatose.

After the way we'd gone at it, I should be worn-out and sound asleep, but my eyes were wide open and my brain was going to short circuit. As soon as Autumn and Brian were married, I'd get on a plane and leave. Nothing and no one was going to get in the way of that happening. Not even Dylan. And that was my problem.

My heart was trying to fall for him, and I had to put a stop to that. This trip wasn't just about me. It was also my promise to my sister on her deathbed to make our shared dream come true. Somewhere on some foreign beach, she was waiting for me. If I fell in love with Dylan, I wouldn't be able to leave him. My gaze traveled over him. He had the cover pushed down to a few inches below his waist. I hovered my hand over his chest, wanting to feel him against my palm. Instead I pulled away, afraid I'd wake him.

I didn't know what to do. Stop seeing him altogether, or at the very least, slow things down. Not spend every night at his place like I'd fallen into the habit of doing. If I put some distance between us, I could better protect my heart, which even now screamed in protest at this idea. I needed time to think, and I couldn't do that here, lying next to him.

There had been something desperate in the way his eyes had locked on me as his body covered mine, almost like he was memorizing me. Was he already thinking of my departure? For the first time since I'd had this dream to travel the world, I wasn't bouncing in my seat, raring to go.

As quietly as possible, I slipped out of bed, grabbed my camisole and boxers, and then made my way to the living room. After slipping on my clothes, I sat on the sofa, wrapping the afghan Dylan kept on the arm around me. Moonlight came in through the glass doors, enough that I could easily see my surroundings. Dylan's owl hooted in the distance, and I was even going to miss hearing him.

"You can't sleep either?" I asked Daisy when she padded into the room, sitting at my feet. She whined. "Ah, you think I should have stayed in bed with your daddy? Is that it?"

She put her chin on my knee, staring up at me with those soulful brown eyes. "I don't know what to do," I confided to her as tears fell down my cheeks.

I scratched her nose, and she crawled onto my lap even though she knew she wasn't supposed to be on the sofa. It was as if she understood that offering her doggy love was more important than furniture rules. Or maybe she just didn't like tears. I didn't like them either, but they always came when I thought of Natalie. God, I missed her with an ache that would never go away.

"I can't break my promise to my sister, Daisy. Tell me you get that."

CHAPTER THIRTY-SIX

~ *Dylan* ~

I WASN'T DAISY, BUT I GOT it. What little hope I'd had that Jenny might give up her plans to take off were crushed at hearing her conversation with my dog. I backed up in the hallway, returning to my bedroom.

If she hadn't made a deathbed promise, would she have decided to stay? It had sounded like she would have at least considered it. A part of me understood her need to keep the promise, but another part resented that someone now dead meant more to Jenny than I did, and I was a bastard for thinking that.

Even sound asleep I'd reached for her, finding only a cold sheet where she should have been. Truthfully I was glad I'd heard her talking to Daisy. Until tonight there'd been that little sliver of *maybe* in my mind. Funny. I loved being in love, but for whatever reason, the fates were apparently aligned against me. Having a slew of women's numbers in my contact list didn't appeal to me. I wanted to love a woman who loved me back, and only me. One I could trust not to find another man in our bed when I returned from a trip.

I thought Jenny could be that woman. Unfortunately she had a promise to keep. And that was still my hang-up about telling her I'd wait for her to return home. I refused to be the reason she felt guilty if she met a man on her travels that she wanted to bring back to her hotel room.

Jenny never came back to bed, and I passed the remainder of the night planning how I'd begin to step away from her. I did my best to ignore the ache in my chest, and I absolutely ignored the burning in my eyes.

Always an early riser, I walked out to my living room at six, expecting to see Jenny curled up on the sofa. She wasn't there. In the kitchen I found a note taped to the coffee maker. Snatching it, I scanned the words.

Good morning, Dylan.

I have a ton of errands to run today for Autumn, so I'm taking off early. The coffee's ready to go, just push start. Last night was amazing. You're one hot cop. Just wanted you to know that. So, I'm going to be really busy helping Autumn get ready for her wedding. I might not get to see as much of you as I'd like before I leave. I'll call you.

Jenny

She was as much as running. After overhearing her conversation with Daisy, I shouldn't have been surprised. I read the note one more time before crushing it in my hand. Damn it. Hadn't I decided only hours ago to do the same thing…put distance between us? I put my hands on the counter and bowed my head. Evidently my heart wasn't very good at protecting itself.

Daisy whined, nudging my leg with her nose. "Don't ever fall in love, Daisy my girl. No good will come of it." She barked, which I took as agreement. I could just stand here, feeling sorry for myself, but I had a big day ahead of me. There was a police captain I had to deal with and a mayor's daughter to arrest.

I sat in a corner booth in Mountaintop Pancake House waiting for the mayor. My mood wasn't good.

"Morning, Chief."

I nodded to the mayor as he slid into the booth. "Jim John." This wasn't going to be a fun conversation.

Our waitress poured coffee into the mayor's cup and

then refilled mine. I ordered an omelet and hash browns, with a side order of bacon to go, Daisy's reward for being a good dog. She was tied to a post right outside the window where I could keep an eye on her. It hadn't taken her long to locate me, and her gaze was fixated on me.

"The meeting went well. Pretty much how I expected," Jim John said after ordering sausage and a double stack of pancakes.

I managed not to roll my eyes. The man had been ready to throw me to the wolves if it came down to it. "So we're good?"

"Of course. What's going to happen to your old partner? He really flipped out, didn't he? 'Course any man that bangs another man's wife deserves what's coming to him."

Ironic he should say that considering what I now knew. "I don't know." No way was I going to talk to him about Jack. Whatever I said would be all over town by the end of the day.

The waitress returned with our food, and I waited while Jim John poured an ocean of syrup over his pancakes.

"I wanted to catch you up on a few things," I said. "An e-mail came in this morning from the DA. They're not going to charge Gertie Jansen. Said she acted in self-defense."

He nodded. "I got that e-mail, too."

Figured he probably had, but that really wasn't my agenda for this meeting. "You good with that?"

"It is what it is." He shrugged, then dived back into his pancakes.

That didn't tell me what he really thought, but I let it drop. Personally I couldn't have been happier that Gertie wasn't headed for a trial. There were two issues we needed to discuss, and I debated which one to bring up first. Both were going to make for an unhappy mayor. I decided to save his daughter for last.

"We need to talk about Captain Moody." That got his

attention.

He set his fork down on his empty plate. "About?"

"He's dirty. I know it and you know it." I pushed my plate aside. Jim John glanced around as if worried that our conversation would be overheard, but I'd kept my voice low. No one was listening to us.

"I know no such thing. He told me you're out to get him. That you'd manufactured fake evidence against him."

No surprise that Moody had been bending the mayor's ear. "I don't have to manufacture anything where he's concerned. He's been stealing from the department, probably for years. What are you afraid of, Jim John?" I hoped he'd level with me, but I didn't expect him to.

"Don't know what you're talking about." His gaze shifted away.

"He knows about your secret daughter, doesn't he?"

His face paled as he glanced around us. "This isn't the place to have this discussion."

"No problem. I'm going to drop Daisy off at the station. I'll meet you in your office."

"Not there either. Just follow me. You can bring the damn dog." He threw a few bills on the table and walked out the door.

We ended up at the city park, sitting at a picnic table near the creek. There was no one else here this early in the morning, so I let Daisy off her leash, knowing she wouldn't venture far.

Jim John leaned forward, resting his elbows on his knees. "What is it you think you know?"

That his secret wasn't as secret as he thought. "Three years ago Moody somehow found out that you'd had a brief affair and that you have another daughter. Her name is Isabelle Bradley, and she's ten years old. He's been blackmailing you ever since."

Jim John sucked in a breath, then blew it out. "How'd

you find out?"

"Moody doesn't know how to keep his mouth shut. He told Jansen a while back, and Jansen told his wife." Jenny's father had hinted that Jim John had skeletons in his closet. He'd also hinted that since Moody and Jansen had been tight, Jansen probably knew. So I'd paid Mrs. Jansen a visit early this morning. I didn't even have to ask her what she knew. Her life with Jansen came pouring out. The mayor's secret had been among the many things she'd told me.

"What if she tells anyone else?"

"Gertie won't say anything, but I have to wonder who else Moody's blabbed to."

"I didn't mean for it to happen… my affair with Sarah." He buried his head between his knees.

Ah hell. I was sitting in a public park with a crying mayor. It didn't get any better than this. Daisy cocked her head at the grunting sounds coming from Jim John. She eased up to him and whined. When that got no response, she licked the side of his face. I seriously considered slipping away, leaving the two of them to their misery.

He lifted his head, pushing Daisy away. "I take care of them financially."

Not my concern, nor was it my place to judge him. "I'm going to fire Moody."

Panic lit his face. "You can't. He said he'd tell my wife if I do anything he doesn't like."

"Maybe you should tell her first. How many other people do you think he's told besides Jansen? Eventually your wife is going to hear. Better it comes from you." I was starting to feel like a priest holding confession. "Think about it. In the meantime I'll take care of Moody."

Daisy brought me a stick, dropping it at my feet. I threw it, and off she went. He didn't ask how I was going to deal with Moody. I sure would have, but then I never would have put myself in this position. "I'd advise you not to answer any phone calls from him from now on."

"That's actually a relief to hear." Jim John stood. "I want to know when it's done."

I almost snorted. It sounded like he thought I was going to kill the man. "Sit down, Jim John. There's something else we have to talk about."

"I've heard enough bad news this morning."

"Sit," I said when it seemed like he was going to walk away. "We need to talk about Stephanie."

He sat, his shoulders slumping in defeat. "I'm listening."

"Her blood test came back. She was over the legal limit." I hadn't been here long enough to decide if he was a good mayor. His personal life and family were definitely screwed up, though.

He let out a weary sigh. "She almost killed that boy. Charge her with a DUI. Maybe she'll think twice next time."

I sure hadn't expected it to be that easy. Even if he had ordered me to drop the charges, I wouldn't have. Hopefully Stephanie would learn a lesson from this.

"We done here?"

"Is Stephanie home?"

"Yes. Probably still asleep."

"I'll send Gene Lanier and Sarah Griffin to bring her in. You might want to warn your wife. If we do it this morning, I can probably push things through, get her in front of a judge this afternoon. You going to cover her bail?"

"I should probably let her sit in jail tonight, but yeah, I will."

He walked away, his shoulders slumped. The meeting had gone better than I'd hoped, but I was mentally drained. Mostly because I hadn't been able to go to sleep after I'd gone back to bed, and I was missing Jenny Girl like the very devil.

"Come on, Daisy. We have a bad man to deal with." I

ran a critical eye over her as she trotted to me. Her ribs were still showing, although not nearly as badly as when I'd found her. It was her enlarged nipples that had me frowning.

"Anyone seen Captain Moody?" It was early afternoon, and the man had yet to show his face. If I didn't know better, I'd think he knew he was losing his job and had made himself scarce.

"He's not been around all day," Kim said.

If I were still giving out points, Moody would have been deducted a truckload for an unexcused absence. I went to my office, got out my phone, and called him.

"This is your chief," I said when he answered. "Be in my office at five." I hung up before he could respond since I didn't want to hear any excuses as to why he couldn't come in. Next I buzzed Gene Lanier, telling him I needed to see him.

"Close the door," I said when Gene walked in.

"Am I in trouble?"

"Not today, but Moody is. He'll be here at five, and I'm taking his gun and badge. I want you in here as a witness so he doesn't go making up lies afterward. You're going to hear some things that you can never repeat, capisce?"

Gene nodded. "I can't say I'll be sorry to see him go. He's bad news. But he's not going to go away without a fight."

I smiled. "Maybe not, but I have a few tricks up my sleeve. You think we scared Stephanie straight?" I'd stayed away from that, making myself scarce when they'd brought her in. The mayor and I had to work together, and I wasn't about to put myself between her and her father.

"I hope so. She seems genuinely sorry. Said she can't sleep at night because when she closes her eyes, all she sees is Sean's mangled body."

"Hard way to learn a lesson. Let me know when her court date is."

"Will do. Anything else, Chief?"

"No, just be back a few minutes before five."

I got busy planning my meeting with Moody, half hoping he'd come at me so I could throw his ass in jail. If nothing else, it helped keep my mind off Jenny. For a while. But she was there in my thoughts, refusing to go away. I kept asking myself one question. What if I did tell Jenny I'd wait for her? What was the worst that could happen? She'd meet someone and fall in love. If that happened, I didn't want her to feel guilty.

As far as I knew, she'd never been in love. I had. It was a wonderful and beautiful thing to love someone, until they didn't love you anymore. Then it was like walking into a wasteland where everything was dead. But it didn't have to be that way for Jenny.

The right thing to do was to let her go.

CHAPTER THIRTY-SEVEN

~ Jenny ~

HOW WAS IT DECEMBER ALREADY? I think the last two months passed so fast because of my time with Dylan. Time really does fly when you're having fun, I guess. I'd only left him this morning, and already I was missing him. It was cowardly of me to take off, leaving a crappy note. I should have told him to his face that I needed time away from him, but I was afraid I'd admit to how I really felt about him. If he knew he was halfway to stealing my heart, he might try to talk me out of going, and I might agree. I think if that happened, the guilt would eat away at me for breaking my promise to Natalie.

It was finally starting to feel like winter. We'd had a few snow flurries this morning, but they'd melted before hitting the ground. I glanced out the window. The trees were bare, the mountains an ugly brown. As soon as Autumn and Brian were married, I'd go. I'd even turned in my notice to Angelo. He wasn't happy, but I'd never hid my plans from him.

Travel brochures I'd collected over the years covered my kitchen table. I sipped my coffee, staring at the budget up on my laptop screen that I'd made for my world tour with a sense of excitement and dread. My tips during leaf season had been exceptionally good. Adding the money my parents had gifted me toward my trip, I had surpassed my goal. That would mean I could travel longer than I'd planned.

That should make me happy, but it didn't. Why did I

have to meet the perfect man now? If Dylan had waited to walk into my life in a year or two, it would have been perfect. Would he even consider waiting for me? A year would go by fast, right? No, that wouldn't be fair to him.

"Damn it." I squeezed my eyes shut against the sting of tears. How did one choose between a promise made to the most important person in my life and love? Not that I loved Dylan yet… Okay, maybe a little. I just didn't know. What if I gave up my dream, Dylan and I got married, and ten years later ended up divorced?

A hysterical-sounding laugh burst out of me at having us already married. After what he'd been through, the last thing he probably wanted was another wife. In which case, there really wasn't a future for us, just some good times until he moved on. Should I risk my dream on the slim chance that Dylan and I could find something special that would last a lifetime?

My phone rang, Autumn's name coming up on the screen. "Hey."

"What's wrong?"

"You got that from one word how?" I heard Autumn's snort in my ear and couldn't help grinning.

"Because I know all your heys and that wasn't a happy one. I just finished my last appointment, so I'm going to swing by Mary's, get us some of her mouthwatering chocolate cheesecake slices. Be there in twenty. Have me a glass of wine poured."

She hung up before I could protest. Autumn was an interior designer, a good one. She'd helped me make my tiny apartment cozy on very little money. There was no one I'd rather pour my heart out to right now than her, unless Savannah was here, too, to join us.

"Let's call Savannah," I said as soon as Autumn walked in the door.

She handed me a white paper bag. "Cheesecake and

wine first, then we'll call her. Mary said, 'Tell Jenn the answers are in the stars.' I just dug my nails into my palms to keep from going bug-eyed on her. What does she know that I don't?"

"I don't know how to read the stars." If only I could, then maybe I'd be able to see a future with Dylan. My lips quivered. "How does she even know I need answers?"

"The woman's spooky, that's for sure." Autumn wrapped her arms around me, giving me a bestie hug. "Whatever this is, we'll figure it out, okay? As soon as we eat." She eyed the cheesecake slices as I put them on a plate. "That's at least five pounds right there that I shouldn't touch if I want to fit into my wedding gown, but you mean more to me than a dress."

God, I loved her. Without Autumn, I'm not sure I would have survived losing Natalie. My parents had been wrapped up in their own grief, and I hadn't wanted to add to their sadness. Savannah had been there for a few days, but then she'd left for New York. It had been mostly Autumn I'd turned to. She had held me, cried with me, sometimes rocking me like a baby during the hardest days of my life. I burst into tears, suddenly missing my twin with a bone-deep ache.

"Oh, sweetie, you're thinking of Natalie, aren't you?"

Unable to speak, I nodded.

She picked up one of the glasses I'd filled with wine, handing it to me. "Drink up, then start talking."

I downed half the wine. Setting the glass back on the table, I buried my face in my hands. Somehow, between sobs, I managed to tell her how torn I was between Dylan and my promise to Natalie. "I don't…" I peered at her through watery tears. "I don't know what to do. I could love him, Autumn. Like I've never loved another man. But I promised Natalie I'd go to all the places we dreamed of going together."

"Sweetie, the two of you were barely out of high school when you made that promise. Loving a man forever wasn't even on the horizon for either of you to take into account. If Natalie knew what Dylan meant to you, she'd be the first to tell you to go for it."

"Maybe." I blew my nose into the paper towel she handed me. "I don't think he can ever love me like he loved his wife."

Autumn's eyebrows lifted. "Whoa. Where did that come from?"

"I don't know," I wailed. Maybe I did know. It had been the pain I'd seen in his eyes when he'd talked about her. "I'm such a hot mess."

"Tell me this. If he asked you not to go, what would you do?"

"He's not going to ask that, so it doesn't matter." Would I stay, though? Maybe. Probably.

"If he does, you need to ask yourself one thing. If you gave up your dream…because it was that along with your promise to Natalie, right?"

"That's true. Wanting to travel the world has always been more than just my promise." I glared at her. "You were supposed to go with me in her place."

"And I would have if I hadn't met Brian. He's my soul mate, Jenn. Choosing him was the easiest thing I've ever done." She took my hands in hers. "Can you honestly say that if Dylan did ask you to stay, that you'd never resent him for it someday?"

Tears pooled in my eyes again. "I don't know. What if he's my soul mate but I'm not his?"

"Only one way to find out. Talk to him, tell him how you feel."

"I'll think about it." I probably wouldn't, though. The thought of Dylan never loving me like he had his wife was a brick wall I couldn't tear down. And did I even want to try? "Do you think you only have one soul mate in life?"

"No, but I do think you love each one differently."

I laughed through my tears. "That makes absolutely no sense." I poked holes in the last half of my cheesecake. "We were just going to be a fling, you know? I'm not supposed to be sitting here talking about soul mates and crying over the thought of leaving him."

Autumn put her hand on my wrist, holding it still. "Stop killing your cake. You can't leave until after my wedding, so spend the time between now and then with him, see how it goes. Nothing says you have to step on that plane when it takes off."

I smiled at my friend through watery tears. "I love you, you know."

"I know. Let's see if we can run down Savannah. Then I need to head home and get ready for my first appointment in the morning. A couple retiring here from New York bought the Miller house and want a complete redo. I hope Brian can love a bald woman because I have a feeling I'm going to pull all my hair out before I'm done with them."

"You'll be brilliant as always, and she'll be thrilled with it when you're finished."

Autumn laughed. "I love your faith in me. Call Savannah."

I picked up my phone, putting it on speaker.

"'Lo," a sleepy voice said.

Autumn and I exchanged glances. It was midafternoon. Savannah had never been one to take naps. "Hey, Savannah."

"Jenn! Is Autumn with you?"

"I'm here," Autumn said. "Sounds like we woke you."

There was silence, and we heard the rustle of bedsheets and a man's voice. "Oops," I whispered to Autumn.

"Hold on a sec." A few moments later we could hear a door close. "Hey, you two. This is a great surprise."

Yet it didn't sound like she was all that happy to hear from us. When she'd first arrived in New York and we would call her, she would scream when we called, and would excitedly tell us everything going on in her life. Now we couldn't get any details out of her when we called.

"How's the wedding planning going, Autumn?"

"Everything's pretty much done. We can't wait to see you. It'll be like old times, the three of us together again."

"About that—"

"No!" Autumn and I both yelled together.

"You listen to me, Savannah Graham," I said. "If I have to come to New York and drag you home for Autumn's wedding, I will. You know I mean that." How could she even consider not being here for Autumn? "You've had the date for almost a year now. That was plenty of time to work it into your busy schedule."

Autumn put her hand on my arm, shaking her head, but I didn't care if I was upsetting Savannah. I was the maid of honor, but Savannah was Autumn's only bridesmaid. She damn well was going to be here. She'd promised.

Someone banged on the door in whatever room Savannah had gone to, and we heard muffled voices. She must have been holding her hand over the phone. Even though the man's voice was muted and we couldn't understand the words, he sounded angry.

"Listen," Savannah said, coming back on the phone. "I have to go. I'll call you soon."

"Savannah..." She was gone.

Autumn stared at the phone, a frown on her face. "Something's not right."

"Yeah, she's definitely not the Savannah we know and love. At least we'll be able to see for ourselves how she is when she gets here."

"I just wish we knew what was going on with her," Autumn said, glancing up at me with worry in her eyes.

So did I.

CHAPTER THIRTY-EIGHT

~ Dylan ~

MOODY WAS LATE, OF COURSE. "You got those restraining orders ready for me to sign?" I asked Gene while we waited for my captain to show his face.

He handed me a manila folder. "Here you go. I hope he doesn't decide to shoot us both."

"A distinct possibility." I laughed when Gene paled. "Good thing I'm a faster draw, huh?" I wouldn't put it past Moody to make some dumbass move, so my gun was sitting on my lap, hidden by my desk.

"Here he comes," I said at hearing Moody's voice down the hallway. I glanced at my watch. "Ten minutes late. The man knows how to push my buttons."

Gene dragged his chair over to the wall. "I'm going to sit over here where I can keep an eye on him."

"Have a seat, Mr. Moody," I said when the man paused in the doorway. He eyed Gene for a few seconds, then sauntered to the chair as if he didn't have a care in the world. He had to suspect that at the very least he was in trouble, so the smirk on his face told me he thought there was nothing I could do to him. He was about to learn differently.

"Put your gun and badge on my desk, Mr. Moody." Out of the corner of my eye I saw Gene tense. I was twitchy myself, having no clue how Moody would react to that, but I wanted his gun off his person ASAP.

Moody narrowed his eyes. "The fuck's going on here?"

Since I was about to fire him, I let his language go

without comment. "Your gun and badge, please." My hand was on my own weapon, my finger on the trigger. I wasn't taking any chances with the fool. Seconds ticked by as Moody stared hard at me, probably debating whether or not he could get away with shooting me.

"So I'm suspended? The fuck I do now?"

"We'll discuss it as soon as you turn over your weapon and badge."

Never taking his eyes—brimming with hatred—off me, he put his hand on his holster. I was pretty sure Gene was holding his breath along with me. The next few moments were like a movie playing in slow motion. Moody unsnapped his holster, put his hand on the barrel of his gun, then paused. I didn't want to shoot a soon-to-be ex-cop in my office, but I would if I had to. I didn't so much as blink as I held Moody's stare.

Gene had his hand in his coat pocket, and I was certain his finger was on the trigger of his gun. That made three of us ready to perform our own rendition of the O.K. Corral. I let my eyes grow cold, let Moody see that I dared him to try to pull a stupid stunt. When the man's gaze flicked away, I relaxed…a little.

"This is bullshit." Moody slammed his gun down on my desk, followed by his badge.

"Now the throwaway you have in your boot. Put it on the desk, too." I was guessing, but my hunch was confirmed when he pressed his lips together.

"That's my personal gun."

"And against regulations for you to be carrying on the job. You'll get it back when we're done." Unfortunately I didn't have grounds to confiscate it or I would. He reached down, and I tensed again. Apparently he decided not to be stupid because he put the .38 on my desk, alongside his department-issued weapon.

I opened my desk drawer and put both guns and the

badge in it. No reason to honey my way up to it, so I just spit it out. "Mr. Moody, you're fired." I'd been waiting to say those words since the night I'd caught him sitting at my desk, playing poker and drinking.

He shot up out of his chair. "The hell you say. We'll just see about that." He took out his phone and punched the screen, then put it to his ear.

"If you're calling the mayor, don't bother. He's not going to answer." I glanced at my watch for show. "Right about now, he's telling his wife about his illegitimate daughter." I heard a sharp gasp from Gene, but I kept my eyes on Moody. "As of now, your days of blackmailing Mayor Jenkins are over. Sit down. We have more to discuss."

Refusing to admit defeat, my erstwhile captain kept the phone to his ear. "You need to call me," he said.

Good. Jim John had taken my advice not to answer a call from Moody. "Sit down, Mr. Moody, or I'll throw you in a jail cell right now. Believe me, I have cause to slam you with a baker's dozen worth of charges, and I will if you don't cooperate."

"You won't get away with this." He sat.

Oh, but I would. I'd barely begun to show my hand. I opened the folder Gene had given me. I signed my name on the first page, then held it up. "This is a restraining order on you to keep away from the mayor."

I signed all the rest, ignoring Moody's attempts to see what all I was putting my name on. When I finished, I waved some more pages in front of him. "These are restraining orders keeping you away from me and all the officers of the Blue Ridge Valley Police Department, the town manager, and the councilmen." I dropped them on my desk, then picked up three more. "These are blank except for my signature, intended for anyone else you might decide to harass or threaten.

"Before you say a word," I said, holding up my hand,

"there's more." I pretended to study the report I pulled out of my desk drawer. "Aside from putting your family on the department's payroll at an exorbitant rate, and aside from your outrageous charges all over town, there's this." I handed him a copy of the proof of his outright stealing from the department's pension fund. His face paled when he saw what I'd uncovered, which made me gleeful. I shouldn't delight so much in a cop's downfall, but this one deserved what he had coming.

"Yeah, thought no one would stumble on that, didn't you?" He didn't answer, not that I was expecting him to. "A word of advice, Mr. Moody. When you set yourself up as the treasurer of your fellow cops' pension fund, don't write checks to yourself for bogus expenses."

Gene's expression went from looking at me with shock at hearing that bit of news to glaring at Moody with the kind of disgust one would have when realizing you'd stepped in dog shit. "Can I kill him now?" Gene said.

I regretfully shook my head. "As much as I'd love to give you that pleasure, you're too valuable to have to arrest for murder." I turned a hard eye back to Moody. "Tell me why I shouldn't put handcuffs on you, take you on the walk of shame so the men and women you were supposed to protect don't find out what a piece of scum you are?"

"I want a lawyer."

"I bet you do." If I'd thought he hated me before, that was nothing compared to the way he looked at me now. As long as he was around, I'd be watching my back. Time to make that problem go away. "You have two choices, Mr. Moody. Stick around Blue Ridge Valley and I'll have no choice but to arrest you. If that isn't to your liking, be gone by Friday. By 'gone' I mean you disappear so far away that I lose my desire to find you. Because I'll be looking. Don't ever doubt that." I leaned across my desk, putting my face as close to his as possible. "And if you do decide to get stupid and come after me or anyone under my protection, I will throw your ass in jail. That you definitely shouldn't doubt."

I hadn't been sure how he'd react to my threat, so I waited. Moody's face turned lobster red, his breaths coming in erratic bursts. For a minute I thought I'd have to call for paramedics.

"That badge you wore, Mr. Moody, represented honor, integrity, and dedication to the people you swore to protect, which included your fellow cops." I took his shield back out of the drawer and curled my fingers around it. "Contrary to what you seem to think, this piece of metal is not a ticket to steal. I'm being beyond generous here by even considering letting you walk away when you've shamed every cop on this force. Which will it be? A jail cell or a new town you can terrorize?" I asked, keeping my voice deceptively soft.

As much as I wanted to throw him in jail and lose the keys, charging him with crimes that would send him away for most of his life, I was doing Jim John a favor by encouraging Moody to disappear. A trial would ruin the mayor because all of Jim John's secrets would come out. At this point I only wanted the mess that was Moody gone so my cops could forget he'd ever existed.

Moody walked out without answering. I lifted my gaze to the security monitor on the far wall and watched him until he stormed out the lobby door. He'd apparently forgotten I had his throwaway gun, but I wasn't complaining about that. Not that I doubted he had more weapons at home. I'd never run a man out of town before. It was kind of fun.

"Holy Mother Mary," Gene murmured.

I swung my gaze to Gene. "Think we've heard the last of him?"

"Don't know, but Chief, you ever decide to come

down on me, just say, 'be gone by sundown' and I'll heed the warning. You're damn scary when you want to be."

I laughed, couldn't help it. "Hope Moody thinks so." While Gene slid his chair back in place, I slipped my gun back into my holster.

"It was common knowledge around here that Moody had something on the mayor, but I never would have guessed Jim John had a secret daughter."

"Yeah, about that. Not a word, okay?"

"No one will hear it from me. We all knew Moody was up to no good in a lot of ways, but to steal from our pension fund? That burns."

"Yeah, I know. Gather the troops for me. I need to tell everyone Moody's gone."

"You got someone in mind to replace him?"

"Why? You interested?" I hoped not. He was more valuable as a detective and too mild-mannered to control a bunch of cops.

"Not even."

"I didn't think so. Yeah, I have someone in mind." I debated telling him but decided I wanted to get his reaction. "Sarah Griffin."

A big smile appeared on his face. "She'll do you a good job."

"I don't doubt it. Now round up everyone you can. I'll be out in a few minutes to talk to them."

After he left, I tidied up my desk when what I really wanted to do was call Jenny and ask her to come over when she got off. A lot had happened today, and I wanted to share it with her.

Letting out a sigh, I went to let Daisy out of jail. She not only hated Moody, but she was so afraid of him that sometimes she shook whenever he was around, and other times I feared she would attack him. My dog was obviously a good judge of character. I'd put her, along with her bed and a rawhide, in an empty cell while I dealt with terminating Moody.

"You're safe now. The bad man's gone." After moving her bed and rawhide back to my office, I headed for the front, Daisy trailing along behind me. With the exception of Moody, she loved all the other officers. She trotted around the room, stopping for a few seconds to greet each of her friends. I pretended not to notice a few of them slip her a dog treat.

"Listen up," I said when everyone was present. "Mr. Moody is no longer a member of this department." Applause broke out before I could continue. I hadn't expected anyone to have a problem with that, but I was happy to have it confirmed.

"If he contacts any of you for any reason, I want you to let me know immediately. Capisce?" All my officers nodded. I'd decided not to mention the restraining orders. It was enough that Moody knew about them.

"That's it. Those coming off shift, go home. Those heading out, be careful out there.

"Come on, Daisy, my girl. Let's go home." When I passed Vincennes, I gave serious consideration to taking Daisy home and then coming back for a beer and pizza. It wasn't like Jenny and I weren't still friends, but seeing her? I'd only be torturing myself with what I couldn't have.

Later that night I lay in my bed, staring at the ceiling, listening to my owl hunt for his dinner and feeling lonelier than ever. I passed the hours until sunrise debating my decision to let Jenny go without telling her how I felt, but I'd known from the beginning that she was leaving after Autumn's wedding. She'd set a deadline on our time together, and I would honor it.

CHAPTER THIRTY-NINE

~ Jenny ~

IF I DIDN'T HAVE TO stay for Autumn's wedding, I'd get on a plane today. "I thought maybe he'd call me."

Autumn glanced over her shoulder. "You're the one who left a stupid note. You call him."

"He probably hates me." We were at Autumn's future home, where I was having a one-person pity party because my best friend wasn't being very sympathetic. She adjusted the silver-framed photo of her and Brian, taken last year on their vacation to St. Thomas.

"I've seen the way he looks at you. He'd want to hear from you, so stop your whining and pick up the phone."

"How does he look at me?" I was pathetic, reaching for any little crumb that might prove Dylan had feelings for me.

"He can't take his eyes off you. It's true," she said when I shook my head.

It wasn't like I was in love with him.

"I don't know, are you?"

"Didn't mean to say that out loud," I grumbled. I just really missed him.

"Well, you did." She frowned when I refilled my wine-glass for the third time. "Are you sure you want to drink that? You've gone through half the bottle already."

"What? You're the wine police now?" Yes, I wanted to drink it. All of it. Until I couldn't remember Dylan's name.

"Don't get snotty with me, Jenn." She pulled out the dining room chair next to me. "I'm sorry you're hurting, but drinking yourself sick isn't going to solve anything. And you do get sick if you drink too much."

That was true. I pushed the glass away. I pressed my palms against my eyes, hating all the crying I'd been doing lately. Somehow my tears were mixed up between Natalie and Dylan, each one calling to me, asking for my love, my allegiance. How was I supposed to choose between the sister I loved more than anyone in the world and a man I could love like no other, but offered only an uncertain future?

"You thought you'd kept your heart safe." Autumn wrapped her arms around me as I bawled like a baby. I hadn't realized Dylan had stolen my heart until it was too late.

"So what are you going to do about it?" She let go of me and went to the kitchen, returning with a paper towel. "Sorry, I don't have any tissues here."

I wiped my face. "Leave." I hiccupped. Soon I'd be on my way. I just wished it were today. Right now.

"Maybe you should talk to Dylan, tell him how you feel."

"It's been four days. If I meant anything to him, he would have called by now."

"Have you considered that he hasn't called because he's respecting your wishes?"

"Well, he shouldn't."

Autumn rolled her eyes. "Do you even know what you want?"

"I have to go, so it really doesn't matter, does it? I won't break my promise to Natalie. Besides, Dylan's not looking for a serious relationship,"

"He told you that?"

"Yeah, when we first got together." I put my hand on my chest. My heart hadn't healed from losing Natalie, and it was breaking all over again.

"I told you how he looks at you, like you mean something to him. Maybe he's changed his mind."

My heart gave a flutter of hope, but I crushed it. I almost told her that Natalie promised I'd feel her with me, but Autumn wouldn't get it. Maybe Connor and Adam would because only twins could understand the connection that lived in our souls. They would get how much I needed to know she was with me.

"Come over and have dinner with me and Brian tonight. I'll make lasagna."

I forced a smile. "There's an offer I can't refuse." Although I wanted to. All I really wanted to do was to go home, eat a tub of ice cream, and cry.

By late Friday morning I was ready to paint my apartment or wallpaper everything in sight or start collecting cats. Anything to get my mind off Dylan. I was going stir-crazy sitting in my apartment, missing a man who didn't want me. I'd tried to read, but after staring at the same page on my Kindle until the screen went blank, I gave up on that. Turning on the TV hadn't worked. The apartment was spotless since I'd gotten up at the crack of dawn and cleaned it from top to bottom. I'd gone through my clothes, deciding what I'd take. Not much, since I'd be moving around a lot.

I finished making a list of the things I needed to do before leaving, then looked around. Now what?

My phone buzzed, my mom's name coming up. "Hey. What's up?"

"Hi, honey. Dad and I visited Sean this morning. I knew you'd want to know that he's been moved out of ICU and into a room."

"That means he's out of danger, right?"

"Yep. He's listed as stable now."

"Fantastic." We talked for a few more minutes, and after hanging up, I decided I'd go visit Sean. It was something to fill the time before I had to go to work.

On the drive to Asheville I turned the volume up on my radio and sang along with the songs. Anything to keep from thinking about Dylan. At the hospital, after finding out Sean's room number, I took the elevator up to the third floor.

I turned the corner and ran into a brick wall. "Oomph."

Large male hands grasped my shoulders. "Sorry… Jenny?"

Dylan's voice washed over me like warm sunshine. I squeezed my eyes shut to keep from curling into his chest and wrapping my arms around him.

"Are you okay?"

No, I wasn't. "Sure." I blinked open my eyes, glancing behind me. When I tried to step around him—because I really needed to get away before I did something stupid like cry, or worse, kiss him—he caught my wrist.

"Were you on the way to see Sean?"

Not trusting my voice, I nodded. Dylan's fingers felt like a brand on my skin, hot and possessive.

"I just came from his room. He's sleeping right now."

"Oh, okay. Well, I guess I'll come back some other time."

He rubbed his thumb over the inside of my wrist. I wasn't sure he realized he was doing it, but it was sending my senses into overdrive. My arm tingled all the way up to my shoulder, and if my lady parts got any hotter, I was going to combust.

"Jenny?"

"Hmm?" Whatever the question, the answer was yes.

"I noticed a coffee shop next door. Let me buy you a cup."

"I don't think that's a good idea." What happened to answering yes to whatever he asked? Self-preservation, that's what.

"Please, Jenny. I…" He swiped a hand through his hair. "Just two friends having a cup of coffee, okay?"

My stupid heart sank to my stomach at hearing him describe us as just two friends, even though I was the one who'd left him with no more than a cowardly note. He put his hand on my shoulder. My body responded to his touch like one of Pavlov's dogs. I squeezed my legs together, willing the aching need to go away.

I guess I took too long to answer because he captured my hand. "We'll walk. Easier than moving our cars."

Five minutes later we were seated at a corner table, an iced coffee in front of me, a hot coffee for Dylan. He'd held my hand all the way over, which confused me. Holding hands had always felt like an intimate act between a man and a woman. Why was he touching me? I wished he'd just go away. Being with him again, even if only to talk, was messing with my head.

My hungry gaze roamed over him. The man was mouthwateringly sexy wearing his cop uniform—beige cargo pants, a dark brown Henley shirt, a brown leather bomber jacket, and the gun holster on his hip.

Handsome, dangerous, and not mine.

CHAPTER FORTY

~ Dylan ~

WHAT WAS I ABOUT? IT was obvious Jenny was uncomfortable, but leaving me with nothing but a note hadn't set well. Yeah, I knew her plans and why she had to go, but there was more to it than that. I'd thought long and hard about it, and the only thing I could come up with for her sneaking out the way she had was that her feelings for me scared her. I could understand that. What I felt for her for sure scared me.

Maybe it wasn't fair to push her to admit there was more between us than friends with benefits, but I needed to know. If she'd only ask me, I'd wait for her however long it took to get the travel bug out of her system, to keep the promise she'd made to her sister. I'd always been a one-woman man, and Jenny was the woman I wanted. If that meant waiting for her, so be it.

"I wasn't expecting to run into you at the hospital." Yeah, I was stalling, not sure what to say.

She stirred the whipped cream into her iced coffee. "How's Sean?"

"Getting better every day. He'll have months of physical therapy ahead, but he'll be okay."

"It was nice of you to visit him."

She still wasn't looking at me, which bugged the hell out of me. "Actually I came to see his parents to let them know that we charged Stephanie with a DUI." That got her attention, and she lifted her eyes to mine. I could drown in those damn green eyes.

"I can't say I'm surprised, but maybe it will be a wake-up call."

"Her father hopes so." Her gaze returned to her coffee, which she'd barely touched. I still didn't know what I wanted to say, but I better spit something out because she was on the edge of her seat, ready to bolt.

"How have you been, Jenny?"

"Peachy. I've been just peachy."

I frowned. What had I done? She was the one who left me a fucking note. "I'm clueless here, Red. Couldn't you have talked to me instead of leaving a note?" I hadn't meant to say that, but now that it was out, I let the question hang in the air.

"Obviously, that was fine with you since you haven't once tried to call me."

Now it was my fault? I studied her face, saw the confusion and regret swirling in her eyes and realized that she had an internal battle going on. She did feel something for me, and as for me, I wanted her more than my next breath.

"Ask me to stay, Dylan," she said, her gaze on the straw she poked around in her iced coffee.

I almost did. But how long would it be before she resented me for not only stealing her dream but for forcing her to break a deathbed promise? I did the only thing I could for her. "No, I won't do that, even though I'm tempted. If you don't go, you'll regret it. Then there's the promise you made to your sister. You have to go, but I'm not telling you anything you don't already know."

"You're not." Her shoulders slumped. "Truthfully I didn't mean to say that."

By all appearances, she was having second thoughts, and I had the feeling it would be easy to talk her out of it, which I think she wanted me to do. It wasn't my decision to make. She had to choose between me and a deathbed promise.

"Do you need a ride to the airport?" I hoped she said no. The last thing I wanted to do was watch her get on a plane.

"No, my parents are taking me." She stood.

"Can I have a good-bye hug?" She walked into my arms when I held them out, and Christ, I didn't want to ever let her go. At hearing her sniffle, I put my hand on the back of her neck, closing my eyes as I leaned my chin on her head.

"Hush, Jenny Girl," I said, stroking her hair when a sob broke free from her. "This time next month, you'll be standing on a warm beach somewhere while the rest of us here are cursing the snow. Just be smart and careful, okay?" The world was a scary place these days, and I clamped down on my protective instincts before I begged her not to take off for foreign places by herself.

"I will." She slipped out of my arms and turned to leave, but not before I saw the tears streaming down her cheeks. "Tell Daisy I'll really miss her."

If I wasn't mistaken, that message was meant for me. I watched her walk away, the ache in my heart growing with each step she took.

"Good-bye, Jenny Girl," I whispered.

Christine's ghost returned.

"*Hello, Dy.*"

I groaned at hearing the voice in my mind. "*I thought you were gone for good.*" I pulled my pillow over my head, but she was still there.

"*I thought so, too, but I came back to help you. Why are you letting her slip through your fingers?*"

So now my dead wife was giving me love advice? Weird. "*Now you sound like Garrett. Are you talking to him, too?*"

She laughed. "*Maybe I'm channeling him.*"

Oh, joy. Both of them in my head at once? "*Get out of my mind, Christine. I'm not going to talk to you about Jenny.*"

"*You're a fool for letting her go, Dylan.*"

That was probably true. I struggled up from sleep, annoyed that when troubled, my mind was still conjuring up my wife's voice. It had been a long day. Wary of my mood after I'd returned from the hospital, my officers had kept their heads down. Even Daisy had anxiously followed my every move, her worried eyes never leaving me.

"Stop watching me," I snapped at seeing her sitting a few feet from my bed. When she whined and hung her head, I sighed. "I'm sorry, girl. It's just that I'm having a hard time right now. Nothing you did."

That seemed to placate her. She barked in answer, then returned to her bed. An hour later I gave up trying to go back to sleep. Was I making a mistake letting Jenny go? She'd all but said she'd stay if I asked. I didn't know the right answer. My hesitation was because I couldn't get past one thing. If she loved me, I wouldn't have to ask her to stay. If she loved me, I would be more important than the dreams of two young girls. So I wouldn't ask, and she wouldn't stay. End of story.

The week before the wedding I spent the days getting my station in order. To keep my mind off Jenny, I was in my office early and still there late. I rode with each of my uniformed officers, observing how they handled calls, and then discussing ways they could improve. They seemed to appreciate it. Doing evaluation rides had been a part of Moody's job description, but I'd learned he'd never once ridden with any of them.

Sarah was promoted to captain, and Kim was just as excited to be promoted to junior detective status.

There was an air of pride in their department from my

officers these days that had been missing when I'd arrived on the job. Their new uniforms had arrived this morning, and they hadn't wasted any time changing out of the puky-green ones. Dressed in the black cargo pants and dark blue Henleys, even their posture was straighter.

"Do I look badass?" Tommy asked from the doorway of my office.

I let my gaze travel over him. "Do you even have to ask?" He was getting ready to go out on the late shift, and like the morning people, as soon as he saw his new uniform, he'd headed for the locker room to change.

"Just making sure my eyes weren't lying." A big grin crossed his face. "I never thought we'd get cool uniforms. As far as all of us are concerned, you're a rock star, Chief."

With that, he walked away. I stared at the empty doorway as a strange combination of contentment and a sense of loss enveloped me. I'd known when I accepted the position as chief of police that I would do a good job. I'd come here expecting to do just that, although I'd thought it might take longer to win my officers' loyalty. What I realized now was that they had been desperate for guidance and discipline. That I'd been able to give them what they needed was thanks in large part to Garrett and how he trained and treated his cops.

Picking my phone up from my desk, I put my finger on his name in my contact list to give him a call.

"If you ask nicely, I'll give you your job back," he said in greeting.

"Demote myself from chief to detective? I don't think so."

"Then why are you calling me, other than because you love me?"

"That I do." I leaned back in my chair. "I'm calling because I decided it was time to thank you. Something I should have done long ago."

"For what?"

His gravelly voice would always be one of my favorite sounds. "For making me the cop I am today. Not to get mushy on you, but I was thinking about that just now, how you took a green kid and made him into something he could be proud of."

"Fuck, Dylan, you're gonna make me cry."

I smiled at my phone. "When's Derrick going to get you to clean up that foul mouth of yours?"

"The man loves my foul mouth."

"So not going there." At his laugh I swiveled my chair, gazing out the window, thinking of the last time I'd seen him. To my shame, I'd not once thought of Jack since Garrett had hauled him away. "How's Jack doing?"

"I pulled in some favors and got him into a special treatment center. He'll never be a cop again, but if he sticks with it and once his therapist signs off on his mental state, I've arranged an interview with a PI friend."

Jack as a PI? "I'm sorry it came to that."

"You're not to blame, son. We each choose what road to travel. He just took a wrong turn is all, but he'll get back on track. How's that sexy woman of yours?"

"Leaving Sunday morning for her world tour."

"You're smart in a lot of ways, Dylan, but in some you're a dumbass tool. If it were Derrick trying to leave me, I'd move mountains to keep him. Think about that while you're crying in your beer."

He hung up on me. I set my phone back on the desk. Derrick wasn't Jenny. He hadn't made a deathbed promise to his twin. It wasn't the same thing. And Derrick would never think of leaving Garrett because he loved that man without question. I didn't have that from Jenny.

CHAPTER FORTY-ONE

~ *Jenny* ~

AUTUMN AND I WERE SO frustrated. Jackson, Savannah's boyfriend, had been glued to her side since they'd arrived two days ago for the rehearsal dinner. He'd even refused to let her attend Autumn's bachelorette party. He was also her manager, and apparently he was controlling one hundred percent of her life.

We were at Autumn's house, the one she would officially start living in with Brian tonight. We had four hours before the limos arrived to take us to the church, and we were both excited that we'd finally get to spend some alone time with Savannah.

"I guess we should consider ourselves lucky Jackson's letting her out of his sight long enough to get dressed with us," Autumn said as we waited for Savannah to arrive. "Why does she let him boss her around like that?"

"If you think about it, her mother's always been the driving force in Savannah's life. It's like she's been trained to be obedient to an authoritarian figure." I pulled the plastic off my dress.

"Well, that's just sad. The only time I can remember seeing her really happy was the year she was with Adam."

"Yeah, they were honest to God in love. Hopefully she'll confide in us when she gets here." I held my dress against me and looked in the mirror. Autumn was having a Christmas themed wedding. Mine and Savannah's dresses were an emerald green, and we would be carrying red tulips. The dress was gorgeous.

"I wish she'd come back alone so we could have spent more time with her," Autumn said. "I don't think—"

The doorbell rang. "She's here." I opened the front door. Savannah stood on the other side with Jackson, and I caught the tail end of what he was saying to her. "...don't talk about us."

"No men allowed," I said, grabbing her arm and pulling her inside before I shut the door in his face. For good measure I turned the lock.

Autumn and I smothered her in hugs. When I pulled away, her eyes were brimming with tears. Savannah Graham was a striking woman. Not classically beautiful like so many models, but her features were unique. Raven-black hair that fell halfway down her back and her gray eyes were the things you noticed first about her. In elementary school, the kids used to make fun of her, saying she had ghost eyes. They also called her beanpole.

Her skin was creamy and flawless, and she was tall and at least fifteen pounds lighter than the last time I'd seen her. Personally I thought she was too thin. She was also extremely shy, which I blamed on her mother for doing her best to crush everything that was special about Savannah except her looks. Regina Graham, a former model herself and a force to be reckoned with, had grown up in the valley. When she'd gotten pregnant with Savannah, she'd moved back. She never told Savannah who her father is.

It was only a guess on my part, but I think the pregnancy was an accident, and that Mrs. Graham resented Savannah a little for it. From the day Savannah was born, she'd been raised to be a famous model, and—another guess on my part—Mrs. Graham was living her glory days through Savannah. I wasn't too fond of Savannah's mother.

"I miss you two so much," Savannah said.

Autumn narrowed her eyes. "Could have fooled us. You never call, never come back for a visit."

"Autumn," I said, shaking my head at her. This wasn't a day for us all to end up in accusations and tears.

"I'm sorry," Savannah said, her voice quivering.

"Well, you're here now, and that's all that matters. Time to break out the champagne." I was determined to spend what little time the three of us had together laughing the way we used to.

I took Savannah's hand and pulled her with me to the living room. Autumn and I had spread pillows around the coffee table, where we had a bottle of champagne chilling in an ice bucket. Plates of treats—chocolate-covered strawberries, iced tea cakes, thin slices of banana nut bread with cream cheese (Savannah's favorite), and caviar on toast points—surrounded the ice bucket.

"Here's to besties, to love, and to happiness," I said after filling the crystal champagne glasses. We clinked glasses.

"To friendships that last forever," Autumn said.

Savannah smiled. "Especially to that." She took a small sip of champagne, then set it aside.

"By the way, you're doing my makeup today," Autumn said to Savannah. "I figure you know all the tricks to make me a beautiful bride."

"I do know a few, and I'd love to."

"Awesome. The plan for today is a few hours of girl time and then we'll get dressed. Two limos will be here at five to take us to the church. My parents will be in one, and I'll ride with them. You two will ride in the second one."

"Why isn't your mother here?" Savannah asked.

"Because my dad said he wanted to ride with her, so…" She shrugged.

Savannah and I exchanged glances, both of us knowing that Autumn never came first with her mother, even on her wedding day. Autumn's parents were a revolving door of on and off together. At the moment they were off. But that was another story, and I was selfishly glad it was just the three of us together.

As Autumn and I ate, I noticed that Savannah wasn't, but her eyes greedily followed each morsel we put in our mouths. I picked up a slice of the banana bread, put it on a napkin, and set it in front of her.

She shook her head. "I'm not allowed… I mean I'm not hungry."

Autumn's gaze zeroed in on Savannah. "I call bullshit, Savannah Graham. You're too skinny and you're looking at this food like you haven't had a decent meal in ages. Who doesn't allow you to eat? Your mother? Jackson?"

"I can't…I mean I don't want to talk about Jackson. Or my mother. Not today."

From what I'd heard Jackson say, she was under orders not to talk about him, but I didn't tell Autumn that. It would only set Autumn off even more, and Savannah was obviously already close to losing it.

I put my hand over Savannah's. "Here's the deal. Whatever's going on in your life right now, we're here for you if you want to talk. In the meantime, we haven't seen you in over a year, and we're going to have fun for a few hours like we used to. That means we're going to drink champagne and eat these delicious treats, reminisce and laugh. What goes on in this room this afternoon, stays in this room. So today, eat to your heart's content. Mine and Autumn's lips are sealed. Okay?"

Savannah's gaze slid over the goodies on the table, and then she smiled as she looked from Autumn to me. "It's marvelously okay."

"Thank God," Autumn said. "I thought I was going to have to cram that banana bread down your throat."

"Remember when it was my sixteenth birthday and my mother gave me a bowl of fruit with a candle stuck in the middle?" Savannah grinned at Autumn. "You were so mad about that when I told you the next day."

I laughed. "Yeah, she got Mary to make a chocolate fudge cake piled high with icing. We hid in Connor and Adam's tree house and ate the whole thing."

"It was so good," Savannah said. "I think that was only the third time in my life that I'd had cake."

Autumn scowled. "That's just wrong."

"Well, we're going to make up for that today." I refilled our champagne glasses, then put two of each treat in front of Savannah.

Savannah popped a chocolate-covered strawberry into her mouth. "I could eat a dozen of these." She ate another one. "Speaking of Connor and Adam, how are they?"

"They're doing great. Their log home business is doing very well and keeping them busy." I wondered if she still had feelings for Adam. "Both are still single."

"They'll be at my wedding and the reception." Autumn slyly eyed Savannah. "Adam asks about you sometimes."

Savannah's gaze lowered to the table, hiding whatever was in her eyes at the mention of Adam. "Is he happy?"

"I don't think he's been happy since you left him."

I shot Autumn a warning glance. We were just getting Savannah to loosen up, and I didn't want her crawling back into her shell.

"You should see some of their log homes," I said. "They're beautiful."

"I'd like to someday." She looked at Autumn. "I always thought you'd end up with Connor."

Autumn's eyes widened. "Why would you think that?"

"I don't know. The two of you seemed to have a special connection."

That was true. No one could make Connor laugh the way Autumn did. And whenever she'd gotten in trouble, which was often, his was the shoulder she'd cry on.

"Well, I did have a crush on him in the sixth grade, but

then along came Larry Stanley. He gave me that mood ring for Christmas, and when it turned blue, he told me it was because I loved him." Autumn grinned. "How can you argue with a mood ring?"

"Yeah, you loved him until the ring turned your finger green." I grinned at her. "You threw it back at him."

"Oh, right. I'd forgotten that. Well, how was I supposed to love a boy who made my finger turn green?"

We reminisced, laughed, and ate the goodies for another hour. It was like old times, but I reminded myself that it was temporary. Both Savannah and I would be leaving the day after Autumn's wedding. That led me to thinking of Dylan and how much I was going to miss him.

"What about you, Jenn?" Savannah said. "Anyone special?"

I shrugged. "Kind of. I've been seeing Dylan Conrad, our new police chief."

Autumn fanned her face. "And he's hot, hot, hot."

"But I'm leaving Sunday, and he was just someone to have fun with for a little while. Nothing special." The lie was bitter on my tongue. Dylan Conrad was beyond special.

Autumn snorted. "Keep telling yourself that, Jenn." She glanced at her watch. "Crap. We're running out of time. We still have to do pedicures and our nails."

Growing up, we'd had fun giving each other pedicures and manicures, so Autumn and I had decided we'd do that today with Savannah. We got our toes and nails filed and painted, laughed some more, and then I watched Savannah do Autumn's makeup and hair.

She really was an expert at both things, and when she was finished with Autumn, she turned to me and raised a brow. "Yes, please," I said.

Finally it was time to put on our dresses. Savannah and I helped Autumn into her gown. I blinked back tears at knowing our girl time was over. Savannah hadn't opened up to us, and I couldn't help thinking she was terribly unhappy.

"I think you're the most beautiful bride I've ever seen," I said, taking Autumn's hand. Putting my doubts aside, I prayed that my friend had found her happily ever after.

"You really are." Savannah took Autumn's other hand and then mine, forming a circle. "I know it doesn't always seem like it lately, but I love both of you," she said. "Please don't give up on me."

I squeezed her hand. "Never."

"Never," Autumn echoed.

The doorbell rang, letting us know the limos were here. Our time together was up, and after tonight we'd each be going our separate ways. As I blinked back tears, already missing my two best friends, I saw they also had tears in their eyes.

"Friends forever," I said, pulling them both into a hug.

Savannah slipped her arm around my waist. "It doesn't seem right that Natalie's not here today."

I swallowed past the lump in my throat. "I know." But I was going to find her again, somewhere out there in the world.

CHAPTER FORTY-TWO

~ Dylan ~

TOMMY AND KIM PAYTON HAD volunteered for traffic control for Brian and Autumn's wedding. Personally I thought they saw it as another chance to show off their new uniforms. I sat in my car across the street from the church, observing the comings and goings. Okay, I was actually here to catch one last glimpse of Jenny.

I'd been invited to the wedding but had decided being near her wouldn't be good for her travel plans. I didn't trust myself to let her go. If I got anywhere near her, I'd lose my control and do something stupid like carry her home and tie her up until she missed her flight. Not something a cop should do.

Two limos pulled in, stopping in front of the church. Jenny and a tall woman with black hair emerged from the first one, wearing identical green dresses. The black-haired woman was gorgeous, but I only had eyes for Jenny Girl. Although she was lovely in her formal gown, her hair piled in a fancy do on top of her head, I preferred the girl who liked jeans and hats. A few steps before entering the church, she turned and scanned the parking lot. Was she looking for me?

Autumn and her parents got out of the second limo. I smiled at the vision in white daintily walking up the steps, knowing that under all that lace was a woman with an outrageous sense of humor. She and Brian were Jenny's friends, though, so I doubted I'd be spending time with them in the future. That was too bad. I liked them both.

From the church, the wedding party and guests would travel in a caravan to the Blue Ridge Valley Country Club. Deciding I'd played stalker long enough, I started the engine. There was nothing for me here.

★★★

It had been almost two weeks since I'd last had a glimpse of Jenny as she'd walked into a church, looking so beautiful in a green dress that I was sure had matched her eyes. And now Christmas Eve had arrived, a day I dreaded.

Instead of getting drunk to forget Christine as I'd planned, I sat in my living room, void of any decorations, drinking a cup of coffee and thinking of Jenny. Even Daisy missed her, often sitting in front of the door, staring at it around the time Jenny would usually arrive. I knew exactly how she felt.

When I'd crossed paths with Jenny's father yesterday, he'd told me she was in Greece. I stared at the velvet box I'd set on the coffee table, a necklace I'd bought to give her for Christmas before she'd left me that damn note and then disappeared from my life.

Almost every one of my officers had invited me over for Christmas dinner, but I'd politely declined. This was a time for families, not to have a lovesick man hanging out with them.

Daisy apparently sensed my mood because she sat, staring at me with that worried look I was getting used to seeing on her. I opened the jewelry box. The platinum heart and chain with an emerald on the heart that matched Jenny's eyes had caught my attention as soon as I saw it. I'd thought of the gift as symbolic. I might have never said the words, but I was going to give her my heart.

Garrett's words bounced around in my head. *Don't let her slip through your fingers.* I snapped the lid closed.

"It's true, Daisy. I am a fool." She tilted her head as if not sure whether or not she should agree. "Who's your favorite cop? Tommy?" At hearing his name, she barked. "Good, then you won't mind staying with him for a while?" She went to the door, making me laugh. "Ready to be rid of me, are you?"

I got out my laptop and started making a list. When I had everything I needed to do down, I went to bed and slept through the night without any ghosts giving me advice.

CHAPTER FORTY-THREE

~ Jenny ~

I ZIPPED UP MY HOODIE AGAINST the chilly December wind blowing in from the Aegean Sea. After two weeks in Greece, I was supposed to leave for England tomorrow. Natalie and I had been here together shortly after we graduated high school, but before we could finish the rest of our trip, she'd gotten sick. When the debilitating headaches and nausea didn't get better, we flew home, only to find out she was going to die. The ache in my heart had never gone away.

Since arriving here, I'd explored the island, revisiting all the places we'd gone to together. God, I missed her. Traveling wasn't the same without my twin at my side. I didn't feel her with me. She had moved on to a better place while I'd hung on to a promise that I'd thought would bring her back to me.

Along with being lonely, I was worried about Savannah. She wasn't the same happy girl who'd left the valley to make her dream come true. She'd refused to talk about what was going on in her life during the three days she'd been home. Instead of traipsing the world, I should be home where I could try to find out what was going on with her. Autumn would be back from her honeymoon in a few days, and we could make a trip to New York, see for ourselves what the deal was with our friend.

And then there was Dylan, my real reason for being miserable. I lifted my head to the star-filled sky. Was Natalie up there, looking down on me? "I know I made a promise, Nat, but I think I made a mistake. I miss him something awful. You would understand if I went home, wouldn't you? I need to know if he misses me as much as I do him."

"He does."

Oh, great. Now I was hearing Dylan's voice in my head.

"Turn around, Jenny Girl."

I pressed my hand over my heart to keep it from exploding out of my chest. He wasn't here. He couldn't be. It was only because I missed him so much that I was hearing his voice.

"You're not really here," I whispered, afraid to turn and see nothing but sand behind me. He chuckled, the sound traveling through me slow and easy like warm syrup.

"Are you sure about that?"

No, I didn't know anything anymore. I turned and there he was, but to make sure, I closed the gap between us so that I could touch him. I put my hand on his chest, right over his heart, feeling it beat against my palm.

"You're real. How?" So many questions crowded my mind, but when he wrapped his arms around me, surrounding me with his warmth, nothing else seemed important.

"Your father told me where I could find you." Dylan put his mouth against my ear. "I came to tell you something."

"Something good?" I said through my tears.

"I guess you'll have to decide that." He stepped beside me and, with his arm around my shoulders, led me to a bench.

Maybe I was dreaming. I still couldn't wrap my mind around him really being here. My eyes soaked him up. He was gorgeous, so sexy wearing a cream-colored cable-knit sweater, jeans, and hiking boots. I'd told myself repeatedly before leaving that I wasn't in love with him. What a fool

I'd been.

He enfolded my hand between both of his. "I forgot to give you your Christmas gift before you left."

"You came all this way just to give me a Christmas present?" Disappointment crashed through me that he hadn't come to… I don't know. Ask me to come home? Tell me he loved me? I forced a smile that I didn't feel.

"Partly." He reached behind him, pulling a thin jewelry box from his back pocket and handing it to me.

I opened the black velvet box to see a silver heart and emerald necklace. "It's beautiful, Dylan."

He took it out. "Turn around."

Obeying, I pulled my hair up so he could hook the clasp. His fingers lingered on the back of my neck, sending a shiver down my spine. "Thank you. It really is lovely." I still didn't understand why he'd flown all the way here just to give it to me when he could have mailed it.

"Before you thank me, you should know the caveat that comes with it. You may decide you don't want it."

His whiskey-colored eyes captured mine, holding my gaze prisoner. He picked up the heart, rubbing it between his fingers. "I didn't come to take you home, but to tell you that I love you, and I'll wait for you, however long it takes. This necklace is my way of saying you have my heart in your care. If you want it."

I'd never seen such vulnerability in his eyes before. Sadness, yes, when he'd talked about his wife. Other than that one time, he'd always been confident and sure of himself. But now he let me see how easily I could hurt him. And he loved me! My heart sang with joy.

This man, oh God, this man. I climbed onto his lap, straddling him. "I want it." I peppered kisses over his face. "I want it forever."

A beautiful smile lit his face. "You just made me a very happy man, Red."

"Well, in case you haven't figured it out yet, I love you, too." That earned me a kiss that curled my toes.

"Ah, young love. Do you remember how it was, Sophia?"

I lifted my head, eyeing the elderly couple standing only a few feet away, their hands clasped together.

The woman smiled fondly up at the man. "I do, and it is still so." She glanced back at us. "Blessings on you both. May the love I see in your eyes last a lifetime and beyond," she said before they walked away, her head resting on the man's shoulder.

"Thank you," I whispered as they retreated. Although she'd been a stranger, her blessing seemed like a gift, one I would cherish.

Dylan chuckled as he trailed a hand down my cheek. "You're blushing."

"I was afraid she could read my mind."

He raised a brow. "And if she could have?"

"She would have blushed too, knowing all the things I want to do to you."

"Now you have my attention."

Happiness bubbled up, making me laugh. "Where are you staying?"

"About that. My luggage is being held at your hotel. I was hoping you'd invite me to share your room with you." He slid his hands up my thighs.

I pushed off him. "Let's go, roomie." We had things to talk about, but all I wanted right now was Dylan naked in my bed.

We ran, holding hands and laughing, back to my room. As soon as the door closed behind us, he pushed me up against it.

"Your luggage—"

"Later." His mouth crashed down on mine.

As our tongues tangled in a quest for dominance, he

pulled the zipper down on my hoodie, pushing it off my shoulders and down my arms. I wanted his sweater off, but then we'd have to separate, so I settled for wrapping my legs around his waist. He slipped his hand under my T-shirt, trailed his fingers up my spine, and unhooked my bra.

"Dylan, please."

He tore his mouth away, and seconds later I was naked from the waist up. "Please what, Red?"

I looked into eyes turned stormy with desire, my breath hitching at knowing all that heat was for me. He'd traveled thousands of miles to offer his heart into my keeping without being sure how I'd respond. How could I not love him?

"Please make love to me."

"I love you," he said as if reading my mind. He curled his arms under my knees, walking us to the bed.

"I love you back." I would never get tired of telling him. Before I realized what he planned to do, we were falling. I yelped, getting a laugh from him as he took the brunt of the fall with me landing on top of him.

He rubbed his thumb over my bottom lip. "Always love me back, Jenny Girl."

"Always. I promise." Something in the way he'd asked for my love made me wonder if he was thinking of the woman who'd broken his heart. It couldn't have been an easy thing for him to trust in love again. Yet he was here, bravely trusting me. I would never be her. Ever. I wanted him to know that.

"Always, always, Dylan. I will die loving you." I smiled down at the man who had stolen my heart the first time I'd seen him, even though it had taken me too long to admit it. Now that I had, he was mine and I was keeping him. "I will never make you regret loving me."

Tears pooled in his eyes, which made my own eyes water. I traced my thumb over his bottom lip. "And don't forget, we've been blessed to love a lifetime and beyond."

"I'll never forget, my Jenny Girl."

He blinked his eyes dry, then pulled my mouth down to his. When he slid into me, joining our bodies, it was different from any time before. We were in love, and that changed everything, even how it felt when his hands roamed lovingly over me. He loved me all through the night until I laughingly begged for mercy. I fell asleep wrapped in Dylan's strong arms, happier than I'd ever been.

☾

"Wake up, beautiful girl."

I groaned as I turned away, pulling my pillow over my face. "Go away."

An amused male sigh reached my ears. "And last night you said you loved me. Not so much in the morning, Red?"

"I'll probably hate you all of our mornings if you're always this cheerful."

"Even if I bring you coffee and hot spanakopitas?"

My nose twitched when the rich aroma of the pastries and coffee drifted my way. "In that case, I might like you a little. Gimme." I pushed up against the pillows and bit into the savory spinach, feta cheese, and egg pie. "So good," I murmured.

Dylan grinned from his spot on the edge of the bed. "I thought that might win me some points."

I snorted. "Like you need more. You've won the game."

His smile faded as his eyes searched mine. "Have I?"

Did he even have to ask? I set down the pastry. "Yes. Don't you know that?"

"When I said I hadn't come to take you home, I meant it." He wrapped his fingers around my ankle. "I understand you not only had a dream to travel long before we met, but that you made a promise to your sister. I would never ask you to give that up. Before you left, I almost told you that I loved you."

"Why didn't you?"

His gaze shifted to the hand he had on my ankle. "Because I knew there was the possibility you might meet someone. A sexy Italian who spoke accented *amore* words in your ear. Or possibly a brawny Scot in a kilt that you couldn't resist peeking under. I wanted you to be free if that happened."

Oh, Dylan. You sweet, wonderful, amazing man. "That's something you'll never have to worry about…well, I can't promise I won't peek under a kilt if the opportunity presents itself. You know, just to learn the answer to the age-old question."

He grinned. "You can look but not touch. How's that?"

"Deal."

His smile faded, and he stared intently at me. "I want you to know that I'll wait for you, however long it takes before you're ready to come home. You're it for me."

Happiness filled me, warming all the places that had been cold since the day I'd lost my twin. I put my palm on his cheek. "Who do you love?"

He leaned his face into my hand. "Jenny. Just Jenny."

There was nothing better he could have said to put to rest any lingering fear that his heart belonged to another woman. I smiled up at him. "I love you more."

"Do not."

"Do too." That resulted in a round of wrestling and tickling, and when we were both laughing so hard we could barely catch our breath, he rolled on top of me and stared down at me. "Where do you go next?"

"I have a flight to London this afternoon, but—"

"Can I come with you? I have two weeks before I have to return."

Before he interrupted me, I was about to say that I wanted to return home with him, but two weeks traveling with Dylan? That would be so awesome.

"If that's not okay, I understand," he said when I didn't answer.

"Crazy man. Of course you can come with me. I want you to. And when it's time for you to go home, I'm coming with you."

"Are you sure? You've talked of nothing but seeing the world since we met."

I could tell I'd pleased him. "And I still want to, but with you by my side. You get two weeks of vacation a year?"

"Actually I negotiated three weeks before I left. The mayor owed me a favor and was feeling rather generous."

I clapped my hands. "Fantastic. Every year we'll pick a country to visit."

"Although that was Plan B, it was my favorite one."

"What was Plan A?"

"To find you, tell you I loved you, and then send you on your way."

Somehow I'd found the perfect man to love. "You're not getting rid of me that easily. So how does Italy next year sound?"

He pursed his lips as if thinking, then said, "Who knows, maybe for our honeymoon."

My heart tripped over itself. While neither one of us was ready to talk marriage, that he was mentioning the possibility moved our relationship into a whole new realm.

"Well, I have heard that Italy is for lovers." I could already imagine us in a villa by the sea, the windows open and sheer white curtains billowing in the air while we made love.

"And we'll have to come back to Greece someday since I'm only getting a glimpse of the country this time around."

"Definitely." I loved Greece and wanted to experience it with him.

He rolled off me, then pulled me onto my side to face him. "Will you move in with me when we get home? I mean, you might as well. You'll be spending all your time in my bed anyway."

"Ha! Pretty sure of yourself, Chief."

"No, I'm just hoping."

His hand was on the bed between us. I curled my fingers around his. "The answer is yes."

"Thank you." He brought my hand to his lips and kissed it. Then his expression turned serious. "I should mention that we're going to have about a dozen kids."

"Huh?" I gulped. "I was thinking two or three someday. In the future." If we get married, I silently added.

"Nope. Somewhere between nine and a dozen if the vet's right."

At his amused grin, I punched his arm. "Don't scare me like that." Then it hit me. "Daisy's pregnant?"

"She is. Must have happened right before I found her. It would have been noticeable sooner if she hadn't been so undernourished. The vet said she'll deliver in about three weeks."

"We need to go home."

He chuckled. "Another reason I love you. You love my dog as much as I do."

"Almost as much. You have a slight edge over her."

"That's nice to know." He leaned over me and kissed me long and hard. "Back to Daisy," he said when we came up for air. "I want to keep her puppies."

"All of them?"

"Yeah. I guess we could find them good homes, but how would we know for sure they were being treated right? Before I left, I asked Connor to scout out some land

I can build a log house on. Adam said he would fast-track it and have whatever I decided on finished in six months. It would mean a houseful of rambunctious puppies in my apartment for a while, but we could manage it for a short time."

"If we don't get evicted."

He laughed. "There is that. We'll worry about that if it happens."

"Okay."

"That's it? No telling me I'm out of my mind?"

"Nope. The more the merrier, I always say."

"You can't possibly know how much I love you," he said. "And we're still going to London. Daisy wouldn't dare have her puppies before we get home."

He picked up a lock of my hair and wrapped it around his fingers. "I think we're done talking. I have other things in mind at the moment."

I waggled my eyebrows. "You by any chance bring your handcuffs, Mr. Policeman?"

A wicked smile curved his lips. "No, but I'm very good at improvising. Let me show you."

Turned out my man was very creative.

COMING AUGUST 2ND . . .

All Autumn

AUTUMN STRATTON HAS IT ALL. Or so she thinks until she catches her two-timing husband with his pants around his ankles. There is much Autumn can forgive but infidelity isn't one of them. Since she obviously can't trust her judgment in men, she decides they are only good for one thing…

Connor Hunter has been friends with Autumn since the first grade, and she's like a sister to him. That changes the day she accidently flashes him. After viewing something he shouldn't have, Connor is seeing his friend in a whole new light. When she says all she wants now from a man is a fling, Connor is all in. Having watched his twin brother fall apart because of a woman, Connor has no intention of giving any female the power to hurt him that way.

Autumn and Connor agree that friends with benefits is the perfect solution for both of them. They are friends and will never hurt each other. That's the plan, anyway. But as happens, the best-laid plans often go awry. And when they do, the quirky residents of Blue Ridge Valley decide to take matters into their own hands, all in the name of love.

ACKNOWLEDGMENTS

ROMANCE READERS—YES, YOU. IT'S IMPOSSIBLE to adequately thank you for the love and support you give authors. I wish I could personally meet each and every one of you so I could give you a hug. I'm blessed by the friendships I've made with readers the world over, and from the bottom of my heart, thank you for reading my books. I love you all.

Book bloggers, you guys rock! I want to name you here, but I'm petrified I'll miss some of you. Just know that I appreciate so much the support and love that you give authors.

To Jenny Holiday, my friend and critique partner, thank you for… well, where do I start? With the friend love or with the sometimes crazy e-mails between us that makes us laugh or just knowing that we're there for each other? Or what about our Skype plotting sessions or your critiques that make my stories so much better. I guess here I'll just say thank you and I love you, and then I'll write you a mushy e-mail!

Miranda Liasson, you have no idea how much I love and value our long, chatty phone conversations. You have a very weird sixth sense about when to call me—somehow knowing when I need a pep talk or a good laugh. Thank you!

AE Jones, we write different romance genres, but we sure do make awesome beta readers for each other. Keep sending me those outrageously funny stories to read.

Ella Sheridan, not only are you a great author, but you make one hell of a copy editor/proofreader. Thank you for keeping me from embarrassing myself. Maybe someday I'll figure out commas, but don't count on it.

Jennie Conway, I'm sorry that we didn't have a chance to "shine" together, but I'll always remember that you helped me make this book better. Thank you!

To Sandra's Book Salon Facebook group, you all are the best! Thank you for all the love and support and especially for the laughter! I can't wait to see who you cast for Dylan and Jenny.

To everyone who has read and then posted reviews for my books, I'd kiss you if I could. Although you'd probably rather I didn't, but tough. Seriously, though, reviews mean everything to an author, so thank you, thank you, thank you!

To my family—Jim, Jeff, and DeAnna—love you guys so much!

ABOUT SANDRA . . .

BESTSELLING, AWARD-WINNING AUTHOR SANDRA OWENS lives in the beautiful Blue Ridge Mountains of North Carolina. Her family and friends often question her sanity but have ceased being surprised by what she might get up to next. She's jumped out of a plane, flown in an aerobatic plane while the pilot performed death-defying stunts, gotten into laser gun fights in Air Combat, and ridden a Harley motorcycle for years. She regrets nothing.

Sandra is a Romance Writers of America Honor Roll member and a 2013 Golden Heart Finalist for her contemporary romance *Crazy for Her*. In addition to her contemporary romantic suspense novels, she writes Regency stories.

Sign up to Sandra's newsletter to get the latest news, cover reveals, and other fun stuff:

https://bit.ly/2FVUPKS

Join Sandra's Facebook Reader Group:

https://bit.ly/2K5gIcM

Follow Sandra on Bookbub:

www.bookbub.com/authors/sandra-owens

CONNECT WITH SANDRA:

Facebook: *https://bit.ly/2ruKKPl*

Twitter: *https://twitter.com/SandyOwens1*

Goodreads: *https://bit.ly/1LihK43*

Follow Sandra on her Amazon author page:

https://amzn.to/2I4uu2Y

47494958R00183

Made in the USA
Columbia, SC
02 January 2019